RAVENSMERE

A Novel of 19th Century Rural Dorset

MARILYN PERKS

TABLE OF CONTENTS

ACKNOWLEDGMENT

I want to thank my editor and mentor, Jeanette Windle, for her hard work and dedication in helping me learn my craft as an author. Her critiques were detailed and professional. When I felt like quitting, she boosted my confidence and helped me press on to the finish line. How grateful I am that God brought us together.

CHAPTER ONE

Geneva Everson had hope. And that hope was backed with a carefully laid plan. In the past few weeks, her mood had brightened so much it didn't matter what hateful things Uncle Alex said or did. She could brush them off knowing she would soon be free of him.

While her uncle drank his second cup of tea in the kitchen and read the morning newspaper, Geneva washed up the breakfast things in the scullery. Hanging up her damp apron, she glanced in the mirror. This summer of 1830 had been a wet one. Despite that, the sunny breaks between showers had brought blond streaks to her light brown hair, a smattering of freckles across her small nose, and a peachy blush to the apples of her cheeks.

Her eyes were unusual. They were green and amber both, but not a mixed hazel hue. Rather, the inner circle of the iris surrounding the pupil formed a narrow band of rich amber followed by a much wider band of turquoise green. While still alive, her mother had always assured Geneva that her unusual eyes were beautiful. At the moment, they looked exhausted and rimmed with dark circles. Her work dress, which had once fit her perfectly, hung loosely over her small bosom.

If disturbed by what the mirror revealed, Geneva couldn't be too surprised. In the past fortnight, her workload had doubled. In addition to cooking, cleaning, and hauling water for laundry, she had toiled over a hot stove, bottling and preserving for the winter months that lay ahead.

Refusing to be discouraged, she adjusted her curly tresses to hide an unsightly scar on her forehead and got on with her morning job of cleaning the parlor. Beginning with the mantelpiece, she dusted the clock and ornaments, then set them aside. Pouring drops of linseed oil onto a cloth, she rubbed and polished the oak slab from one end to the other.

Satisfied with its clean, shiny surface, Geneva reached for her uncle's collection of three porcelain British soldiers. As she set the last one down, it tipped over too close to the edge of the mantelpiece. Her heart thumped in her chest as she tried to catch the much-loved ornament. But it was too late. Landing on the stone hearth with a crack, the porcelain soldier shattered into numerous pieces.

"What was that?" Uncle Alex bellowed from the kitchen. His boots thumped on the floorboards as he strode down the hall and into the parlor.

Moving away from the hearth, Geneva held trembling fingers to her lips. "I'm terribly sorry, Uncle Alex. It was an accident. I didn't mean to break it."

Alex Brigham's eyes darted from the smashed ornament on the hearth to the surviving pair on the mantelpiece. "You clumsy oaf! Without the drummer boy, the collection is worthless. It was the most beautiful item ever brought to my pawnshop."

"Please, Uncle Alex, don't be angry," Geneva pleaded. "I can make it up to you. I'll make your favorite steak-and-kidney pie for dinner. You always like my flakey crusts."

Her uncle stooped down to pick up the porcelain fragments. "By gum, you owe me far more than that. But if you're lucky, I might be able to fix this."

Sitting down at a small desk in the corner of the parlor, Uncle Alex cursed and fussed over the odd-shaped pieces. Geneva watched him surreptitiously. Over the last few years, his face had weathered, his chin had doubled, and his round belly put a strain on the buttons of his waistcoat. But he was still a force to be reckoned with—strong and confident with anyone who opposed his business methods or his strict rules written in stone.

Their home occupied the rear quarters of Uncle Alex's pawnshop in the small hilltop town of Shaftesbury. This was situated in the county of Dorset in the middle of the south coast of England. Since the turn of the century, breweries had become the mainstay of the town's economy. Thanks to Shaftesbury's growing prosperity, Uncle Alex's pawnshop was doing well. Although the income he earned was an honest one, Geneva hated that it came at the expense of the downtrodden. Everyone was familiar with the three brass spheres that hung outside the shop, medieval symbols of a pawnbroker. And like her, many of them had little regard for the grumpy man known as the Pinchpenny of Shaftesbury.

Uncle Alex drew a sharp breath and pounded his fist on the desk. "It's no good. Even if I glue it together, it won't look right."

Heaving himself to his feet, he paced around, scratching his belly, pulling the tufts of his side whiskers, and rubbing his greasy forehead. After several turns around the room, his eyes brightened. He reached for Geneva's flute case on a bookshelf.

Geneva dashed forward. "What are you doing with that?"

"I'm taking it to my shop," her uncle stated bluntly. "Since you're so careless with my things, you can do without yours for two months."

"No, please, Uncle Alex, my flute belonged to Mother. Don't take it there. It could be sold by mistake." Geneva grabbed for her flute case, but Uncle Alex shoved her back, baring yellowed teeth.

"Don't defy me, you wicked girl! Now get out of my way and make sure dinner is ready at six o'clock—and not a minute later."

Her uncle stomped out of the room with the case tucked under his arm. Geneva jerked at the violent slam of the door. Overwhelmed with frustration and disappointment, she picked up her marmalade cat and held him against her cheek. "Oh, Pookie, why do things always go wrong? It's not fair."

Walking over to the parlor's bay window, Geneva looked out across the magnificent view of the Blackmore Vale. This day in mid-August had dawned with such a glorious sunrise that she felt a pang of guilt for her own fears and worries. The rolling hills were stunning, a patchwork of fields and hedgerows in countless shades of green with small hamlets and church spires receding into a distant lavender haze. In her opinion, the view must be one of the best in all of England.

As she stroked Pookie's silky coat, Geneva's thoughts went to her mother. Life wouldn't be filled with so many trials if she hadn't died. The day after her burial, Uncle Alex's true colors came to light. Geneva had been only eleven at the time, yet he'd forced her into her mother's role as unpaid cook and housekeeper. Geneva hated being used and mistreated like a piece of property. If she did the slightest thing wrong or spoke out of turn, he inflicted harsh punishments, making her life a living nightmare. Now that she was eighteen, he no longer used the belt. But he'd found other forms of punishment—like confiscating her flute.

As much as Geneva loved this view and her comfortable home, her departure couldn't come soon enough. Without her uncle knowing it, she'd been saving some of her earnings for the coach fare to London, a journey of well over a hundred miles. Her neighbor Mrs. Gilbert had a kind sister who lived near Belgrave Square. She'd promised Geneva temporary lodging and help in finding work as a governess. But with this vexing setback, London would have to wait for two more months. Geneva could never leave home without her flute, the one treasured possession she still had to remind her of her beloved mother.

Later that afternoon, Geneva placed an armload of folded linen in the upstairs cupboard. She longed for a brief nap to rest her weary bones, but she was expected shortly at the vicarage for her weekly ironing job. Changing into a clean summer dress, she stepped out the side entrance of her home.

Adjacent to the small courtyard, Geneva's kitchen garden was brimming with onions and herbs. Zinnias growing against a sun-drenched wall had peaked in a dazzling array of pink, yellow, and orange. Normally, she would stop to enjoy the bumblebees humming from flower to flower. But not this afternoon, as the black cloud of disappointment had robbed her of such pleasures.

Geneva made her way down the shady side of High Street to St. Peter's Church in the town square. Next door to the church, a group of farm laborers and tradesmen had gathered outside the portico to the town hall. As she drew near, a farm laborer raised his voice to speak.

"My boots are worn out from walking to every hiring fair in this county. I've stood for hours in the hot sun with not one offer of work for the harvest. What am I supposed to do? I've got rent to pay and a wife 'n' five kids to feed."

A tradesman placed his hand on the laborer's shoulder. "I hear you, my friend. You're not alone. Hundreds of men like you are searching for work."

"I've been forced into crime," a younger man admitted in a hushed tone. "If I didn't go poaching at night, I'd starve."

Geneva's heart went out to him. She could hear the despair and hopelessness in his voice. His face was thin and haggard with protruding cheekbones. His clothes, worn and faded, hung from his body like a tattered flag on a windless day.

Pulling her gaze from the young man, Geneva noticed Todd Billings in the crowd. A carpenter by trade, Billings was a chum of Uncle Alex's from their school days. He'd often grumbled about the mass production of furniture that threatened his livelihood.

A fellow tradesman standing next to Billings climbed onto a mounting block and called out to the crowd, "Give me your ear, my friends. Did you know that your present state of poverty has its roots as far back as the thirteenth century?"

Interested, Geneva paused beneath a lamppost to listen.

"It was back then that small land holdings were first enclosed into bigger farms. Prior to that, men like you could be their own masters. They had rights of access to common land where each man was self-sufficient, farming the strip of land allotted to him."

"Why can't we go back to those good days?" a tall man shouted from the back. "You're a tradesman. You could take a group to the officials and tell them to break up the land. It should be shared by everyone."

The tradesman shook his head. "I wish I could, but it's not legally possible. Over the centuries, private property laws have enabled wealthy landowners to purchase more and more land. Now they have so much power they've shut down small farms and monopolized the agricultural industry. The result is a surplus of farm laborers like you folk."

"That accounts for our low wages," another farm laborer called out. "They've got us hooked around their little fingers, and there's nothin' we can do."

As the gathered crowd grumbled and complained amongst themselves, Geneva noticed a tall, lean man about thirty years of age who'd stopped to listen as well. His fashionable beige trousers and the tailored trim of a maroon tailcoat across broad shoulders set him apart from everyone else in the square. A top hat, black leather boots, and a gold watch chain hanging from his waistcoat completed the picture of a well-to-do man. Who could he be? A proud landowner who had come to put the grumbling workers in their place?

Advancing forward to the portico, he waved an arm in the air to draw the crowd's attention. "Excuse me! May I have a word with you?"

The man's strong baritone voice broke through the angry chatter. The gathered men turned toward him, some with suspicion and anger etched on their faces but others looking more willing to hear what this newcomer had to say.

As the crowd quieted, the man's baritone voice dropped in volume. "Thank you for allowing me to speak. I shall never know the full extent of your poverty and suffering. But believe me, I do sympathize with your struggles to survive."

Geneva was surprised at his words. This was no proud landowner but a real gentleman with compassion for the underprivileged.

"To be fair," the man continued, "some landowners do care for the welfare of their workers. Sadly, they are outnumbered by the vast majority who are governed by self-interest. I, for one, am grieved by landowners and farmers who profit at the expense of underpaid workers. You may ask what the solution is. Well, I believe the answer is education—for *all* classes of society, including folk like you. A good education can pave the way to better paying jobs and a higher standard of living."

Tensions easing, the men nodded in agreement. They soon broke into smaller groups, still grumbling about hungry families, unpaid bills, and barely enough coal to cook. Just then, Todd Billings approached Geneva, a concerned look on his face.

"Miss Everson, what are you doing here? Your uncle wouldn't want you hanging around a laborers' gathering."

From a corner of her eye, Geneva noticed the gentleman who'd spoken approaching as well. "You're right, Mr. Billings. I'm leaving now. But it was interesting to hear these things, especially how education could improve lives."

As Mr. Billings walked back to his fellow tradesmen, the gentleman drew closer. His expression was so intense Geneva felt intimidated until a smile brightened his face.

"Good afternoon, miss. It appears you and I both have an interest in the plight of the poor." He removed his top hat, revealing a mass of dark, wavy hair. "Please allow me to introduce myself. Daniel Cavendish at your service."

Geneva curtseyed politely. She liked his chocolate-brown eyes, bronzed skin, and the shadow of a beard on his strong jaw. "How do you do, sir. I'm Geneva Everson. I'm so glad you spoke to these men. An education won't meet their immediate needs, but at least they now know there are some gentlemen who care for their welfare."

"Well, the solution I propose requires time, but I'm confident such changes will come about in our lifetime."

"I hope that's true." Geneva hesitated before going on to ask, "Do you live here? I don't recall seeing you before."

"No, I came to Shaftesbury for a meeting. My father and I are bankers. We had a request from your local bank to assist them in their transition from private provincial to joint stock."

Geneva gave a smiling shake of her head. "I'm not sure what that means, but your father must be pleased that you followed in his footsteps."

"Definitely. He often mentions it. Forgive me, but I overheard your friend speaking with you. It's a shame your uncle would object to you listening in. Does he live nearby?"

"Yes, he's the local pawnbroker just down the street. I live with him and work in his shop on his busiest days. Some of his customers are these farm laborers. It's terrible when they're forced to pawn a blanket or a teapot in order to eat. I try to help with secondhand clothing when I can get such and baking from my oven. But it isn't nearly enough."

Geneva didn't mention that the second-hand clothing she'd given away was mostly clothing Uncle Alex no longer wore to the point he hadn't even noticed its disappearance. Mr. Cavendish smiled at her appreciatively. "That is very kind and generous of you. I'm sure the poor you've helped love you for it."

"Oh, no!" Geneva interjected quickly. "Please don't give me credit for what little I do. Helping those in need always cheers me up, so in truth, I am receiving more than I've ever given."

The look in his chocolate-brown eyes turned suddenly sympathetic. "Please forgive my boldness, Miss Everson, but it is distressing that it should take helping the poor to bring cheer into your life. Do you have no other family than this uncle?"

Geneva lowered her eyes from the seeming pity in his kind gaze. "No, my father died before I was born, and Mother passed away when I was eleven."

"I'm so sorry to hear that. It must have been hard to grow up without either parent."

"Well, I wouldn't say I've grown up quite yet. I'll be nineteen next month." Geneva gave a little chuckle. "People say I should have been named Michelle since I was born on Michaelmas, the day that honors St. Michael the archangel."

"Michaelmas Day. That would be the twenty-ninth of September." For a long moment, Mr. Cavendish seemed lost in his thoughts, his eyes intent on her face. "Michelle is a nice name. But I prefer Geneva. It reminds me of Lake Geneva in Switzerland. A painting of that lovely lake hung in my dormitory at boarding school. It was so serene and comforting that it helped to ease my homesickness during the first year."

"I'm so glad it did. The artist would be pleased to hear that."

Geneva thought of all the gentlemen of Shaftesbury she often passed on High Street, always too busy with their important lives to acknowledge her with a smile or a nod. Yet this clearly distinguished gentleman had not only introduced himself but chatted with her in a friendly, kind manner. Given her unhappy state since morning, the brief encounter had lifted her spirits.

She gave him a warm smile. "It was lovely talking with you, Mr. Cavendish, but I'm running late for my next engagement, so I'd better be on my way. I hope your bank meetings are successful and that you have a safe journey home."

He bowed politely. "I'm delighted to have met you, Miss Everson, and thank you for your kind wishes."

Geneva turned to thread her way through the still-milling groups of laborers toward the street that would take her to the vicarage. When she reached the far side of the town square, she looked back. Mr. Cavendish hadn't moved an inch, his gaze still fastened intently upon her retreating figure. What could such a gentleman find of so much interest in a small-town orphan girl like herself?

She spun around and quickened her pace.

CHAPTER TWO

On a sunny morning a week later, Geneva pulled out the last weed from her kitchen garden and threw it into a basket. Without stopping to rest, she swept the paving stones and dumped the dirt into a rubbish bin. Unless every crack was cleaned out, more annoying weeds would take root, adding another task to her heavy workload.

She was pinching off a few sprigs of rosemary and thyme for dinner that night when she heard a coach coming up the side lane. A rattle of wheels and the clink of harness-chains became louder. Then a post-chaise carriage with a team of four horses came into view. It stopped just outside the courtyard gate.

Shading her eyes from the sun, Geneva watched an older man of slight build and frizzy grey hair climb down from the coach. The expression on his pale face was solemn. A disgruntled businessman with a complaint against her uncle?

Opening the gate, the man entered the courtyard and gave Geneva a formal nod. "Please forgive me for coming without prior notice, miss. My name is Harold Bradshaw, junior solicitor with Ingleford Legal Services. Mr. Gregory Clarke, my superior, has sent me with a message for Miss Everson."

"I'm Miss Everson," Geneva replied. "But shouldn't it be my uncle, Mr. Alex Brigham, you wish to see? If you go around to the front, you can enter his shop."

"I'm not here about your uncle, miss. The message concerns you and a family matter."

Geneva had no family except Uncle Alex, so what family matter could this man possibly mean? She looked her visitor over. Surely such a mild-looking older man wasn't the sort to take advantage of a young woman. She stepped toward the side entrance into the house. "Very well, sir. Please come this way."

Geneva led the solicitor into the parlor and took his hat. "Do make yourself comfortable, sir. I'll be with you in a moment."

Hanging his hat on the hat rack, Geneva nipped into the kitchen and removed her soiled apron. After washing and drying her hands, she returned to the parlor. Her visitor stood looking out the bay window.

He turned to face her. "Upon my word, you have a wonderful view from here."

"Yes, the best blessings in life are often free. Won't you sit down?"

Mr. Bradshaw lowered himself into a comfortable chair near the hearth. Geneva sat down across from him, eager to hear what he had to say.

The solicitor leaned forward slightly. "Miss Everson, since I'm rather pressed for time and not very good at small talk, forgive me if I come straight to the point of my visit. Mr. Clarke and I are solicitors for your father, Mr. Adam Everson of Waterton. He sent me here to deliver a letter to you."

Geneva shook her head. "I'm sorry, sir, but you've made a mistake. You're right that my father was Adam Everson, but he lived with my mother in Newminster, not Waterton, wherever that is.

He was a sailcloth manufacturer who died in a factory fire while Mother was pregnant with me."

The solicitor frowned. "Excuse me, miss, who told you that?"

"My mother told me. When my father died, Uncle Alex opened his home to her. Everson is a fairly common name, so I'm sure you've just come to the wrong house. I'm not the person you're looking for."

The solicitor took a paper from his breast pocket and held it out. "Please read this. It should make things clear for you."

Geneva was beginning to question her wisdom in inviting this man inside, however harmless he appeared. Reluctantly taking the paper, she cast her eyes over the heading: *Marriage Registration*. As she read the details, she saw her mother's name: Elizabeth Harriet Brigham. This was followed by her father's name, their signatures, the date in November 1810, and the name of a parish church located in Waterton.

A tingling sensation ran down Geneva's spine. "Is this a valid document?"

"Yes, miss, it's verified by the seal in the lower corner."

As Geneva read the words again, confusion and disbelief churned in the pit of her being. It felt as if she were floating on a sea of contradiction where nothing made sense. "I don't understand, Mr. Bradshaw. Why would my mother make up a false story?"

The solicitor shifted awkwardly in the chair. "Miss Everson, it's not my place to speak of personal matters, but under the circumstances, I have no alternative. I'm not surprised your mother hid the truth from you. She had a valid reason. Four months after your parents' wedding, she had an . . . an unfortunate indiscretion. Your father was so distraught at her infidelity that he ended the marriage."

Geneva stood up, hands clenched and cheeks flushed. "I don't believe that! How dare you come into my home speaking of such things. My mother was a close friend of the vicar's wife. She had a fine reputation as a virtuous lady."

"I understand this is shocking news," Mr. Bradshaw said calmly. "But please sit down. There's more we need to discuss. First, do you remember a Mr. Daniel Cavendish who spoke with you at a laborers' protest in your town last week?"

"Yes, I remember," Geneva admitted cautiously.

"He's your father's godson."

Geneva sank back down to the edge of her chair, eyes wide, as the solicitor continued. "When Mr. Cavendish heard your surname mentioned, his interest was sparked so much that he introduced himself to you. After hearing certain things you shared with him, he finished his bank meeting and immediately returned to Waterton to inform his godfather of your existence."

Geneva's heart thumped in her chest. "Good heavens, are you saying my father is really alive?"

"Yes, miss, he most certainly is. Mr. Cavendish might have told you this himself, but he believed it should be your father's decision to take action, not his. Now, Miss Everson, I've been your father's solicitor for a long time. I remember clearly that it was early March 1811 when your mother was sent away from your father's home. You told Mr. Cavendish you were almost nineteen years old and born on Michaelmas Day. I've already visited your vicar to confirm your date of birth from the parish records. A simple calculation is all that's needed to confirm your mother was at least two months pregnant when she left. It's most unfortunate that neither she nor her husband were aware."

Despite this man's insinuations about her mother, Geneva couldn't deny her natural curiosity. A question she'd kept bottled up much of her life suddenly forced its way out. "So do I resemble my father? No one has ever said that I look like my mother."

"Yes, you do, actually, especially the distinctly hued rings of your eyes, like some rare jewel. I see now why Mr. Cavendish was so sure you are your father's daughter. Heterochromia is what they call it, your father once told me. It is said to run in families, certainly in yours by some of the family portraits."

Mr. Bradshaw cleared his throat as though embarrassed to have been caught discussing such personal details. After removing a letter from the same breast pocket out of which he'd taken the marriage registration, he handed the letter to Geneva. She broke the seal and read.

> Dear Miss Everson,
>
> As you read this, I expect you are as overwhelmed as I was upon hearing news of you from my godson, Mr. Daniel Cavendish. I am very anxious to meet you, so I extend this invitation for you to visit my home in Waterton. I do hope you are brave enough to come. Please know that Harold Bradshaw is a loyal and trustworthy gentleman who will ensure your safe journey.
>
> Eagerly waiting your arrival,
>
> Adam Everson

Geneva's hands were trembling by the time she finished reading the letter. Could it really be that the father she'd lost before her birth was truly alive? She glanced from the letter to the marriage registration. Though she was no expert, the signature of Adam Everson certainly looked the same on both pieces of paper. Tears trickled down her cheeks as her mind swirled with thoughts too fragile to grasp. The essence of who she was and where she'd come from had been uprooted and turned upside down.

Across from her, Mr. Bradshaw was looking uncomfortable at her emotion. He once again cleared his throat. "I don't mean to rush you, miss, but will you come with me? My driver is waiting, and the horses are ready for the journey."

Geneva stood up and gripped the edge of the mantelpiece to steady herself. "I've never left home before. I . . . I don't know if I should go to parts unknown with a stranger."

The solicitor's uncomfortable expression softened into kindly concern. "I understand, miss. Perhaps it would help knowing that my wife has come with me. She's waiting in the coach."

Geneva moved to the window and peered out. The shadow of a woman was visible in the rear seat of the post-chaise carriage. "So just where is this place called Waterton?"

"It's a small village in the southwest corner of Dorset, a half-mile from the coast. A good seven or eight hours by coach, allowing for a meal break, rests, and time to change the horses at the posting stations. Ingleford is the closest big town."

So nowhere near Newminster, the town where her mother had purportedly met and married her father. Why would her mother lie about that? What other secrets had she withheld from her daughter?

Turning around, Geneva asked, "Could you tell me something more about my father? Who is he? What is his profession? Did he ever remarry? Does he have other children?"

The solicitor scratched his cheek. "Dear me, Miss Everson, you do have a lot of questions. But I guess you have reason to wonder if your mother never told you about your father. Adam Everson is a landowner with a sizeable country estate near Waterton. He also served for many years as justice of the peace. And no, he never remarried after your mother. He wasn't young when he married her—forty years to your mother's eighteen—and never showed any interest in remarrying once she left. If he'd gone through the formal process of divorce, I would know. But he does have several nephews and a niece."

Geneva's head was swimming. This was all just too much to take in. She paced back and forth, still stunned by the knowledge that her father had been alive all these years and that her mother had lied to her. If he was alive, why hadn't her mother taken Geneva to meet him? Maybe her mother had her reasons. She wasn't even sure she wanted to meet a father who'd thrown her mother out and never troubled himself to check on her over the years. If he'd bothered, he'd have known he had a daughter.

On the other hand, Geneva had always longed for a father like other girls. She'd tried to imagine what her father might be like from the few details she'd been given. This was an opportunity to find out for herself what her mother had hidden from her—and maybe even why.

She stopped her pacing and turned to face the solicitor. "Mr. Bradshaw, how long will the visit last, and how will I return home?"

The solicitor tapped a finger on his armrest. "I can't really speak for Mr. Everson's plans for your visit. But I'm certain your father would pay for your return trip if at any point you wished to return home."

Swinging around again to stare out the window, Geneva tried to think practically. At worst, this journey and experience could be beneficial for her eventual work as a governess in London. Besides, she'd planned to leave as soon as possible, so why not today? She had been her uncle's slave for long enough. Leaving him in the lurch with no hot dinner and a basket of dirty laundry was no more than he deserved.

Considering the misery she and her mother had been through, the most compelling reason to accept Adam Everson's invitation was the chance to find out what had really caused the break-up of her parents' marriage. Only then would she have peace of mind.

Confident in her final decision, she faced Mr. Bradshaw. "Very well, sir. I'll come with you. I'll get ready as quickly as I can."

The solicitor sighed with relief and leaned back in the chair. Geneva sat down at her uncle's desk. She had no intention of asking her uncle's permission to go. He would immediately forbid such a trip. In fact, if he knew this man was in his parlor, he wouldn't hesitate to throw the elderly solicitor out on the street.

Instead, Geneva wrote a brief note explaining where she was going and requesting that Uncle Alex please take care of her cat while she was gone. She also removed her birth certificate from a file of official documents her uncle kept in a desk drawer. Wherever she ended up, she'd need that identification.

Leaving the note on her uncle's desk where he'd see it the moment he sat down, Geneva went upstairs and changed hurriedly into a green day dress with a black waistband. After giving her hair a cursory brush, she tied it back with a black ribbon, then quickly packed a bag with dresses, nightwear, toiletries, and her Bible with her birth certificate tucked between the pages.

As she did so, she glanced around the bedroom. Hard as her life had been, Geneva was suddenly reluctant to leave the only home she'd ever known. Not to mention her darling cat, her only source of comfort since her mother's death. In earlier years, Geneva's strong faith in the Lord Jesus had given her joy. But when her desperate prayers had done nothing to keep her mother from dying, that joy had evaporated. While she hadn't lost faith in her

Savior, things had never been the same, and her once-eager interest in spiritual matters had faded into the background.

With one last look around, Geneva picked up her bag and
descended the stairs. One day she'd get her flute back. She might
even be able to take Pookie with her once she'd established herself
in a new life. Until then, she'd have to live without both.

In the kitchen, Geneva placed bowls of food and water on the
floor, then stroked her cat's marmalade coat. "Good-bye, Pookie.
I'm trusting that Uncle Alex will take good care of you, but I'll
miss you very much."

After gathering her cloak and bonnet from where they hung
on a peg by the hat rack, Geneva tied the bonnet sash under her
chin and left her cloak draped over an arm. Mr. Bradshaw had
already hurried forward to take her bag and retrieve his own hat.
Together, they exited the side entrance and made their way across
the courtyard to the waiting coach.

As the coach left Shaftesbury behind, descending to the low-lying
farmland of the Blackmore Vale, Geneva glanced out the rear window for a last view of her hometown perched on the hilltop. It
seemed strange to experience both apprehension and glee at the
same time. Apprehension about venturing into the unknown. Glee
for every moment that widened the distance between Geneva and
her uncle. Her mouth curved into a slight smile as she imagined
the look on his face when he read her note. It didn't matter how
angry Uncle Alex would be. By then, she'd be far away in Waterton
and free of his domination.

"I saw that smile!"

At the humorous tone, Geneva turned to the solicitor's wife, who sat next to her. A pleasant older woman with plump cheeks and a button nose, she had a distinct twinkle in her eyes as she went on, "Do share what you find amusing."

Geneva cleared her throat. "Well, I was thinking about my uncle. He's been my guardian since my mother died. He'll be quite lost without me to cook and clean for him."

"And that makes you smile? I sense there is something more to this story. It's not difficult to hire a housemaid. Can your uncle not afford one?"

"Oh, yes, he can afford a housemaid *and* a cook."

Geneva couldn't prevent bitterness from tinging her words. Losing the twinkle in her eyes, Mrs. Bradshaw glanced down at Geneva's red, chafed hands. Quietly, she said, "I can see that you work very hard, Miss Everson. I'd say you've earned a little pampering. This visit will be a refreshing and relaxing time for you."

Geneva managed a smile. "How kind of you to say so, Mrs. Bradshaw. That's the sort of thing my mother would have said to me. Not a day goes by that I don't think of her. As for my uncle, you are right that there is more to the story, especially after my mother died. Let's just say I have reasons not to grieve if I never see Uncle Alex again. If I still had Mother's loving presence, my life would be much different."

Mrs. Bradshaw patted Geneva's hand. "Never mind, dear. Life's difficulties are what make us stronger. You'll be looked after very well at your father's home, but life is never smooth even in the best of circumstances. One thing we can count on is God's love for us."

She glanced across to her husband. "Isn't that true, Harold?"

The solicitor's fond smile made him suddenly less formal. "Indeed it is, Mildred. Human love often fails, but God's love is constant."

Turning her head back to the coach window, Geneva gazed out at fields of lush grain and pastures of grazing cows. She wanted to believe God's love was constant. But her experiences in life told her the opposite. And it wasn't just *her* bad experiences but those of her mother Elizabeth as well as her mother's older brother Alex.

Once she was old enough to understand, her mother had explained that Geneva's maternal grandparents had died when Elizabeth was only five and Alex ten years old. Thankfully, a childless couple, Dr. Dewhurst and his wife, had taken them in, never formally adopting the siblings but becoming their official guardians. Sadly, Alex had been so traumatized by the loss of his own parents that he'd become increasingly naughty and rebellious. When his foster parents could no longer cope with his behavior, they'd sent him to an excellent boarding school.

That hadn't helped. Alex hated school, and when he came home for holidays, his behavior grew even worse. Once his education was completed, Dr. Dewhurst had given him enough money to start his own business. Since Alex's one and only school friend, Todd Billings, lived in Shaftesbury, Alex had moved there to establish a pawnbroker's shop.

In contrast, Elizabeth had remained with the Dewhursts and was raised as their beloved daughter. She had a governess who provided her with an excellent education along with drawing, needlework, and flute lessons. It suddenly made sense to Geneva that her father might be a landowner rather than a tradesman. Elizabeth's social standing as the daughter of a well-respected doctor made it not unheard-of to marry into the gentry class. It was incredible to think that Geneva's mother had lived in wealth and comfort until her world came crashing down with an allegation of adultery. Where was God's love when Elizabeth had been

ripped from a life of privilege to become an outcast and her brother's unpaid servant?

Geneva swallowed hard, fighting to hold back her tears. She
understood now why her mother had lied to her. She hadn't
wanted her daughter to know of her disgrace or the heartless
behavior of Geneva's father. But what had actually happened to
make such a lie necessary? Geneva knew her mother well and was
certain she'd never betray her husband.

By now, Mrs. Bradshaw had fallen asleep, her head tipped to
the side. Across from the two women, Mr. Bradshaw was looking
out the window, deep in thought by his expression. Angling her
body for a better view, Geneva followed his example, taking in
panoramic vistas of Dorset's windswept downlands and beautiful
forests of beech, ash, and ancient gnarled oaks. Midday, the coach
stopped at a wayside inn for luncheon. There were further stops
for tea and to have the horses changed at the posting stations.

The sun had begun its descent to the west when Geneva
noticed a tall structure on the horizon. She broke the silence. "Mr.
Bradshaw, do you know what that tower is in the distance?"

The solicitor craned his neck to see what she was pointing out.
"Oh, marvelous, we're nearing our destination. That's Ingleford's
clock tower."

Within another half hour, the horses were clip-clopping on narrow cobbled streets. Once the coach reached the market town's central square, Mr. Bradshaw rapped on the roof, signaling for the driver
to stop. Waking at the halt, Mrs. Bradshaw sat up straight, one hand
smothering a yawn. Her husband pointed across the square.

"Before we go on, let me point out a few places for you, Miss
Everson. The guildhall there with the clock tower is home to Ingleford's civic government. And that building with three arches is the
corn exchange where merchants trade grain and determine prices.
That building on the corner is Ingleford's Joint Stock Bank."

The final building Mr. Bradshaw indicated was Georgian in style with elegant symmetry and arched windows. Wide steps ascended to a grand front entrance where two impressive columns rose to the roofline. Two small boys sat on the steps munching apples.

Geneva eyed the building with interest. "Isn't that where Mr. Cavendish works?"

"Yes, he's the assistant manager. His father is the executive bank manager."

Mr. Bradshaw rapped on the roof for the driver to move on. As the coach continued to the south side of town, Geneva noticed a sign that read Ingleford Racecourse. "I've never seen a racecourse before. Would that be horse racing?"

"So I'm informed, though I haven't actually been there. Betting on the races is the main attraction, and since I'm not a gambler, it holds little interest for me."

Just then a large, grey stone structure distracted Geneva from the racecourse. It appeared to be some kind of fortress with two square towers flanking the main entrance. Guards manned the upper battlements. The latticed entry gate was raised, but just as the coach passed by, it began to lower on thick iron chains. The sharp prongs along the bottom looked like shark's teeth closing down on its prey. Geneva gave a sudden shiver at the horrifying image.

Beside her, Mrs. Bradshaw spoke up. "It is quite intimidating, isn't it?"

Geneva drew her gaze from the lowering gate to look at the solicitor's wife. "Frightening is what I'd call it. What is that place?"

"Hawkley Castle Prison. A good reminder for people to behave themselves," Mrs. Bradshaw said flatly.

"Which you, miss, of course, don't need to worry about," Mr. Bradshaw broke in hurriedly. "From here it isn't far to the village of Waterton where your father's estate is located."

Geneva didn't respond to either spouse. Apprehension was beginning to build in her with the knowledge that they were so close to her destination. As the coach left Ingleford, she removed her bonnet and smoothed back her loose strands of hair, hoping to make herself more presentable.

The long ribbon of winding road soon gave Geneva her first glimpse of the English Channel's misty-blue waters. The coach passed more woodlands, rocky outcroppings, and fields where laborers swung scythes under the hot sun. When they came to a fork in the road, Geneva spotted a signpost that read: Waterton ¼ Mile.

"We're nearly there," Mrs. Bradshaw announced brightly. "That babbling brook to your left is the Celandine River."

Once past the signpost, they soon came to rows of stone cottages with flowering vines around the doors. Further on, they arrived in the heart of the village, evidenced by the tall pillar of the market cross. People were milling around numerous shops. Others were resting on benches outside a white-washed establishment identified by a brightly painted sign, The Bell and Crown. Presumably the local inn. Across the intersection was a church, partially shaded by plane trees.

From here, the coach turned onto a side road called Manor Lane. After they'd crossed a bridge over the Celandine River, they passed a forest on the north side. To the south lay more fields, woodlands, and a small lake sparkling in the sun. Then a sign chiseled into stone came into view: Ravensmere Estate. A side road that veered off to the right held another stone sign: Everson Quarry.

Mr. Bradshaw directed a kindly smile at Geneva. "Well, Miss Everson, we've reached your father's home. You were a brave young lady to come all this way. I have a feeling your life will never be the same."

CHAPTER THREE

A head through the trees, Geneva caught a glimpse of gabled peaks and chimney tops. The coach turned left onto a pebbled drive. As they passed under an archway set within a stone wall, a large manor house came into view. It had the appearance of a fortified castle with crenellated walls, a turret, and an oriel window. Stables lay to the east and a walled garden to the west. The coach stopped at an arched entrance porch.

"I'll take you in, Miss Everson," Mr. Bradshaw said. "After you've been introduced, my wife and I shall be on our way."

Geneva smiled at the couple who had been her traveling companions for a good portion of the day. "Thank you for everything. You've been awfully good to me, including the nice luncheon along the way."

"You are most welcome," Mr. Bradshaw responded. "And don't be nervous. Your father is a kind, generous man."

Mrs. Bradshaw put her arm around Geneva. "So nice meeting you, dear. You're a sweet girl. Just be yourself, and they'll love you."

Geneva squeezed her hand. "Thank you, and God bless."

Getting out of the carriage, Mr. Bradshaw took Geneva's hand to help her down. As her feet touched the ground, a soft cooing of doves was suddenly overruled by the raucous call of a raven. The sooty bird swooped over the drive and soared on a current of air before landing on a top limb of a nearby sycamore.

Geneva turned to the solicitor, who was retrieving her travel bag from the coach. "Can I guess that is where the name Ravensmere comes from?"

A slight smile crossed Mr. Bradshaw's face. "That's right, miss."

Just then, the massive front door swung open. A man somewhere in his forties with thinning hair, wearing a dark suit and white necktie, emerged from the entrance porch and approached them. "Good afternoon, Mr. Bradshaw. I trust your trip went well."

Mr. Bradshaw handed the man Geneva's bag, then introduced, "Miss Everson, this is Stanway, your father's butler."

Geneva acknowledged the introduction with a warm smile. The butler simply bowed in return. "I'm glad you've arrived safely, miss. Please allow me to show you both inside."

Geneva waved a final farewell to Mrs. Bradshaw before following the butler and Mr. Bradshaw into the entrance hall. Stanway hung Geneva's traveling cloak on a peg. "Please, miss, come with me this way through the Great Hall."

Having never set foot in a manor house, Geneva turned her head from side to side as she followed Stanway across an enormous hall, taking in fine oak furnishings, the stained glass of an oriel window, and a suit of armor standing near the fireplace. Portraits hung on wood-paneled walls under the carved timbers of an amazingly high ceiling. As she craned her neck she spotted ravens carved in ebony perched on corbels in each corner.

A small anteroom led from the Great Hall into a sitting room where the scent of well-polished furniture hung in the air. From a window, the late afternoon sun cast its rays through the crystal prisms of a lampstand, sending rainbows across a gorgeously hued Persian carpet. A bust of William the Conqueror rested on a Chinese cabinet. Above it, a tapestry depicted what appeared to be the Battle of Hastings.

There were also more ravens, this time carved into the woodwork surrounding a fireplace. Grouped in front of the fireplace sat rose-colored armchairs. Four of these were currently occupied.

Stopping in the doorway, Stanway announced, "Mr. Harold Bradshaw. Miss Geneva Everson."

As he ushered Mr. Bradshaw and Geneva ahead of him into the room, the four occupants of the armchairs rose to their feet. A petite elderly lady walked forward, a gnarled hand gripping a walking stick.

"How do you do, Miss Everson. I'm Mrs. Louise Everson, Adam's mother."

That made the old lady Geneva's grandmother. She curtseyed. "It's a pleasure to meet you, ma'am. Thank you for your hospitality in having me stay here."

The elderly lady gave the shortest of nods, then turned to Mr. Bradshaw. "On behalf of my son, I want to thank you for bringing Miss Everson to Ravensmere, a long and tedious trip, I'm sure."

The solicitor bowed. "Thank you, ma'am. Please give your son my regards. My wife and I enjoyed Miss Everson's company very much."

He bowed again to Geneva. "If that's all, Miss Everson, I shall take my leave now. Good day to you, and once again my wife and I wish you all the best."

As he left the room, Mrs. Louise Everson stepped closer. Geneva's apprehension grew as the old lady looked her up and down. "Adam is in his upstairs lounge at the present. He wishes to have his first meeting with you in private. Before that, our housekeeper will take you to your room so you can settle in. I must say we were shocked to hear about you. Did Mr. Bradshaw tell you about Ravensmere?"

"No, ma'am. He just said that my father had a large country estate."

"I see. Well, the invitation to visit must have been hard to resist."

The woman's pointy nose, big eyes, and tiny mouth gave her the appearance of a mouse, but her assertive manner projected aggression. Tamping down the urge to answer in kind, Geneva said quietly, "No, ma'am. I had a hard time knowing whether or not to come, especially since I'd never left home before."

"But you were bold enough." The old lady gestured to a stout, big-bosomed woman with dark hair and pale skin. "This is my daughter-in-law, Mrs. Mary Everson, the widow of my late son, Frederick."

Geneva curtseyed. "How do you do, ma'am."

"Gracious, I wasn't sure what to expect," the stout woman replied with a high-pitched voice. "I'm glad to see you're a polite girl. Let me introduce my second son, Robert. You'll meet his brothers tonight."

A tall, lanky man in his middle or late thirties stepped forward. "How do you do, miss." Pushing spectacles up a long nose, he indicated a young woman with blond ringlets framing a pretty face. "This is my wife, Tess. She's been eagerly awaiting your arrival."

Tess stepped forward with a warm smile. From her appearance, Geneva guessed her to be with child. "Welcome to Ravensmere, Cousin Geneva. This has been such a big day for you. I don't know how I would handle such a life-changing event."

"No doubt she's worn out from the journey," Mary said. "Would you care for tea and refreshments, Miss Everson?"

"No, thank you. We stopped for tea before we arrived in Ingleford."

"Well, we don't want to keep Mr. Everson waiting." Mary frowned at Geneva's crumpled cotton dress and loose hair dangling around her face. "Tess, ring the bell pull. I'm sure our guest will want to tidy up after her long journey."

Within moments, a woman who looked to be in her fifties entered the room. She wore a black dress with a white apron and cap. A set of keys jingled at her waist. Mary turned to Geneva. "This is Mrs. Fox, our housekeeper. She will take you to your room to tidy up before you meet your father."

As Geneva started to follow the housekeeper, her newfound grandmother stepped forward, frowning. "Before you go up, let me be clear about one thing. Adam has a heart condition. The doctor has given strict orders that he's to have no upsets. Keep that in mind while you are visiting with him."

"Yes, ma'am, I won't forget."

"Good. Before dinner, Mrs. Fox will bring you here to meet the rest of the family."

Geneva followed the housekeeper through the Great Hall and down a wide hallway. Climbing an oak staircase, they came to a grandfather clock on the upper floor. Geneva peered down a long corridor, dark and gloomy with minimal light and reddish-brown wallpaper. A console table displayed Chinese blue-and-white vases and outside each door, griffin sconces hung on the walls.

The housekeeper looked over her shoulder. "Come along, Miss Everson. Those doors lead to family bedrooms. The guest bedrooms are on the east wing."

A few paces further, they turned right onto a narrow corridor. Halfway down, Mrs. Fox unlocked a door and pushed it open. "Here we are. I hope you'll find this satisfactory."

The floorboards creaked as Geneva stepped into a small room furnished with a bed, night table, washstand, bureau, and wardrobe. A porcelain clock stood on the fireplace mantelpiece. Spread across the bed was a gorgeous silk eiderdown in a pretty shade of smoky blue and multiple pillows with ruffled edges.

After such a grueling day, Geneva longed to climb into bed. Instead, she walked over to the window. Below was a courtyard partially enclosed with outbuildings. Across the back lane, a farmyard was visible through a coppice of oaks. But what made the view lovely were the distant green pastures and gently curved hilltops.

A woman in her thirties slipped into the room and placed a jug of steaming water on the washstand. She had a slim, willowy body and thick auburn hair under her cap. Mrs. Fox indicated the newcomer with a gesture. "Miss Everson, this is Emily, our head housemaid. While you freshen up, she'll unpack your bag and hang your dresses in the wardrobe. If ironing is needed, she'll see to that as well. When you're ready, ring the bell pull, and Stanway will take you to Mr. Everson's lounge. Is there anything else I can do for you?"

"I don't think so. Thank you for bringing me up."

As Mrs. Fox departed, Geneva turned to Emily with a smile. "Goodness, I'm not used to having things done for me. My uncle would have a fit if he could see me now."

"I'm happy for you, miss. I think it's wonderful that you're here."

"Thank you, but I'm not sure if everyone is happy that I'm here." Geneva opened the wardrobe door and bent forward.

Emily took a step closer. "May I ask what you're looking for, miss?"

"I had a bad experience with rats when I was a child. I'm just checking for any signs of them."

"Oh, no, Miss Everson. Mrs. Fox and I run a tight ship. You won't find rats in this manor house."

A half hour later, Stanway escorted Geneva to the master's suite in the hallway leading to family bedrooms. Geneva's apprehension reached new heights as the butler tapped on the half-open door.

"Miss Everson is here, sir. Are you ready to receive her?"

Geneva heard the rustle of a newspaper, then a quiet baritone voice. "Yes, by all means, Stanway. Please bring her in."

As Geneva entered a cozy lounge with comfortable furnishings and potted ferns, an older man stood up from a leather chair. For someone Geneva knew to be sixty years of age, Adam Everson looked well-preserved—slim, upright, and clean-shaven, with still-thick, ash-grey hair. Geneva gave a shy curtsey.

"It's nice to meet you, Mr. Everson. Thank you for sending Mr. Bradshaw with the invitation."

He didn't answer immediately, his breath quickening as though he'd been running a race. As his silence grew awkward, Geneva raised her eyes to meet his. Her own breath quickened at what she saw just as he exclaimed, "Dear Lord, Daniel was right! You have the Everson eyes—green with amber. And your mother's beautiful features. You *are* my daughter!"

He sank back into his armchair, a hand on his chest. Remembering her grandmother's admonition, Geneva worried the shock had been too much for him. But he lowered his hand and smiled tremulously.

"Geneva, I've been waiting on tenterhooks for your arrival, hoping my godson was right but convinced he had to be wrong.

But the eyes—that's a rare family trait. I've never seen such eyes outside the Everson family, and it has often skipped generations. That you and I should both have the Everson eyes—it is as though designed by our Creator to confirm that you are indeed my daughter."

Geneva could hardly contain her own astonishment as she looked into the same eyes that greeted her in the mirror every morning—the narrow amber circle around the pupil, the turquoise green filling the rest of the iris, the dark, thick fringe of eyelashes.

"Oh, yes, this is amazing. I brought my birth certificate that states you are my father. I thought there might be a mistake until just now. I've never dreamed they might have been inherited from my father. Certainly my mother never told me such."

As she spoke, Geneva pulled the birth certificate from her pocket and handed it to the man she now knew beyond doubt was her father. Adam looked it over and smiled. "Yes, Daniel mentioned you were born on Michaelmas Day. Another proof you are my daughter. If I'd only known Elizabeth was pregnant when—"

He broke off, then gestured to a leather chair next to his. "Please, sit down. We have much to talk about and so much to learn about one another."

As she sank into the offered armchair, Geneva glanced out a bay window to a lovely garden. Clearly it was a topic of interest to her father, by the stack of gardening periodicals piled on a table beside his armchair. There were also two medicine bottles labeled Tincture of Digitalis and Tincture of Hawthorn—most probably for the heart condition her grandmother had mentioned.

Crossing his legs at the ankles, Adam leaned back in his chair, his narrow features lit up with joy. "Geneva, you have no idea how delighted I am to be a father of such a beautiful daughter. I was shocked when Daniel came with news of you. If I'd known of your existence earlier, please believe I would have come for you. It's tragic that I missed your childhood but such a blessing that you've arrived now safely."

Geneva responded to his wide smile with a diffident one of her own. "Well, at first I didn't believe you were alive. Not until Mr. Bradshaw showed me the proof on paper. I was so bewildered I didn't know what to do. Now that I'm here, I know it was the right decision. It was nice having Mrs. Bradshaw with us. She and her husband were kind to me."

Geneva had no idea how to talk to this father who was a stranger to her. She felt herself rambling as she told about the journey, rest stops, her first glimpse of the sea. Adam listened with seeming interest. But as the minutes passed, his bright expression grew serious, and he rubbed the side of his neck.

As Geneva finished her tale, he said heavily, "I'm glad you enjoyed the journey, Geneva. But I expect you're aware now of what happened in the past and why your mother left my household. I gave Mr. Bradshaw permission to speak of it."

Geneva lowered her eyes to her hands, folded tightly in her lap. "Yes, he told me about it. I was deeply shocked as Mother had told me a very different story—that you were a sailcloth manufacturer who died in a factory fire. She wasn't the type of person to tell lies. But in this situation it's easy to understand she wanted to guard her reputation, not just for her sake but mine as well."

Geneva lifted her eyes to meet Adam's green-amber gaze squarely. "Let me be clear that I don't believe the allegation against her. Mother was an honorable, well-respected lady, devout in her faith, who never missed church, and wouldn't dream of acting contrary to godly principles."

Adam let out an unhappy sigh. "I don't deny her good qualities. But my first wife had good qualities too. They aren't always enough."

"Your first wife?" Geneva repeated blankly. "So—you were married before my mother? She never mentioned that either."

An expression of deep pain and sadness crossed Adam's face. "There is no reason she would since I never spoke of that sad time to Elizabeth. I married Rachael Prout when I was thirty. She was indiscreet with her lover and brought shame upon me before finally running off with him. It was the worst time of my life. When I heard she'd died of consumption, I vowed to never marry again. But ten years later, I met your mother at a country dance. She was so lovely and charming I asked her guardian, Dr. Dewhurst, for permission to court her. We were married on the second day of November 1811, not quite eleven months before your birth, and were married for just four months before our marriage ended."

He let out a weary sigh before continuing, "About my wife's indiscretion—it would be inappropriate for me to speak of the details. All you need to know is that I witnessed the immorality with my own eyes. This lounge connects with our two bedrooms."

He pointed to the door on the right. "That was her room. When I entered unexpectedly, I found our coachman in bed with her. I went berserk. It was clear evidence of adultery and grounds for her expulsion."

Geneva searched his face. "Her expulsion? Even if she was guilty, which I'm sure she wasn't, why were you so quick to throw her out? Couldn't you have given her a second chance?"

"Geneva, you have no—" Adam broke off in a coughing fit. Rubbing at his chest, he recovered his breath. "You are an innocent child, so you have no idea what betrayal does to a man. It was bad enough with Rachael. But Elizabeth as well? I was done with marriage. I wanted her out of the house so I could be alone to lick a new set of wounds."

"But why did you send her to my uncle?" Geneva asked tensely. "He is a cruel man. No matter what she'd done, she didn't deserve that. Why didn't you at least send her home to the Dewhursts?"

"That wasn't possible. The doctor and his wife had gone to do missionary work in Natal, South Africa. Dr. and Mrs. Dewhurst were always caring for others—the reason they took in your mother and her brother when they were left orphans."

Coughing again, Adam dabbed at his forehead with a handkerchief. "There's more, Geneva. Something I deeply regret. A fortnight after Elizabeth's departure, I received a letter from her. I assumed she was begging to return. Reconciliation was out of the question, so I threw the letter unopened into the fire. I received two more letters at later dates. I threw those in the fire as well. Now I can't help but wonder if those letters were informing me of her pregnancy. I'm sorry, Geneva. If I had known, I would have done the right thing by bringing her back."

Geneva swallowed hard, unable to move an inch as she digested her father's horrifying confession. In her mind's eye, she could see the letters bursting into flames and shriveling up into ashes, sealing the fate of mother and unborn child. She wanted to turn back the hands of time. She wanted to scream and lash out. She wanted to weep, but her anger wouldn't allow it.

"How could you do that?" she burst out. "You were responsible for her. You have no idea what she went through. How she suffered. Did you just erase her from your mind as if she never existed?"

"Of course not," Adam responded. "I loved your mother. I didn't want to expose her to the publicity and humiliation of divorce, and certainly I had no plans for remarriage myself. So I devised a plan. I asked Mr. Bradshaw to send a letter to Alex Brigham with false news that Elizabeth's husband had died and had left her a jointure in his will. If he would provide her with protection and a comfortable home, then he would receive the jointure as compensation. Alex replied without delay. He was happy to open his home to his sister."

"Happy?" Geneva's anger boiled into furious speech. "Uncle Alex wasn't happy to take my mother in. He was just happy to get the money. I doubt Mother knew about this agreement, and I'm glad for her sake. It's easy to guess what he did with the money. That year she moved in is when he bought property in a better part of town where his business would flourish. He earned a good income from his pawnshop, but he was too miserly to spend it. He dismissed his paid housekeeper and forced Mother to work like a South Indies slave!

"After she died, I had to take over. If I made a mistake, he beat me with his belt. Sometimes he made me sit for hours with the coal scuttle turned over my head. My worst ordeal was when he locked me in the storage closet. Maybe he really didn't know there was a rat behind the boxes. Either way, he went off to the pawnshop, where he couldn't hear my cries of terror."

Surging to her feet, Geneva pushed her hair back from her forehead. "See this scar? It's a testimony to his drunken violence. He struck me. When I fell over, my head hit the corner of the cast-iron stove."

Adam swayed in his chair, a hand rising to his brow as if he were dizzy. "Believe me, Geneva, if I had known of your suffering, I would have come to your rescue. I'm so sorry! Please forgive me."

A scarlet flush crept over Geneva's cheeks. "After what I've been through, why should I forgive you? I could have grown up in this manor house with sisters and brothers, stability, and privilege. You stole my first eighteen years and ruined the life of my innocent mother. Don't ask me to forgive you. It will *never* happen!"

Spinning around on her heel, Geneva marched out of the room and down the hall to the privacy of her bedroom.

CHAPTER FOUR

An hour later, Geneva removed a cold, damp cloth from her face and looked in the mirror. Thankfully, her reddened, puffed eyes had returned to normal. The dinner hour was fast approaching. She knew that gentry dressed up for dinner, so she put on her best dress, a soft muslin fabric in a pale shade of mauve, the bodice with ruffles and pleats, and a sash tied at the waist. Hopefully, it would do. After brushing her hair until it shone, she pinned it up loosely and left a cluster of curls trailing down her back.

She had just finished when Mrs. Fox arrived and escorted her downstairs to the drawing room. It seemed packed with people, all of whom rose to their feet as Geneva entered the room. Her heart sank when she caught sight of the stunning gowns the female family members were wearing—silk, satin, and organza with exquisite embroidery, mother-of-pearl beads, and shimmering puffed sleeves. Compared to them, her dress looked like something from the parish donation bin.

"Good evening, my dear." By his bright, cheery tone, Adam had recovered from the stress of their initial meeting. "May I have the pleasure of introducing you to the rest of the family. You've met my mother, my sister-in-law Mary, her second son, Robert, and his wife, Tess. But let me introduce you to my eldest nephew, Captain Jack Everson."

Geneva had already noted the four family members she'd met earlier. Now a tall, handsome gentleman with deeply-tanned freckled features stepped forward. His ginger hair shone with pomade, and his bright-blue waistcoat was like nothing Geneva had seen in her small hometown. As she curtseyed, he proffered a smile that didn't reach his pale-blue eyes.

"How do you do, Miss Everson. I can't deny that I'm astounded to have you here. But I trust your brief visit will be a pleasant one."

His slight emphasis on "brief visit" made Geneva doubt her welcome, but she answered politely, "Thank you, sir. I'm sure it will be."

"And this is Philip, my youngest nephew," Adam said. "He's the vicar of our parish church."

Another gentleman, shorter and stockier than Robert or Jack with a mass of curly brown hair, moved forward. "Miss Everson, what a delight to meet you. I don't know many young ladies willing to take on a household of strangers. How brave you are."

His smile, at least, was so warm and welcoming, Geneva couldn't doubt its sincerity. He turned to a slim woman as tall as himself with glossy nut-brown hair, braided and pinned up in coils. "Please let me introduce my wife, Claire."

Claire beamed at Geneva. "I'm so happy to meet you. And I'm looking forward to introducing our children to their new cousin. We have two—Paul and Hannah. They're at home with Nanny."

"I'd love to meet them," Geneva replied. "Children are such a blessing."

"Last but not least," Adam cut in, indicating another young woman standing at the back, "may I present my niece, Katherine, the youngest of Mary's children."

"Hello, Miss Everson. I couldn't believe it when I heard about you. A feather could have knocked me over." Like her mother, Katherine had pale skin and dark hair, but hers was styled into the latest fashion of tight curls and loops. Though an attractive young woman, her pretty features were diminished by a cheerless, almost sullen expression.

Adam cleared his throat. "Do sit down, Geneva. Will you have a glass of sherry?"

Geneva hesitated. Drink had caused trouble with her uncle. Perhaps it was best to avoid it. "No, thank you, but I do enjoy grape cordial, if you have it."

"We certainly do. Dr. Whitmore advises me to have it every day. Stanway will pour you a glass."

As Geneva thanked the butler for her fruity drink, Tess sat down on a nearby sofa and patted the cushion beside her. "Come and sit here, Miss Everson. It's nice to have someone younger than me in the house."

Geneva sat down. "Please, call me Geneva."

Adam took his own seat. "Well, this is a momentous day. Not just for Geneva but for all of us. Now that I've met her, I have full assurance she is my daughter. Our resemblance to one another is unmistakable."

His mother waved her fan across her face. "Adam, I'm shocked to hear you say this. Has this girl bewitched you?"

Adam raised an eyebrow. "What on earth are you suggesting, Mother?"

"Do I have to spell it out?" the elderly woman hissed. "This girl has much to gain by claiming to be your daughter. You shouldn't trust someone you've just met. And even if she truly is Elizabeth's daughter, she might be as deceitful as her mother."

Outrage swelled Geneva's breast. "Mrs. Everson, that's not fair to my mother. She was good and honorable and—"

"Hush, girl!" Mary cut Geneva off with a wave of her arm, then turned to her brother-in-law. "Adam, you know Grandmama

Louise is right. Have you lost your good judgement? Yes, she may look a bit like Elizabeth. But resemblances are subjective."

"I have to agree," Jack spoke up. "Being Elizabeth's daughter doesn't mean she is yours. But in fairness to Miss Everson, her mother's actions are not her fault. She deserves a measure of respect during her brief visit."

Again, the emphasis on "brief visit." Geneva was quickly feeling unwanted. Adam gave her a reassuring smile as he responded firmly, "Bradshaw has investigated all these facts and is completely satisfied with Geneva's identity. She was born less than seven months after Elizabeth left Ravensmere. Her birth was registered by the parish vicar with the name of the father recorded as Adam Everson. I have her birth certificate right here."

Adam took from his breast pocket the birth certificate Geneva had handed him and held it up. Reaching over, Jack took it from his hand. "Here, let me take a look. Ah yes, the date does indicate she was conceived before your wife departed. But that hardly proves she's your daughter versus the consequences of your wife's—well, let's just call it an indiscretion. Or it could be a forged document designed to deceive you."

"Forged?" Adam snatched the document from Jack's hand. "That's not only ridiculous, but impossible. After all, Daniel discovered Geneva just a week ago. And she's made no claims of being my daughter. It was Bradshaw who approached her on my behalf. After he also confirmed that she's been known in that town as the daughter of Elizabeth Everson and niece of Alex Brigham since her birth."

He gestured toward Geneva. "As to being my true daughter, just look at her. She has not only her mother's beauty but the Everson eyes. The only Everson in this room besides myself to inherit that trait."

Geneva was already speechless with rage at the aspersions being cast on her mother. Now she froze as every eye focused on her face. If she weren't a lady, she'd throw her grape cordial at the entire bunch.

Philip broke the awkward silence. "Uncle Adam is right. Anyone with eyes in their head or who has ever walked through the Ravensmere portrait gallery can see she's inherited the Everson eyes, which is more than the rest of us. In any case, it's rude to discuss our cousin as though she were not sitting right here in the room with us."

As Geneva sent him a grateful smile, Tess broke in. "You're quite right, Philip. And it's not just her eyes. The shape of her ears, the mouth line, the dimples in her cheeks are all identical to Uncle Adam's. What other proof do you need?"

"It is not to any of you that Geneva need offer proof," Adam said, slipping the document back in his pocket. "Now if you will all cease this unkind and offensive discussion, I have something important to say." Rising to his feet, Adam moved toward the fireplace. Hands on his hips, he glanced from face to face with a grave, unyielding expression.

"The matter of Geneva's paternity is settled, so I will not hear it raised again. Nor will I tolerate any insults toward my daughter. Whether in my presence or absence, *all* of you will give Geneva the respect and courtesy she deserves or face consequences. Have I made myself clear?"

His mother's lips were pursed so tightly her mouth had disappeared, but she said nothing further. The others showed acquiescence, if not agreement, except for Jack, whose face was completely blank of expression. Only Philip spoke up.

"Yes, Uncle Adam, we understand, and I'm sure everyone will act accordingly."

Returning to his chair, Adam focused his gaze on his daughter. "Geneva, I know you're angry with me concerning your mother. I won't argue with you on events that happened before your birth. But I do hope that one day you'll forgive me. While I can't change the past, I can offer you now protection, comfort, and a bright future. I have no wish whatsoever for you to return to Shaftesbury. Will you stay here and make Ravensmere your home?"

Silence came over the room. Glancing around, Geneva saw a mixture of shocked and angry expressions. Only Tess and Philip offered encouraging smiles. It wouldn't be easy living here with the support of so few. But Geneva could hold her own. Besides, if she was really serious about discovering the truth and vindicating her mother, she had no alternative but to stay.

Squaring her shoulders, she lifted her chin. "Thank you, Father. I would be delighted to stay at Ravensmere."

"I'm glad to hear it." Adam glanced at the mantel clock and called out, "Stanway, is there a crisis in the kitchen? Dinner should be ready by now."

The butler appeared so quickly he must have been loitering just outside the drawing room door. "I beg your pardon, sir. Mrs. Fox just informed me that dinner is served."

Stepping up beside Geneva, Adam offered his right arm with a courtly bow. Geneva quickly swallowed her last sip of grape cordial and rose to her feet to take his arm. As her father escorted her with great formality from the room, Jack offered Grandmama Louise his arm. The two followed Adam and Geneva at a slow, dignified walk. The others trailed behind in order of marital status and age.

Entering the dining room, Geneva marveled at the delicious aromas coming from a sideboard. Soft green wallpaper created a pleasing mood. Oak beams crossed the ceiling while French doors provided a view of the garden. Illuminated with glowing candelabras, a long mahogany table sparkled with crystal glasses and sterling silverware. Adam seated Geneva to his right at the head of the table.

When everyone had taken their place, Philip gave thanks. "Father in heaven, we thank you for your bountiful blessings and for the safe arrival of Cousin Geneva. Bless her, O Lord, and by your grace may we each do our part in helping her to adjust to her new home. In Christ's name we pray. Amen."

While Stanway served soup from a steaming tureen, Tess placed her napkin in her lap and glanced across the table. "Cousin Geneva, I'd love to hear about your life in Shaftesbury. Will you share with us?"

"Well, compared to growing up in a beautiful manor like this, it's not very interesting. From an early age, Mother gave me reading, writing, and arithmetic lessons. She also taught me to play the flute and to read music. Sometimes I've played in church during the offertory. I was awfully nervous at first until I got used to it.

"Anyway, Mother thought a good education would enable me to become a governess. After she died, I kept reading the educational books the vicar loaned to me. English history books were my favorite, though I don't get much time for reading. Most of the time, I'm occupied with domestic work or helping in my uncle's pawnshop."

As Geneva trailed off, there was silence around the table as though these gentlefolk had no idea how to respond to her simple narrative. Then Tess spoke up. "I love the sound of the flute. Did you bring it with you?"

Geneva swallowed a spoonful of creamy potato-leek soup. "No, I couldn't. Uncle Alex locked it away in his pawnshop as punishment. Though if I'd known I was going to stay here, I'd have brought my cat at least. He's very special to me."

"I love cats too," Claire spoke up. "I can see how he must have been hard to leave. And your home. You must miss it. And your family there too, this—Uncle Alex, you said?"

Geneva shook her head. "I miss my cat, but not my uncle. He was never kind to me or my mother, so in truth I'm glad to be away from him."

"But your flute," Tess interjected. "You're a grown woman. Why would your uncle punish you like a child needing correction?"

Geneva shrugged. "I broke something when cleaning. Uncle Alex doesn't need much reason. Especially when he drinks. If he's read the note I left for him, I'm sure he's angry enough to be into his second bottle of gin by now. Another reason I'm thankful not to return there."

"Good gracious!" Grandmama Louise lowered her spoon. "Your uncle sounds like a terrible man. He'd better not come poking around here."

For an instant, Geneva believed her grandmother was actually expressing sympathy until the elderly lady looked her up and down, adding acidly, "I can spot an opportunist from a mile away."

Geneva was no fool. She got the innuendo but chose to ignore it. Adam placed a dab of butter on his crusty roll. "Well, Geneva, I'm interested to know what you think of this grand old manor."

Geneva was more than relieved to turn the conversation from her past. "It's fascinating and beautifully furnished. May I ask when it was built?"

"Certainly. Sir Callum McCormack, an Everson ancestor of Irish descent, built the Great Hall in 1487."

"Oh, that was shortly after the Battle of Bosworth when Henry VII became the first Tudor king."

Adam smiled. "That's right. Your knowledge of history is good."

"Sir Callum also built our parish church," Philip said, "of which I'm honored to be the current vicar. McCormack means 'son of raven' in the original Gaelic. The 'mere' in Ravensmere refers to our small lake. And since ravens have inhabited this area for centuries, you can see how the estate's name came about."

"Yes, I've seen the ravens," Geneva answered. "And all the carvings around the manor."

"You'll be interested in the portrait of Charlotte McCormack," Adam said. "It was from her that we've inherited our unique eyes. She became the heiress of Ravensmere in 1649. Several years later, she married Sir Tobias Everson, a Knight of the Shire. I'm the fifth generation of Eversons to own Ravensmere. I enjoyed my years serving as justice of the peace, but managing the estate has always been the most rewarding."

"Jack is the manager now," Mary put in with maternal pride. "After my husband died, Adam instructed Jack in all things pertaining to the estate, farm, and quarry. I'm so grateful that he financed all three of my sons' education. They attended boarding school and university at Eton. After Jack graduated, Adam purchased him a commission in the Royal Navy, for which I can never thank him enough."

"Jack did very well in the Navy," Katherine added. "He rose quickly to be captain of his own ship. A fellow officer told me he was known for his skill as a military strategist. Just three years ago, his ship fought in the Battle of Navarino against the Ottoman Empire."

She looked over at her brother. "You earned substantial prize money for that, didn't you?"

Jack brushed a speck of lint from his sleeve. "The prize money was inconsequential compared to serving my country. But my responsibility and loyalty to Uncle Adam comes first. When his health began declining not long after Navarino, I retired and came home. It has been my pleasure to free Uncle Adam in any way I can from the stress of estate management."

Grandmama Louise nodded approvingly. "He's doing a marvelous job, isn't he, Adam? It's good to know the estate is in such capable hands. And it's a blessing to have my grandchildren living with us. Except for Philip, of course. He and Claire live at the vicarage. Robert does well financially from his published books. He's an ornithologist. He studies birds throughout the region, and Tess draws the illustrations for his books."

Robert sent his wife an affectionate smile. "Tess is a great artist with an incredible eye for detail, which is probably why my books are so popular. I studied the natural sciences at Eton. My first books were on the seabirds and raptors of Dorset. I'm studying songbirds for my next book. Jack is the businessman of the family, but I'm cut from a different cloth. I have a strong bond with the land and wildlife of our heritage. Perish the thought that we might lose it or have someone dare to take it from us."

Tess patted his hand. "That's not likely to happen, dear. Perhaps Cousin Geneva would like to hear about the estate itself."

"Yes, of course," Adam spoke up. "Our estate is midsized with roughly fifteen hundred acres. While many landowners subsist just on their tenant income, we receive additional income from our quarry as well as the land we farm, which is used for grain production, dairy, and poultry. We try to follow the latest practices in scientific husbandry, not just for profit but because we feel it's important to set an example to other farmers."

"That's a good Christian principle," Geneva said approvingly. "I'm sure your laborers must appreciate that. Scripture teaches that caring for others is the best example of all. Isn't that true, Cousin Philip?"

Philip glanced at his uncle. "Well, I'm sure most are appreciative. Not all welcome change of any sort."

Adam spoke up firmly. "I can assure you, Ravensmere has an exemplary record of caring for our employees. And we try to set an example to *all* the working men and women of our parish."

Stanway and Mrs. Fox cleared away the soup bowls and served thin slices of roast sirloin beef, fricassee of rabbits, and silver servers filled with an array of vegetables. Drizzling gravy onto her meat and potatoes, Geneva tucked into the mouth-watering meal with gusto.

The last course was a rich and creamy trifle. This was followed by coffee, which Stanway served in the drawing room. Geneva contributed to the conversation as best she could, but after such a hearty meal and long day, her eyes began to droop. Mary suddenly spoke up.

"Stanway, has Miss Geneva's room been prepared for bedtime? She might want to retire early tonight."

"Yes, ma'am, Emily anticipated that. Her room is ready."

Thankful for the considerate suggestion, Geneva smiled warmly at her new aunt as she set her coffee cup down. "I think I will go up now, if you don't mind. It's lovely to have met you all. And thank you for the delicious meal."

The men all rose to their feet courteously. Adam stepped forward to give Geneva a kiss on the cheek. "The pleasure is ours, my dear. I couldn't be more delighted to have you with us. Sleep well tonight. I shall look forward to seeing you at breakfast."

Geneva curtseyed and made her way to the staircase. On the upper landing, the floorboards creaked beneath the carpet as she passed the griffin sconces. In the candlelight, their eagle beaks and sharp claws looked more menacing than by daylight. Normally, she'd be dog-tired from a day of physical work. But today it was the emotional strain of her new situation that exhausted her.

At least the family were doing their best to be polite. Still, knowing that some of them resented her presence made Geneva feel uncomfortable. She'd done nothing to offend them except be born. And it was hardly her fault that she was as shocking a surprise to the family as they'd been to her.

Oh well, things were sure to get better in time. But that didn't quell her outrage for the way her mother had been treated. What a preposterous notion that the godly woman Geneva had known would allow a coachman into her bed. Geneva knew her mother better than these people did. One day, Lord willing, she'd unravel the truth and clear her mother's name.

A jug of hot water was waiting in Geneva's bedroom, undoubtedly carried up by Emily. After undressing, Geneva luxuriated in a sponge bath, then donned her cotton nightgown. With sheer delight, she slipped between the snowy-white sheets of the prettiest bed she'd ever seen. It was incredible to think her mother had once lived here as mistress of Ravensmere.

The silky eiderdown pulled up to her neck, Geneva snuggled down and listened to the sounds of the manor. The creak of wooden beams. The hoot of an owl on the rooftop. The footsteps of a maid extinguishing candles outside her door. It wasn't until she imagined Pookie's comforting body next to her that she finally drifted off to sleep.

CHAPTER FIVE

The following morning, Geneva was awakened by a tap on the door. A moment later, Emily came in. "Good morning, Miss Everson. I've brought your tea tray."

As Geneva lifted her head, Emily placed a tray on the bedside table, set with fine bone china and a fresh yellow rose in a vase.

"Thank you, Emily. Does this happen every morning or just today?"

"Every morning, miss. It's a family tradition. Did you sleep well?"

Geneva sat up and pushed her tangled hair back from her face. Last night she'd awakened damp with perspiration from a horrible dream—her mother being cast out on a cold, wet night, disgraced and penniless. It wasn't until early dawn that she'd finally slept again. "Yes, I did, but only for part of the night."

Another maid entered with a jug of steaming water. Emily introduced her. "This is Samantha, one of the housemaids. When you've gone down for breakfast, she'll clean your room and make the bed."

Emily opened the wardrobe. "Which dress would you like to wear today?"

"The pale blue one should do," Geneva replied.

Emily laid the dress at the foot of the bed. "Will you need help with your hairdo?"

"My hairdo? No, thank you. It's quite simple. I can do it myself."

"Very well, miss. If that's all, I'll be on my way. Don't hesitate to ring if you need me."

An hour later, Geneva headed downstairs to the dining room. Conversation and a clatter of silverware immediately died as she entered the room. A glance around told her she was the last family member to arrive. Curtseying, she cleared her throat. "Good morning. I'm sorry if I'm late for breakfast."

Adam, Jack, and Robert had risen politely upon her entrance. Adam came to her side. "No, my dear. For breakfast we serve ourselves, so a few minutes don't matter. You still look a little tired. Was the bed unsatisfactory?"

"Not at all, it's very comfortable. I'm sure I'll sleep better tonight."

"Well, come over here to the sideboard. Stanway has set out a selection of tasty dishes, so take whatever you fancy."

Geneva thanked him and helped herself to kippers, a poached egg, and grilled tomatoes. Once she'd taken her seat next to her father, Stanway walked over with a silver coffee pot. "Will you have a cup, miss?"

"Thank you, Stanway. Goodness, I'm not used to being waited on. I feel a bit guilty for not fetching my own hot water and making the bed."

Mary shook her head. "Gracious, that would be totally inappropriate. It would certainly raise eyebrows with the servants."

"I'm not surprised you feel that way, considering your life till now," Adam said. "But you'll soon grow accustomed to our ways and even come to enjoy the ease and time for other pursuits having servants provides."

Glancing at the worn cuffs of Geneva's dress, Mary gave an audible sniff. "Well, I'd say one of the first orders of business should be to summon Mrs. Lockwood to the manor. You remember our seamstress, Adam. She designed Katherine's last-season wardrobe, including the ballgown you so admired. She can take Geneva's measurements and get at least a few basic dresses made quickly. We don't want the girl walking around in rags."

Geneva gritted her teeth to bite back a sharp rejoinder, but her father looked pleased. "Excellent idea, Mary. I'll leave that in your capable hands. Order anything you think my daughter needs."

"Oh, no, Father, that isn't necessary," Geneva protested. "I don't want to be taking advantage. Besides, I've always made my own dresses. If you feel my wardrobe is inadequate, I can sew new ones myself if I can just get a few fabrics."

"Nonsense, child," Adam responded. "You are my daughter and should dress accordingly. If you'd been raised in your proper position here, you'd have been choosing ballgowns along with Katherine. It is my pleasure to rectify that injustice now. In fact, I insist on it."

Geneva argued no further. "Yes, of course, Father. I wouldn't want to put you to shame. Thank you, Mary, for thinking of it."

The older woman gestured away Geneva's thanks but looked pleased at the courtesy. "It is a small thing. And do call me Aunt Mary. You are, after all, my niece, it would seem."

"Well, well, it seems our new cousin is settling in nicely to her new position." From the opposite end of the table, Jack's chuckle held no genuine mirth. "Let's not pretend a new wardrobe isn't what any girl who's spent her life as a servant would want. Tell me, what would your uncle think now of the fine company his missing housemaid is keeping? In fact, maybe someone should inform him. After all, he is still your guardian, is he not?"

Geneva lowered the fork she'd been using to debone a kipper. "I won't pretend I'm not as delighted as any girl to have some new dresses. As to Uncle Alex, I told him where I was going in the note I left. But you're right, Cousin Jack. This afternoon, I'll write to let him know I won't be coming home."

Her father turned his gaze to the French doors that led from the dining room to his garden. "Well, it appears we have another sunny summer day. After breakfast, I shall give you a tour of my garden and an introduction to the portraits in the Great Hall."

Adam looked down the table at Jack. "What's on your agenda today? Have you heard when the farm equipment is arriving?"

"Yes, today's the day. I'll meet with the bailiff this morning. After that, I'll be in Ingleford on a business matter."

"I hope you haven't forgotten we have guests coming for dinner tonight," Mary said. "Angus Fairfax and Nigel Spooner are coming with their wives."

"We haven't forgotten," Robert said. "Mr. Fairfax is a distinguished acquaintance, Cousin Geneva. And Mr. Spooner is Jack's long-time friend. You will enjoy meeting them."

"Just do us a favor by not bringing up your drunken Uncle Alex," Katherine interjected caustically.

"Or his pawnshop," Grandmama Louise added. "We've worked too hard to build up this family's position to have the Everson name associated with such a vulgar, low-class man."

For the first time, Geneva felt a desire to defend her uncle, but only because she shared his "vulgar" bloodline. Just then Jack got up from the table. "If you'll all excuse me, I have work to do."

He offered Geneva a hollow smile. "Enjoy your time with the seamstress, Cousin Geneva."

Once he'd departed from the dining room, Tess reached for a slice of toast. "Geneva, dear, you must come to my bedroom this afternoon. I think you're the same size as me. If you wish, I could loan you an evening gown for tonight."

Geneva's eyes sparkled. "Would you? Oh my goodness, you've saved the day."

After breakfast, Geneva donned a blue bonnet that matched her dress and stepped out the front entrance porch with her father. As at dinner the night before, he held out his arm for her to take. But she still had feelings of resentment toward him, so she looked the other way, pretending not to notice.

Dropping his arm, Adam led the way through a gate in a stone wall to a perennial garden surrounded by a low boxwood hedge. Color and texture abounded. Weather-beaten statues competed with towering sunflowers. Benches were well-positioned beneath climbing vines.

"This is amazing!" Geneva said, unwillingly impressed. "You must have an artistic flair to design all this."

Adam squeezed a lavender head to release the fragrance. "I took my time in the planning stages. After studying garden designs from the Roman era to the present day, I decided to create my own unique place. As you can see, my garden occupies a full acre on this side of the manor. The stone wall keeps animals out, but more importantly, it gives me a sense of refuge from the world. This perennial garden is just the first of several such enclosures."

"It's lovely—like a small paradise."

"I'm glad you find it so." Adam wiped at the corner of his eye. "I never thought I'd stroll through here with a daughter at my side."

He led Geneva along a brick path and under a wrought-iron archway to the next enclosure—a water garden with a natural pool and trickling waterfall. Rocks and pebbles lined the edges with an arrangement of flowering plants, shrubs, and a weeping cherry tree. As Geneva peered into the crystal-clear water, she spotted goldfish swimming between lily pads and water ferns.

"My goodness, it must have taken months to create all this."

"It did," Adam responded somberly. "That was the best part of it. Planning all this kept me focused throughout that dreadful year after your mother departed. First, creating the blueprints, then overseeing construction. Daniel's father helped too. His ideas and suggestions were excellent."

Geneva raised her eyes to a dense area of bushes and trees beyond the garden wall. "I see you've left an untouched wilderness out there. Is that where the ravens live?"

"Yes, they build their nests and raise their offspring there. When the leaves drop in the autumn, you will see some of the nests. The natural world has its own beauty, so we've left it untouched. It's been quite a while since I took a short stroll through there."

Adam led the way through another arch to a rose garden with a fountain reflecting back the rainbow hues of the roses. "This garden was built by my father, Henry. It's a shame he never lived to see the additional enclosures I created."

As they passed under the last archway, gingko trees offered a shade garden with a variety of ferns and hostas. In the center was a round gazebo built of stone. As Adam took her inside, Geneva admired a wicker settee, tea table, and colorful jute rug.

"What a charming place. I can just imagine you and Mother having tea here." Geneva broke off, feeling her cheeks turning red as she realized the tactlessness of her musings.

Adam kept his gaze riveted on a bee buzzing against a windowpane. "No, Geneva, this place was built after Elizabeth's departure. But I've spent many afternoons in here, not having tea but with a book and a glass of whiskey."

His description sounded so lonely that Geneva's heart went out to him. Adam turned toward her, his expression dispirited and sad. "I feel quite tired. Let's go back inside now and I'll show you the family portrait gallery."

Adam led the way from his shade garden to the French doors that led into the dining room and down the main hallway to the Great Hall. After the heat of the garden, the cool air indoors felt good. Geneva glanced up at the timbers of the high ceiling and the carved ravens perched on corbels. "What year did you say the manor was built—1487?"

"That's right. The Great Hall with the solar and buttery was the first section to be built. More additions were built at later dates. The fireplace you see provided the servants with a place to cook. The family dined here and entertained guests. The upstairs solar was a private sanctuary for the family. It now serves as an exceptionally nice bedroom for my mother. On the ground floor below it, we have the wine cellar. On the other side of the hall, the buttery was a place where travelers and strangers could come for free food and drink. Today it's our library."

"It's all fascinating," Geneva said, "but I'm longing to see the portrait of Charlotte Everson."

"Ah, yes, come this way." Adam led her to the fireplace and pointed to a painting above the mantelpiece. "First of all, that is Sir Tobias Everson—your great-great-great-grandfather and Knight of the Shire."

Geneva shook her head in wonder. "I am still amazed that I should be related to such a man. Look at the raven taking food from his hand. Was it his pet?"

"I doubt it, but he obviously befriended the bird. The portrait of Charlotte, his wife and heiress of Ravensmere, is to the right."

Geneva studied the head-and-shoulders painting of a young woman. The artist had not failed in reproducing the unique green and amber of her eyes. Adam led her along a row of additional portraits that represented distant uncles, aunts, and cousins.

Geneva paused at a portrait of a much younger Adam, robust and handsome, leaning against his horse with his elbow resting on the saddle. She studied the painted eyes so like her own and Charlotte's. "Goodness, I feel light headed. Yesterday morning, I knew nothing about my past. Now I have all these faces looking at me—a line of ancestors who made me who I am today."

Smiling tenderly, Adam took his daughter's hand. "How lovely to hear you say that, Geneva. I can feel it in my bones that you and I will become close to one another."

Still uncomfortable at his touch, Geneva found an excuse to pull away by stepping back to examine the portrait of Charlotte once more. Just then, a thought occurred to her. "Did you ever have a portrait of my mother painted?"

Adam seemed to hesitate before stating, "Yes, I did. In fact, I commissioned it before our wedding from a well-known London portrait painter. He finished it not long after we returned from our honeymoon."

"That is wonderful! I have no sketches to remind me of her appearance. May I see her portrait?"

Adam hesitated even longer before answering apologetically, "I'm sorry, Geneva. I no longer own the portrait. You must understand how devastated I was when your mother—well, I had it removed the same day she left. My impulse was to destroy it, but Jack felt it would be far more justice to allow it to be sold at auction to the highest bidder."

The tenderness Geneva had been feeling toward her father vanished in a blaze of anger. "You *sold* my mother's portrait? How could you do such a thing? I don't care what you say. She was *not* an adulteress. There must be some way we could get it back."

Adam grabbed the back of a chair to steady himself. "I'm sorry, but that is impossible. I deliberately chose not to know who purchased the portrait. Try to see this from my point of view and not just yours. I hope you never have to endure the pain of betrayal, so don't judge me."

He took a deep breath, one hand again clutching at his heart. "Can we not just focus on today and rejoice that my godson found you and that my daughter has come home?"

His expression of weary pain melted Geneva's fury as much as his words. Up to this point, she had been enjoying her father's company. He'd seemed as kindly and generous as Mr. Bradshaw had said, and she did want to get to know him. If he truly believed her mother had betrayed him, his actions were understandable.

Of course, Geneva knew otherwise and was still determined to prove that. But in the meantime, she could indeed rejoice at finding a father. And she hadn't missed his clutching at his chest. The last thing she wanted was to provoke the kind of upset Grandmama Louise had warned against.

"I am happy too that Mr. Cavendish found me," she responded gently. "I can't put the past completely behind me because I know with all certainty Mother would not do what you claim. In time, I will discover the truth and put your own heart at ease. But for today at least, I too will rejoice that I have found a father."

She saw tears brimming her father's eyes. He opened his mouth to speak but was interrupted by several loud raps. Stanway hurried down the entrance hall to open the front door. "Good morning, Mr. Cavendish. Mr. Everson is expecting you. Please come in."

Stepping past the butler, Adam greeted his visitor with a handshake. "Hello, Samuel. I'm glad you got my message. You've come at a good time. Come and meet my daughter. Geneva, my dear, may I present my great friend, Mr. Samuel Cavendish."

The smartly-dressed gentleman approaching Geneva was clearly Daniel's father with the same tall stature, chocolate-brown eyes, and dark, wavy hair, though Samuel's hair had silvered at the temples. Geneva curtseyed. "How do you do, sir. It's an honor to meet you. I'm so glad I met your son in Shaftesbury."

Samuel's smile was warm, his gaze kindly. "The honor is mine, Miss Everson. I, too, couldn't be happier that my son brought the two of you together. This must be a huge change for you."

"It is. I feel quite spoilt sitting back while others do all the work."

His eyes twinkled. "A much-wanted change, I should think. My son couldn't come with me today due to other appointments, but he's looking forward to meeting you again soon."

"That will be nice. I hear that you and my father have been close friends for a long time."

"We have. Our shared interests in garden design created a lasting bond between us."

"Not to mention our mutual love of chess," Adam added. "Geneva, I hope you don't mind if Mr. Cavendish and I go up to my lounge. We have a few things to discuss. Later on, we'll continue our tour of the manor. If you want to join the ladies, you'll find them in the library."

As Geneva's father and Samuel Cavendish retreated down the main hallway, Geneva entered the library. Compared to the drawing room, this room had a relaxed feel with comfortable seating, a table for hobbies, a pianoforte, cabinets, and shelves lined with books of all sizes.

Grandmama Louise raised her eyes as she pulled a needle through her cross-stitch. "Ah, look at this, ladies, a newcomer to our sewing circle. Do sit down, Geneva."

Tess moved over on the sofa so Geneva could sit next to her. "We're doing needlework. If you have none of your own, would you like to start a sampler? I have one in my sewing box. Or would you prefer to read? We have history books you might like, or I could show you Robert's ornithology corner."

Geneva hesitated. "Well, I do sew, but have never tried a sampler. In truth, I find history books more interesting."

Looking up from her own needlework, Katherine said snidely, "Yes, I'd think you'd want to rest your hands. By the callouses and chafing, one might guess you were a washerwoman."

"That wasn't kind, Katherine," Tess responded with a frown. "Need I remind you Geneva has more right here than you do?"

Katherine's cheeks flushed to a bright red as Tess and Geneva walked over to a bookcase and a glass cabinet filled with taxidermy birds, skeletons, nests, and eggs. Tess pulled two books from the book shelves. "This is Robert's first book. And here's one on British history."

Geneva was peering into the cabinets. "What a marvelous collection. I feel like I'm in a museum."

She opened Robert's book. "And what beautiful illustrations. You really did all these?"

"Yes, Robert and I make a good team. I had art lessons growing up. Little did I know they would enable me to make illustrations for my future husband's books. We have wonderful outings to study birds. I think I know every footpath in the district."

She placed her hand on her stomach. "Of course that will soon need to be put on hold when our child arrives in early January. Or maybe even in time for Christmas."

"How exciting," Geneva responded fervently. "I've never had siblings, so it will be wonderful to have a baby in the house."

"Yes, it will," Grandmama Louise spoke up. "It has been too long since we've had little ones in this house. We'd once thought that Katherine—"

She broke off, her mousy features unexpectedly abashed. Without raising her eyes, Katherine snipped off another length of thread. "In case you're wondering what she's referencing, Geneva, I was engaged three years ago to a high-ranking officer in the army. Sadly, Charles was killed in the line of duty."

The sudden desolate expression on her face touched Geneva's heart. "I'm so terribly sorry to hear that."

"Well, I got over it. Last year, I had another marriage proposal." Letting out a deep breath, Katherine glanced out the window. "In the end I thought I could do better, so I turned him down."

"Well, I'm sure you'll find someone else."

"I'm not so sure about that. I'm twenty-four now, practically an old maid, and no one suitable has come along. It wouldn't bother me if I had something worthwhile and productive to fill my life."

Geneva glanced at the pile of music books near the piano. "Are you proficient at the piano? If so, you could give lessons."

Aunt Mary rolled her eyes. "Really, Geneva, ladies of the gentry don't lower themselves to giving music lessons. *You* might, coming from the working class, but not my daughter."

Tess frowned at her mother-in-law. "With all due respect, Geneva is hardly working class anymore. She is your niece and my cousin. More importantly, she is Uncle Adam's daughter."

Aunt Mary looked mildly ashamed. "I suppose you're right, though Geneva's mother was little above working class herself. Just because her guardian was a doctor—oh, well, that's ancient history. In any case, arranging a new wardrobe can't come soon enough. Once it arrives, at least your cousin will *look* like one of us."

"Oh, for heaven's sake!" Tess took Geneva's arm. "Come on, let's leave these ladies to their needlework. Would you like a tour of the east wing?"

"I would love that!" Geneva responded fervently. Anything to get away from her other female family members! She left behind the books Tess had given her, planning to retrieve them later. As she followed Tess down the main hallway, Geneva glanced through open doors, noting the butler's pantry and his office. "May I ask where the servants sleep?"

"Certainly." Tess pointed to a door at the end of the hallway. "That's the entrance to the kitchen wing. A spiral staircase leads up to their quarters on the top floor. The rest have quarters above the stables."

Just then, a broadly-built man with bald head and bushy grey side-whiskers emerged from a corridor on the right, a black Labrador at his heels.

"Hello, Mr. Blackerby," Tess called out. "Since you're here, I'd like to introduce you to Miss Geneva Everson. Geneva, this is Mr. Blackerby, Ravensmere's bailiff."

Mr. Blackerby bowed deeply. "It's a pleasure to meet you, miss. I just had my daily meeting with Captain Everson. He mentioned you'd arrived yesterday. I hope you'll be happy at Ravensmere."

"Thank you, sir. I'm sure I will be." She hesitated, then her curiosity overcame her diffidence. "Please, Mr. Blackerby, if you wouldn't mind, I've never been on a big estate. What is the role of a bailiff?"

Mr. Blackerby smiled. "You might call me the farm manager. I oversee the farm laborers' daily work. I also make sure the tenant farmers' rents get paid and any orders from Mr. Jack are carried out. Even evict the occasional tenant who isn't up to the mark."

He winked at the last statement. "Anyway, you'll likely see me around quite a bit. My wife and I and our two sons live in the bailiff cottage out at the farm. You'll be welcome to stop by and meet the family any time."

As the bailiff departed, Tess took Geneva into the corridor from which he'd emerged and pointed out a closed door on the left. "That's Jack's office. He calls it the hub of the estate since he manages everything from there. And down here we have the billiard room."

Tess led the way into a large room dominated by a billiard table. Leather chairs and card tables dotted the room, and a grand piano stood beneath a window. A deer head was mounted on one wall while a navigational map of the world presided above the fireplace. French doors led to a terrace with a driveway leading to Manor Lane.

"We all enjoy this room for music and tea out on the terrace," Tess said. "But Jack uses it the most. Every week or so, he entertains his friends and business associates. Robert says it's like a gentleman's club—cigars, drinks, billiards, gaming, and all the things men discuss. It isn't really Robert's scene or Uncle Adam's, so they rarely join in. And of course as vicar, Philip feels he shouldn't participate in anything that might be considered gambling. But Katherine's fiancé often came over for a game of billiards. Both being military men, he and Jack were good friends."

Tess sighed. "I feel badly for Katherine. She used to be such a cheerful, warm-hearted person. I don't like to speak ill of my mother-in-law, but I think she was wrong to discourage Katherine from accepting her second marriage proposal."

"Why would she do that? Did she have a good reason?"

"Not in my opinion. This is my first cousin Edwin Northcott we're talking about. He's well-educated and charming in every way. He'd be a wonderful husband for Katherine, at least in my opinion. But his plans were to serve as a missionary in Tahiti, which means he'll never be wealthy. My mother-in-law threw a fit and managed to convince Katherine she'd hate the tropical climate, not to mention living a life of poverty and sacrifice. Katherine turned Edwin down, but I think she's regretted it ever since."

"Thank you for telling me," Geneva said. "Now I understand her sarcasm and cold manner—a sign of her unhappiness."

Geneva wandered around admiring pictures of naval battles until she came to a walnut cabinet. Bending over, she peered through the glass doors. "Oh, what lovely porcelain figures of Bible characters. My uncle's collection is nothing compared to this. Is that Noah holding a hammer and saw?"

"You guessed right. Do you know who the others are?"

"Let's see. Moses holding the tablets of the law. Eve with her apple. David and Goliath. From what I've seen in Uncle Alex's pawnshop, they must be very valuable."

"Maybe, but nothing compared to what used to be kept in there."

Geneva straightened up. "That sounds intriguing."

"Yes, these shelves used to contain a collection of Japanese Netsuke carvings. Your grandfather and great-grandfather accumulated them over many years. They were so exquisite and valuable that an art dealer described them in a newspaper column. Uncle Adam regretted that. He said it was an invitation for thieves. Sure enough, a thief broke that window near the piano and climbed through. He smashed the glass of the cabinet, and took the carvings. Uncle Adam was devastated."

Geneva could well imagine, remembering Uncle Alex's fury over her breaking one porcelain soldier of far less value. "So was the thief caught?"

"No, the authorities were baffled by the case. Of course, I only know what I was told as it was long before I married Robert."

Tess's statement brought another query to Geneva's mind. "Tess, I hope you won't mind if I ask you something. Did Robert ever tell you about the coachman who seduced my mother?"

Tess grimaced. "He did tell me, but not much. He doesn't like to be reminded of the terrible scandal. I just know the coachman hadn't been with the family long. Still, your father trusted him enough to give your mother riding lessons. Afterward, Adam realized the coachman probably used the lessons to form an inappropriate relationship with Elizabeth."

Geneva pursed her lips. "Really, Tess, my mother wasn't like that. If someone tried something inappropriate, she'd report it to her husband immediately."

"I don't know, Geneva, and neither do you. After all, she was just a young girl then, younger than me, no older than you. In any case, I hope you won't ask the servants about it. Most of them weren't here at the time. Even if they were, it's none of their business."

"I have to ask someone," Geneva said with annoyance. "How else will I learn what happened?"

"Geneva, do your instincts tell you she was innocent?"

"Yes, and my memory of her good character."

"Well, if you're sure in your heart, then relax and put it out of your mind."

"Out of my mind? I can't do that. I want to clear her name."

"Well, I'm sorry, but I can't help you." Tess strolled toward the piano. "Do you mind if I play for a while? Sometimes your father's discussions with Mr. Cavendish can be lengthy. If you want some fresh air and exercise, you could explore the estate and walk up to the Stillberry Stones. It's an ancient burial chamber with a wonderful view of the surrounding countryside."

"That sounds delightful," Geneva said. "I've never had the time or freedom to explore like that. I think I will."

Tess pulled out a folded paper from a bookshelf and handed it to Geneva. "Take this with you. It's a map showing the footpaths around the estate. We don't want you getting lost."

CHAPTER SIX

Putting on her bonnet, Geneva stepped out the door to the rear courtyard of the manor. Several women servants were sitting on the rim of the water well drinking coffee. When they saw her, they stood up.

Geneva approached them. "Hello, I'm Geneva Everson. I'm heading out for a walk to the Stillberry Stones."

Brushing flour from her apron, an older woman gave a quick curtsey. "How do you do, miss. I'm Lily, the cook. This is Becky, my kitchen maid, and Mabel, the scullery maid. I'm delighted that you've come to be with your father."

"Thank you, Lily. You're an excellent cook. Last night's dinner was wonderful."

"Don't mention it, miss. It's a nice day, so enjoy your walk."

Geneva left the courtyard and walked out to the back lane, which a signpost identified as Raven's Lane. Examining the map, she decided to start with a walk through the farmyard, then follow the footpath that looped south to the coast and northeast to the Stones. After passing through a coppice of oaks, Geneva came to numerous farm buildings forming a loose half-circle around a well pump.

The farmyard scene was a beehive of activity filled with the clamor of voices as each laboring man, woman, and child went about their work. A wagon was filled to capacity with wheat sheaves. Two men passed the tied bundles to the workers, who carried the sheaves to the stacking yard near the barn. One man was poised precariously on a ladder leaning against a hayrick. He was packing the hay down and trimming it in such a tight, symmetrical way that the cone-shaped dome looked like a work of art. Beyond the skill and danger involved, the pressure would be on to complete the task while the current sunny weather lasted.

Geneva skirted around the workers to peer through the barn's open doors. The interior design was simple: a series of A-shaped timbers with cobwebby crossbeams rising up to a thatched roof. Though the air was thick with pungent odors, rows of animal stalls displayed fresh beds of hay. Feed sacks were stacked one upon the other, and bulky equipment for tilling the soil occupied an entire corner. Not far from the doors, two cats basked in the sun, licking their paws.

On the gabled side, Mr. Blackerby, the bailiff, and a group of laborers stood around a strange contraption built mostly of wood with a metal wheel and an attached handle. Was this the new piece of equipment Jack had mentioned at breakfast?

Putting his hands on his hips, Mr. Blackerby groaned. "Good grief, don't be such a sissy! It's only a threshing machine."

He pointed to a tall, burly man in the group. "Turn that wheel and don't stop until I tell you."

The man did as he was told but was clearly unnerved by the machine's constant whirling and humming. Blackerby pointed to another man. "And you! Come over here and feed the sheaves onto the moving rollers."

As the men followed his instructions, Mr. Blackerby nodded approvingly. "That's good. Once inside, the sheaves are beaten and rubbed, then moved along to the shaker. That's where the grain and chaff are separated from the straw. It falls into the hopper down there. Then it's poured into sacks and taken to the mill. The old method of threshing with flails is finished. With this machine, just three or four men can do what used to take twelve men. You should consider yourselves lucky to be among those chosen for winter work."

"What will happen to the other laborers?" one in the group asked.

Mr. Blackerby shrugged. "They'll be laid off. My job is to get you trained and familiar with this machine. Don't worry about the noise. You'll get used to it after a week or so. Now, switch your positions and let's try again."

Geneva pitied the men who would be laid off because of machines. Charity would be their only means of survival through the cold winter months ahead.

Pressing on, she took a well-used footpath through the countryside east of the manor. Laborers were tying wheat sheaves and propping them up in stacks, and in fields now reduced to wheat stalks, women gleaned for kernels left behind. Continuing southward, Geneva enjoyed the change in the landscape—a panorama of open grassland with thickets of juniper and gorse. The small lake fed by the Celandine River shimmered in the sunlight. In the shallows, blackbirds were perched on the fluffy heads of cattails, their carefree songs drifting with the summer breeze. Eventually, the footpath linked up with a well-used dirt road known as Quarry Lane. As it ascended to higher ground, Geneva noted stunted hawthorns and rabbits darting around rocky outcroppings. Then finally, as she rounded a thick clump of gorse, Everson Quarry came into view.

In contrast to the beauty of the fields, this place of industry was a scar on the landscape—a huge area cut into the limestone rock. Ugly piles of rubble were scattered about. Men were pounding their sledgehammers and shouting to one another. A steam crane belched smoke as it lifted a massive square-cut stone onto a wagon. The entire area was like a community of its own. Geneva had already identified a blacksmith's workshop, storage barns for machinery, and stables for the animals and wagons. The only place pleasing to the eye was a single well-kept tenant cottage with flowers cascading from window boxes. Undoubtedly, the quarry foreman's home.

From here, an uphill footpath took Geneva to the coastal chalk cliffs, giving her a close-up view of the sea in all its beauty and magic. She gloried in the fresh air filled with the scent of salt and seaweed. Light glittered and danced on the crests of rolling waves. Gulls soared on the wind, calling *keer keer* to one another.

Moving closer to the edge of the cliff, Geneva looked down about seventy feet to a small cove sparkling with turquoise water—Cox Cove, according to the map. She caught glimpses of a path descending through dense gorse to a sandy beach below. What a delightful place. One day when feeling adventurous, she might go down to paddle and search for shells.

As Geneva headed in a northeast direction, the path came to an abrupt stop at a stone fence.

Looking at her map, Geneva identified the fence as the boundary of Everson farm. Thankfully, someone had built a wooden ladder stile to climb over. Geneva managed the rungs with no difficulty. But as she jumped down to the other side, she heard the sound of tearing fabric and nearly toppled over at the sudden tug on her body. Regaining her balance, she stared with dismay at the long rip in her skirt, and the jagged edge still hooked to a splinter in the wood.

Annoyed with her carelessness, Geneva climbed back up to the second rung and tried to release the fabric. But as she fumbled, the splinter's sharp spike pierced the soft pad of her forefinger. As she winced with pain and applied pressure to the wound, Geneva was distracted by the sound of pounding hoofbeats. The sound was distant at first but quickly grew until Geneva could feel underfoot the approaching vibrations of a galloping horse.

Moments later, a horse and rider came thundering around a bend in the bridle path not far beyond the stone fence. Geneva immediately recognized the rider—Mr. Daniel Cavendish. Catching sight of Geneva, he pulled on the reins and called out to his horse, "Whoa, Victor!"

Startled by the sudden pull on the bit, the horse whinnied and pranced about in a circle as Mr. Cavendish exclaimed, "Miss Everson, I can't believe it's you! How delightful that we should have another chance meeting."

"It certainly is," Geneva replied, trying again to discreetly tug her skirt free. "Though I'm afraid you've caught me at an awkward moment."

Mr. Cavendish's sharp gaze had already taken in Geneva's odd posture and dress twisted around her body. "Well, what perfect timing. Let's see if I can help."

His saddle creaked as he slipped to the ground. Placing his top hat on the cantle of his saddle, he approached Geneva with long, fluid strides. A step up to the second rung brought him close to Geneva's side. He frowned at the trickle of blood on her finger. "What happened here?"

"A splinter did it, a rather large one. It tore the skirt of my dress."

"Well, we'd better take care of your wound first." The hint of a smile curving the corner of his mouth, Mr. Cavendish pulled out his monogrammed handkerchief and wrapped it snuggly around her finger. Tying it off with a knot, he smiled. "There, that should stop the bleeding. Now, let's see about your dress."

While easing the fabric back and forth on the jagged spike, he turned his gaze to Geneva. "I'm happy that you've come to Ravensmere, but I have a feeling it hasn't been easy for you."

Geneva raised her brows. "You're a perceptive man. It hasn't been easy. The family is polite, but I don't seem to fit in. In some ways I feel like an intruder."

"You've only just arrived. In many ways, you fit in very well. You'll adjust soon enough." The fabric broke free. Mr. Cavendish pulled out his pocketknife, sliced the splinter off, and tossed it into the bushes.

Geneva breathed a quiet sigh of relief. "Thank you, Mr. Cavendish. I'm much obliged for your help."

"My pleasure, Miss Everson." He took her hand to help her down. "And, please, do call me Daniel. After all, your father is my godfather. That makes us almost family."

"Then thank you, Daniel." Geneva gave him a grateful smile as she shook out her now-free skirt. "And if we're almost family, you should call me Geneva."

They strolled toward Daniel's horse, now munching blades of grass. "Well, Geneva, how are things going with your father?"

"I must say he's a kind man. I'm to be fitted for a new wardrobe. What makes it difficult is that only he, Tess, and Cousin Philip regard me as his legitimate daughter. The rest are too stubborn to admit it."

"I'm surprised to hear that, especially for your grandmother. There's nothing to question. Beyond the impeccable documentation of your birth, your eyes are a lovely feminine version of your father's, unmistakable to anyone who has known the Everson family."

Geneva's heart welled with gratitude. "Mr. Cavendish, I mean, Daniel, I'm so glad we met and that you took news of me to my father. In a way, you've saved my life."

Daniel shook his head. "I didn't save your life. I was simply God's instrument in his providential care over you. It was his will that you should be united with your father."

"Are you sure of that? How do you know it wasn't fate?"

"I'm sure because of God's character revealed in the Bible. He isn't passive. Since creation, he has governed the world and all people with his wisdom and holy purposes. Nothing happens outside of his will."

Geneva turned her head away. If that were true, why would God let her father burn her mother's letters? Or allow her mother to die of an infectious fever? "You have strong views on the Christian faith. How did that come about?"

"Well, while I was at Eton with your cousin Philip, we became chummy with students who had been influenced by the teachings of John Wesley and George Whitefield. As we studied the Scriptures with them, both of us realized that only faith in Christ's atoning work on the cross could save us. We were born again, and our lives were changed forever."

"That's so interesting to hear. I, too, learned about their teaching from my vicar. Is that when Philip chose the clergy for his career?"

"Not immediately. His calling came the following year."

"And you chose banking."

"Yes, around that time I received an inheritance from my aunt. It enabled me to become a shareholder at Ingleford's bank. One doesn't have to be a vicar to serve the Lord."

"Yes, I suppose that is true." Geneva glanced at Daniel's top hat resting on the saddle. "You seemed to be in a hurry before you stopped to help me. I hope I haven't made you late for wherever you're going."

"Not enough to matter. I'm off to the fishing town of St. Aubrey for a music practice. I'm the pianist in a piano trio."

"That's nice. I hope to hear you play one day."

"I'd be delighted. I should be on my way now. If you want a shorter route back to the manor, take this bridle path down the hill. When you reach the road, take a right turn to the manor." Daniel donned his hat and swung effortlessly into the saddle. "Goodbye, Geneva. I look forward to seeing you again soon."

As he picked up speed and galloped across the grassland, Geneva watched his coattails flying in the wind until a dip in the landscape took him from her sight. Continuing on, she began the steep climb to her intended destination at the top of the hill.

Reaching the summit, she took several paces through tall, yellow grass to the Stillberry Stones, built on a small mound of earth. All that remained of the prehistoric burial chamber was a horizontal capstone supported by three vertical stones not more than ten feet high. As Geneva circled around, she ran her hand over each stone, crusted with lichen and eroded from nature's forces over vast stretches of time.

But as interesting as the tomb was, the glorious view meant much more to Geneva. Turning around, she lifted her arms to the breeze and took in the sweeping view of rolling farmland and the pale-blue waters of the English Channel. She could see the church bell tower in Waterton, the meandering route of the Celandine River, and a distant glimpse of slate roofs at the edge of the sea. Could this be the fishing village where Daniel Cavendish was headed?

As she leaned back against a stone hewn by ancient man, Geneva turned her thoughts to her parents. Had they hiked up together to this very place before heartbreak had driven them apart? Resentment rose up in her at the memory of her father's horrific allegations against her mother, stealing Geneva's enjoyment of the moment.

Her bewilderment was as strong as her resentment. Her father's allegations just didn't make sense considering Geneva's own memories of her mother. Uncle Alex's closest neighbor, Mrs. Gilbert, had befriended Elizabeth when she came to Shaftesbury and continued to befriend Geneva after Elizabeth's death. She'd often mentioned to Geneva how she admired Elizabeth's gracious acceptance of her sad situation. In general, the townsfolk disliked Alex, but Elizabeth had been loyal and respectful to her brother no matter what. Her good attitude was a reflection of her character. God-fearing. Hardworking. Honest to a fault. For someone to suggest Elizabeth Everson had fallen into adultery was utterly absurd and illogical.

Geneva stepped forward and picked up a rock. With all her strength, she hurled it down the hill, where it plopped into a mass of prickly gorse. Who was this coachman who had ruined her parents' marriage? Where did he go, and how would she find him? She needed help with such a difficult quest.

Filled with frustration, she tucked loose strands of hair under her bonnet and set off down the bridle path Daniel had suggested. Once down the hill, it became a country lane bordered on either side by a hedge. Not wanting to be late for luncheon, she picked up her pace until she heard a man's anxious voice on the other side of the hedge to her right.

"Hurry up, Joseph. Help us fill the bucket before someone comes."

Stepping closer, Geneva peered over the top leaves of the hedge to a thicket of wild blackberry bushes. Three men and a young boy were crouched down picking ripe berries and tossing them into a bucket. The men were painfully thin, their clothes worn and tattered. As the boy picked, he stuffed a handful of berries into his mouth, sending purple juice running down his chin and onto his already stained shirt.

Unaware of Geneva's presence, the three men worked feverishly to fill the bucket—until the boy happened to notice her and raised his pointed finger. "Da! Look!"

The men stood up, worry etched on their faces as they spotted Geneva's face peeping over the hedge. The boy's father spoke up. "It's only a few berries we need. Please, miss, don't tell no one. Without these berries, we got nothin' to feed our families tonight."

Geneva took in the man's straw-like hair, patched trousers, and a muddy sock poking through the broken toe of one boot. "I won't tell anyone. You have my word."

"That's mighty good of you. The law got no mercy for farm laborers who trespass on the private land." With a smile, the man wiped a berry-stained hand down the front of his smock. He had a gentle face, lined and weathered from hours of labor in the sun. But behind his smile, his eyes betrayed the horror of abject poverty, unrelenting hunger, and many sorrows known to him alone.

Geneva's heart twisted in compassion. "Excuse me, but my father owns this farm. I know he wouldn't mind you picking these berries. No one else seems to be picking them, so please take all you want."

The man's mouth fell open. "Lawks, we didn't know you were his daughter, miss. It's not as bad as it looks. We're doin' this on our lunch break."

"Well, then, you're using your time wisely. Do you live nearby?"

"Yes, miss. We live in the last three cottages on McCormack Lane. I'm Harry Whipple, and these are my friends Cyrus Rook and Charlie Badger. And this is my son Joseph."

"I'm glad to meet you. I might be able to bring you some food, if my father allows it."

"Thank you, miss. What a kind lady you are." He glanced at the bucket of berries. "I think we got enough for our dinner tonight so we better get back to work."

"Well, if anyone stops you, just tell them you have permission from the landowner to pick here."

"Right you are, miss."

The boy's father picked up the bucket. As the group tramped away across the field, the boy's skinny legs struggled to keep up with the three men. Before they disappeared through the trees, the boy turned and waved a purple-stained hand. "Goodbye, Miss Everson!"

CHAPTER SEVEN

Later that evening, Geneva stood before her bedroom mirror admiring the evening gown Tess had loaned her. The exquisite silk taffeta in a soft shade of peach with short, puffed sleeves and a beautifully embellished skirt would certainly help her fit in with tonight's important guests.

Not long after the family had gathered in the drawing room, Stanway announced the arrival of their guests. Adam introduced Geneva to Mr. Angus Fairfax, the chief magistrate of Ingleford. A tall, strapping man in his mid-forties with bushy eyebrows and a ruddy complexion, he bowed respectfully.

"Miss Everson, it's a pleasure to meet you, but I confess that I'm somewhat puzzled. I was not aware my dear friend Adam had a daughter." The magistrate sent Adam a perplexed look.

"I understand your confusion, Angus," Adam replied calmly. "My daughter arrived just yesterday, and we're still reeling from the events that brought her to us. It's a private and rather delicate matter related to Elizabeth, my former wife who passed away some time ago. I'm overjoyed that Geneva has agreed to stay and be part of the family."

Brows knit together, Mr. Fairfax studied Geneva's eyes for several moments until a big smile revealed white teeth. "Well, dash my wig! There's no doubt looking at you that Adam is your father. I'm overwhelmed and hardly know what to say."

Clearing his throat, he stepped back, gesturing to a fashionably dressed woman, her hairdo a spectacle of flowers, feathers, and jewelry. "Let me introduce my wife, Lady Abigail."

Geneva curtseyed. "How do you do, Lady Abigail? I'm pleased to make your acquaintance."

The lady pressed her hand to her sapphire necklace. "Miss Everson, how nice to meet you. What a joy and comfort you'll be for your father in his old age."

Jack stepped forward to introduce the next guest. "Cousin Geneva, may I introduce Mr. Nigel Spooner."

Geneva greeted the gentleman. He was around Jack's age with high cheekbones, small hazel eyes, and hollowed cheeks. His dark brown hair was straight and brushed back from his face.

"I'm pleased to meet you, Miss Everson. I'm sorry that your mother passed away. How happy you must be to have a new family. This is my wife, Felicity."

Geneva curtseyed to a petite lady wearing a deep burgundy gown. "It's a pleasure to meet you, Mrs. Spooner. I shall enjoy getting to know my family's close friends."

"Then I will invite you over soon to meet my daughters," Felicity responded affably. "The oldest is close to you in age."

"Indeed!" Adam agreed heartily. "Now shall we all sit down and make ourselves comfortable?"

As they took their seats, Adam massaged his hands and glanced around. "Would anyone care for an aperitif? We have sherry, vermouth, champagne, and pastis."

While Stanway busied himself at the liquor cabinet, Mr. Fairfax eased himself into a chair next to Adam. "Well, my dear friend, we're honored to be your first guests since the arrival of your daughter. I love the pleasant surprises that life can bring—as I'm sure you do, Miss Geneva."

"It's more than a surprise, sir," Geneva answered earnestly. "My life has been turned upside down."

"And no doubt for the best," Lady Abigail said. "So how would you describe your first full day at Ravensmere?"

Geneva thought for a moment before summarizing. "A time of discovery. Father showed me his garden. I've learned about my ancestors. And I had a lovely walk around the estate and out to the chalk cliffs. Cox Cove is beautiful. One day I'll go down to collect shells."

Jack leaned forward in his chair. "I don't recommend that, Cousin Geneva. The path leading down is unstable and liable to give way unexpectedly. If you want shells, the sandy beach near St. Aubrey is your best bet. We could arrange a picnic if you like."

"Oh, I'd love that!" Geneva responded eagerly. "I also went up to the Stillberry Stones and had a great view, far and wide. Do you live nearby, Mr. Fairfax?"

"Not too far," he replied. "We live at Morlington House, a farming estate northwest of Waterton. We specialize in grain production."

"Oh, I thought my father said you were the chief magistrate in Ingleford." Geneva shook her head in confusion. "I must have misheard."

Mr. Fairfax chuckled. "You didn't mishear. I have excellent tenants who handle the farming, and my cousin serves as the land agent. That frees me up for my magisterial work in Ingleford."

Nigel Spooner took a sip of vermouth. "Morlington House is a fine example of Georgian architecture. I'm in the process of building a Georgian home myself, which I trust will prove as superior as yours. In fact, the quarry here at Ravensmere is providing the stone."

Mr. Fairfax looked interested. "Well, you could hardly find better quality. Where are you building your new home? If I remember, you have quite a nice little manor near Porthaven, do you not?"

"Little being the operative phrase," Nigel responded. "With my shipping concerns growing and my oldest daughter soon to launch on society, I felt it was time to give my family a setting worthy of our position."

"Will your new house have a view of the sea?" Grandmama Louise asked.

"Oh, yes, it certainly will," Felicity interjected. "I ensured that when Nigel chose the land. We love to watch the ships coming and going."

Adam turned to Geneva. "In case you're wondering, Geneva, Porthaven is a seaport just eight miles from here. That's where Nigel bases his shipping and other business interests. He has long been a patron of our quarry's products. One of these days, we'll have to give you a tour of the area now that you have seen the estate."

"I would enjoy that," Geneva said politely. "I did see your quarry today on my walk. It is indeed impressive. I wondered where all the stone I saw ended up."

"Not all in my new house, you can be sure!" Nigel's small eyes crinkled in a smile. "My father was in the stone-shipping business before me, Miss Everson. After he passed away twelve years ago, I inherited his business and property at the docks. I purchase stone from local quarries and have it transported to the quayside. After it's cut and shaped by masons, it's shipped by sea to waiting customers."

"He is being modest," Jack cut in. "In truth, Nigel has built up his father's business concerns to great success. I've admired his intelligence and ambitious nature since our school days at Eton. I was his errand boy, and he has certainly not proved me wrong."

Nigel chuckled and swallowed the last of his vermouth. "Well, you were a good errand boy when you were lower form and I could still order you around. But that was long ago. You have had ample success of your own. It is not I who can claim to be a hero of Navarino. In any case, Ravensmere has always been a special place for me, even back to our school days when you so unstintingly offered its hospitality. Offering my business to your quarry is a small enough return."

After more chitchat, Stanway stepped into the drawing room to announce dinner. As she and her father led the formal procession into the dining room, Geneva saw that the table setting was even more lavish than it had been to date, no doubt to impress their influential guests. As centerpiece, a beautiful three-tiered crystal server was laden with unblemished grape clusters, apples, and peaches. Vases were stuffed with roses, and the light from five-branch candelabras gave a lustrous sparkle to the women's jewelry.

Once all were seated, Adam welcomed their guests with a toast. Then Stanway and Mrs. Fox served an amazing array of dishes from the sideboard. Pan-fried mackerel and trout. Matelot of eels. A haunch of beef with Madeira sauce and buttery asparagus and beetroot. Conversations and polite laughter followed as everyone chatted about the summer's garden parties, croquet matches, and evening soirees.

When a break came in the conversation, Tess turned to Geneva. "You mentioned enjoying your walk around the estate this morning. You were gone long enough I was a bit worried you might have lost your way or come to some other misadventure. I'm glad to know I was wrong."

Geneva dabbed her mouth with her napkin. "Actually, you weren't totally wrong. I managed to tear my dress climbing carelessly over a ladder stile. It was fortunate that Daniel—Mr. Cavendish—came by on his horse. He stopped to help me get down."

"Daniel is always a gentleman," Tess said. "That doesn't sound too bad of a misadventure."

"No, but, well—" Geneva hesitated before going on with determination. "The real adventure was on my way back, and it was not in fact my misadventure. I came across three farm labor-ers and a boy picking wild blackberries on their lunch break. They work on this farm but said they had nothing else to feed their families tonight. My heart went out to them."

Setting her napkin down, she looked over at Adam. "I have not had opportunity to ask, but may I have your permission, Father, to take some food baskets to these families?"

Adam took a sip of wine before lowering his glass to the table. "I approve of charity work, Geneva, but not with specific individu-als. If you give one family food, or three as you said, they'll come to expect it. And if the word spreads, we would have endless beggars knocking on our kitchen door. If these people were truly from our estate and not claiming so to seek your sympathy, then they receive the same wages as others. They should learn to survive on those like everyone else."

"They are struggling to survive every day," Geneva argued. "That little boy's eyes were hollow, his legs as thin as sticks. When I look at this elaborate dinner we're having, it doesn't seem right he should go to bed hungry. If the others are receiving the same wages, perhaps their families too are going hungry. In my uncle's town, I've known farm laborers so desperate they're forced to poach and steal even knowing they could hang for such crimes."

Her mind went to the young laborer who'd confessed to such a crime at the protest where she'd first seen Daniel Cavendish. "If it is not proper to take them food baskets, could not a shilling or two be added to all of their wages? This meal alone must cost more than such a pay rise."

Geneva broke off as she caught stony glares and frowns from the women of her family. Her passion on the topic had undoubtedly crossed the line of proper behavior for a young gentlewoman. Even Adam was frowning as he said sternly, "Geneva, we don't change wages on a whim. Now, let's talk about something else. This conversation is inappropriate for the dinner table."

Seeing her downcast face, Mr. Fairfax addressed himself smoothly to Geneva. "Miss Everson, please don't think we have no regard for the poor. In fact, this part of England has had a system for almost forty years that guarantees a minimum wage so no one will die of starvation. Perhaps you've heard of the Speenhamland System."

Geneva shook her head with what she hoped was convincing meekness. "No, sir, I haven't."

"Well, it began in 1793 when magistrates met in the town of Speen in the county of Berkshire. A bad harvest had brought a sharp increase in the price of grain. Britain's population had grown significantly, and due to the Napoleonic wars, grain could not be imported from Europe. The ruling classes feared not only starvation amongst the poor but a revolution as well. To prevent this, they devised a system of parish poor relief that topped up farm laborers' wages based on the price of a loaf of bread and the number of children a man had."

Geneva didn't want to irritate her new family members again, but she simply could not hold her words back. "Then the system must not be working, Mr. Fairfax, or perhaps it has not kept up with the prices of food. Because those laborers I met today are not just enduring severe poverty but most clearly face starvation as well."

This time there was no mistaking the thunderous expressions around the table. Jack lowered his knife and fork. "Cousin Geneva, perhaps you're unaware that landowners like your father pay high taxes to fund the poor relief. It puts a huge burden on estates like ours."

"And mine as well," Mr. Fairfax said. "But that's not the only issue, Miss Everson. Farm laborers aren't worthy of higher pay. They're illiterate and have no special skills."

"Yes, I've heard that they're denied a parish education."

"And for a good reason. We don't want them getting above themselves. It could upset the status quo. They're paid for their strength and obedience and nothing more."

"Like beasts of burden," Geneva muttered under her breath. She hadn't thought anyone could hear her, but Adam coughed so hard the vein in his forehead bulged.

"That's enough, Geneva! We'll have no more talk of this." He turned to Mr. Fairfax. "Please, excuse my daughter, Angus. She has much to learn."

Stanway's entrance just then with the second course was a welcome diversion. The mouth-watering aromas of curried rabbit, pigeon pie, and orange-glazed Cornish game hens filled the room, stirring up appetites for another round of culinary delights.

Grandmama Louise broke into the tense silence as Stanway spooned a portion of game hen onto her plate. "Lady Abigail, this dish reminds me of the orange trees and beautiful plants in your conservatory. Have you heard about Ingleford's flower show and garden party next Monday?"

"As a matter of fact, I have," Lady Abigail responded calmly, looking in no way perturbed by or interested in the recent conversation. "I'm arranging a party to attend. Are any of your household planning to go? It would be a delight to see you there."

As they chattered on about the upcoming event and other topics of conversation, Geneva thought about Harry Whipple and his little boy. Right now, Joseph was probably licking every drop of blackberry juice from his plate.

Three hours later, following desserts of jellies, chocolate mousse, and gooseberry pie, the ladies retired to the drawing room for coffee while the men separated for cigars and brandy in the billiard room. As the ladies made their way across the Great Hall, Geneva's new aunt, Mary, took her arm and whisked her away to the privacy of the library. Shutting the door, she spun around on Geneva, her dark eyes flashing angrily.

"You dreadful girl! Your conduct at dinner was *disgraceful*. I thought you were a polite young woman. Let me make clear that a lady does not discuss wages or hanging offences with gentlemen. Your father told you it was inappropriate, yet you continued with no restraint." Her eyes narrowed, she wagged a forefinger in Geneva's face. "My suspicions about you were correct. You've barely arrived, and you're already meddling in our affairs!"

Geneva pulled back from her aunt's wagging finger. "Please, Aunt Mary, I just care about the poor. All I want to do is help them."

"Maybe so, but you're an outspoken and opinionated girl. If you don't control yourself, you'll lose your good standing in society and become a disgrace like your mother."

Geneva raised her chin and hardened her voice. "Very well, I'll try to be more tactful. But don't ask me to stop defending the downtrodden. That would be a sin."

CHAPTER EIGHT

On the eighth day since her arrival at Ravensmere, Adam invited Geneva for an afternoon walk through his garden. Now that September had arrived, the slanted rays of the sun cast a golden haze from one end of the garden to the other. As they passed a bed thick with black-eyed Susans and purple coneflowers, Adam smiled at Geneva. "I'm so pleased that you've settled in over the past week and made a friend in Tess especially. Before long, you'll meet her parents, Mr. and Mrs. Carrington."

"I'm looking forward to the birth of her child."

"So am I. I long to hear the sound of a baby's cry again here at Ravensmere."

Taking the brick path, they enjoyed a stroll around the fish pond and into the rose garden. Adam dabbed his forehead with his handkerchief. "I'm feeling quite tired. There's a bench and table over there. Let's have a rest in the shade. I've asked Mrs. Fox to bring out a tray of cold beverages shortly."

He smiled tenderly at his daughter. "Grape cordial for you and lemonade for me. Do I have that right?"

Geneva's heart warmed to his smile and tender consideration. Squeezing his arm linked in hers, she offered a wide smile in return. "Exactly right, Father."

They sat down side by side on the bench. Adam moved a hand over the weathered wood of the armrest. "I have bittersweet memories of this bench. This is where I proposed to your mother. I remember it clearly. It was this time of the year. It might have been this very day of the month. She was wearing an ivory frock, and her white parasol shaded her face from the sun. Gracious, I haven't thought about it for such a long time."

Geneva glanced up at the clusters of pink roses dangling from the arbor. "You couldn't have chosen a more romantic place. She must have been thrilled."

Adam shifted his position toward her. "Geneva, are you happy? I think you are. You've become more relaxed over the past few days. I trust that you've finally laid the past to rest."

Geneva lifted questioning eyes. "I'm not sure what that means."

"Well, I'd hoped that you'd come to terms with your mother's indiscretion."

She shook her head slowly. "You're mistaken, Father. I knew my mother better than you did. She was loyal to everyone, even my beastly uncle."

A strange knocking sound came from the sycamores beyond the garden. Moments later, a raven swooped down and alighted on the rim of the fountain.

Adam turned his attention back to his daughter. "You're mature for your age, Geneva, but in some ways quite naïve. Everyone is vulnerable to weaknesses, even the most noble of characters. You would do well to keep that in mind as you journey through life."

Geneva's body tensed at his words. For just a moment, a cloud of doubt threw her off balance. Was she self-deceived in extolling her mother's virtues? Were her memories and natural instincts all wrong? No, that wasn't possible. She was a level-headed person, and her father was simply too old and stubborn to see things differently.

Adam observed her expression. "I can see you don't want to share your thoughts, Geneva. Perhaps it's best that we never speak of this again. Do you agree?"

"Yes, I think it's wise unless something makes it necessary."

Her father turned his gaze to the fountain. "I brought you out here for more than just a walk. I've been thinking seriously about my life. I've felt quite good in the last few days and hope that I have many more years ahead of me. But since one can't know for sure, I want you to know that I've seen my solicitor and have included you in my will. It's wise to have things in order for the future."

The strain in his voice made Geneva wonder if he was worrying about his heart condition. Or was it the discussion regarding her mother that had put a deep furl in his brow? Anxious to restore the harmony they'd been enjoying, she responded graciously. "Thank you, Father. I appreciate that very much."

Just then the housekeeper arrived with the tray.

Adam sat up straight. "Ah, here's my lemonade and grape cordial for you. I'm feeling quite thirsty."

Mrs. Fox set the tray down, both glasses beaded with cool condensation. As the housekeeper retreated from the garden, Geneva had an idea. Standing up, she said, "I'll be right back, Father. I'm going to pick something for you in the perennial garden."

Geneva made her way down the brick path to the perennial enclosure at the far end of the garden. The lavender was past its prime, but as she picked a stem and sniffed, the fragrant scent still stimulated her nasal passages in a pleasing way. Going to work, she picked a generous bunch of equal length and tied them together with a pliable stem. With this held a few inches from her father's nose, his tensions would soon melt away.

Returning back down the path, Geneva paused in the archway that led into the rose garden. She could see the table with its drink tray and the bench, but not her father. Had Adam gone to the cool shade of the gazebo where he could rest more comfortably?

She moved forward but stopped again, eyes widened in shock, as her new position gave her a better view of the bench. Her father hadn't left the bench but was slumped over on his side, one cheek pressed against the armrest. Even at this distance, she could see his face was a frightening shade of dusky blue. Something was terribly wrong!

Lifting her skirt, Geneva ran down the path, calling at the top of her voice. "Father, I'm coming. Hold on!"

At the bench, she dropped the lavender. Falling to her knees, she shook Adam's shoulder. "Father, I'm here. What's wrong? Please, wake up!"

There was no response. She shook him again. "Dear God, help him!"

But Geneva's cries were in vain. It was too late.

Adam Everson was gone.

The next morning, Geneva left her bedroom to join the family for breakfast. Heavy grey skies had moved in overnight, making the upstairs hallway darker than ever. As she made her way past the griffin sconces, the grandfather clock chimed on the ninth hour, the reverberating tones sounding like a church bell tolling for the departed one.

Last evening, the coffin had been placed in the drawing room. With the curtains closed, candles lit, and everyone still in a state of shock and disbelief, Philip had led them in lengthy prayers and Bible readings. Following that, a light supper was served. Then everyone retired to the privacy of their bedrooms.

Descending the stairs, Geneva found the rest of the family already seated in the dining room. As she entered, their chatter came to a stop and all eyes fell upon her. She took her seat unobtrusively, her glance going automatically to her father's empty chair.

"It's a terrible sight, isn't it?" Aunt Mary said harshly.

Geneva swallowed back sudden tears. "Yes, it seems so strange that he's no longer with us."

Jack fixed a somber look on Geneva. "We aren't the only ones flummoxed with Uncle Adam's sudden passing. I had a word with Dr. Whitmore last night. He came by to give his condolences. He was quite perplexed by Uncle Adam's passing. He said his condition had declined recently and wondered if a sudden upset had triggered a fatal heart attack."

Aunt Mary lifted her grapefruit spoon and aimed the pointy end at Geneva. "You were the last person with him. What went on between you, pray tell?"

Geneva didn't like the tone of her voice. "I've already told you, Aunt Mary. Father was tired from our walk around the garden. Mrs. Fox brought out some beverages. I picked some lavender to bring to my father. When I returned, I found him slumped over. Dr. Whitmore is wrong. Father told me he'd felt good over the last few days."

Jack thumped his fist on the table. "How dare you contradict our doctor! He's the finest in the county. It's not hard to imagine you upsetting my uncle with more tales of woe about your wretched uncle and miserable past."

Heat rushed over Geneva's cheeks. "I did nothing of the sort. Are you suggesting I caused his death?"

"Stop it, both of you," Grandmama Louise exclaimed. "My nerves can't take it. Jack, don't make things worse than they are. You're the head of the family now. Show some leadership."

Jack straightened his shoulders. "I already have. While you were all weeping on your beds yesterday, Robert and I met with Philip. We've made arrangements for the funeral on Monday. Mother, you have two days to prepare for a gathering of friends after the burial. I suggest you get on with it."

Aunt Mary raised her hands. "Only two days? Gracious, there's so much to do. Stanway, tell Mrs. Fox I'll meet with her after breakfast. Katherine, you can help me. Tess can take charge of the flowers."

She glanced at Geneva. "You can write the invitations for refreshments in the Great Hall. That'll keep you out of our hair."

As the others discussed details, Geneva finished her coffee and got up. "Excuse me. I have no appetite for breakfast. If you need me, I'll be in my bedroom."

Yesterday, Geneva had managed to keep her emotions at bay. But today her personal regrets, compounded with Jack's and Aunt Mary's mean-spirited attitudes, were too much to take. Filled with conflicting emotions, she flopped onto her bed and wept into her folded arms.

Adam had wanted to form a close relationship with his new-found daughter, yet she'd kept him at arm's length. She'd hardly listened when he talked about his past work as justice of the peace. She'd shown little interest in his garden blueprints and diagrams of fountain pumps. Under normal circumstances, she would be interested in such things, but intrusive thoughts of him burning her mother's letters had made it impossible.

As her crying eventually turned to deep, shaking sobs, Geneva heard a tap on the door. The head housemaid Emily stepped in.

"I heard you crying, Miss Geneva. Is there anything I can do for you?"

Geneva raised her head. "Thank you, but I don't think so—unless you could keep me company for a while."

The housemaid came to the foot of the bed. "I'd be happy to, miss."

"Will you sit down?"

"No, miss, I'd be in trouble if Mrs. Fox caught me." Emily looked sympathetically at Geneva's tear-streaked face. "This is a hard time for you. But it's good that you had the chance to meet your father before he passed away."

"I wish we'd had more time to get to know each other. One of the benefits might have been his willingness to share more about the past." Geneva got up and closed the door. "Emily, I shouldn't be asking you this, but do you know about my mother who was sent away from the manor?"

"Yes, miss, I was here at the time. I was fifteen years old."

"Really? Do you remember what happened with my mother?"

"I remember it all, but we're forbidden to speak of private family matters."

"Well, my father told me just a little. He said he caught my mother in bed with the coachman, but he wouldn't say anything more. He said it wasn't proper for a man to speak to a young lady about such things. But you could tell me—one woman to another. I would never say or do anything to put your job at risk."

"Do you promise?"

"Yes, this is important to me."

"Very well." Emily drew a deep breath. "It happened the night Mr. Adam and Mr. Jack were invited to a gentlemen's evening at Mr. Fairfax's home. Afterward—well, there was a lot of talk amongst the servants. I heard tell that the master and his nephew had come home earlier than expected. Stanway unlocked the front door to let them in. The two went straight upstairs to bed. Stanway locked up again and was checking the doors and windows one last time like he always does. That's when he heard a terrible commotion coming from upstairs."

"What kind of commotion?"

"Yelling and shouting and things banging and crashing from the upstairs bedroom wing. Stanway ran upstairs, thinking someone was hurt. By the time he got there, Mr. Jack had come out from his room. The noise was coming from the master suite. Both of them dashed into your father's lounge and found your mother's bedroom door wide open. Your mother was in her bed. Drake was stark naked, being punched and knocked about by your father. Stanway managed to restrain Mr. Adam, but he was so angry he turned around and lunged toward your mother as if he was going to strike her. Stanway said Mr. Jack was quick. Apparently, he blocked his uncle's way to your mother and begged him to stop or he'd regret it for the rest of his life. Your father must have to come to his senses. He went to his own bedroom."

Emily paused to draw a deep breath before continuing. "Next thing, Drake took off down the hallway toward the servants' stairwell. Stanway and Mr. Jack were chasing after him. From our bedrooms, we heard the Chinese vases crashing from the console table to the floor. Then suddenly Stanway was calling out, 'Stop him! Stop him!' Anyone not still sleeping came rushing out of our bedrooms. I got to the spiral stairwell just in time to see Drake racing down the stairs with a bundle of clothing under his arm. Stanway was at his heels, and Mr. Jack right behind."

Geneva sat down on her bed. "Oh Emily, what a terrible thing for you to witness. And what about Robert and Philip? They must have been teenagers then. Did they witness all this?"

"No, miss, they were still at boarding school. Mr. Jack had finished his studies and had returned home. The ladies couldn't hear. Their bedrooms are on the south wing."

"And what about my mother? What was she doing? Didn't you go down to help her?"

Emily shook her head emphatically. "Oh, no, miss! It wouldn't have been my place to interfere. But Stanway returned a few minutes later calling for Mrs. Fox to tend to your mother. None of the rest of us ever set eyes on your mother again. Your father was so furious he wouldn't let her out of her room until a week later when she was sent away. Mrs. Fox was the only one allowed in to serve her."

"So what happened to the coachman?" Geneva asked. "Who was this man? How could he have been allowed to walk off scot-free after such behavior?"

"Well, his full name was Nicholas Drake." Emily sighed. "Such a handsome young man, not much older than Captain Everson and so polite and efficient none of us could believe he'd do such a thing. He'd been here less than a month, so none of us knew him well. He told us in the servants' hall that his grandfather was born in Tavistock, over in Devon, the county next to ours. That was the birthplace of Sir Francis Drake, the famous sea captain. Mr. Drake fancied himself as one of Sir Francis's descendants. As to what happened to him—"

Emily gave another quick shake of her head. "I never saw him again, so he must have left that very night after he was dismissed. Captain Everson was only eighteen at the time. He wanted to protect the family's reputation so he warned the staff never to speak of that night, not to Mr. Adam and certainly not outsiders. If we did, we'd be dismissed. I'm sure your father preferred to have Drake leave with no more punishment than losing his position than have him dragged before a magistrate. That would start every tongue in the county wagging. But of course, there was talk in any case when your mother was sent away."

"So no one here at Ravensmere has seen this Nicholas Drake since he left?" Geneva asked.

"I haven't heard otherwise. But I can truly speak only for myself."

Geneva got up and looked out the window. "This is so distressing, Emily. I can't believe my mother would betray her husband."

"I understand, miss. We all want to think well of our loved ones. Don't stay up here. Come downstairs and be with your family."

Turning to face the housemaid, Geneva raised her chin resolutely. "You're right. If I don't write the invitations in time, I'll never hear the end of it."

CHAPTER NINE

That next Monday afternoon, All Saints Church in Waterton was filled with friends and parishioners who had come for Adam Everson's funeral. Heads turned to view the mourning family as the Eversons entered the nave and made their way down the north aisle to their box pew at the front.

Taking her seat, Geneva tugged at her neckline. Tess had loaned her a black dress for the occasion. It was beautifully made, but the fabric was heavy and tight at her neck. Discreetly trying to stretch it with her fingers, Geneva glanced into an adjoining chapel where an ornate tomb displayed the effigy of an armored knight upon an alabaster altar. Nudging Tess, seated next to her, she whispered, "Whose tomb is that?"

"Sir Tobias Everson," Tess whispered back.

How amazing to think that he was her direct ancestor, the Knight of the Shire. Geneva turned her gaze to the baptismal font decorated with Tudor roses and winged angels blowing trumpets. Above the altar in the chancel, Christ the Shepherd was depicted in a glorious stained-glass window. It was indeed a beautiful church with its stone walls and floors provided by Ravensmere's own quarry, from what Philip had once mentioned.

As the pipe organ played on, Geneva forgot the pomp of her surroundings, turning her thoughts instead to the dreadful day of her father's passing. Their final amicable walk in the garden. Her anguish in finding his slumped body, limp and lifeless. Geneva lifted her eyes to the gold cross on the altar. If it was indeed God's providence for her to meet her father, then his timing was truly miraculous considering how little time had remained to Adam.

Following hymns and Bible readings, Philip, dressed in clerical vestments of black and white, climbed up to the pulpit to deliver the funeral sermon. Geneva listened attentively, especially to his closing words.

"So when our mortal bodies have been changed to immortal bodies, then the words of Scripture will be fulfilled. O death, where is your victory? O death, where is your sting?" Philip spread his arms wide as though in invitation. "Let us all give thanks to God, for it is through his Son, Jesus Christ, that this victory is ours."

A more somber expression came over his face. "You have heard me say this before, but let me say it again. Faithful church attendance and good works are commendable, but they cannot save you. Nor can baptism or the partaking of Holy Communion. As we contemplate our own mortality today, let us be ever mindful that only personal faith in Christ's substitutionary death on the cross can guarantee our forgiveness of sin and gift of eternal life."

As Philip closed his Bible, Geneva glanced across the aisle to where Daniel Cavendish sat beside his father. He was nodding approval at Philip's words, but in that moment he turned his head to catch Geneva's gaze. His firm lips curved slightly in a brief smile of encouragement before he turned his gaze back to the pulpit.

After Philip's sermon, Jack went to the front to deliver Adam's eulogy. He spoke well, citing Adam's contributions to the community and his work as justice of the peace. But toward the end, the eulogy seemed to become more about Jack and all the things Adam had done for him. After drawing chuckles over amusing anecdotes, his expression suddenly switched to sorrow, and he spoke as if Adam were in their midst.

"Of 'all the uncles in the world, I was honored to be your nephew. I shall miss our billiard games and cigars by the fireside. But most of all, I shall miss you—my mentor, my father figure, my friend."

A lump grew in Geneva's throat. Her father would be happy to know Jack had ended his eulogy on such a personal note.

After most of the parishioners had departed, the Eversons, the Cavendish family, and others of Adam's closer friends crossed the churchyard to gather for Adam's burial. The air was so still Geneva could hear the sound of doves cooing in the bell tower. But overhead, billows of dark clouds occupied the sky, threatening rain at any moment.

As Philip recited comforting Bible verses, Geneva grieved afresh for the loss of her father. But the occasion also evoked unbidden thoughts of her mother's burial, memories so vivid they brought tears to her eyes. She'd been eleven years old, her heart stricken with unbearable despair. Just one thread of hope had kept her on her feet: the assurance that her mother was free of suffering and safe in the arms of Jesus.

As the coffin was lowered into the ground, Geneva brushed her tears away and turned her gaze to the other members of her new family. Grandmama Louise's shaking body was supported by Tess and Robert. Katherine had buried tears against her mother's shoulder. Philip's wife Claire looked suitably sorrowful. In contrast, Jack's demeanor was cool and reserved. Could he not shed a tear for the dear uncle he'd so lauded in his eulogy? Or had the military instilled in him a stoic acceptance for such occasions?

While earth was cast into the grave, Philip read from his prayer book. "For as much as it has pleased Almighty God of his great mercy to take unto himself the soul of our dear Adam Everson, we therefore commit his body to the ground, earth to earth, ashes to ashes, dust to dust, in the sure and certain hope of the resurrection unto eternal life through our Lord Jesus Christ."

He closed his prayer book and glanced around. "Let us pray together. Father in heaven, I thank you for the life of Uncle Adam, and I pray that you will comfort those who mourn for him. Help us to abide in you, O Lord, and to love one another as Jesus did in laying down his life for us. In his name we pray. Amen."

Geneva lifted her head. As they walked across the grass, weaving around headstones, she felt the first drops of rain on her cheek. No sooner had they reached the brick path than the heavens opened with a ferocious downpour of rain. Umbrellas opened. Clearly, many of the group had come more prepared than Geneva. Jack raised an umbrella above his mother's head. Robert did the same for Tess and Grandmama Louise.

Geneva made a dash toward the shelter of their waiting carriage, but before she could get too wet, she found an umbrella sheltering her from the storm. Glancing up, she met Daniel's warm chocolate gaze. She smiled tremulous thanks as she took his hand to step up into the carriage.

At four o'clock that afternoon, those guests invited to Ravensmere for the funeral reception began arriving. Stanway announced each name as they stepped into the Great Hall. Before long, the din of chatter filled the hall, echoing in the upper reaches of its fifty-foot ceiling. A multitude of candles illuminated the room. Flowers perfumed the air. Stanway served champagne while maids weaved amongst guests with silver platters of savory canapés and sweet pastries.

Geneva felt overwhelmed to be in the company of magistrates, members of parliament, retired military officers, bankers, and businessmen. Expensive broadcloth, gold watch chains, and brass buttons proclaimed their wealth. Their wives, in no less expensive gowns and towering hairdos, fluttered their fans as they probed Geneva with superficial questions. She answered each with courtesy, but when the opportunity arose, she picked up a glass of her favorite grape cordial and slipped away to a quiet corner where a potted palm provided a measure of privacy. But having taken just a few sips, she heard a familiar baritone voice.

"Geneva, are you all right?"

Turning around, she found Daniel's tall frame looming above her, the expression in his eyes one of concern. "Yes, I'm fine, thank you. I just need a moment to catch my breath, so to speak."

"I see. Would you prefer to be alone?"

"No, I'd be happy to have your company. Other than my family, I know so few of these people."

Daniel stepped closer. "Geneva, I have not had opportunity to express my sincere condolences for your loss. We have all been shocked to hear of your father's sudden passing. I'm so sorry and wish you'd had more time with him."

"I do too. I was only just getting to know him. In many ways, he showed himself gentle and caring as I'm sure he was with you."

Daniel inclined his head in agreement. "I was blessed to have him as my godfather. I have many fond memories of him, especially my twelfth birthday when he introduced me to archery with a new bow and arrow. I loved it. In the years to come, my parents hosted many competitions in our garden."

Geneva smiled. "What a great gift for you. May I ask where your home is?"

"Wyncombe Hall is my father's estate. The side lane is just a quarter mile from the village."

"Is it a farming estate like Ravensmere?"

"No, but we have a demesne that provides for the needs of the household. My great-grandfather made his fortune producing pottery up north in Staffordshire. When he died, my grandfather entered banking and moved here for the warmer climes."

"This is a lovely part of England, but without my father here, I feel out of place. When I walk through the gardens he so loved and other places we spent time together, I can't believe he's not there."

"I understand. I'm here to help you if you feel lonely or need a friend."

"Thank you. I'm surrounded with everything a person could want or need, yet I have a perplexing problem."

"Yes, I can see it in your eyes. May I be of help?"

"It's concerning my parents' break up. I'm sure you're aware of it."

"Yes, I am."

"Well, I don't believe my mother was unfaithful. I won't say who, but someone gave me information about the events that led to her expulsion. Nicholas Drake was the coachman who allegedly seduced her. He'd been working here for less than four weeks when it happened. I don't suppose you remember him."

"No, I was only ten at the time. All I recall is the change in your father and his obsession with his garden. Are you hoping to find this Drake?"

"Yes. And when I do, I'll confront him and demand to know what happened."

Daniel's eyebrows shot up. "Have you then learned such information that would lead to finding him?"

"Not much," Geneva admitted. "Just that he was a handsome man who fancied himself as a descendant of Sir Francis Drake."

"That is indeed not much, but . . ." A broad smile brightened Daniel's face. "It is not nothing either. You have a name, his reputation for good looks, and his propensity to identify with the well-known explorer. To solve this mystery, you simply need persistence and a good deal of patience. My own work takes me afield quite often, including travel by stagecoach on occasion and stops at coaching inns. It would be a simple matter to inquire in these places if a Nicholas Drake has found work as a coachman. You never know, I might find him or someone else who knows him."

"Goodness!" Geneva's eyes sparkled. "I was hoping to find someone who could help me but did not expect such a generous offer. I do not know how to thank you, Mr. Cavendish."

"Daniel, remember?" He glanced back between the fronds of the palm. "From the way they are looking around, it appears your family has noticed your disappearance. Would you care to cross the hall with me and mingle with the guests?"

Geneva took his arm. "Thank you, Daniel. I would be most appreciative of your company."

Halfway across the Great Hall, Daniel and Geneva paused under a chandelier where Grandmama Louise was chatting with a small knot of people that included Katherine and Tess. Her grandmother's petite frame was dwarfed by a tall gentleman with a shock of red hair.

"There you are, Geneva." Grandmama Louise held a lace hanky to her chest. "I was wondering where you'd gone. I want you to meet Tess's father, Mr. Jacob Carrington, and his wife, Fiona. Mr. Carrington is a former member of parliament. He owns a prestigious hotel in Porthaven."

The red-headed gentleman bowed his head. "How nice to meet you, Miss Geneva. A long time ago, your father gave me a book of poems by Rabbie Burns—a perfect gift for a Scotsman like myself."

He pulled a small volume from a pocket and held it out. "It would give me great pleasure to pass this on to you as a token of my sympathy."

Accepting the gift, Geneva caressed the book in her hand. "Thank you, Mr. Carrington. I shall treasure it. I have one consolation over my father's passing. He died in his beautiful garden surrounded with roses and birdsongs."

"Oh, how poignant!" Fiona, a plump, older version of Tess, exclaimed. "And so good that Adam was united with his lovely daughter."

A pretty middle-aged lady smelling strongly of *eau de cologne* cleared her throat. "Is anyone going to introduce me to Adam's daughter?"

Tess stepped forward with a smile. "I'm so sorry, Aunt Lydia. Cousin Geneva, may I present my mother's sister, Mrs. Lydia Northcott of Porthaven."

Geneva greeted Tess's aunt with a curtsey. The older woman smiled kindly. "Lovely to meet you, dear. Now that I've seen your unusual eyes, I can understand why word of them is getting around. My condolences for your loss, and yours too, Mrs. Everson. It's tragic when a mother outlives her sons."

"Indeed, it is." Grandmama Louise sighed heavily. "First my dear Fredrick and now my firstborn. Well, we may have lost Adam, but we've gained his daughter, so we ought to be thankful for that."

"And how is your son, Mrs. Northcott?" Geneva was surprised it was Katherine who had asked the question. The eager expression on her otherwise sullen face was more than Geneva had ever seen. "Edwin has been in Tahiti for—has it been a year now? Have you had news from him recently?"

Lydia's pleasant expression faded. "Yes, I received a letter from him last month. But I cannot imagine you would be interested in what he wrote."

"No, you're wrong." Katherine's tone held sincerity. "I enjoy hearing about his work."

"Well, if you must know . . ." Lydia waved her fan over her neck. "Edwin writes that he's been instructing the natives on building latrines. As they work, he shares the gospel with them. By bedtime he's quite exhausted in a good sort of way, knowing that he's fulfilling the Great Commission."

A maid approached with a platter of canapés. By the time Geneva and Daniel had each selected one, their chatting companions had been hailed by other guests. But just then, two well-dressed, prosperous-looking men stepped toward them. Daniel introduced Geneva to Mr. Edgar Baines and Mr. Peter Farthing, Ravensmere's two principal tenant farmers.

A short, portly, grey-eyed man, Mr. Baines gave Geneva a deep bow. "How do you do, Miss Everson. Your father's sudden death was a great shock to me and a huge loss for our community."

Geneva managed a smile. "Thank you, sir. It is indeed a great loss."

In contrast to Mr. Baines, Peter Farthing was tall and wiry with a medallion hanging in the ruffles of his white shirt. He bowed politely to Geneva. "Miss Everson, I have one reason to be thankful at this sad time—that we have Captain Everson to look after the estate."

Geneva followed his glance across the Great Hall to where Jack stood with Nigel Spooner beneath the portraits of Ravensmere's founders. He was leaning forward with one elbow propped on the mantelpiece, seemingly in a deep conversation with his friend.

"Yes, clearly my father trusted my cousin to place Ravensmere in his care." Geneva chose to change the subject. "So, Mr. Farthing, I've heard that you oversee Nightingale Farm on the northeast side of the estate. What a charming name for a farm. Do you mind if I ask what sort of farming you do?"

"I don't mind at all, miss. Your father's estate is blessed with the best soil a farmer could want—a light, sandy loam. For that reason, both Mr. Baines and I specialize in grain production. Mostly wheat and barley, as that yields the greatest profit. Though this year's harvest is cause for concern due to unseasonable weather."

"Not to worry," Mr. Baines said. "Rainy afternoons are perfect for a tankard of ale with friends at the Bell and Crown Inn. Don't you agree, Mr. Cavendish?"

"Once in a while, yes," Daniel said. "New ideas are often born in the midst of lively conversations. Will you excuse us, gentlemen? I want to introduce Miss Everson to my sisters and their husbands. They've come all the way from Blandford Forum."

The reception eventually came to a close, and Geneva joined her family in bidding the guests a good evening. When the last guest had departed, she went upstairs to prepare for a light supper in the dining room. Hanging up Tess's gown in the wardrobe, she changed into one of the dresses she'd brought with her, this one a deep plum shade appropriate for mourning.

She was searching through her top drawer for a pair of stockings when she came across her Bible. She hadn't read it since Easter, Geneva realized guiltily. She flipped through the pages until she noticed a smudged ink splat. Turning back to the page, she read a verse she'd underlined many years ago. The verse immediately followed the Lord's Prayer in the sixth chapter of the Gospel of Matthew.

> For if ye forgive men their trespasses, your heavenly Father will also forgive you: But if ye forgive not men their trespasses, neither will your Father forgive your trespasses.

Geneva smoothed the dog-eared corner of the page. She wasn't the sort of person to hold a grudge. She preferred to forgive and let bygones be bygones. On the other hand, some things were inexcusable, and letting people off the hook didn't seem right even if they had apologized. No other human being knew the extent of the things she'd endured with Uncle Alex. But God knew, and she was sure he understood why she did not feel she could forgive her uncle.

As she put the Bible back in the drawer, Geneva noticed Daniel's monogrammed handkerchief laying on her chemise, a memento of their encounter at the ladder stile. She stroked the embroidered initials. What a contrast to Uncle Alex were Daniel's kind, thoughtful ways. How he'd hurried home after their first encounter to share the news of her existence with his godfather. And today's expression of willingness to help her find Nicholas Drake.

Geneva picked up the folded handkerchief. Such a meaningful keepsake deserved a better place than the drawer of her bureau. Tucking it instead into the pocket of her dress, she put on a fresh pair of stockings and went downstairs to join the family.

CHAPTER TEN

Geneva was surprised to see Samuel Cavendish join the family for supper that night. Grandmama Louise had informed her coolly that they would all be gathering together following the meal to await her father's solicitors for the reading of Adam's will. Had Adam bequeathed his best friend something important that required Samuel's presence at the reading?

After the meal, the family retired to the drawing room, where coffee was served to the ladies and glasses of port to the men. Settling into a comfortable armchair, Jack opened a silver snuff box. "Mother, I must commend you for your selection of refreshments this afternoon. They paired perfectly with the champagne."

"Thank you, Jack. Tess did well with the flower arrangements. They came all the way from the hothouses in Bath."

Jack inhaled a pinch of snuff. "I'm all in favor of flowers, but we have far more than we need. Stanway, tell Burrows to deliver half of them to the church tomorrow."

"Very good, sir," the butler replied. "I'll pass the message on."

"That's kind of you, Jack," Grandmama Louise said. "You've done well managing our affairs at this difficult time."

Samuel sipped his port. "Philip deserves a word of praise for the funeral service. Your selections from Scripture couldn't have been more comforting."

"All glory to God," Philip replied. "The flowers are indeed beautiful, but they remind me of a Scripture from the prophet Isaiah, the fortieth chapter and eighth verse: 'The grass withereth, the flowers fadeth, but the word of our God shall stand forever.'"

Geneva was mulling over Philip's words when she heard the scrunch of carriage wheels coming down the drive. Jack got up and peered through the rain-streaked window. "Ah, the solicitors are here—a bit earlier than we thought. Stanway, we'll gather in the dining room, and you can show them through."

Gulping the last of her coffee, Geneva followed the others to the dining room. With nightfall fast approaching, the curtains had been drawn and a candelabra placed in the center of the table. When everyone was seated with Jack at the head of the table, Stanway ushered in the two solicitors.

The older solicitor led the way to two vacant chairs at the far end of the table. He bowed his head to Grandmama Louise. "Good evening, ma'am, I'm so sorry for the loss of your eldest son."

Grandmama thanked him and introduced Geneva to her father's senior solicitor, Mr. Gregory Clarke.

The portly man nodded his head. "How do you do, Miss Geneva. My deep condolences to you and all your family. I shall miss your father—a fine man and a distinguished member of our community."

Mr. Bradshaw flashed Geneva a smile. "How nice to see you again, miss. I just wish the circumstances were happier."

As they took their seats, Mr. Clarke opened his leather case and placed a document on the table. "Well, let's get down to the business at hand. I'll begin by reading the relevant parts of the will. Please save your comments or questions for the end when I shall answer them."

He placed his spectacles on his nose and cleared his throat. "I, Adam Nathaniel Everson of Ravensmere, in the parish of Waterton, being of sound mind and memory do hereby make, publish, and declare this to be my last will and testament, hereby revoking all prior wills and codicils at any time heretofore made by me. I hereby name and appoint Mr. Samuel Cavendish to be the executor of my estate."

Glances of surprise went around the table. Shifting in his seat, Jack acknowledged Mr. Cavendish with a nod. So this was why Daniel's father was present. Geneva studied Mr. Clarke's calm face as he continued to drone through paragraph after paragraph of legal jargon. Why had her father chosen an outsider as executor of his estate? Would not his heir, Jack, be the logical choice?

Finally, Mr. Clarke came to the bequests Adam had stipulated in the will. An annuity for his mother and niece. A French chaise lounge for Mary. A Swiss mantel clock for Robert. Adam's seventeenth-century Tyndale Bible for Philip.

As the solicitor turned to the next page, Jack leaned forward and placed his elbows on the table. He had chosen subdued apparel for the occasion, but as the moments ticked by, Geneva noticed a distinct sparkle of anticipation in his pale-blue eyes. Pulling her gaze from her cousin, she listened as Mr. Clarke continued reading.

"Next, I bequeath fifty pounds to Alex Brigham of Shaftesbury on the condition that no further bequests, either physical or monetary, will be granted in his lifetime. To my nephew Captain Jack Everson, I bequeath my collection of rare books, my John Constable painting, and my Italian humidor cabinet. To all three of my nephews, I hereby declare that for the rest of their lives they will continue to benefit from their monthly allowances issued from the estate."

Jack abruptly straightened, his elbows sliding off the table, hands dropping to his lap, but not before Geneva saw that his fists were balled so tightly that his knuckles had blanched. His jaw tightened, his expression darkening, as Mr. Clarke went on.

"Finally, being of sound mind, I leave in trust all the remainder of my estate, including all property, financial investments, the quarry, farm, and manor to my one and only daughter, Miss Geneva Everson, formerly of Shaftesbury. It is for her benefit during her lifetime or until she chooses to marry, upon which, the entire estate will become the property of her husband."

Jack's face was now scarlet with rage. Leaping to his feet, he shouted, "I do not accept this! Uncle Adam promised I would be his heir. Since my childhood, I've been groomed to be master of Ravensmere. How dare you tamper with a will that was drawn up years ago!"

Mr. Clarke pulled the spectacles from his face. "Captain Everson, settle down. We don't tamper with wills. Your uncle amended his will three days after Miss Geneva arrived at the manor. It was a quiet Sunday afternoon as I recall. Everything was carried out in a professional manner with my assistant signing as the second witness. I assure you this is a sound legal document."

"It's not possible," Jack countered. "I knew my uncle well. He wouldn't change his will unless he was under pressure or influence. Mark my word, I shall contest this in a court of law."

He turned to Geneva, the cold fire in his pale-blue eyes turning them to ice. "You're the one behind this. Ever since you arrived, you've been manipulating my uncle for your personal gain. You're nothing but a fraud and a common thief willing to take advantage of a vulnerable man."

Geneva gasped with shock at his spiteful accusations and the barrage of insults that followed. Jack's tongue lashed with such force that he sprayed spittle across the mahogany table. Grand-mama Louise fell into a state of panic, crying for her smelling salts. Philip moved to the edge of his seat as though anticipating a physical confrontation.

Then Mr. Bradshaw stood up and shouted above Jack's voice, "Captain Everson, stop this at once! If you don't sit down and control yourself, we'll have no choice but to send for the authorities."

Jack's chest heaved up and down, his nostrils flared. He glanced around at his family's horrified faces, clenched his fists, and lowered himself to the chair. Bradshaw kept a stern gaze on him.

"Thank you, Captain Everson. Now let me make one thing clear. Mr. Clarke and I have a lot of experience in dealing with these matters. Go ahead and contest the will if that is your wish. But I guarantee you will not win. Mr. Clarke and I can testify with full confidence that Adam Everson was *not* under duress or undue influence from Miss Geneva or anyone else. He exhibited a calm, level-headed, and rational demeanor throughout the entire process."

"He's right, Jack." Samuel said. "Adam and I shared many things of a personal nature. Including his concerns for the future of his newfound daughter. You know that Adam's estate has no entail that requires a male heir. Adam told me of his plans to change his will when he asked me to be his executor just last week. Surely you recognize Miss Geneva's legal right to be her father's heiress."

Geneva's mind raced as the reality of Samuel's words sank in. After her last conversation with her father, she'd expected to receive some provision, but certainly not the entire estate! The thought of owning such vast property and heading the most prominent family of the parish was daunting. She was a working-class girl, familiar with cooking, scrubbing, and ironing. What did she know about such high and mighty things?

In the intervening moments, Jack had fallen silent. The scarlet rage on his face had faded to pallor, and he appeared to be in a daze, stunned and bewildered.

"Give my grandson a few moments," Grandmama Louise said in a croaky voice. "Can't you understand what a terrible blow this is to him?"

"I can understand," Philip spoke up. He turned to Mr. Clarke. "Jack has done so much to serve Ravensmere. Surely my uncle has left some authority to him."

"I was coming to that," Mr. Clarke replied. "Adam appointed Mr. Samuel Cavendish to be Miss Geneva's guardian and trustee of her estate—the reason I requested his presence tonight. But Adam retained a high regard for Captain Everson's work as estate manager. He hoped that Mr. Cavendish would have him continue in that capacity."

"I have no qualms about that," Samuel said. "Adam often praised his nephew's management skills. Of course as trustee, I will need to begin with a full audit simply to satisfy myself that everything is in good order."

Robert pushed his spectacles up his nose and turned to Geneva. "I must say I am as shocked as my brother. Good heavens, this means you're the new mistress of Ravensmere—a mere child and virtual stranger who arrived on our doorstep not ten days ago."

Tess squeezed his arm. "Robert, you shouldn't belittle Geneva. Like it or not, she's Adam's daughter born in legitimate wedlock and a direct descendant of Sir Tobias Everson. And it is not her fault she is a virtual stranger to her family."

"Hear, hear! Nothing could be clearer than that," Philip agreed genially. "Geneva deserves respect and a warm welcome as the new head of the family."

Jack curled his lip. "If you expect that of me, then your head is in the sand." He glared at the solicitor. "Are you quite done, Mr. Clarke, or do you have another shattering announcement to make?"

Mr. Clarke cleared his throat. "I'm finished, Captain Everson, and ready to answer any questions you have."

Still seething with anger, Jack got up, his fingers curled like claws. "What questions could there be? This would appear to be a *fait accompli*, and as you say, there's nothing I can do to change it."

Turning on his heels, he stomped out of the room and slammed the door shut. His mother held tightly clasped hands to her bosom. "I'm terribly sorry, Mr. Clarke. I do apologize for my son's anger."

"Thank you, Mrs. Mary. I hope for Miss Geneva's sake that he settles down in due time. Since you have no questions, Mr. Bradshaw and I shall be on our way." The elderly solicitor tucked the document into his case and stood up. "Thank you for the opportunity to serve you. Should you need me in the future, don't hesitate to come to my office in Ingleford."

As everyone left the dining room, Mr. Cavendish took Geneva aside. "Please don't be discouraged. With time and patience, I'm sure Jack and the rest of them will adjust and open their hearts to you."

Geneva cast a worried glance over her shoulder. "I don't know about that, but I hope you're right."

"Well, just remember that I'm your guardian. If you have any problems, big or small, please have a message sent, and I'll come as soon as possible."

"Thank you, that's comforting to know."

He smiled and took her hand in a fatherly way. "Take care of yourself and try to sleep well tonight. I'll return tomorrow at eleven, and we'll look over your estate finances together. I'll bring Daniel as well since he'll serve as my deputy trustee when needed."

Geneva bid him a good night. As she turned toward the stairs, Tess called out to her. "Geneva, we're having hot chocolate in the library. Won't you join us?"

"No, thank you, I'm awfully tired. Please say good night to the others for me. I'll see you at breakfast in the morning."

Geneva made her way to her bedroom. The night was so wet and cool that Emily had slipped a bedwarmer between the sheets. After washing and donning her nightgown, Geneva removed the bed warmer to the hearth, then climbed into her warm nest.

But despite her exhaustion, sleep did not come easily. The news Mr. Bradshaw had brought to Shaftesbury was shocking enough. Tonight's events were staggering, their implications unsettling. Above all, the seeds of animosity were planted between her and Jack. Now that she was mistress of Ravensmere, Jack had every reason to resent her or even hate her for displacing him as the heir apparent. Likewise her female family members. How would she cope with their constant snide remarks and critical stares following her every move?

But even more, Geneva detested false accusations. First, those against her mother and now, against her. Shouldn't her father have anticipated that his amended will would throw the family into chaos? Perhaps he believed that it would make up for the terrible consequences of his actions toward her mother and Geneva's own life over these almost nineteen years.

If so, her father was wrong. It was too late to forgive him. He was gone, and her new life lay ahead of her.

CHAPTER ELEVEN

The following morning, Geneva gripped the oak banister as she made her way down the staircase. She hadn't slept well. Her neck ached from tension, and the thought of joining her family in the dining room for breakfast took away all appetite. After Jack's angry outburst the previous night, what would he do today? Throw more insults and caustic comments at her?

Descending the lower flight of the stairs, Geneva was taken aback to find the family member she most dreaded waiting for her at the bottom.

"Good morning, Cousin Geneva." He glanced down the hall briefly and lowered his voice. "Before we join the others, may I have a brief word with you?"

Geneva paused on the bottom step. "Yes, what is it?"

"I've had time to think. I want to apologize for my bad behavior last night. The things I said were simply inexcusable. I will be honest that this isn't easy for me. I feel betrayed by Uncle Adam after all his promises to me. But that is not your fault. So I hope you will forgive me, and I plead for your patience while I adjust to this unfortunate reversal in my life."

Geneva cast a dubious eye over her cousin. He sounded sincere, but his quick turnaround gave her an uneasy feeling. How could his fierce opposition dissipate so quickly? Or was his seeming change of heart just a cover for ulterior motives? If so, it would be interesting to see how long the charade would last.

"I wasn't expecting an olive branch," she said in a cool tone. "Especially one offered so soon. But if you can be cordial, I'll do the same."

"Absolutely!" The smile Jack turned on her was admittedly charming. "That's all I want. After all, we are family, dear cousin. We all want the best for Ravensmere and peace within our household."

Geneva wasn't convinced, but she nodded. "Fine. Then shall we go in for breakfast?"

"Not yet." To Geneva's surprise, Jack bowed graciously and offered her an arm. "Before that, there is one small formality that must be observed now that you are mistress of Ravensmere. Will you come with me to the Great Hall?"

Still wary, Geneva took Jack's arm and allowed him to lead her down the hallway. As they stepped into the Great Hall, she was surprised at a sea of faces looking her way. On one side, the servants stood in a row according to their status from butler and housekeeper down to scullery maid. On the other side, the entire Everson family stood waiting for her.

Geneva held back, but Jack urged her forward. "Don't be shy. This is an important day for you. I've gathered everyone here to welcome you in your new capacity."

He turned to the servants. "Most of you are already acquainted with our cousin. But today I present her to you as your new employer—Miss Geneva Everson, mistress of Ravensmere."

A murmur of welcoming voices sounded throughout the Great Hall. Looking around, Geneva saw both smiling faces and expressions of shock that the newcomer was now head of the household. Clasping her hands, Geneva shifted awkwardly from foot to foot.

"Thank you for your welcome. I'm grateful for what my father has given me, and I promise to do my best for you. But please be patient. I have so much to learn."

Stanway stepped forward. "Don't worry, miss. We understand how you feel. We'll do everything we can to make the transition easy for you."

"Thank you, Stanway. While I think of it, would it be permissible for the servants to have an extra hour of leisure today? After the hard work they did for the reception, I think they deserve it."

Stanway didn't change his usual stoic expression, but Geneva thought she caught approval in his gaze as he bowed respectfully. "Beg your pardon, miss. I wasn't expecting that. Very thoughtful of you."

Mrs. Fox moved forward beside Stanway. "And you mustn't be afraid to ask for help. You've rarely used the bell pull, so I hope you'll avail yourself of it."

"Thank you. I'll keep it in mind." Out of habit, Geneva bobbed a quick curtsey. Gasps and snickers came from the servants and a groan of dismay from Aunt Mary. Jack grinned broadly as he led a red-faced Geneva into the dining room and guided her to the head of the table where Adam had once sat. "This is your seat now, Cousin Geneva."

Sitting down, Geneva sniffed the scent of white roses laid around her place setting. "Goodness, the flowers are lovely. Who put them here?"

"I did." Jack went over to the sideboard and began filling his plate from the serving dishes. "I thought you might want to enjoy them while they are still fresh. There is an abundance of flowers if you'd like to have a vase or two carried up to your room or any-where else you choose."

Geneva was unwillingly impressed with his thoughtfulness. She joined the rest of the family helping themselves at the side-board. Katherine added scrambled eggs to her plate and scowled at Geneva. "Why did you offer the servants time off? They're used to having extra duties."

"I'm aware of that," Geneva responded evenly, spooning por-ridge into a bowl. "But I'm familiar with hard domestic work so I can sympathize with them."

"Just be careful you're not soft with them," Aunt Mary inter-jected, carrying her plate to the table. "It just makes them lazy. Tomorrow Mrs. Lockwood will deliver your wardrobe. I'm sure that will keep you busy. When you're done, we'll go over your responsibilities as mistress and cover the important points on eti-quette for a lady of your position."

Jack cracked a boiled egg open and reached for the salt. "I've been thinking about Cousin Geneva's bedroom. Now that she's mistress, she should be moved to her mother's former bedroom." He sent Geneva a warm smile. "I'm sure you'll be happy with it. It has a sunny exposure with a view of the gardens."

"I was about to suggest that," Aunt Mary said. "I'll tell Mrs. Fox this morning. It will need a thorough cleaning, and your father's lounge will need some feminine touches. Hopefully, you can move in tomorrow."

Geneva drizzled cream over her porridge. "That sounds excit-ing. But what will happen to my father's bedroom?"

"You must think of the future," Grandmama Louise said. "When you marry, that will be your husband's bedroom."

"Indeed," Jack said. "Let's pray that whoever she chooses, he will not only love her dearly but care for the estate as Adam did. Well, now, later this morning, I should write a letter to Alex Brigham asking for him to send your flute. I'm looking forward to hearing you play for us, Cousin Geneva. And your cat. Those were the two items you were missing, were they not? Or are there other items I should request as well?"

"No, Pookie and my flute are the only items of value I left behind." Putting down her spoon, Geneva reached out a finger to touch the white rose petals. "You are all so kind to me. I appreciate it very much, but may I be so bold as to ask for one other thing?"

"By all means." Jack cocked his head inquisitively. "What is it?"

"Well, it's regarding those three laborers and that little boy I met while on my walk. May I have permission to take food baskets to their families?"

"Oh, yes, I quite forgot." Jack looked over at his grandmother. "You don't object, do you, Grandmama?"

The old lady fiddled with her napkin ring for a moment. "Well, one does have to be careful with charity. We don't want the laboring folk becoming dependent on handouts. But I suppose it wouldn't hurt just once."

"Thank you, Grandmama Louise. I'll see to it right after breakfast. Who should I talk to about it? The cook?"

"Mrs. Fox would be the one to make such arrangements," her grandmother responded sharply. "Never ever go over the housekeeper's head if you wish to maintain discipline among your staff!"

"And don't dally if you intend to carry out your charity after breakfast," Aunt Mary added. "Samuel Cavendish and his son will be here to meet with you at eleven. They will not be happy if you keep them waiting!"

Geneva sighed inwardly. So much for an improved relationship with her female family members. "Don't worry, I'll be back in time."

Geneva tucked into her porridge, then finished off a slice of toast with ginger marmalade. Excusing herself from the table, she made her way down the hall to the housekeeper's sitting room. She was several paces away from Mrs. Fox's partially opened door when she heard a raised voice.

"Oh hogwash, how can you say that, Lily? The girl has been here for less than a fortnight. The captain was born here and groomed to be his uncle's heir. Don't talk about the *law*. By all moral rights, *he* should be master of the manor."

Geneva came to an abrupt halt. There was no reason to feel shaken at Mrs. Fox's outburst. After all, the housekeeper was right. Jack had every reason to believe he should be master of Ravensmere. And the servants who'd watched him grow up to support his claims. Maybe this was not the time to be approaching Mrs. Fox with her unconventional request.

But, no, that would be cowardly. Geneva hadn't asked to be mistress here. Her father had wanted it. And a forthright manner was the best way to start off. Backing up a few steps, Geneva strode forward so that her shoes tapped audibly on the stone flags. As she neared the housekeeper's door, she called out, "Mrs. Fox, are you there? May I have a word with you?"

By the time Geneva reached the sitting room door, it had swung wide open and Mrs. Fox appeared, cheeks tinged with pink. Behind her stood Lily, the cook, looking embarrassed and even slightly scared.

"Yes, miss, do come in. Lily was just on her way out."

The cook scurried out the door as Geneva entered the small sitting room. Mrs. Fox stood respectfully at attention. "Please come in and make yourself comfortable. I had hoped I might receive instructions from you or provide answers to your questions."

"Thank you." Geneva looked around as she took a seat in a chair next to a desk piled high with household accounts and other paperwork. "What a bright room and so nicely decorated. I love your plates on the wall and the colorful cushions on your sofa. And please, do be seated as well."

As Mrs. Fox took a seat, Geneva went on. "As to questions, I'm sure I will have many in coming days. But for now, my only instruction is to have food baskets made up for three families of laborers. I want each one to have enough for several meals."

Mrs. Fox compressed her lips tightly but nodded. "Certainly, Miss Geneva. I will give orders for the kitchen maid to prepare them with Lily's guidance."

"Thank you. And when they're ready, I'll need a lift to the estate farm cottages to distribute them. Could you please inform the coachman? What's his name? I've forgotten."

"Burrows, miss. Stanway will inform him." Mrs. Fox's expression thawed slightly as she added, "It's kind of you to help those in need."

As Geneva smiled, she noticed a framed pen-and-ink sketch of a young boy on the mantelpiece. "That's a charming little picture. Is it a family member?"

Mrs. Fox's expression thawed even further. "No, but it's someone who was very special to me: Billy Jasper. Stanway has a talent for sketching. He drew that picture shortly after Billy came to us from the orphanage."

"It's lovely. Does it look like him?"

"Oh yes, Stanway got his features just right. I've always liked children, so I used to volunteer at the orphanage every week. Billy was such a nice boy. When he turned eight, Stanway hired him as stable boy. I took him under my wing to make sure he'd settle in well. But a few weeks later, I was shocked to find out he'd packed up his things and departed without a word to anyone. Captain Everson organized an extensive search, but he was never found."

"That must have been very difficult for you," Geneva said, catching a faraway, sad expression in the housekeeper's eyes.

"Yes, it was," Mrs. Fox responded with a sigh. "But it was a long time ago. Not long after Mr. Adam's second marriage, in fact. I remember because he was gone by the time—" She flushed and finished awkwardly, "Well, by the time your mother left us. By now he'll be grown up and married with his own children, no doubt. Wherever he is, I hope he's happy."

Glancing at the clock, the housekeeper stood to her feet. "I beg your pardon, Miss Geneva. I've been rambling far too long. I'll go now and see to those baskets."

A half hour later, Geneva stepped out to the rear courtyard and climbed into the waiting carriage. Three baskets covered with blue-checkered tea cloths had been placed on the seat across from her. Burrows drove the carriage down Raven's Lane in the direction of the village. Before reaching Waterton Road, he turned right onto McCormack Lane, shaded by numerous trees.

Geneva was disheartened at the shabby state of the tenant cottages rented by farm laborers employed on Everson land. The rubble-stone cottages were filthy from smoke and grime. Gaping cracks were visible in the exterior walls. Flakes of green paint clung to front doors. Small yards were littered with rocks and brambles.

At the second-to-last cottage, Geneva spotted Joseph playing outside with a ball made of rags. She tapped on the carriage roof, and Burrows pulled over. She'd no sooner stepped down with a basket on her arm than Joseph dropped his ball and rushed down the path to meet her.

"Miss Everson! Ma and Da said you'd forgotten 'bout us. What's in the basket?"

"Lots of good things. Is your mother inside?"

Without a word, Joseph streaked to the cottage door, calling out, "Ma! Ma!"

Following slowly, Geneva noted an emaciated goat tethered to a pole and a tiny vegetable patch picked clean except for a few onion stalks. A broken window was stuffed with rags, and a drainpipe dangled precariously from the eaves. As Geneva neared the front door, a young woman appeared. She was as thin as her husband and son except her belly, well advanced in pregnancy. Straggly hair poked out from under a grey kerchief, and a toddler dangled on her hip.

"Miss Everson, mercy me, I'm surprised that you came! I'm Anna, Harry's wife. Will you come in? I just made a pot of tea."

"Thank you, Anna. I'm sorry I took so long in coming." Geneva stepped through the door into a small room furnished with only one table and wooden chairs. A small fire on the hearth offered meager heat. "A lot has been happening at the manor. Did you know that my father died?"

"No, miss, I'm sorry to hear that."

"Well, I'm the mistress now. But I won't have any authority until I come of age. My grandmother and aunt have been good in allowing me to bring this food."

Geneva set the basket on the table. Joseph reached up and grabbed at the checkered tea cloth covering it. "Can I see, Miss Everson?"

Anna smacked her son's hand. "Mind yer manners, boy! That's no way to behave with a lady."

But her own hand was trembling as she lifted the cloth. "Glory be! Joseph, climb onto a chair and look at this. Your da won't believe it! Butter and cheese. Oatmeal and flour. A joint of gammon. Carrots, turnips, 'n' apples. And what's this? Fruitcake! Oh, Miss Everson, thank you. 'Tis so kind of you."

Geneva held Anna's toddler while Anna poured tea into chipped cups and cut three slices of cake. Glancing down, she saw that the floor was littered with straw. In one corner, the straw had been piled into a makeshift bed where two more children were sleeping under a threadbare blanket.

Following her gaze, Anna spoke up. "Those are my daughters, Alice and Milly. I'm expecting another around Christmas. Harry hopes it'll be another boy this time. When boys turn seven, they can help in the fields. Like Joseph here. He's already working with his da a few days a week. It may not be much, but every extra penny helps. Once harvest is over, Harry will be laid off, and I won't deny the winter don't look too good."

"I heard about the layoffs," Geneva said sympathetically. "I'm awfully sorry. It's due to the threshing machines, isn't it?"

"Yes, we hate them awful things. All the big farms in the parish have them now. I wish I could earn money myself. But it's not easy when I've got the kids to mind an' another on the way."

Joseph took his last bite of cake. While he licked his fingers, a thought came to Geneva's mind. "Anna, maybe there is something you could do to earn money. Not just you but other women in your situation. I don't know if you've heard of Shaftesbury. That's where I lived until I came to Ravensmere. The wives of laboring men there are often employed in cottage industries like spinning cotton and making buttons and gloves. The factories haven't taken over entirely. If you're interested, I could look into it and see if it's possible here in Waterton."

Anna lowered her slice of cake to the plate. "I've heard of cottage industries but I know nothing about spinning wheels or button making."

"I'm sure someone would teach you as they do in Shaftesbury."

Anna let out a sigh. "Lawks, it sounds good. But I don't want to get my hopes up in case it comes to nought."

"Well, for now, it's just an idea," Geneva cautioned. "But a good one in my opinion. My guardian is coming to the manor later this morning. He's a good man. I'll mention it to him, and we'll take it from there."

Anna's eyes brimmed with tears. "Miss Everson, 'tis wonderful that you brought this food basket today. But workin' hard to pay the bills would be so much better than charity."

Geneva smiled. Then she noticed the young boy eyeing the slice of cake on her plate. "Joseph, perhaps you could do a job for me. Will you run outside and tell the coachman that I want the other two baskets brought in? After we've taken them to your neighbors, you can gobble up my slice of cake."

Grinning from ear to ear, the child bolted out the door as fast as his skinny legs would take him.

CHAPTER TWELVE

Samuel and Daniel Cavendish arrived at the manor at eleven o'clock sharp. Geneva was waiting punctually in the Great Hall as they walked in and handed their hats to the butler.

"Good morning, Miss Geneva," Samuel said. "I've been worrying about you and Captain Everson. May I hope things are going better between you?"

"Well, actually, they are," Geneva said. "Even before breakfast, Jack apologized for his angry outburst."

"Really? So soon?" Daniel queried.

"Yes, that was my thought. I'm perplexed that he would be resigned so quickly to his loss, but I'm not complaining. I'm just grateful to have peace in the house."

"Jack is a mature and reasonable man at heart," Samuel responded heartily. "Last night he was in a state of shock. Now he isn't. We should give him the benefit of the doubt. Now, let's go down to see him."

Samuel clearly knew where he was going, so Geneva was happy to let him lead the way down the main hallway. Turning onto the east wing, Samuel paused outside the door Tess had once pointed out as leading to Jack's estate office. It stood wide open, and Jack stepped into the doorway. "Good morning, gentlemen, Cousin Geneva. Please come in."

Following on the heels of her companions, Geneva looked around. The office was a large, comfortable room with a Persian carpet, a desk, and a massive oak cabinet in one corner. A worktable occupied the middle of the room. Near the hearth, a celestial globe rested on its stand between two winged chairs in red velvet. Jack's naval commission hung above the fireplace.

As they entered the room, Jack greeted the men with handshakes. "I'm awfully embarrassed about last night. I was devastated that Uncle Adam had changed his will so quickly. But that is no excuse for my explosive reaction. I've already begged Cousin Geneva's forgiveness for my bad behavior. Now I hope you'll forgive me as well."

"Your behavior isn't my concern," Samuel answered coolly. "But your accusations against Miss Geneva were horrendous. You knew your uncle. Do you really think he could be so easily manipulated by a young girl, even his own daughter?"

"Not now, but in my anguish, I did entertain such thoughts." Jack waved a hand toward his worktable. "Mrs. Fox has brought coffee. Would anyone have a cup while it's hot?"

"Would you like me to pour?" Geneva offered, trying to be helpful. If only she knew the proper etiquette of being mistress here!

Jack smiled ingratiatingly. "Thank you, cousin. That is a kind offer. Now, gentlemen, do sit down and make yourselves comfortable."

Geneva took a seat behind the coffee tray. As she poured the steaming dark liquid into cups, she eyed with delight the jeweled colors dancing across the table, product of sunlight shining through a stained-glass window. They were reflected in a jeweled walking stick Geneva had seen Jack carry before, now leaning against the desk.

Noticing her interest, Jack spoke up. "This room used to be a chapel, Cousin Geneva. Redmond McCormack, who built this wing of the manor, was Catholic and a very pious man who wanted a chapel for family worship. Sir Tobias Everson, on the other hand, was Church of England with little interest in religious matters. When he took ownership of Ravensmere, he converted the chapel to an office and replaced the religious stained glass with his own heraldic glass. Do you see the colorful quatrefoils, sheep, and griffins? Those were symbols from his belt and sword."

"It is very impressive," Geneva agreed diplomatically, though she wasn't sure how she felt about converting a place of worship to an office. "A great reminder of the family's history."

Samuel swallowed a generous gulp of coffee. "Well, Jack, let's get down to business. I have heard nothing but good in your management of Ravensmere. So I see no reason why you should not continue as estate manager as Adam stipulated, if you are willing to do so, of course. Your remuneration will remain the same."

"Thank you, sir. I certainly am happy to continue serving Ravensmere—and my cousin." Jack gave Geneva a warm smile.

Samuel looked over at her. "Miss Geneva, I expect you'll have many expenses with a new wardrobe and other needs or wants that arise from time to time. Those bills will be sent to me for payment out of your bank account. Daniel and I will audit the financial books this morning. Before that, we should open them up so you can see what you've inherited."

"Of course," Jack responded smoothly. "I've prepared for that."

Walking over to his desk, he took three black ledgers from the top drawer and brought them back to the table. "Cousin Geneva, why don't you take a seat next to me so you can see the entries in question as I explain them to your guardian."

Pulling her chair close to Jack, Geneva listened as he spoke at great length about the double-entry system of account keeping. His penmanship was beautiful and his columns of figures perfectly aligned. But when Geneva's eyes reached the bottom of the page and she beheld the grand total of stocks and bonds and estate income, she covered her mouth with her fingers.

"Good heavens, I . . . I had no idea. Cousin Jack, there's no need for me to see more. You've explained things well, and I trust your accounting skills."

"Are you sure?" Daniel said. "Don't you want to see the farm and quarry ledgers?"

"No, thank you, but there is one thing I want to ask. I delivered a food basket to Harry Whipple's wife this morning. I was saddened by their state of poverty. Anna wants to earn extra money so they don't have to rely on charity. Is it possible for women like her to have cottage industry work of some sort?"

"Humph, what a kind young lady you are!" Samuel said. "But you should be aware that work of such nature pays very little."

"Perhaps," Geneva said quietly. "But I think I know how Anna would respond to that. She'd say low pay is better than no pay."

"In that case, I could have a word with a textile merchant I'm acquainted with through the bank. I can't guarantee it will be fruitful, but I'll do my best and let you know what the prospects are."

"Thank you, Mr. Cavendish. I'll look forward to hearing from you."

Jack gulped back the last of his coffee. "Meanwhile, would you care to see a map of the estate?"

Geneva's expression brightened. That sounded definitely more interesting than more columns of incomprehensible numbers. "Yes, I want to learn more about the estate."

Samuel reached for a ledger. "Well, Miss Geneva, while you're busy with that, Daniel and I shall get on with the audit."

While father and son took over one end of the worktable with the three ledgers opened wide, Jack pushed aside the coffee tray to unroll a map across the other end, securing the corners with paper weights. Geneva swept her eyes over the colorful details drawn with a three-dimensional effect. "This is beautiful. A piece of art. I feel like a bird looking down from the sky."

She touched the surface. "What kind of paper is this?"

"Parchment made of calfskin." Jack went on to point out the village, manor, farm, quarry, and the two tenant farms, each comprising three hundred acres. "This is Mr. Baines's farm to the southeast and Mr. Farthing's to the northeast. As you can see, we have other tenant holdings ranging in size from residential cottages to thirty-acre parcels. Our biggest—I beg your pardon, your biggest—source of income is derived from rent. The balance comes from farm products and the sale of limestone from Everson Quarry."

"This is very helpful. Now I can picture the entire estate and community." Geneva searched the map for McCormack Lane and placed her finger on the parchment. "That's Harry Whipple's home where I went this morning. I noticed that cottage repairs are needed. Is it possible to have work done?"

Jack rubbed a hand along his jaw. "That would be my bailiff's decision—Mr. Blackerby. He's responsible for building maintenance and rent collection. I appreciate your compassionate heart, cousin. But the truth is that laborers' cottages aren't high on the priority list."

"Why not?" Geneva demanded heatedly. "In God's eyes, the poor are just as important as the rich."

"I don't deny that," Jack responded calmly. "But the rent they pay is also minimal, which makes it impractical to spend a lot on maintenance."

"It's just a broken window and drainpipe," Geneva argued. "Can't you at least ask Mr. Blackerby to have a look?"

Jack's expression didn't change, but after a pause, he shrugged. "Of course, if that is what you want, I'll tell Mr. Blackerby to drop by."

At the other end of the worktable, Daniel stood up, a ledger open in his hands. "Sorry to interrupt, but I see the quarry income has declined significantly over the past two years. Is there a specific reason for such a change?"

Jack frowned. "Yes, actually. It's an unfortunate situation due to increasing competition. Several quarries down the coast have expanded considerably. They produce stone more quickly than we can, and their transport costs by sea are cheaper. Builders with large projects have been turning to them rather than us. As a result, I've been forced to accept smaller contracts like the one for Nigel Spooner's new Georgian house."

"Isn't it possible to increase your rate of production?" Daniel asked. "After all, if these other quarries can do so, why not here?"

"It's not that simple. It would require additional equipment and steam cranes, which are expensive to buy and maintain. We'd need larger stables for the increase in oxen and wagons. The overhead would be huge for such an ambitious project. Adam and I had frequent discussions about this. His declining health was a concern, so he wanted to avoid the stress of change and expansion. He was content to keep the quarry as it had always been—a family business meeting the needs of our own community."

Daniel's eyebrows rose. "Knowing Adam, I'm surprised to hear that. I was under the impression he wanted to keep abreast of progress and stay competitive."

"And why would you assume that?" Samuel gave his son a stern look. "Your conversations with your godfather were hardly about estate business. Jack has long been in his uncle's confidence when it comes to managing the estate. If Adam was content with a modest family business rather than tearing up his estate like the big industrial quarries, then who are we to question it? Let's finish this audit. We'll plan for another at the year's end."

Daniel didn't respond to his father's rebuke, his expression unreadable as he continued pouring over the ledger page. Geneva glanced at the clock. "Mr. Cavendish, Daniel, won't you both join us for luncheon when you're finished? It would be nice to have you. Cousin Philip and Claire are coming as well."

"That sounds jolly good," Samuel said. "We'd be delighted."

While the two Cavendish men delved into the ledgers once more, Geneva walked over to the oak cabinet. She'd learned enough working for Uncle Alex to estimate the rich patina and worn edges as a good two centuries old. The lavish carvings were outstanding: shells, artichokes, and acanthus leaves. She reached for the knob. "Cousin Jack, I hope you don't mind if I have a look in here."

"Don't do that!" At Jack's sharp tone, Geneva released the knob and jumped back. Jack strode over, his expression vexed. "Can't you see the latch at the bottom? Unless you release it first, you'll break the knob. Furniture that old needs to be handled with care!"

Geneva put her hands behind her back, unnerved by Jack's sudden change of mood. Her cousin opened the left side of the cabinet, revealing six shelves holding an array of historic scrolls and books. He smiled warmly as though he hadn't just barked at her. "These are the manorial records that date back to Sir Callum

McCormack. Dry conditions and even temperatures are essential for their preservation."

Geneva had endured enough lectures on the proper care of antiques from Uncle Alex to know Jack had cause on his side. Somewhat mollified, she asked meekly, "May I read one of them?"

"Not these, I'm afraid, unless you are fluent in Latin. From feudal days until 1732, all estate records were written in Latin. If you wish, I'll show you one of Sir Callum's." Putting on a pair of white gloves, Jack eased a large book out from the shelf. With a delicate touch, he opened it to the center page and held it forth for her to see.

"Oh goodness, I love the first capital letter!" Geneva exclaimed. "The colors and embellishments are beautiful. How old is this?"

"Over three hundred years."

"Are there any written in English by more recent generations? I'd love to read about their personal lives."

"There are a number in English, but unfortunately, they're all legal and administrative records, which is why they're rarely looked at. It is a pity there are not more personal accounts. Factual records are essential of course, but the lives of our predecessors are far more important. That's why I put great store in our family portraits. Each one is a link in the continuity of the Everson family line—from Tobias to your offspring. Speaking of which, now that you're the head of the family, we ought to have your portrait painted. Would you like that?"

Jack's earlier transgressions were swept away in a rush of delight. Maybe he wasn't anything like Uncle Alex, as Geneva had begun to fear. "Thank you, Cousin Jack. How kind of you to suggest it and what an honor."

Shortly after one, the family and guests were seated around the dining room table. Stanway served salmon soufflé with a medley of creamed vegetables and crusty rolls.

Geneva sipped her grape cordial. "I have interesting news. Anna Whipple was grateful for the food basket I took her, but she said paid work would be better than charity. Mr. Cavendish is going to look into a possible cottage industry for her and other women on the estate who might be interested."

"That's an excellent idea," Philip said. "Work of that sort has many benefits. Women can determine their own work hours and mind their children at the same time. Grandparents can partake, and even small children can do simple tasks."

"You paint a rosy picture," Robert objected. "I've heard that wage disputes are rampant in cottage industries. It's a competitive system for the merchants. Any slump in trade conditions results in reduced income for the workers."

Katherine turned to her brother. "Oh, Robert, why must you be such a wet blanket? Nothing is perfect in this world, so we do the best we can. I support Geneva in this. In fact I'd like to help her."

Geneva lowered her knife and fork, surprised at her cousin's unexpected support. "That would be wonderful. Do you really mean it, Katherine?"

"Absolutely, as long as Mr. Cavendish allows it."

"Why wouldn't I?" Samuel responded. "I'm pleased to hear this. If things work out, I could connect you with a merchant in Ingleford. You're a mature and forthright young lady, Miss Katherine. You'd do well with an appointment at his office."

"Thank you. If this has a positive outcome, I can help financially as well. Uncle Adam was generous with the annuity he gave me."

"I'm glad to hear that. Yes, Adam was a generous man. I miss him terribly." Samuel turned his attention to the flowering clematis in the window. "I had a stroll in my garden early this morning. If it wasn't for Adam, I wouldn't have had the inspiration to create my own garden paradise. His enthusiasm was infectious."

"How lovely to hear that," Grandmama Louise said. "My son touched many lives, especially as justice of the peace. He lived up to his title, always just, without favoritism or discrimination."

Daniel reached for the salt cellar. "Well, our local justice system will be put to the test very soon. I heard from a bank client that they had trouble near Salbridge last night. That's only five miles from here. The previous day, a landowner received a letter from Captain Swing demanding a wage increase for his farm laborers. He met with them and agreed to a rise of three pence, but that wasn't good enough for them. In retaliation, a gang of laborers swarmed into his farmyard late last night and burnt a hayrick to the ground."

"That's dreadful!" Geneva exclaimed. "But who is this Captain Swing?"

"He isn't a real person. He's the invisible figurehead of those laborers who are protesting their wages. Most laborers are illiterate, but there's always someone willing to write letters for them."

"Was anyone arrested?" Robert asked.

"Several, so I heard. I pity the worst offenders."

Jack knitted his brows into a frown. "You pity them? Why? They're criminals worthy of punishment."

"You know I don't condone violence, but I do sympathize with them. They're honest men driven to crime by hunger."

"Will they go to prison?" Geneva asked.

"Some will—the fortunate ones. The worst offenders will be transported to Australia. The journey itself can be a death sentence. Only the strongest can survive three or four months of filth and disease in a prison hulk."

Geneva looked approvingly at Daniel. As when she'd first met him, he displayed a compassionate heart for those in need. "I agree with Daniel. One cannot condone violence. But it could have been prevented if the landowner was more charitable to these desperate men. Three pence is nothing. If he'd offered them food and coal to feed and warm their families, it might have quelled their anger and eased their worries."

"Well said!" Philip spoke up. "A master should care for the welfare of not just his household but his employees as well. The church provides poor relief, but that is *not* the solution. Charity shouldn't be a substitute for a living wage. It robs men of their independence and dignity. In some instances, it causes them to turn *against* their benefactors. In my opinion, Cousin Geneva's desire to help Anna Whipple into the cottage industry is the better one."

"You're right of course, Philip," Samuel agreed. "But with regards to Anna's husband and other farm laborers, raising wages isn't always practical. And laborers are most commonly unskilled for alternative work. I am well aware of the grief it caused Adam in having to lay off his laborers for the winter months. Weeks before he died, he mentioned the new threshing machines made by J. Fulton, a local craftsman. He believed the time had come to purchase one and that your tenant farmers were of the same mind. You know more about this than I do, Jack."

"Yes, I do," Jack said. "Uncle Adam had a valid reason for turning to mechanization. The large payroll through the threshing months was a financial burden. He estimated that Fulton's moderately priced machine would, in the end, yield a better profit margin. We've used threshing machines before—poorly made and not worth a shilling. But Fulton's patent is excellent, designed with the help of a millwright, a carpenter, and a blacksmith."

"I understand all that," Philip said. "But until alternate forms of employment are available, charity must continue. If Cousin Geneva is interested, she could join other volunteers in bringing produce to the church on Saturday afternoons. That would coincide with the issuing of the laborers' poor relief in cash payments. Uncle Adam was always generous with such contributions, though he never participated personally."

Geneva perked up. "I'd be delighted to volunteer with whatever produce Ravensmere can spare. Maybe Katherine would like to join me." Her glance toward her cousin held challenge. Was Katherine really softening her attitude?

To Geneva's surprise and satisfaction, Katherine nodded. "Yes, I certainly will, as long as I'm not occupied with my work concerning the cottage industry. Geneva has reminded me that we ought to obey God's commands by caring for those who are least amongst us."

Geneva glanced around at the family's expressions. She wasn't the only one surprised at Katherine's words. Claire reached over to give her sister-in-law's hand a squeeze. "Dear sister, I can't thank you and Cousin Geneva enough. What a great asset you will be to our parish charity team."

CHAPTER THIRTEEN

Geneva's head was spinning. This was the second day since she'd become mistress of Ravensmere, and it had been a busy one. She'd just spent two hours with Aunt Mary learning all the dos and don'ts and rules of protocol pertaining to ladies of the gentry. Her main role as mistress seemed to be acting as a gracious hostess, always mindful of the needs of others. When it came to the ceremony of pouring afternoon tea, she'd practiced each step repeatedly until it met her aunt's approval.

As housekeeper, Mrs. Fox was Geneva's representative in the manor. She was responsible for domestic accounting, ordering supplies, and managing the female servants except for the cook and those under her. Geneva was confident she'd soon master the art of meal planning, but until then Mrs. Fox would guide her. Aunt Mary had stressed the importance of not becoming familiar with the servants. They deserved respect but nothing more. This was challenging since Geneva had already formed a friendship with Emily, the head housemaid.

Geneva made her way up the stairs to her new bedroom, which the maids had finished cleaning. She couldn't believe her father's suite had become her private domain. But not all such reflection was pleasant. As Geneva reached the upper-floor landing, her thoughts turned to the dreadful night that had forever changed the course of her mother's life.

Taking several paces to the right, Geneva glanced at the door to her father's lounge. Within that suite were husband and wife bedrooms. The servants' stairwell was at the north end of the hallway. Geneva's tension rose as she visualized the scene Emily had described. A naked Nicholas Drake, clothing stuffed under his arm, fleeing down the spiral stairs while Emily and other servants peered down from the top floor.

Geneva was grateful for Jack's quick response in preventing Adam from attacking her mother in a fit of anger. Who knew what might have happened otherwise. But how had her mother responded? And if innocent, why had she not cried out for help when Drake invaded her bedroom? Had she been too frightened to speak?

Geneva entered her lounge. Mrs. Fox and the housemaids had been busy. The air smelt like lavender. Her father's leather chairs had been replaced with two matching armchairs in pale green upholstery. A gold carpet gave the room a cozy feel. Crossing over to the window, Geneva fingered the soft fabric of ivory curtains. Outside, her father's rose garden looked lovely—not a weed in sight and the pathways swept clean.

Geneva turned her gaze to the bench where she'd sat with her father on that last day. The words he'd spoken only minutes before his untimely death reverberated in her mind. *Everyone is vulnerable to weaknesses, Geneva, even the most noble of characters. You would do well to keep that in mind as you journey through life.*

It was true that some of the most venerated characters in the Bible had fallen into sin. But to assume this happened to every noble person was just plain wrong. Certainly, her mother's life had been an open letter, and anyone who read it could testify to Elizabeth's high moral principles. At one time, that weather-beaten bench had been a joyful place where Adam had proposed to his young bride. Now it was a place of sorrow where he'd drawn his last breath.

Wiping a tear from her cheek, Geneva crossed the threshold into her bedroom. New lace had been hung from the canopy of the four-poster bed. A vase of freshly picked flowers brightened the dressing table. Figurines of lords and ladies added elegance to the mantelpiece.

Geneva was admiring a botanical print on the wall when Mrs. Fox appeared at the door, linen draped over an arm. "Excuse my intrusion, miss. I didn't know you were here. My apologies that the room is not quite ready yet."

Geneva gave the bedroom an appreciative scan. "Well, I must thank you for what you've done already. I never dreamt I'd ever have such a pretty room." She walked over to look out the bedroom window. "Goodness, there's a magnolia growing up the wall. My cat Pookie will love it. Whenever he wants to come in, he can just climb up the trunk and slip through this open window."

Mrs. Fox set her load of linen on the canopy bed. "Yes, miss, a lucky cat to be sure. When you're finished here, the maids will make up the bed and have everything ready for the arrival of your new wardrobe."

Geneva turned around from the window. "I'm looking forward to that. But please, before you go, I want to ask you something. I understand you were already housekeeper at Ravensmere when my mother lived here."

Mrs. Fox paused halfway to the door. "Yes, I've been here a long time, miss."

"Well, I heard that my mother was confined to this room before her departure and that you looked after her."

"That's correct. It's what your father wanted and not for me to judge."

"I'm not afraid to judge," Geneva said. "He was cruel to keep her locked up like a prisoner. You were her only companion. She must have been very upset by what happened. Could you share with me how she was and what she said?"

The housekeeper pursed her lips. "Miss Geneva, with all due respect, I must take offence to your questioning. I've served your family faithfully for many years. Just ask Stanway. He'll vouch for my impeccable record."

Geneva was taken aback at Mrs. Fox's sharp tone. The housekeeper seemed flustered, and her chin was quivering. "Mrs. Fox, I don't understand. Why are you so defensive?"

"I'm not defensive. I'm embarrassed to be asked such pointed questions. In spite of your mother's serious indiscretion, she still maintained a degree of propriety by not talking to me about her personal affairs. I was her subordinate. Surely you understand that by now."

"Yes, I do. But this is very important to me, and you're the only one who knows what happened."

For a moment or two, Mrs. Fox glanced down at the floor and rubbed her forehead. Then lifting her gaze to Geneva, she spoke with confidence. "Very well, I'll tell you. When I was sent upstairs to attend to her, I found her weeping on her bed."

"Was this soon after the event?"

"Yes, not long at all."

"What was she wearing?"

"An ivory negligee. Her husband had gifted several to her. This crying continued on and off for several days. I was kind and gentle without being familiar. She expressed how sad and distraught she was to be leaving the family and the manor. I helped with her bathing needs and toilette. I brought her meal trays, but she ate practically nothing. At first, I thought it was a sign of her remorse and repentance, but as the day of her departure neared, she became angry and demanding."

Geneva stiffened. "That doesn't sound like the mother I knew. She was always courteous and respectful even to those who mistreated her."

"Well, I'm glad she improved as the years went by. She wanted to take Emily as her lady's maid. Your father wouldn't allow it. Then she fussed about her suitcase. It wasn't big enough. She wanted a trunk for all her dresses."

"Mrs. Fox, this isn't making sense," Geneva interrupted. "To be frank, I find it hard to believe what you're saying."

The housekeeper lifted her chin. "I am not a liar, Miss Geneva. Your mother must have known there would be consequences to the choice she had made. I gave her what she needed the most—a Bible."

Scanning the top shelf of a bookcase, Mrs. Fox found the Bible and pulled it out. "Here it is. I don't know why she didn't take it with her. I brought it to her the day before she left the manor. It belongs to you now."

Geneva took the Bible Mrs. Fox pushed toward her but simply returned it to the shelf. "Thank you, Mrs. Fox, but I expect she had her own Bible. Someone needed to repent on that dreadful day. I assure you it wasn't my mother!"

The following Saturday afternoon, Geneva collected a large basket of eggs from the henhouse and carried them out to the farmyard. Burrows had prepared the horse and cart. As she set the basket down at the rear of the cart, Mr. Blackerby emerged from his tenant cottage, his black Labrador, Max, bounding behind him.

"Good afternoon, Miss Geneva, I heard about your charity work. My word, the laboring folk of the parish will be glad to see all this food."

Lifting his nose, Max sniffed the back of her cart. Geneva gave the dog a pat on the head. "I'm glad I can help them. Miss Katherine wanted to help as well but she's in Ingleford this afternoon concerning her work for Waterton's cottage industry. This is all produce from the farm except for those bundles tied with string. Lily said she could spare white beans from the pantry. They are very nutritious, and I thought the more the better with so many laborers laid off for the winter months."

"The layoffs are unfortunate, miss," Mr. Blackerby agreed. "I've worked here a long time and never thought a threshing machine would replace the manual use of a flail. But times are changing, and so is husbandry."

His words brought a sudden thought to Geneva's mind. "Mr. Blackerby, do you mind if I ask when you started as bailiff?"

The bailiff looked surprised at the question. "It must be twenty-five years now, miss. Why do you ask?"

"I wondered if perhaps you could help me with something. If you were here nineteen years ago, did you know Nicholas Drake, who was the coachman then?"

Mr. Blackerby's expression lost its geniality. Cautiously, he answered, "I knew him, yes, but not well at all. He wasn't here for long."

"Well, I'm anxious to find him so I can ask him some questions. Do you know where he might have gone?"

"I know where he went when he left here," Mr. Blackerby admitted. "But I doubt it will help you now, miss. I had a very early appointment with the seed merchant in Porthaven that morning after the . . . the incident. I left before dawn and was not aware of Drake's dismissal. On my way, I passed him resting beside the road with a heavy bag. I was puzzled he hadn't brought the estate carriage so I assumed he must be on personal business. I stopped to offer him a lift. He was much obliged and asked to be dropped off at the harbor."

"So how did he seem?" Geneva asked eagerly. "Did he speak of his plans?"

Mr. Blackerby shook his head. "You must remember, miss, at that point I had no idea he'd been dismissed for cause. If I'd known why he had left Ravensmere on foot, I certainly would not have offered my services. As to plans, he said nothing to me, and I did not see him again after I left him at the harbor. Perhaps he took the ferry up the coast. Or he may have taken stable or coach work at one of the inns in Porthaven. Quite a comedown from his respectable position at Ravensmere. No good family would ever hire him without a letter of recommendation."

"Yes, that is true. Well, thank you, Mr. Blackerby. This information could be quite helpful."

"Glad to be of assistance, miss. I should go up to the manor now. Captain Everson is expecting my daily report."

Geneva secured her egg basket with bunches of hay and covered the provisions with sackcloth. When she was done, Burrows assisted her into the seat. A few minutes later, they arrived at the parish church.

Under the cool shade of plane trees, three couples from the parish had already arrived with donations in their carts. Stepping down from the cart, Geneva introduced herself. "Lovely day, isn't it? I'm Miss Everson from Ravensmere. I have some produce here from our farm."

With Burrows's help, Geneva quickly added her donation to those already being mounded up on tables by other volunteers.

There was a good variety of root vegetables, a pile of used clothes, and even a jumble of kitchen items. Ravensmere's contributions included rounds of cheese, blocks of butter, bags of stone-ground flour, along with the eggs and parcels of white beans.

Once unloaded, Geneva strolled over to the church. Passing under a gothic archway to an enclosed porch, she spotted her cousin Philip and two other men seated at a table with open books and cash box. Laborers and their family members were gathered to one side. As a man at the table called out a name, a laborer stepped forward. Coins were counted into the laborer's hand and a mark made in the open book. When he stepped back, another name was called out.

Sympathy tugged at Geneva's heart as she eyed the group. Their clothes were grey and drab, their footwear nothing but strips of leather sewn together, their heads bowed in subservience as they shuffled forward to receive their weekly relief.

Returning outside, Geneva saw that Philip's wife Claire had arrived and walked over to offer her services. She was soon stationed at a table, measuring out small sacks of flour and beans, chunks of cheese and butter, and mounds of potatoes for laborers who approached with empty baskets. She added a half-dozen eggs for each until they ran out.

Women and children stood in the line as well. One stooped old lady offered a toothless grin. "Thank you, miss. Me husband will go corky over this."

Geneva recognized the next two men in line as Cyrus Rook and Charlie Badger, the other two laborers who'd been picking blackberries with Harry Whipple and his son Joseph. Cyrus Rook gave his chunk of cheese a sniff. "Look at this, Charlie. No more cold spuds for lunch. What a treat to have bread 'n' butter with cheese for a change."

Just then, the Whipple family emerged from the church, the little ones clinging to Anna's skirt, Harry with their toddler in his arms, Joseph carrying their empty basket.

"I can't believe this, Miss Everson!" Anna exclaimed as Geneva piled the basket high. "What a blessin' you are! We're still enjoying the victuals you brought four days ago."

Geneva handed the heavy basket to Harry. "Well, I have more good news about the cottage industry we spoke of."

"Really? So soon?" Anna asked.

"Yes, my cousin Miss Katherine offered to help. Yesterday, she met with a textile merchant in Ingleford. If you could wait until I'm finished here, I'll tell you all about it."

"Of course. Harry, let's wait under the trees near the river."

More people were crowding up to Geneva's table, some with clothing draped over their arms. Chipped, stained bowls and plates as well as battered kitchen utensils peeked from baskets. As the crowd thinned, three laborers sauntered toward Geneva. She recognized them as Everson Farm laborers laid off for the winter like Harry and his friends.

The shortest man, who looked to be in his forties, was almost skeletally thin, his hollow cheeks covered with pockmarks. "Hello, miss, I'm Gus McGavin. Would ya happen to have any coal? We're runnin' short at my cottage."

"No, I'm sorry, Mr. McGavin. I haven't seen any coal, but we've got some good victuals. Here you are." Geneva had run out of fresh produce, but passed him a selection of flour, beans, and a portion of cheese and butter. Adding the parcel of beans to his basket, Gus wrinkled his brow. "Thank you, miss. But these take a long time to cook, so we can't eat 'em till we get more coal."

It hadn't occurred to Geneva that even free food was no help if there was no fuel to cook. Something else for her to look into.

As Gus moved away disconsolately, his two other friends came forward. One introduced himself as Ted Norton and thanked her for the donation.

Then the tallest man stepped forward, a stem of straw dangling from the corner of his mouth. Geneva didn't care for the haughty look on his unshaven face as she doled out the same items she'd given his companions. He took the food, but rather than giving thanks, he sneered, "We were hopin' for a meat bone, not just beans! Ain't that true, Gus?"

Gus didn't answer but chewed on his lip until his companion jabbed him in the ribs. "Don't stand there like a dunce! Say somethin'!"

Gus's chin quivered. "Well, yah, a soup bone would be nice, miss."

Gritting her teeth, Geneva looked up at the sneering laborer. "I'm sorry, but there is no meat or bones, just as there is no coal. What is your name, sir?"

His sneer deepened. "Simon Harfield. We were laid off from your farm last week. That's why we don't have so much as coal to cook your beans!"

Geneva managed to keep her tone calm. "I'm aware of that, and I'm sorry, Mr. Harfield. But if you're not content with what we have to offer here, then you needn't come back."

He tossed the beans into his basket. "Oh, I'll be back all right, seeing as thanks to you I have no other way to feed my family. Oh, yes, I know you're the new boss at Ravensmere. The secret daughter of the late Adam Everson and that wife of his who got thrown out for immorality. Lawks, what a story that is! You sure got tongues waggin' in the village."

Geneva was so taken aback she hardly knew what to say. While true enough, how dare he make it sound as though there was anything illicit about her parentage! Were all the villagers really gossiping so unkindly about her? A hot flush of anger rose up her neck and face.

"Good day, Mr. Harfield!" she said sharply. "I have better things to do than listening to you."

The three laborers were the last in line, the tables now empty of donations. Geneva walked over to Ravensmere's coachman. "Burrows, I'll be ready to leave shortly. I have just one more thing to do."

Still irked at Simon Harfield's behavior, Geneva strode across the grass. It wasn't as though she was responsible for his layoff. On the contrary, she was a good part of the reason he had food to take home today. Words of thanks weren't even required, just ordinary respect!

Geneva found the Whipple family beneath a maple, the older children happily chasing winged maple seeds in their twirling descent to the ground. Joseph ran to her with his typical enthusiasm. "Miss Everson, have you got work for us?"

"I think I do, for your mother and for you as well." Geneva sat down on the grass beside Anna. "I'm excited with the news Miss Katherine brought from Ingleford. Two days ago, she had an appointment with Mr. Roscoe, a textile merchant who buys material for clothing. He has a workshop where his employees use patterns to cut the fabric into pieces for shirts and trousers. His agent, Mr. Baldwin, delivers the pieces to outworkers and collects them after they've been sewed together. If you can sew a fine seam, then you're qualified to do it."

"My Anna sews beautifully," Harry said proudly. "But with four wee ones and another coming, I don't see how she can sew enough to satisfy this man."

"She can work at her own pace," Geneva assured. "And if Joseph can help by doing odd jobs and minding his sisters, she could work faster and earn more. But it wouldn't be just Anna. My cousin, Miss Katherine, is meeting with Mr. Baldwin today. He's hoping Waterton might supply a good number of outworkers. That would make it more profitable and worthwhile for him to bring the fabric pieces to our village."

"That won't be no problem," Anna said eagerly. "You saw the crowd that came for poor relief today. I'm sure almost every woman here and more would want to work for Mr. Roscoe."

"That's good. Miss Katherine will be your overseer. She'll purchase the scissors, needles, pins, and candles you'll need. She'll help with any problems and make sure that you get your proper wages."

"Lawks, I'm lookin' forward to meetin' her," Anna said. "I'll talk to my neighbors so I can let her know how many women are keen to work."

Harry got up from the grass. "Why do you say women, Anna? I just got laid off, and we got the winter ahead of us. I don't care if it's women's work. I'll put my hand to it. After all, every penny counts."

CHAPTER FOURTEEN

For a country village such as Waterton, the bustle of activity and throng of people gathered at the market cross for the midweek market was impressive. Geneva had joined Robert, Tess, and Katherine in strolling to the village for a special event: traveling performers who would provide entertainment for this week's market.

The weather was sunny and warm, and vendor stalls made the weekly market a feast for the senses. Baskets brimmed with colorful vegetables. Spicy smells wafted through the air. Goats bleated in corrals. And women jibber-jabbered as they bargained for the best prices available.

From her new wardrobe, Geneva had chosen a dress with a forget-me-not print to wear that day. The neckline was trimmed with lace, and the full skirt reached the ankle of her dove-grey shoes. Meandering with her cousins through the crowd, Geneva admired bolts of fabric, pottery, and leather gloves. Arriving at the baker's stall, she was surprised to find Daniel there chatting with Tess's mother and aunt.

"How nice to you see you, Daniel," Geneva beamed.

Daniel tipped his hat. "And lovely to see you. I was just recommending the baker's Melton Mowbray pies to Mrs. Carrington and Mrs. Northcott—the best by far."

Tess touched her mother's arm. "Why didn't you tell me that you and Auntie would be here? I would have invited you to join our party."

"We didn't have time, my dear. When we heard the Macaw Performers would be entertaining, we came right away. Miss Geneva, you remember my sister, Lydia Northcott, don't you? You met her at the gathering following your father's funeral."

"Yes, of course." Geneva smiled at Tess's aunt. "If I remember correctly, you live in Porthaven, eight miles from here."

"Yes, and not far from my sister and her husband. One day you must all come for tea. What do you think of Waterton's market?"

"I'm enjoying it very much."

"Waterton always offers an excellent market, though I am somewhat disappointed with today's produce. The pumpkins and squash are barely half their normal size."

"I noticed that," Geneva responded. "Mr. Farthing, one of our tenant farmers, told me all the crops have been affected by the unseasonable weather this summer."

"Well, all this sunshine is blinding my eyes," Katherine commented tartly, rubbing at her forehead. "If we are going to converse, can we not find a place out of the sun?"

"Of course," Daniel said agreeably. "Let's walk over to the plane trees at the church."

As they strolled toward the church, Mrs. Carrington smiled at Katherine. "I'm impressed to hear that you are bringing the cottage industry to this area. What are the latest developments?"

Katherine's face lit up with enthusiasm. "We already have fifteen households wanting employment. Next week, all wanting to participate will gather at the church hall to meet Mr. Baldwin and learn what they must do."

"That's exciting for you. Your mother must be proud of the work you're doing."

"She is, if surprised. It is not something she ever thought I could do." Katherine turned to Mrs. Northcott. "Speaking of proud mothers, how is your son doing with his labors for the Lord in Tahiti?"

Mrs. Northcott suddenly lost her smile. "Actually I did not want to spoil the pleasure of this outing, but the latest news I've had of Edwin is troubling."

Tess touched her aunt's arm. "What is it, Aunt Lydia?"

Mrs. Northcott sighed unhappily. "A letter came from Edwin yesterday. It was weeks coming from Tahiti, so I have no way of knowing how Edwin is at this moment. But the letter mentioned he'd been terribly sick with his second bout of dengue fever."

Katherine edged closer, concern creasing her forehead. "Oh, no, I feared something like that might happen. Missionaries face so many dangers."

"I'm sure he is much better by now," Tess consoled her aunt. "After all, you said this was his second bout, so he survived the first well enough."

Looking down from his tall height at his sister, Robert added teasingly, "It's a good thing you turned down his offer of marriage, Katherine. I can't see you coping with disease in a tropical jungle."

"Robert, what a thing to say!" Tess scolded her husband. She turned to her aunt. "Edwin is young and strong. With God's help, I'm sure he's already made a full recovery by now."

Katherine lowered herself to a bench. "I seem to have lost my energy all of a sudden. I hope you don't mind if I rest here for a while."

"I'll stay with you," Tess volunteered, giving Robert another reproachful look. Seating herself, she glanced down the road. "Listen! I can hear music. The Macaws have arrived."

Geneva could now hear it too. She made out tin whistles, squeeze boxes, and tambourines. Daniel turned to Geneva. "If you want the best view of the performance, you will want to stand at the market cross." He offered his arm. "Shall we go together?"

By the time Daniel led Geneva to the market cross, a colorful company of performers were wending their way through the crowd. They stopped when they reached the village pump a short distance from Geneva and Daniel. The market crowd gathered around, clapping their hands to the lively rhythm of the music. Moments later, four couples began a choreographed dance, kicking up their heels and leaping about in frolicking jigs.

Geneva had never seen anything like this in Shaftesbury. The women's dresses were in bright shades of scarlet, yellow, and blue. Cheap earrings dangled from their ears and their glossy brown hair shone in the sun. Over to the side, four young boys tapped tambourines against their thighs. Each boy had a parrot on his shoulder with scarlet, yellow, and blue plumage that matched the women's dresses.

"Where have such colorful birds come from?" she asked Daniel with astonishment. "And how do they keep the birds from flying away?"

"They're macaw parrots from the jungles of Mexico," Daniel replied. "As to why they don't fly away, their wings are clipped after they've been captured."

As Geneva noted the four boys' clear enjoyment in their performance, her thoughts went suddenly to the pen-and-ink sketch she'd seen in Mrs. Fox's sitting room during her first consultation with the housekeeper. "Maybe that's what happened to Billy Jasper!"

"Billy Jasper?" Daniel's deep baritone asked. "Should I know that name?"

Geneva hadn't realized she'd spoken aloud. Turning, she looked up to Daniel's inquisitive gaze. "Billy Jasper was a boy from a local orphanage hired at Ravensmere for stable work. Mrs. Fox told me he took off one day without a word. I just wondered if maybe he linked up with people like this. After all, to an eight-year-old this must seem a better life than mucking out stables day after day."

"You could be right," Daniel agreed. "Still, a life on the streets is a chancy thing for an eight-year-old, especially one who has known nothing but the structure of an orphanage. Is anyone trying to track the boy down?"

"Oh, this wasn't recent," Geneva clarified. "It was after my parents married but before my mother left, so a good twenty years. But Mrs. Fox still seems to grieve over his going."

The music continued through amazing performances by jugglers and acrobats. When it came to a close, audience members went forward to toss coins into upturned hats conveniently set at the performers' feet. Daniel threw in some glittering half-crowns, then returned to Geneva.

"I'm glad you had opportunity to be here today, Geneva. One of their best performances I've seen."

Just up the street, a vendor was selling beverages. Daniel purchased two bottles of ginger beer and offered one to Geneva. She was thirstily enjoying the sweet, tart beverage when two men strode up to a neighboring stall. One called out, "Does anyone know where the wattle fence vendor is? His stall is usually around here. We haven't been able to find him."

The beverage vendor leaned out of his stall. "He left an hour ago. Said he'd sold the last of his stock."

The first speaker turned to his companion. "I had hoped to get that fence up today. But I guess we'll have to come back next week."

The beverage vendor leaned out again. "No point comin' back next week. He won't be here. He said he was closing up his stall and not makin' fences no more. At least not around here."

"What do you mean not around here?" the first speaker demanded. "Has he moved his business to a new location? Is it nearby?"

The beverage vendor scratched his head. "Just across the ocean. From what he said, he's emigrating with his family to Canada. Only came to market today to sell out the rest of his stock."

"So what are we supposed to do for fences? Is there another vendor of such around here?"

"I'm sorry, sir. I can't help you with that. Would you like a cool ginger beer?"

Still grumbling, the two men each purchased a beverage. As they wandered off, shaking their heads and muttering to one another, Geneva's gaze followed them thoughtfully. She was fully aware of the need for woven fences by farmers and gardeners alike. The manor's kitchen garden utilized quite a few to keep out rabbits and rodents. Could this sudden lack of supply be an opportunity?

Daniel bent his head toward her. "Are you all right, Geneva? You seem somewhat perturbed."

Geneva turned her contemplative gaze on him. "I'm not perturbed, but I do have an idea. Do you think wattle fence hurdles could be made at Ravensmere?"

Daniel gave a chuckle as his glance followed the departing men. "Are you thinking to seize a business opportunity?" His expression sobered. "Actually, it's not my area of expertise, but I would think it's quite possible. Certainly, your estate has plenty of the necessary raw materials, willow and hazel especially."

Geneva's face shone with delight. "If you're right, then I could start a wattle fence business at Ravensmere to give jobs to our laid-off laborers." She broke off to frown. "That is, if you think your father would allow it as trustee of the estate."

"Well, he'd need to look into it before making a decision. Starting a business isn't as easy as finding laborers and gathering materials. I'll mention it to Father this evening. In the meantime, I would suggest keeping the idea to yourself until Father has time to consider it. We don't want anyone stealing your brilliant plan before you have opportunity to bring it to fruition."

Tucking her arm in his, he steered her back toward the rest of their group. "Meanwhile, how has the rest of your week gone?" He gave her forget-me-not attire an appreciative glance. "It would seem your new wardrobe has been delivered at least."

"Yes, it has. I'm still waiting for Pookie and my flute to arrive. Cousin Jack said he'd write to Uncle Alex and ask for them to be sent. I've also been pursuing inquiries about my mother. I had a most interesting conversation with Mrs. Fox. I learned that before my mother was sent to Uncle Alex, she was confined to her bedroom for a week. Mrs. Fox was the only person authorized to look after her. She seemed very defensive when I asked for details."

Daniel looked grave. "Perhaps she felt uncomfortable with your questions. After all, it is not a topic that household members would want to revisit."

Geneva stopped dead in the middle of the crowd. "It's not my concern if they don't like it. I need to know what my mother said or did at the time of her alleged adultery. Mrs. Fox wouldn't say anything except for a few things I know to be contrary to my mother's character."

"Then you must look to others for answers."

"I have. I spoke to Mr. Blackerby. I learned that he gave Nicholas Drake a lift to Porthaven the morning after he was dismissed."

Daniel lifted an approving eyebrow. "Well, that's a good start. Next time I'm in Porthaven, I'll ask around the coaching inns to see if anyone has heard of him."

"Thank you," Geneva responded, somewhat mollified. They began walking again. "I do appreciate your help, Daniel, but I must say it all seems like a futile search for a needle in a haystack. Sometimes I am still so angry with my father. Did you know he burned the letters my mother wrote to him after he sent her away? I'm sure she must have been informing him of her pregnancy. If he'd read them, he would have brought her back, and I would have grown up here and not with my beastly Uncle Alex. It sickens me to think of it. You won't see me visiting his grave any time too soon."

"You are being unfair to your father," Daniel rebuked quietly, but his gaze held compassion as he went on, "I'm sorry you've endured so many hardships, Geneva. But you're mistaken in thinking this is a futile situation. Nothing is impossible with God."

Geneva lifted her chin. "I used to rely on God until he stopped answering my prayers and abandoned me. After that, I lost interest in praying and reading the Bible."

Daniel shook his head sadly. "Geneva, God does not abandon believers in Jesus Christ. One of Jesus's names is Emmanuel, which means God with us. Just before his ascension into heaven, Jesus uttered the words, 'Lo, I am with you always even unto the end of the world.'"

"Then why doesn't he answer my prayers?" Geneva demanded hotly.

"He may not answer them as you would wish, but that doesn't mean he hasn't heard and answered. God sees the broad perspective of your life and may want you to wait. Sometimes he allows hardships for purposes we may never know while still on this earth. Either way, they're opportunities for a closer walk with Jesus and the means to grow spiritually. Whatever he does, his goal is for your ultimate good."

As Geneva pondered Daniel's words, she felt for the handkerchief she'd tucked in the pocket of her dress, the embroidered monogram soft against her fingers. "Thank you again, Daniel. You have such interesting things to say about God. You've given me a lot to think about."

CHAPTER FIFTEEN

Later that evening, Geneva entered the billiard room. Jack was preparing cigars for an evening with his gentlemen friends, who would arrive within the hour. Glancing up, he smiled. "Cousin Geneva, what brings you in here?"

"I need to ask you something. I didn't see you at breakfast this morning or at the market with the rest of us. So when I saw you in here, I thought I'd take the opportunity."

Jack straightened up. "I was at a political meeting in Ingleford last night. I didn't get home until the wee hours, so I slept in and had breakfast in my room. Work has kept me too occupied for street entertainments."

Geneva approached to watch Jack fill six shallow boxes with cigars. Besides the aroma of tobacco, she detected hints of cedar, hazelnuts, and honey. Her cousin looked dashing in the outfit he'd chosen for his role as host. Beige trousers fit him perfectly, and a forest-green tailcoat looked marvelous against his ginger hair.

Stanway had been busy preparing the room for the evening's entertainment. A tall vase of flowers stood on the mahogany table, surrounded by sparkling glasses and decanters filled with yellow and amber spirits. Each card table had a vase with a single rose, and the French doors to the terrace stood wide open.

Closing the last cigar box, Jack swept his gaze over Geneva's new evening gown. "My word, for a young lady with little experience, your fashion sense is amazing. The gold dress you are wearing is particularly splendid. When you first arrived, you seemed so young. I was quite wrong. You're a woman and a very lovely one."

A warm flush crept over Geneva's cheeks. "Thank you. I had fun choosing my own styles and fabrics."

"You certainly have a flare for it. Perhaps you'd give me the honor and privilege of escorting you to the Fairfaxes' winter ball in December?"

"Winter ball?" Geneva smoothed the gold material of her skirt nervously. "I've never been to a ball before. I mean, I'd be delighted, but I don't know any dances."

"That can be easily rectified." Jack glanced at the clock. "Would you like to try a few steps now? I have time if you do. We could start with the cotillion, a popular dance with a simple sequence of steps. You'd pick it up quickly."

Geneva looked around the billiard room skeptically. "You mean, right here?"

"Why not? We have the whole room to ourselves." With a smile, Jack took Geneva's hand and led her to a spacious area away from the table. "The dance begins with my bow and your curtsey. After that, we must keep to a four-beat rhythm. As we go, I'll show you how we link arms and dance in a full circle, alternating to the left and right. Are you ready?"

Geneva fought an urge to giggle. "Yes, I'm ready."

While Jack counted the rhythm softly, Geneva copied his light footsteps as he guided her over the carpeted floor, his eyes focused on nothing but her. He was right. It didn't take long for Geneva to catch on. Soon, she was anticipating the variations in steps and twirls. It was so much fun she could have continued much longer.

But Jack's counting eventually stopped. After a graceful bow, he planted a soft kiss on her hand.

"What a delightful partner you are, my dear. The winter ball can't some soon enough." He glanced at the clock once more. "Didn't you come in here with a question for me?"

"Oh, yes, I nearly forgot." Geneva briefly summarized the local shutdown of wattle fence production and her idea for Ravensmere to take it on.

"Humph, that's an interesting proposal," Jack said when she finished. "We have hazels and willows in the southwest corner of the estate. Those are ideal for woven fences. With good management, they could provide an endless supply of material."

Geneva laced her fingers together. "This is wonderful! Daniel Cavendish said he'd talk to his father, my guardian, about it. For the jobs, I'm hoping we could hire our own unemployed laborers from the estate. If Mr. Cavendish agrees to it, could we pay them a little more than the average farmworker?"

Jack rubbed his chin. "Well, that depends. If they're reliable and learn the trade properly, Samuel might agree to a higher wage. But even if he doesn't, we could offer bonuses like new smocks and boots and a shorter workday once in a while."

Geneva liked what she was hearing. She studied Jack's handsome face beneath ginger hair that shone like copper. Only nine days had passed since she'd become mistress. Other than that first understandable outburst, he hadn't failed to treat her with kindness and respect. His encouragement now was a good sign he'd come to terms with the loss of his inheritance and that a warm relationship was growing between them.

"Thank you, Cousin Jack. You've been so good to me. And while I think of it, I want to thank you for something else."

Jack's pale-blue eyes smiled warmly down at her. "What might that be?"

"It's concerning the day when the coachman was found in my mother's bedroom. I'm sure you remember it."

Jack's smile immediately faded. "I do, but it's been a long time. I don't remember much."

"I understand. Apparently, my father went berserk at the time. You came into his suite to stop his attack on the coachman. So you must have seen my mother. Do you remember what she said or did at the time?"

Jack lowered his gaze to study the silver buckles on his shoes. "It's true your father became aggressive, which made the situation tense. And, yes, I did see your mother. She was sitting up in bed shielding her face with her pillow. I can't recall if she said anything. I'm sorry. It isn't a memory I've wanted to retain."

Geneva's shoulders slumped. "Well, I heard that you protected her from my father's aggression and urged him to leave the room. I appreciate that. Thank you."

Jack raised his gaze from his shoes to her face. "I'm touched to hear you say that, but I hope you're not dwelling on the past. You have a new life now and a family who loves you—including me."

Geneva glanced toward the French doors, where bright lanterns and a clatter of carriages provided a distraction. Moments later, gentlemen in top hats and dark cloaks were climbing the steps of the terrace. With relief, she took a step back.

"Oh goodness, your guests are here. I must make myself scarce. Thank you for everything, Cousin Jack. You're a real gem."

Following the church service on Sunday, adults chatted with friends and shared news in the churchyard while children chased each other around headstones. After shaking hands with the vicar, the Cavendish family joined the Eversons in the shade of a yew tree. Geneva's eyes sparkled with anticipation as Samuel turned to her with a smile.

"Well, Miss Geneva, I've had lengthy discussions with Jack and Daniel about your business idea. I didn't know we had a budding entrepreneur with us."

Raising her eyebrows, Aunt Mary sent Geneva a disapproving glance as Samuel continued placidly, "We've done extensive research. It's clear there's a great need to fill the void created by the prior wattle fence maker's departure. We've considered all aspects of wattle fence production, your customer base, required capital, a reliable workforce, to name a few. The key would be to start without delay before someone else seizes the opportunity."

Geneva's eyes widened. "Does this mean you authorize it?"

"Absolutely. Jack has informed me of a good-sized shed behind the dairy that would serve as the workshop."

Daniel stepped forward. "Of course, your workers will need an instructor. Your Mr. Blackerby has an older family member who once worked in wattle fence construction. He is willing to teach your workers the trade during their probation period."

"This all sounds too good to be true!" Geneva exclaimed.

"You are the one who has made it true, Miss Geneva," Samuel corrected with a smile. "Your laborers will be pleased to have year-round work. Of course, you can't employ them all. My suggestion would be to start out with no more than three in order to judge the market for their product."

Geneva turned to Jack. "Which men should those be?"

"Well, Harfield, Norton, and McGavin are the most senior of our laid-off employees. By all rights, the work should be offered to them."

The smile faded from Geneva's face. Those three were the last people she wanted to hire, especially Harfield, the bully who had insulted her.

Daniel gave her a sharp look. "What's wrong, Geneva? Do you have a problem with those choices?"

"Yes, I do," she said firmly. "When they came for charity, they were rude and insulting. They weren't content and wanted things that weren't available."

Aunt Mary gasped. "Good gracious, scoundrels like that don't deserve a dry crust of bread!"

"Be careful, Mother," Philip interjected. "This is what happens when charity wounds a man's ego and crushes his dignity."

"Oh, balderdash, they have no excuse. Work should be given to those who are polite and grateful."

"That's why I want to hire Harry, Cyrus, and Charlie," Geneva said. "They're polite and respectable men."

Jack turned to Samuel with a shrug. "I see no reason not to allow it. After all, the business was Cousin Geneva's idea."

"Very well, Miss Geneva," Samuel said. "You may hire them this afternoon. Assuming they will accept, they can begin on Monday morning."

Geneva flashed Jack a dimpled smile. "Cousin Jack, you're so amazing! No one has ever stood up for me like you just did."

That afternoon, Geneva collected a wrapped Dundee cake from the kitchen and made her way down Raven's Lane with a happy spring in her step. Migrant geese honked overhead as they flew south in a V-formation. Enough leaves had fallen from the ash trees for Geneva to spot several ravens' nests.

The stable boy had been sent ahead with a message to the Whipples' cottage requesting a meeting with Harry, Cyrus, and Charlie. At McCormack Lane, Geneva turned right and continued until she came to Harry's cottage. The broken drainpipe had been repaired, she noted, though not the window. So Jack had kept his promise to some extent.

Anna's smiling face greeted Geneva at the front door. 'Tis good to see you again, Miss Everson. Come on in. The men are waiting for you."

Geneva handed her the parcel. "Here's a Dundee cake to enjoy after the meeting."

"Oh, bless you, I'll put the kettle on."

The three men rose from chairs to greet Geneva. Harry stepped forward. "Welcome to our humble home, Miss Everson."

Inside, Geneva noticed a new table set up in an orderly fashion with stacks of cut fabrics and sewing paraphernalia. Next to it, a half-dozen snowy-white shirts hung from a clothing rack. The floor was well-swept, and the walls had been scrubbed clean with soap and water. Even the air seemed fresher.

"My goodness! You have quite an enterprise going on here. Where did you get the table?"

"Miss Katherine brought it for us," Harry said. "She said it wasn't being used at the manor. She's a kind lady but mighty strict. She brought us soap and said we couldn't work for Mr. Baldwin unless we scrubbed the place down."

Geneva laughed. "Yes, that sounds like Katherine." She glanced at Harry's bandaged thumb. "What happened there?"

"Too many sticks with the needle," Anna said with a chuckle. "We don't want no blood on the white shirts."

"Right," Harry said. "I didn't know women's work could be so hard on the eyes and thumbs. Anyway, have a seat, Miss Everson. You've got us wonderin' why you gathered us together."

Geneva took a seat in the chair he indicated. "I don't want to take more of your time than necessary, so I'll come to the point. I'm starting a new business at Ravensmere."

She paused for a moment. "No, that's not quite right. I'm not starting it, but it was my idea. My guardian Samuel Cavendish and Captain Everson have laid the plans for a wattle fence business to replace the former maker, who has emigrated to Canada. The estate has lots of hazels and willows for the sticks and stems, so they think the business will do well. If you're interested in full-time work with no layoffs, I would like to hire the three of you."

Charlie wrinkled his nose. "We've never made 'em afore, Miss Everson. Why would you want us?"

"Because you're respectful, and I've heard that you're hard-working. Mr. Blackerby has arranged for someone to teach you how to do it, and you'd have enough practice time before we start selling."

Harry leaned forward, elbows on his knees. "Cripes, this sounds mighty good, a lot better than getting' my thumb jabbed every day. We'd be fools to turn you down."

"You can count me in, Miss Everson. Never thought I'd learn a trade." Cyrus smacked his thigh, his broad features beaming. "By Jove, imagine bein' known as a craftsman. That's a step up the ladder!"

Charlie stood to his feet with his scarred but handsome face alight. "You won't regret hirin' me, Miss Everson. I'll serve ya faithful every day."

"And I'll work fast and efficient," Cyrus said.

"I know what I'll do," Harry said in a more somber tone. "I'll make sure we work as a team—gettin' along with each other, respectin' your customers, and makin' Everson Wattle Fence Company the best in the county."

He called out to his wife. "Anna, make a potta tea and cut the cake. We got cause to celebrate!"

CHAPTER SIXTEEN

On the morning of Geneva's birthday, the twenty-ninth of September, she stepped out of her bedroom and made her way to the staircase to go down for breakfast. Jack had just emerged from his own bedroom. As he caught sight of her, a smile spread over his handsome face.

"Good morning, Cousin Geneva. How delightful to meet you here." He took her hand and kissed it lightly. "Happy birthday, my dear, and may you have many blessings in the year to come."

"Thank you, Cousin Jack. Shall we go down for breakfast?"

"First, I have a gift for you. Could we step back into your lounge for you to open it?" He held out a small parcel wrapped in white lace and tied with a black silk ribbon.

"Oh my, it looks lovely. Yes, come to my lounge." Geneva led the way back to her lounge. With the ivory curtains thrown back, the morning light brightened her pale green armchairs and a vase of autumn leaves in the bay window.

Taking a seat, Geneva opened the parcel. Inside, she found a small, flat alabaster box with a gold catch. As she opened it, her breath caught in her throat. A double-string pearl necklace lay on a bed of royal blue velvet, each pearl smooth, round, and iridescent with rosy tones and a rich luster. "Oh, Cousin Jack, this is beautiful, but it's too much. It must have cost a fortune."

"Too much?" Jack replied with a perturbed frown. "No, Geneva, not at all. In the past month, I have come to realize what a breath of fresh air you are in this stuffy household. My mother was worried that you wanted to change things. You have, but it's been for the good of all concerned, especially me."

Moving to the edge of his chair, he reached over to take her hand. "Geneva, there was a time when I thought a sophisticated woman would be best for me. I was mistaken. Your sweet innocence and down-to-earth nature has truly captured my heart. I love you, my dear, and I would be deeply honored to have you as my wife. Will you marry me?"

Geneva was quite taken aback by his out-of-the-blue proposal. But the sincerity of his tone and a tearing up of his pale-blue eyes gave every reason to believe his heart was genuine. She'd forgiven Jack for his nasty outburst at the reading of her father's will. That was all behind them. Since then, he'd been kind and thoughtful, making himself available despite his many business responsibilities. And they'd fit together so perfectly during that dance lesson he'd given her in the billiard room.

But as she glanced down at Jack's hand holding hers, Geneva found her thoughts turning to Daniel. His wise counsel on the things of God. His willingness to help her find Nicholas Drake. She'd definitely developed a closeness with him she'd never felt with anyone else. Could that mean that she loved Daniel? Then again, she wasn't so sure what she felt for Jack wasn't love. Given the uncertainty of her feelings, she was left with only one response.

Slowly, Geneva removed her hand from Jack's caress. "Cousin Jack, I'm flattered with your proposal and ever so grateful for the necklace. But this is so sudden. I can't give you an answer right now. Would you allow me time to pray and think it over?"

Jack's shoulders dropped just a little. "Yes, my dear, you must take all the time you need for such an important decision. In the meantime, I'll do all I can to ensure your comfort. And by the way, I haven't forgotten about having your portrait painted. We must do that soon."

He reached out for the pearls. "May I put them on for you? They'll look lovely with the violet day dress you are wearing."

Turning in the chair, Geneva held back her trail of curls. The touch of her cousin's fingers on her skin gave her goosebumps. When he was done, she noticed his cheeks were slightly flushed. With a deep bow, he offered her his arm. Arms linked together, they descended the stairs to the dining room, where a tall vase of Michaelmas daisies graced the center of the table. Next to Geneva's chair, a table held gifts wrapped in colorful fabrics.

"Michaelmas daisies for a Michaelmas birthday," Jack commented.

Grandmama Louise came to her with outstretched arms and a kiss on the cheek. "Happy birthday, Geneva. My word, nineteen today! Lily has made your favorite breakfast—toad in the hole. Go ahead, dear. Today you must have the honor of being first to serve yourself."

"Thank you, Grandmama Louise. How kind to give me such royal treatment." Geneva helped herself to a generous portion of pudding baked to a golden crisp with spicy sausages poking through. After adding a spoonful of braised tomatoes, she took her seat at the head of the table.

As the others selected their food choices and tucked into their meal, Aunt Mary turned to Geneva. "I'm looking forward to your birthday dinner at Wyncombe Hall tonight. I'm sure Mrs. Cavendish has planned a—" She leaned closer as she caught sight of Geneva's necklace. "Good gracious! Where did you get those pearls?"

Geneva touched them lightly. "Cousin Jack gave them to me this morning. Such a generous birthday gift."

"Good heavens, child, do you realize what you have?" Aunt Mary turned to Grandmama Louise. "He bought her South Sea pearls, the very finest."

"Well, I hope you appreciate it, Geneva," her grandmother said crisply. "A clear sign of your cousin's high esteem for you."

"Indeed it is," Jack said. "I hope you'll wear them tonight, Cousin Geneva. Have you decided what dress you'll wear?"

"No, not yet. The pearls will go well with any color."

Robert glanced at the small table next to Geneva. "Dear me, our gifts will seem insignificant compared to that."

"No, you're quite wrong," Geneva assured him. "Every gift, no matter how small, is of equal importance to me."

Stanway circled the table, pouring coffee. When everyone had finished, he cleared the plates so Geneva could open her gifts from the family. An embroidered reticule from Grandmama Louise. A tortoise-shell hair comb from Mary. A Kashmir shawl from Katherine. Kid gloves in a soft shade of grey from Robert and Tess. Tears were brimming in Geneva's eyes by the time she'd finished.

"I'm overwhelmed. Uncle Alex always forgot my birthday. It's so good to have a family who cares for me."

Geneva was quite taken with Wyncombe Hall as she caught her first glimpse from the carriage window. In the twilight, the Cavendish home was a lovely sight set against a backdrop of stately trees and rolling hills. The style was distinctly Georgian with a hipped roof, triangular pediment crowning the front entrance, and two welcoming torches that blazed on either side of the stairs.

The Eversons alighted from the carriage. When they reached the top of the front steps, the door swung open and a rosy-cheeked butler received them into the entrance hall. As a maid took their hats and coats, Geneva took in the scenic wallpaper, high ceiling, and marble floors. Leading the way down the hall, the butler ushered them into the drawing room and announced their arrival.

Philip and Claire had already arrived. Tess's parents and Nigel Spooner and his wife were there as well. All greeted Geneva with smiles and good wishes. Samuel Cavendish presented her with a posy of pink roses.

"Thank you, Mr. Cavendish." Geneva breathed deeply of the roses' sweet scent. "I've never had a birthday party before."

"Well, it's high time you did," Daniel said. "Welcome to Wyncombe Hall. Your birthday is the perfect occasion for your first visit."

Jack moved close to Geneva's side. "Doesn't Cousin Geneva look lovely in her pale-green gown? Would you believe she designed it herself! I think her fashion sense is marvelous."

"Yes, a step ahead of the latest trends. All she needs is one more thing, if she'll allow me." Grandmama Louise pulled a single rose from the posy and tucked it into the soft curls of Geneva's upswept hairdo. "There! The pink goes perfectly with your dress and pearl necklace."

Geneva blushed at the excessive attention. Thankfully, Samuel came to her rescue. "Well now, you must all make yourselves comfortable while Soames takes care of your drinks. Will you have grape cordial, Miss Geneva?"

"Thank you, I do enjoy it." Geneva took a glass from the but-ler. Jack guided her to a sofa and sat beside her as close as protocol would allow. Geneva looked around the room, so different from Ravensmere's Tudor style. The walls were painted in robin's egg blue with decorative detailing in swags and ribbons. Well-pol-ished Chippendale furniture gleamed, and an impressive Erard grand piano stood in a bay window.

Nigel Spooner sipped his sherry as he turned to Geneva. "Well, Miss Geneva, your cousin Jack has told me about your wattle fence business. How is it coming along?"

"Thank you for asking. It's been ten days since I hired the men. They have all done well with the training. We already have hurdles for next week's market. And the men are happy to have year-round work."

"The business has great potential," Jack interjected. "If things go well, we can expand our customer base by advertising in the Ingleford Gazette."

Mr. Carrington smiled at Geneva. "You're a quick-thinking young lady to fill the void left by the previous fence maker."

"And to think she's only just nineteen," his wife added. "I heard the previous fence maker has taken his family to the wilds of Canada—such a God-forsaken colony with bears and mosquitoes."

"Quite an adventure, I should imagine," Robert murmured. "Tess, think of the new bird species we could study."

Tess waved her hand at him. "Really, Robert, don't even sug-gest it. Mrs. Spooner, I heard that you and your girls attended the harvest garden party in Porthaven. Do share how it went."

Later, the group moved to the dining room and took their seats. Samuel offered a toast for Geneva's birthday. Not to be outdone, Mr. Carrington offered another in his strong Scottish accent. The butler Soames and kitchen maids then served a scrumptious dinner followed by a two-tiered birthday cake iced and topped with sugared berries. The sweet finale couldn't have been better.

When they retired to the drawing room for coffee, Geneva had high hopes that Daniel would play the piano for them. But he'd disappeared. The coffee was served. Robert and Tess were extolling their upcoming book on songbirds when Daniel finally returned, a wooden box in his arms. He brought it straight to Geneva and laid it at her feet.

"What's this?" Geneva asked with astonishment.

Daniel's chocolate-brown eyes sparkled. "It's your birthday surprise."

"A surprise?" Geneva touched her pearl necklace. "My, I wasn't expecting more."

She leaned over to unhook the box's latch. As she lifted the lid, a furry face with whiskers popped up. Geneva clapped her hands together. "Pookie! Oh, my darling Pookie! I thought I'd never see you again."

Gathering the cat into her arms, Geneva held him to her chest. "I have no words to thank you, Daniel. Did you arrange for him to be sent?"

"Not exactly," Daniel responded with a broad smile. "I thought it would be better for the cat if I collected him myself. I took the early coach to Shaftesbury yesterday morning. Since I got back, your cat has been confined to our kitchen and not happy at all. Judging by that purring, he's awfully glad to see you."

"This is amazing! I can't believe you went all that way for me. Did you speak with my uncle?"

"No, but I spoke with his housemaid. She was sure he wouldn't mind parting with the cat. Apparently, your uncle has been more content since he hired extra staff for his shop. He enjoys exploring the countryside in his new horse and carriage."

Geneva turned to Jack. "Did you hear that? He put his legacy money to good use."

"Yes, I heard what Daniel said." Jack's voice held a trace of irritation. "It's about time Alex got a housemaid and stopped acting like a miser."

Geneva crooned sweet nothings in Pookie's ear and rocked him in her arms.

"Are you going to finish opening your surprise?" Daniel interrupted. "There is still more in the box."

Geneva passed Pookie to Jack. Holding the cat at arm's length, he placed him on his grandmother's lap. "Here, Grandmama, you're a cat lover. I'd rather not have his hairs on my clothes."

Geneva had spotted the brown-paper-wrapped package at the bottom of the box. "I think I know what it is."

A smile spread across her face as she pulled back the paper, opened the leather case, and beheld her flute. "I'm so glad Uncle Alex didn't sell it by mistake. Thank you again, Daniel."

"Yes, very nice of you, Daniel," Aunt Mary put in tartly. "But it wasn't necessary. Jack was planning to have them brought here very soon, weren't you, dear?"

"Yes, I'd have had them delivered by now," Jack said coolly. "But my busy schedule prevented it."

Geneva touched the dark-brown cocuswood of her flute. "Well, it doesn't matter now. I've received some lovely gifts today, but Pookie and my flute are particularly special. It seems like they're part of me. Without them, I've had an empty feeling that's hard to describe."

She turned her gaze to Daniel. "Now that feeling is gone, thanks to your kind deed in going such a long way for me."

Daniel took his seat. "Not at all. The journey there and back went smoothly except for one incident at a wayside inn. I had Pookie on a leash, but he managed to break free. Before I could catch him, he scampered into the bushes. I was beside myself. Only a minute before departure did I manage to catch him by the scruff of the neck. It was a long trip, to be sure, but definitely worth it to see you so happy."

He gestured toward the flute. "Is there any chance you could play for us? I'd love to listen."

"So would I," Tess spoke up.

"How about a hymn?" Philip suggested.

"A Scottish song would be nice," Mrs. Carrington said.

"She wouldn't know Scottish songs," Katherine butted in. "Play a classical piece, Geneva."

Grandmama Louise raised her hands. "Stop arguing! She can play another time. Jack has prepared a poetry reading. He has a perfect voice for it."

Samuel leaned forward. "With all due respect, Mrs. Everson, if Miss Geneva is willing to play, I think my son deserves a reward for his efforts."

The old lady pursed her lips tight and stroked the cat.

"I don't mind," Geneva said. "I play better when people are listening. I'll play my favorite folk song, 'The Oak and the Ash.'"

Geneva assembled her flute and stood near the piano. With her fingers placed on the keys, she drew a deep breath and brought forth a haunting melody that immediately captured everyone's attention. Her flute sang with a pure tone for every note, phrase, and trill of the delightful composition. Bringing the song to its peaceful conclusion, she ended on such a tender note that the room was filled with oohs and ahs and claps of appreciation.

"Bravo, Geneva!" Daniel cried out. "You've given us pure poetry in the language of the flute!"

"I should say so," Robert said. "For someone without formal training, Cousin Geneva plays very well."

"Thank you, Cousin Robert. I can't wait to play in Ravensmere's Great Hall. It'll sound wonderful under that fifty-foot ceiling."

"And if I may," Daniel said, "it would be a privilege to accompany you on the piano in the billiard room."

"Yes, a duet for the flute and piano. That would be fun." Geneva laid the flute down. While the others returned to conversation, she carried Pookie around the room, stroking his coat and whispering loving words into his ear.

Only Jack was unusually quiet, his head propped up with one hand, eyes drooping. Returning to the sofa, Geneva tapped his knee, admonishing teasingly, "Cousin Jack, it's not polite to fall asleep when you're a guest at someone's house."

He lifted his head. "I wasn't sleeping, just resting my eyes."

"You must have had an extra-long political meeting last night."

Robert turned his way. "You rarely speak of these meetings. Where do you gather, and what political issues do you discuss?"

Nigel spoke up. "We rent a room at Ingleford's Royal Stag Inn."

"That's right," Jack said. "The central location is convenient since our talks often continue into the night. As to political issues, I'm sure you've heard that the Whig party is pushing for electoral reform. We believe that broadening the vote will only make things worse. Besides that, Parliament has more important issues to deal with."

"That reminds me of an upcoming meeting," Philip said. "Not for political enthusiasts but for the clergy and our local landowners. Angus Fairfax will chair the meeting at the Bell and Crown. He wants to discuss poor relief and the rising price of grain. Since you're the trustee of Ravensmere, he'll want you to attend, Mr. Cavendish."

"Thank you for informing me," Samuel said. "It should be interesting."

With a brief lull in the conversation, Mrs. Cavendish spoke up. "Would anyone care for more coffee or a glass of port?"

Jack glanced at the clock. "Actually, I think we should call it a night, Mrs. Cavendish. This has been a delightful party. I didn't know Cousin Geneva was such a good musician. From now on, I shall keep my office door ajar so I can hear her melodies in the background."

As the guests made their way to the entrance hall, Daniel watched Pookie following on Geneva's heels. "Ravensmere is a great house for a cat. I'm sure he'll love all the nooks and crannies."

"Yes, it's a castle compared to Uncle Alex's home. Thank you again, Daniel. Your kindness is truly remarkable."

"It was my pleasure." Daniel accompanied Geneva down the front steps to the waiting carriage. "I'm just glad I was able to find a free day this week. Next week I'm off to London. Father has banking work for me to do, and while I'm there I plan to research an investment opportunity."

"I'm quite envious of you. Will you have time for other things?"

"Yes, I'll be there for a fortnight. I hope to visit the National Gallery. A symphony at the theatre would be a treat as well. Perhaps one day soon, you'll have opportunity to visit both. It was lovely having you here, Geneva. Do come at any time. You're always welcome."

As Geneva climbed into the carriage, Daniel ascended the stairs to go back in. But Jack blocked his way by stepping forward from a pilaster where he had been standing. "I thought we might have a word before I leave."

Daniel gave him a puzzled look but responded politely, "By all means. Can I be of help with something?"

Jack moved closer. "No, that's the whole point of why I wish to speak with you. You've already done too much. Your bold actions in fetching Geneva's cat and flute have raised eyebrows. You've created the impression that you have designs on her. A tin of sweets would have been a more suitable gift."

Daniel narrowed his dark eyes. "It's not for you judge my actions. I'm her deputy trustee. Since you procrastinated on your promise, it was entirely appropriate for me to make sure Miss Geneva had her flute and cat for her birthday."

Jack widened his stance. "Listen here, I saw the look in your eyes while she played the flute. Geneva is young and vulnerable. She's an easy target for ambitious men, and she doesn't need you baiting her with favors. If I were you, I'd be a lot more circumspect if you don't want to arouse unwelcome gossip."

Daniel took a step forward, making his eyes perfectly level with Jack's. "Really? Everyone noticed the pearl necklace Geneva was wearing tonight. I wonder who gave her that? Only a man with marital aspirations would pay such a price. You may want to follow your own advice."

Daniel sidestepped Jack and walked through the open doorway. Before closing the door, he glanced back. "If you'll excuse me, I have an early start tomorrow morning. Good night."

CHAPTER SEVENTEEN

Geneva's flute playing sounded angelic with the soft tones reverberating in the upper reaches of the Great Hall's timbered ceiling. The closing bars came all too soon with a long note that tested the endurance of her breath. Lowering the flute, Geneva glanced toward the hearth where Grandmama Louise reclined comfortably in a soft chair. The music had lulled her to sleep. Curled up on her lap, Pookie was fast asleep as well.

Since Geneva's birthday a fortnight ago, the cat had settled in well and seemed much at home in his new surroundings. He followed Geneva about with his tail held high, sniffing carpets, rubbing his body against the furniture, and peering into shadowy corners. Every evening, Geneva prepared his supper in the kitchen—a saucer of milk and a bowl of chopped meat with gravy. Best of all, Geneva was sure Grandmama Louise loved Pookie almost as much as she did.

Geneva looked up at the portrait of Charlotte McCormack above the mantelpiece. Her resemblance to her ancestor was uncanny—the same unusual eyes and small, straight nose. Charlotte's husband, Tobias Everson, had ginger hair, which accounted for Jack's hair of the same color. It seemed strange that with all the manorial records in the big oak cabinet, there wasn't at least one personal journal written by these people whose portraits graced the places of honor at the fireplace.

But maybe there were one or two Jack had forgotten to mention. Geneva now owned all those records in his office, she reminded herself. Which meant she had every right to have another look.

Jack was out on the estate that afternoon. Geneva made her way to Stanway's office, where she found the butler seated at his desk, writing in a ledger. "Excuse me, Stanway."

The butler stood up. "Yes, miss, what can I do for you?"

"I want to look through the manorial records. May I have my own key to the captain's office?"

"Certainly, miss. In fact, I should have given this to you before." Reaching into a desk drawer, Stanway brought out a key and handed it to Geneva. "This is your father's master key. It was brought to me when his belongings were cleared out for your move to the master suite. It will open all locks, including the captain's office. Please lock up when you're done, miss. Your cousin is fussy about keeping the estate records private."

"I understand. Thank you, Stanway."

Entering the main floor's east wing corridor, Geneva unlocked the door to the office. The scent of liquor and tobacco still lingered. Walking over to the cabinet, she carefully released the catch and opened the right side. The middle shelf held small leather-bound books. Geneva eased one out carefully.

The book was written in English but was no personal journal, containing only information about tenants and rental income. Other books dealt with surveyors, offences, and legal issues. Geneva persisted until she reached the lowest shelf. Crouching down, she noticed one book with gold print on the spine. The letters had faded over time, but she could decipher a name—Albert Everson.

Pulling the book out, Geneva opened it to the first page. At the top was a date, June 1725, followed by clear, legible handwriting. From the opening sentences, this was no estate record but a personal journal. Had Jack known this was among the estate records? Or perhaps he'd given up in boredom before he'd reached the bottom shelf. Geneva read the first lines with interest.

> Five years ago today, I married my dear Leah. Since then, I have been the most contented man. Yet in the past few weeks, as I have delved into the writings of Redmond McCormack, I have been thoroughly engrossed with Ravensmere's past and the historical events that have shaped the lives of those who have inhabited this unique and intriguing manor.

What had Albert learned that was so absorbing? Geneva closed the journal. It would require a careful read and more time than she had before Jack returned from his business around the estate. Of course, she had every right to remove her own property from the cabinet, but she preferred to avoid any possible objection from her cousin. Taking a book from the closely packed top shelf, Geneva slipped it into the vacant slot left by the journal below. After locking the office, she headed upstairs to her lounge.

Settled into a comfortable armchair, Geneva read the first five pages that described Leah's older brother, Malcolm. He had been a scholar and librarian at Oxford University and had spent hours deciphering the Gothic Script of Sir Callum McCormack's journals. As he translated from Latin to English, Albert had jotted down notes to use in writing this journal concerning the manor's past.

Continuing, Geneva read Albert's description of the events of 1480 when Sir Callum purchased land in the southwest corner of

Dorset. Over the following years, he'd built a house for his family and enclosed the land for the purpose of sheep farming. Sir Callum was amongst many others who produced wool that was highly coveted by the French. But he also believed in free trade and hated the high export duties that provided revenue for the king's wars. Like other sheep farmers, he'd become a professional smuggler, exporting his wool to the continent and importing in return French wine and brandy. Albert had added a comment that if it wasn't for Sir Callum's smuggling, he would have been a respectable citizen in every way.

Turning to the next page, Geneva learned that Sir Callum had built the Great Hall in 1487 to protect his assets and family from raiders, thieves, and customs officers. Ravensmere's isolated location among untouched forests and near an accessible cove had made the manor a safehouse for contraband bound for Porthaven, Ingleford, and northeast to London.

What intrigued Geneva most was Albert's description of an underground cavern connected in some way to Ravensmere. It had the capacity to store over seventy casks of brandy plus weapons and ammunition. Where this cavern was located was unclear. The only clue mentioned in Sir Callum's journal was a V-shaped fossil located in the wine cellar, but what this fossil meant was anyone's guess. On the next page she continued reading.

Of all the McCormacks' concerns, anti-Catholicism under the reign of Queen Elizabeth was their greatest fear. In 1575, rumors of religious persecution in Dorset had alarmed Redmond, the third master of Ravensmere. By then, the Great Hall had become inadequate for their needs. With the help of his son Tyrone, Redmond undertook the grand project of building additions to the manor—a south and east wing and an extension of the kitchen wing to the north. All the hired laborers and craftsmen were extended family members and pious Catholics who had sworn oaths to never disclose the . . .

Geneva shifted her eyes to the top of the next page, but what she read didn't make sense. It was the continuation of a sentence about Liam McCormack's valiant death in the English Civil War and how his daughter Charlotte became his heiress. Leaning closer to examine the binding, Geneva realized that an intervening page between the two sentences had been cut out with a sharp knife. Recently or long ago? Why would someone do such a thing? To hide some information that the missing page had held?

Turning additional pages, Geneva skimmed through an account of Charlotte's conversion to the Church of England and subsequent marriage to Sir Tobias Everson, Knight of the Shire. Following that, Albert wrote in great detail about Parliament's clampdown on tax-evading smugglers. In 1660, new legislation decreed that anyone found guilty of smuggling wool to the continent would be hanged on the gallows. With such a serious warning looming over them, the Eversons made the big decision to convert from sheep farming to crop production. And that lengthy description filled the remaining portion of Albert's journal.

Geneva closed the book. Her annoyance over the missing page had one benefit. She was all the more determined to unravel the mystery of the fossil. The best time to do that would be a quiet Sunday afternoon.

Until now, the wine cellar had been of little interest to Geneva. Located behind the Great Hall, this sunken room was Stanway's domain where he received deliveries of wine and spirits. On this Sunday afternoon, Grandmama Louise and Aunt Mary had gone upstairs for a nap. Katherine had joined Robert and Tess for an afternoon walk along the coastal path. After midday dinner had been served and cleared, the servants had left the manor for their half-day off, including Stanway. Cousin Jack had left after church, where he'd mentioned riding over to spend the afternoon with Nigel Spooner. This left Geneva free to pursue the challenge of finding Sir Callum's cavern.

Pookie followed Geneva across the Great Hall and into the small anteroom. From here, the door to the wine cellar was two steps down, always locked due to the considerable value of wine and spirits. Geneva pulled out the master key Stanway had given her. Sure enough, the key turned easily in the lock. Inside, oak casks and barrels rested on stands while shelves held bottles of wine and spirits. Across the room was another door that led outdoors where deliveries could be unloaded directly into the cellar.

But Geneva had come in search of a stone containing a fossil. Hands on her hips, she looked around. It seemed unlikely that the fossil would be placed in the stone walls. An entrance into an underground cavern suggested a trapdoor. In which case, the orange-tinted flagstones covering the floor offered a possibility.

Starting in the back corner, Geneva bent forward and began a systematic examination of each one. Pookie kept getting in her way, and the light from a narrow window was dim, forcing Geneva to crouch low to see well enough. Her legs soon tired, but she pressed on until something caught her eye a few feet out from the inner wall.

At the edge of one flagstone, she beheld vegetation—two tiny leaves like ferns joined at the base of their stems and not more than a half-inch wide. The preservation of their form was remarkable. If this was what Albert meant by the V-shape, then Geneva had most assuredly found the clue.

The flagstones had been laid tight together, but this one and four more adjacent to it had a small groove between them. To investigate further, Geneva needed a tool of some sort. Glancing around, she noticed a small table. An open box on the table held various tools, including some for opening wine barrels she'd often seen in Uncle Alex's pawn shop. Amongst them, she found a screwdriver. This might do the trick.

Geneva's hands trembled with excitement as she poked the screwdriver into the groove between flagstones. Using it as a lever, she pushed the handle down. With a scraping sound, a three-foot section of the floor became dislodged. Geneva could now see that the flagstones had been glued to a thick slab of wood to form a trapdoor. As she lifted it and glimpsed a dark shaft below, a fusty smell wafted up, forcing her to cover her nose.

Once Geneva pushed the trapdoor to its highest level, the wine cellar's dim lighting revealed a slanted ladder descending about ten feet to the bottom of the shaft. It was wide enough to permit sizeable burdens to be passed up from below. At the bottom of the shaft, she could see a door. Did it open into Sir Callum's cavern as Albert's notes had suggested?

Geneva's heart pounded with excitement but also trepidation. She wasn't particularly fond of descending into dark, dusty, long-unused shafts. Should she wait until she could inform the rest of the family and come back with company?

But, no, this was her discovery, as Ravensmere was her inheritance. She could just imagine the objections from her female family members, especially if she announced that she wanted to explore the darkness below.

Pookie had sauntered over, ears pricked, nose twitching. Shooing the cat into the anteroom, Geneva took a lit candlestick, then closed and locked the wine cellar door behind her. Mustering her nerve, she sat at the edge of the shaft and lowered her legs onto the ladder. By the time she'd descended three steps, cold air had crept up her dress, coiling around her legs like clammy tentacles. The chance of Stanway entering the wine cellar this afternoon was slim. But as precaution, Geneva tugged on a cord that shut the trapdoor. By the light of her candle, she descended more rungs until her feet touched a dirt floor.

Geneva looked around. How strange to find herself beneath the manor's stone foundation. She could now see that the shaft was built of bricks and mortar. A wooden door was scraped and dented from countless decades of use. Setting her candlestick on the dirt floor, Geneva turned the doorknob and pushed with her shoulder and hip. With a creak, the door moved a few inches. Geneva continued pushing until the door swung open, revealing a brick wall a short distance away.

Picking up the candlestick, Geneva entered the manor's underground realm. She immediately realized this was no cavern but a subterranean tunnel that receded into pitch-black darkness. Good heavens, the thought of venturing down there to find the cavern was frightening. What if she encountered rats? What if she took a wrong turn and couldn't find her way back? What if the flame of her candle went out?

Well, she didn't have to go far or take any complicated turns. Counting her steps would help and if she was careful, her candle would burn for well over an hour. As to rats, she'd just have to trust there were none. After all, what could they possibly find to eat down here?

Candle held high, Geneva proceeded down the tunnel. She could now judge it was about four or five feet wide. And she didn't need to worry about her candle going out. Iron sconces were attached to the walls holding partially burned, melted-down candles. The brick walls were damp with seeping moisture and mold. Here and there, chunks of crumbling mortar and brick had fallen to the dirt floor.

Pushing away thoughts of cave-ins, Geneva lit an iron sconce and held her own candlestick high as she followed the passageway. As hoped, there were no signs of vermin, just black beetles scuttling along the floor and disappearing through cracks and holes. A few more paces brought Geneva to a T-junction with a second passageway to the right. She'd investigate that later, but for now she continued straight along the first passageway, counting her steps and lighting more sconces as she went.

But the passageway continued for what seemed an eternity, and after a while there were no more candles to light. By now, the tunnel must have taken her far beyond the manor. She had lost count of her steps and this was no longer an exciting exploration. Geneva was so cold she was shivering, and the musty air made her cough. Worst of all, she had a terrible feeling of isolation as though cut off from the world and utterly alone. Why hadn't she brought Pookie? His comforting presence would have made this easier.

Geneva was about to turn back when she realized the dirt floor underfoot had begun an upward incline. Lifting her candle high, she saw a flight of stairs leading to an arched door with reinforcement straps and an iron ring handle. Perhaps this was the entrance to Sir Callum's cavern or, more likely, an exit to the outdoors.

Hurrying up six stone steps, Geneva grasped the handle and pulled hard but to no avail. She pulled out the master key that had worked so well on other doors, but even before she jiggled it in the lock, she could see that whatever key opened this door would have to be much larger. Well, this quest wouldn't end until Geneva discovered what was on the other side of that door. Meantime, there was still the second tunnel. Since it was on her way back, it would be a waste not to investigate.

Geneva headed back, blowing out the iron sconces as she went. At the T-junction, she turned left into the second passageway. She'd walked less than a dozen paces when she came to a second door. This had the same oversized keyhole as the other tunnel door, but when Geneva tugged on its iron ring, it gave way with a screech of rusty hinges.

Stepping through, Geneva discovered with delight what must be Sir Callum's cavern. It was a good-sized chamber with an arched brick ceiling. Not a barrel, cask, or tub remained from the smuggling days. But other clues indicated that this place must have been used at some point as a Catholic chapel. On the left, an old prayer desk was positioned near the corner where an ornately carved altar held a statue of St. Mary nestled within a wooden niche. This made sense considering the McCormack's religious background at a time when practicing Catholicism could trigger swift reprisals.

But other clues made clear this place had been used long after the era of Catholic persecution and, in fact, recently. Three whale oil lanterns rested on a long oak table in the middle of the cavern, a tall glass bottle of extra oil beside them. A low shelf held a ceramic water crock, as well as pewter mugs, a half-empty bottle of whiskey, and a glass jar filled with smoked beef strips. Someone had been satisfying thirst and hunger down here. Turning the crock's spigot, Geneva discovered that it still held water. If its contents were not yet evaporated, it could not have been here years or even months.

On the right side, two wooden trunks were positioned against the wall. Geneva opened one and found a stash of antique pikes and muskets. The other trunk held moth-eaten blankets that made Geneva cough. The contents of these trunks had definitely not been in use within recent years or possibly generations.

Having seen all she wanted, Geneva was about to leave the cavern when she noticed something odd in the back corner—a vertical beam of wood set within the brick wall. Curiosity urged her to investigate, until she spied three rats crouched together just inches from the beam. Their ugly fangs, beady red eyes, and naked tails threw her back to her worst childhood memory when Uncle Alex had inadvertently—or so Geneva assumed—locked her in the storage closet with a rat.

Every nerve in Geneva's body screamed with panic. She wanted to turn and run for her life. But her insatiable desire to check out the beam wouldn't allow it. Besides, the rats were the ones cornered, not her. Backing up slowly, she set her candlestick down and took out a rusty spike from the trunk that held weapons. Grasping it tight, she rushed at the rats, waving her weapon wildly through the air and shouting, "Get out! Get out!"

Her plan worked. The spooked rats scurried across the dirt floor and, one by one, disappeared through a hole in the brick wall. Not wasting a moment, Geneva dashed over and stuffed the hole with bits of broken brick and mortar until it was plugged enough to keep the hideous creatures from returning.

Heaving a sigh of relief, Geneva returned the spike to the trunk, dusted off her hands, and picked up her candlestick. Holding the light close to the beam, she noticed that the mortar had shrunk away from the wood, yet the beam remained in its place. Geneva pushed tentatively against it. She was startled when the beam shifted just a little. When she pressed harder, it started tilting like a seesaw on a hinge!

Slipping her candlestick through to the other side, Geneva peered in to discover another shaft with a vertical ladder. It had to be another exit. As she wriggled through, she found it to be much smaller than the shaft below the wine cellar. Just big enough for an average-sized man standing upright. A trapdoor lay at the top, but where it opened, she had no idea.

Geneva held her skirt up with her teeth and climbed the rungs to the top. With a little pressure applied, the trapdoor loosened easily. Since she didn't know what to expect, she eased it up only an inch and peeked through. A moment later, she was easing the trapdoor shut, hurrying down the ladder, and slipping under the tilting beam.

Now back in the cavern, Geneva held her breath, listening intently for noises in the shaft. When none came by the time she'd counted to a hundred, she relaxed and wiped her damp brow. It wasn't just the legs of chairs and a table she had seen. Nor the worn bottom of an antique cabinet. She had recognized the brass base of Jack's celestial globe. That second shaft opened in his office.

Geneva might have explored further if she hadn't also glimpsed a pair of well-polished gentleman's shoes walking across that carpet and the distinct scent of a cigar. Jack had clearly returned much earlier than expected from his visit to the Spooners' home. Geneva couldn't imagine what he'd have to say if her dusty, unkempt self had emerged into his office from a dark hole in the floor.

But why Jack's office? Geneva's mind flashed back to Albert's journal and his mention of Redmond McCormack hiring pious Catholics to build the east wing. Jack's office had been their family chapel. Priests had been forbidden to practice mass during that historic period of Catholic persecution. If caught, they could be imprisoned. Or worse yet, be hung, drawn, and quartered at the Tower of London.

Creating a priest hole for their family priest to take shelter was not uncommon in wealthier Catholic residences. What would be more logical than for Redmond McCormack to have built a secret way out from the chapel? If the authorities came to arrest the priest, he could slip down this hole and hide in the underground chapel that had once been Sir Callum McCormack's smuggling headquarters.

Geneva had forgotten her annoyance over the missing page in Albert's journal. His fossil clue had led her to the underground secrets of the manor. All that remained was finding out what lay beyond that locked door at the end of the first tunnel. Tomorrow, Lord willing, she would embark on an outside search for Sir Callum's aboveground portal to what lay below.

The following day, Geneva gazed out her bedroom window to the wilderness beyond the garden wall. Yesterday, she had noted that the long tunnel ending in a locked door ran from the wine cellar in a straight line due west. By her estimation, that placed it underneath the Great Hall, the library, and her father's garden, surfacing somewhere in the forest between the manor and the village. Which certainly made good sense for Sir Callum. It meant he could bring smuggled goods into an unpeopled wilderness and offload the contraband without being seen.

Geneva had no assigned meetings with Mrs. Fox or other tasks for the next hour or so. Putting on the wool work dress she'd brought from Shaftesbury, she slipped downstairs. Neither family members nor any servants were in sight as she donned her cloak and slipped out the French doors in the dining room. Making her way to her father's water garden, she stepped through the gate in the stone wall and waded through tall grasses at the edge of the forest.

From here, Geneva pushed back the low-hanging branches of a cedar and weaved her way around thick tree trunks, moss-covered boulders, and bushy fir saplings. From the treetops, the sudden cawing of ravens drowned out the pleasant twitter of bush tits and chickadees. Soon she came across a narrow game trail. It seemed to be heading in the general direction where she believed the underground tunnel led, so she followed it.

By now, her cloak was soaked from the wet vegetation, her boots caked with mud. As the path twisted and turned, Geneva could no longer see the sun through the autumn foliage overhead and wondered if she was still headed in the right direction. She was debating turning back when she spotted ahead an outcropping typical for this area of Dorset.

The outcropping thrust high enough through the dense forest to let in bright sunshine. Pushing through a few more bushes, Geneva stepped into the warmth of the sun's rays where the Creator's artistry was in full display. Thick green moss clung to the rock. Ferns poked out from crevices. Fleshy toadstools glistened in the sun. From the top of the rock face, ivy cascaded like a green waterfall, intermingled with morning glory and other vines.

The morning glory still boasted a few trumpet-shaped flowers. Geneva reached up to pick one but was startled when the entire waterfall of greenery swayed at her touch. Shouldn't all this vegetation have roots anchored to a solid surface?

It seemed so peculiar that Geneva started pulling at the leafy vines. Large handfuls came away. When she probed even deeper her fingers touched something that looked like a tarry fishing net but much thicker and stronger. Could this be the simple and ingenious answer to the tunnel exit she'd been hunting? It wouldn't take long for vines to grow over netting as they did on a wooden trellis.

With fresh energy, Geneva tugged on the green waterfall. The vegetation swung free of the cliff face easily enough that it was clear Geneva wasn't the first in recent history to tear it loose from encroaching vines. Her mind flashed to the food and drink in the cavern, evidence others had been there in the not-too-distant past. Had her father continued to use the tunnels his forefathers built for his own purposes?

Geneva lifted the curtain enough to slide around to the other side. The dim green light illuminated an unevenly shaped cave where a steep overhang had created a partially roofed grotto in the rock. On this side, she could also see that the entire underside of the matted vines was indeed heavy netting. It had been there a long time judging by large sections that had disintegrated from nature's harsh elements. Geneva doubted it could be old enough to have been strung by Sir Callum himself. Perhaps later generations had replaced the net as needed.

Straight ahead, the back of the grotto slanted down to barely a man's height. Set within this rock wall was the counterpart of the arched wooden door she had found at the end of the tunnel. This had to be Sir Callum's portal for carrying contraband underground.

Walking closer, Geneva studied the door. She'd hoped that like the cavern door this one wasn't actually locked but simply had some heavy latch or bar that had prevented her from opening it from the inside. But all she saw was a keyhole and iron ring identical to that of the cavern door. She gave the iron ring a hard tug. As she'd expected, it didn't budge. Without a key, there would be no entrance this way.

Geneva slipped back out to the sunny side of the netting. The disappointment of finding the door locked couldn't squelch her elation at discovering the tunnel exit. She wanted to shout her discovery from the rooftops. But it was clear the successive generations of her forebears had chosen to keep this a secret, including her own father. Geneva would do the same for the present, and Lord willing, she might even find that key.

CHAPTER EIGHTEEN

Six weeks had passed since the first time Geneva donated farm produce at the church. Since then, she'd continued volunteering on Saturday afternoons. Simon Harfield and his two cohorts had been among those showing up each week for food relief, but they were at least now showing some measure of respect.

The afternoon was cool and overcast as Burrows drove Geneva to the church in the loaded farm cart. The previous night, the plane trees had dropped a glorious carpet of yellow and orange leaves upon the churchyard. Doves flitted from the naked limbs to the top of the bell tower. While Burrows went off for a pint of ale at the inn, Geneva joined the other volunteers and added her donations to the mounds of produce.

She'd just finished when she noticed Philip striding out of the church and over to the food donation tables. Seeing the troubled look on his face, Geneva hurried over to intercept her cousin. "What's wrong? You look worried."

The vicar ran a hand through his curly mop of hair before he eventually responded, keeping his voice low. "Cousin Geneva, do you remember me mentioning that Mr. Fairfax wanted a meeting with landowners at the Bell and Crown?"

"I do. What happened?"

"Well, the meeting was held two days ago. Everyone agreed that the poor relief should be increased in accordance with the recent rise in the price of bread."

"That's good—isn't it?"

"Yes and no. The landowners objected to the subsequent increase in their taxes. I've just learned now from those seeking relief that these same landowners have lowered agricultural wages to compensate. I've also been informed that this has happened in other parishes as well."

"Lower wages? How much are laborers getting now?"

"It's reduced their income from eight shillings, four pence to seven shillings even. That may not sound a big difference, but for them it's a great hardship, close to twenty percent of their income."

The injustice of it infuriated Geneva. "But isn't there something you can do? Or Mr. Fairfax? He is the magistrate, is he not?"

"We can speak out, but the landowners have no obligation to listen. What they are doing is legal if not moral. The worst is that the wage cut has already been put into effect while it will be some time before the higher taxes are actually collected. So the poor are worse off than before the rise was agreed on. All we can really do now is pray for the Lord to intervene and set things right."

Philip glanced toward the church. "The laborers will emerge soon. I need to mention this to the other volunteers so they won't be surprised at the anger they may encounter."

Philip had no sooner done so and headed back when the church doors opened and a crowd of laborers emerged, the biggest Geneva had seen gathered for poor relief. Some faces were dour, others fierce and hostile as the crowd stampeded toward the tables, not bothering to get in line but elbowing their way in and grabbing what they could.

One woman snatched up an almost-full sack of flour from which individual portions were being measured. "Them land-owners are cheats and scoundrels. They'll get their just deserts on judgement day!"

"Bah, let 'em have it now," a man called out. But he peaceably accepted the portions of flour, cheese, and butter Geneva handed him. "Thanks, Miss Everson. Without this, I'd be eatin' nothin' but spuds till kingdom come."

At a neighboring table, a squabble had broken out over turnips and carrots. People were grabbing at the food items Geneva was doling out, forcing her to raise her hands. "Please, slow down. If you will each wait your turn, we have enough for everyone."

But no one was listening. As the disorderly crowd pushed and shoved, a basket of eggs fell to the ground in a sludgy mess. A woman raised her fist to the culprit. "Watch what you're doin', you greedy brute. Go home! You got far more than your share."

Geneva felt powerless in the midst of the mob's fierce indignation. Philip and the other overseers who distributed the poor relief had emerged from the church, drawn by the commotion. Philip called out sternly, "Stop this right now! If you do not stop this, you can forget any further food relief."

But by the time the other overseers had arrived, every table in the churchyard had been stripped bare. Those with full arms hurried away. Those laborers and their families who hadn't been so fortunate left the churchyard, looking discouraged and demoralized.

Geneva had headed back to her own farm cart when Simon Harfield and Ted Norton stepped out from under a nearby tree, both munching on carrots. Simon dropped a carrot top to the ground as he ambled close. "Hallo, Miss Everson. I guess ya heard they cut wages but have kept our poor relief not a penny more."

"Yes, I'm sorry about that. I'm sure Father Philip and the overseers are doing all they can to resolve such injustice."

"Hah! That will be the day." Simon ambled a step closer. "In any case, that isn't what I came to say. I've seen your wattle hurdles for sale at the market. What are you payin' the workers, if you don't mind me askin'?"

Geneva stiffened. "I do mind, Mr. Harfield. It's certainly none of your business, but if you must know, I don't deal with that enterprise personally, so in fact, I have no idea. Have you not been able to find other work yet?"

"There isn't any, at least around here. If I get caught poachin', I'll hang, so I figure I've got to find another way to feed my family. Few days ago, some information came my way you might find of interest. Ya ever heard about a fella called Nicholas Drake?"

Geneva couldn't believe what she was hearing. "Yes, I know of him. Why do you ask?"

A sly look crept over his face. "Well, I hear tell that he got lucky with your mother."

Heat rushed into Geneva's cheeks. "How dare you speak to me like that! For your information, that is a wicked lie."

"Yeah, well, that's what's been said. No one thought twice about Drake until you showed up. But I hear you've been askin' in the farmyard if anyone knows where the man is. And I figure if you're askin', maybe the answer is worth somethin'."

Searching her mind, Geneva drew up a memory of asking Mr. Blackerby about Drake that first Saturday she'd been filling the cart for food donation. There'd been others in the yard, even the laborers who'd helped her carry out eggs and other produce. It didn't really matter who'd been carrying tales. Angrily, she demanded, "And how would you know where Drake is after all these years?"

"My half-brother oughta know. He works on Drake's fishin' boat."

Geneva's eyes grew wide. "His fishing boat? What fishing boat? Where is it? I need to know."

Simon studied her face for a few moments. "Ah, so you really are that anxious to find him! I'll tell ya, but only if ya got a ten-pound note."

"Ten pounds!" Geneva gasped. "That's . . . that's half a year's wages! I don't have that kind of money!"

"But you could get it. Everyone knows you're the mistress of Ravensmere, the daughter of Master Adam's bride. She was kicked out for having relations with Drake. You're a wealthy woman. Unlike us poor folk, you can have that money for the askin'."

Geneva seethed with fury at the fresh dig against her mother. Much though she wanted the information, she would not grovel at the feet of this rude, brazen, vile man. "You won't get a penny from me, Mr. Harfield. And if I hear you are repeating such lies about my mother, I'll—!"

"You'll what?" he interrupted with a sneer. "You think the same isn't being said elsewhere? Or that anyone believes them to be lies?"

Before Geneva could find a retort, she saw Burrows hurrying toward her. The coachman burst into apologetic speech. "Miss Geneva, I didn't know you'd be finished so soon. I'm terribly sorry for keeping you waiting."

"Just take me home, Burrows—the faster the better!"

On the following Wednesday, near the end of October, all the family except Jack had coffee in the library following luncheon. Aunt

Mary had informed Geneva that Jack had gone into the village to meet friends for luncheon at the Bell and Crown Inn. Sipping the dark brew, Geneva glanced out the library window where grounds-keepers were raking leaves into piles destined for a bonfire. Four days had passed since the reduction of farm laborer wages. Simon Harfield's obnoxious words were still fresh in her mind and too insulting to share with the family.

She was still stewing over the memory when she spotted Daniel riding down the pebbled drive. She stood up with a bright smile. "Daniel Cavendish is here. What a nice surprise."

Robert glanced out the window. "Thank goodness! Maybe he can pull you out of your gloomy mood of the past few days."

Geneva waited for Stanway to usher Daniel into the room, then greeted him with a curtsey. "How nice of you to drop by. I'd love to hear about your trip to London. Do sit down. Will you have coffee?"

"Not now, thank you." Easing himself into a chair, Daniel crossed his legs. "It's good to see you all. London hasn't changed—still cramped and smoky. My financial work went well, and I did enjoy the opera but to be honest, I'm glad to be home. The city isn't my cup of tea."

Uncrossing his legs, he leaned forward. "I actually stopped by to inquire if anyone would like to join me for a visit to today's market. A local artist is presenting his work there. I thought we could go for a look and offer support. I've heard his work is quite out of the ordinary."

"I doubt that!" Aunt Mary commented caustically. "Notable artists don't come from country villages like ours."

"I, for one, will have to decline," Katherine said. "Grandmama Louise and I are visiting Philip's children this afternoon."

"Well, I'd like to go," Tess spoke up. "We shouldn't judge until we've seen the man's work." She turned to Robert. "Are you interested, dear?"

"I have no doubt this artist can't compare to your gifts, dear. But if it is your wish to go, I am happy to accompany you." Robert glanced over at Geneva. "And you, cousin?"

Geneva smiled at Daniel. "I would very much like to go. Thank you for thinking of us."

In truth, she was far more interested in conversing with Daniel than the skills of some unknown artist. As they waited on the pebbled drive for Burrows to bring the carriage around, Robert and Tess chatted together, giving Geneva an opportunity to ask Daniel, "Have you heard the news about farm labor wages?"

Daniel's smile disappeared. "Yes, my father gave me a full update as soon as I got home. It's most unfortunate. My father said that he and Philip both tried to convince the landowners to keep wages up. Since neither are directly involved with agriculture, their views carried little weight. I know they did all they could."

"I understand, but it still seems terribly unjust. In any case, I have other news on the matter we've been discussing." Stepping close, Geneva lowered her voice so only Daniel would hear. "One of our laid-off laborers gave me information about Nicholas Drake. Apparently, his half-brother works for Drake—on his fishing boat!"

Astonishment lit Daniel's eyes. "A fishing boat! So much for looking for the man at coaching inns. No wonder my queries were fruitless. I have to wonder how a dismissed coachman obtained funds to acquire a boat. But at least this narrows the matter down. There are many fishing boats moored in Porthaven's harbor. Next time I'm there, I'll ask at the docks if anyone has heard of him."

Geneva's face brightened. "Thank you so much, Daniel! This is encouraging. It may be that I will soon have a chance to confront him and learn the truth of my mother."

CHAPTER NINETEEN

Carriage wheels scrunched on the pebbled drive as Burrows drove the team of horses to the manor's entrance porch. Daniel and Geneva, with Tess and Robert, climbed in for the brief ride into Waterton. At this afternoon hour, the midweek market was crowded with shoppers buying provisions for the week. After they'd alighted from the carriage, Daniel scanned the scene and pointed to the market cross.

"That must be our artist. He was described as a slight young man with dark hair. Judging by the crowd around his stall, he must be as excellent an artist as claimed."

The foursome worked their way through the crowd flocking around the young artist and his paintings. Geneva was thoroughly taken with his scenes of farmyards and wheat fields, snow-covered cemeteries, and ladies strolling on sandy beaches. She turned to Daniel. "Goodness, his work is so lifelike and full of bright tones."

"Indeed, he's a true artist of our romantic era. I think he'll do well."

Robert took out his billfold and approached the artist. "What are you asking for this heron at the lakeside?"

"One pound, sir," the young man answered.

"Good night, is that all? You've got the features of the bird just right. I know because I'm an ornithologist. Here you are."

Robert handed over the money. While the artist wrapped the painting in brown paper, Geneva glanced toward the grassy area at the church. "Oh, look, there's Mr. Baines and Mr. Farthing, our tenant farmers. Shall we be neighborly and say hello?"

"Certainly." Daniel offered Geneva his arm, and the two strolled over to where the tenant farmers were seated on a bench, puffing cigars and watching the activity of the busy market. As Daniel and Geneva approached, the two men stood up and nodded.

"Good afternoon to you both," Mr. Farthing said. "I saw you browsing the artist's paintings. What do you think of his work?"

While the men chatted and shared their opinions, Geneva turned her attention to a commotion at the north end of the market. A tall, skinny man in a red jacket was standing on an overturned crate, a large group of laborers pressed close around him. His voice rose above the din of the market but not enough to hear what he was saying. Some of his audience were shouting and raising their fists. Others turned with angry faces to point toward the church.

Concern growing, Geneva touched Daniel's arm. "Sorry to interrupt, but look over there. Should we be worried?"

As Daniel and the two tenant farmers turned to scrutinize the angry group, the speaker suddenly got down from the crate and strode toward them, his followers close on his heels.

"Good Lord, I don't like the look of this," Mr. Farthing said.

Just at that moment, a familiar voice rang out angrily. "What's going on here?"

Jack's tall, commanding frame stepped out of the doorway of the Bell and Crown Inn, a dark scowl on his handsome face. Striding swiftly toward the man in the red jacket and his followers, he added forcefully, "In case you didn't know, the Riot Act of

1714 forbids public assemblies of more than twelve people. I'd say you're well over that number."

The laborers muttered but fell back as Jack pushed his way through to his two tenant farmers. An eyebrow rose as he took in Geneva's presence with Daniel. But he turned to face the speaker, who had stepped forward.

However passionate his previous speech, the speaker looked calm, his eyes bright and focused, as he swept his hat from his head in polite greeting. "Good afternoon, sirs." His nod acknowledged Geneva. "Miss, I'm Rudy Banks, at your service. My friends and I saw Mr. Farthing and Mr. Baines sitting here and thought we'd come over to ask a few things. Since you're here as well, Captain Everson, we'll ask you too."

Jack folded his arms across his broad chest and looked coldly down his nose at the speaker. "Very well. I know who you are. Speak up, and let's hear it."

"I'm sure you can guess what it's about. Our weekly wage has dropped by one shilling, four pence while the cost of bread has gone up. We're worried about the winter months ahead—not enough income for food, bills, rent, and coal to heat our cottages. Our old folk and little ones are vulnerable to sickness. I've buried two sons this year. Only God knows what next year will bring. We're asking politely for you and these tenant farmers to increase our wages to what they were and to stop using them threshing machines. They're destroying our livelihood and taking away our winter work."

Peter Farthing tapped the ashes from his cigar. "Mr. Banks, it's not possible to return to the primitive farming methods of the past. I'm sorry for your losses, but threshing machines are vital for today's agricultural business. Britain's population is growing, and along with it the demand for more grain."

Mr. Baines spoke up. "I hear what you're saying, Mr. Banks, but you're under no compulsion to work as a farm laborer. You could do what others have done—move to the cities up north. Jobs are always available in factories."

"That's ridiculous," Rudy blurted. "How could I afford to get my family there? And where would we live?"

"Captain Everson, I got a complaint too!" Geneva hadn't realized Simon Harfield was amongst the group of laborers until he shoved his way through and stood before Jack. "You've been breakin' the rules by showin' favoritism. I should have been hired for your wattle fence business. I got way more seniority than the ones you picked. That's like rubbin' salt into my wounds."

Jack pointed his jewel-studded walking stick at his former employee. "Have you no propriety, Mr. Harfield? It's not for you to speak publicly about a private business. Since you don't care if all and sundry hear it, I'll tell you why you were passed over. You're a rabbble-rouser, and your attitude is despicable. Charity was given to you, yet you received it in an arrogant and ungrateful manner. As I live and breathe, you shall never work on Everson land again. If you want employment, I suggest you leave Waterton. No one here will want to hire you!"

As Simon's face turned purple with rage, Jack raised his voice. "You're all aware of our parish relief system that supplements your wages. A system that is funded by the high taxes paid by landowners. Why should they pay more, considering how lazy and unproductive you've become? The system is based on the price of a loaf of bread and the number of children you have. You take advantage of that by marrying young and having large families. Aren't you capable of self-restraint?"

The protestors' faces flushed with anger. Rudy Banks threw his hat to the ground. "You got a nerve to say that! What a harebrained system it is—keeping wages low because the parish tops them up. Your fat profits never trickle down to a better life for us, and I'll tell you why. Landowners are tyrants. They control us by destroying our independence and making us miserable."

The speaker wagged a finger at Jack. "Have a care, Captain Everson. You got influence over people in authority. You could have our rent lowered. You could have them threshing machines ditched and our wages raised to what they were. Be a gentleman. Show the village folk that you're a decent man by doing at least *one* of these things."

While Rudy's fellow laborers clapped and cheered, Jack's face and ears turned scarlet. His pale-blue eyes blazed with anger, and he pointed his jeweled walking stick toward his opponent's face.

"Listen to me, Rudy Banks. It appears to me that the generosity of this parish has given every one of you a sense of entitlement. If I had my say in this, able-bodied men like you would be denied parish relief altogether. I would redirect the tax money to the workhouse for the sick, the elderly, and the disabled who cannot support themselves. Now clear out of here, or I'll call for the authorities!"

It was clear from their furious expressions that the protestors wouldn't take much more. Mr. Banks knocked Jack's walking stick away from his face. It fell from Jack's hand. As it smashed onto the cobblestones, the protestors swarmed in, chanting at the top of their lungs, "Bread or blood! Bread or blood! Bread or blood!"

Grabbing Geneva by the arm, Daniel maneuvered her to a safe distance as protestors picked up handfuls of horse dung and began hurling them at Jack and the two tenant farmers. Other protestors stormed through the market, cursing and shouting. Tables and carts were overturned. Watermelons and other produce smashed to the ground. A bale of hay caught on fire. Shoppers screamed while vendors scrambled to protect their wares.

Into the mayhem strode a constable and half-a-dozen deputies, wielding truncheons and shouting for order. But they were too few in number. The rallying cries continued until the constable had no alternative but to fire his pistol in the air.

Shock rippled through the crowd. Seconds later, the protestors began shoving their way out in a desperate effort to avoid arrest. With the help of bystanders, several of the worst offenders were seized and handcuffed. The rest bolted from the scene, leaving the marketplace in shambles.

Gradually with the help of vendors and village folk, order was restored. Over at the church green, Jack patted the tenant farmers on the back. "Thank you for your help. At least we can rest easy knowing that the worst perpetrators are in the lockup."

Mr. Baines threw a now-filthy coat onto the bench. "Well, whatever punishment they get, they deserve it."

"I should say so," Mr. Farthing added emphatically. "I'm glad you took a firm stand with those rabble-rousers, Captain Everson. Imagine suggesting Ravensmere farms should pay higher wages than has been agreed on by every landowner in the region!"

His words stung an unintended response from Geneva. "How can you say that? Have you no sympathy for their suffering and poverty? Something needs to be done about this! Is there not one compassionate man able to show leadership?"

The two tenant farmers immediately fell silent, but Jack rounded on Geneva, his face darkening. "Have you forgotten yourself, cousin? Women do not express their opinions on such matters. Especially in public. This is none of your affair!"

Daniel stepped forward as though placing himself protectively between Geneva and her angry cousin. "Perhaps they should speak up. We could use a woman's sensitive voice of reason. In any case, many of those men were employees of Ravensmere estate. That makes them Geneva's affair."

Jack glared at him. "No one asked you. Your ideas are dangerous! Keep them to yourself." He waved his hand at Burrows, who had brought the carriage to the churchyard as the crowd emptied. "Take Miss Geneva and the rest of her party back to the manor immediately!"

Geneva opened her mouth to speak, but Jack raised his arm and pointed to the carriage. "I won't say it again. Go on—shoo!"

Geneva climbed into the carriage. A moment later, Robert and Tess joined her. As the carriage started down the lane, Geneva peered out the rear window. Jack and Ravensmere's two tenant farmers had joined the constable and his men, who were leading the prisoners away. Geneva could see neither Simon Harfield's tall form nor Andy Banks's red jacket among them. The prime agitators had evidently escaped. And Daniel, left by Jack's autocratic decree without transport, strode off with the crowd in the opposite direction.

Later that afternoon, Geneva passed by the corridor to the east wing and heard the click of billiard balls. Entering the billiard room, she found Jack leaning over the green felt, body and cue poised to take a shot. With a sharp tap on the white ball, a yellow ball ricocheted off a red ball and rolled into the corner pocket. Straightening his back, Jack ambled around the table, eyes fixed to the balls as he calculated his next shot.

Geneva cleared her throat. "Cousin Jack, may I speak with you?"

He glanced over his shoulder. "Ahh! I had a feeling you would seek me out."

"And so I should." She came close to the table. "The riot in the village could have been prevented if you had handled it better."

"I see. So it's my fault, is it?" He leaned over to take another shot. "How do you reckon that?"

"Isn't it obvious? You were disrespectful toward the laborers and showed no compassion at all. Your insults made them feel like the dregs of society. You could have promised to petition Samuel Cavendish for lower rent and returning wages to their former rates or even an increase. At least to those who are Ravensmere estate laborers. That would have quelled their anger."

Jack took the shot and sunk another ball. "Dear Cousin Geneva, you are the sort of person who takes in wounded animals—and humans. An admirable quality, but in this case you really don't understand. I've been dealing with farm laborers since my teens. I know what they're like. Giving them the upper hand would be a big mistake."

"What do you mean?" Geneva demanded heatedly. "Returning their wages to what they already received is hardly the upper hand. It is simple justice!"

Jack laid down the cue. "Sorry to say, but that's where you're wrong. It would initiate endless demands for more and more. In a way, the protest served a good purpose. The authorities took control by arresting the offenders. That will serve as a deterrent and warning to others. If there's more labor unrest, be assured it won't happen in our parish."

Jack stepped toward Geneva, smiling warmly down at her indignant face. "You're bright and clever, Geneva, and I do value your input. I'm sorry if I seemed harsh earlier. My only excuse is that I was sick with worry when I saw you in danger in that crowd. My greatest concern was removing you safely before the situation turned ugly again. If we could agree to disagree on that topic at least, then things would be much more harmonious between us."

Geneva watched him go to the bell pull. She'd been expecting a heated argument, not kind and diplomatic words. If Jack was trying to pacify her, it wouldn't work. She would always be a voice for the poor. That said, she was warmed by his concern for her well-being.

Returning to her, Jack said jovially, "After this unpleasant-ness, we all need some cheering up. I've already spoken to the rest of the family about a jaunt to the beach. All of them thought it a splendid idea. We'll have a picnic for afternoon tea, and I'll take you for a long walk on the sand. What do you say?"

Geneva's resentment was ebbing away at his bright smile and soothing words. Jack was right about the value of maintaining harmony, and food always tasted better in the fresh outdoors. "Very well, I'm game for a picnic."

Her cousin's pale-blue eyes twinkled. "Marvelous."

The butler entered the room.

"Ah, Stanway, I have some requests. We are going to the sea-side for afternoon tea. Please tell Burrows to prepare the coach and ask Lily to pack a light picnic. And one more thing—a reminder that my guests are coming for billiards tonight."

"Very good, sir. Will you have the usual refreshments?"

"Yes, but this time tell Lily to include Russian caviar and smoked venison." He turned to Geneva. "You'll want to put on something more suitable for sand and wind, my dear. Go upstairs and get changed. We'll leave as soon as the picnic is ready."

CHAPTER TWENTY

The next Sunday evening following an All Hallow's Eve church service, the family gathered around the drawing room fireplace. The wind had picked up that afternoon, bending the upper limbs of trees and scattering leaves abroad. Geneva was thankful for the warm fire, a cozy lap blanket, and the sweet, frothy cup of hot chocolate Mrs. Fox had poured out.

Robert reached for a book on the end table. "Is this the book Tess's father gave you, Geneva?"

"Yes, it's the poems of the Scottish poet Rabbie Burns. My father gave it to your father-in-law originally. Mr. Carrington passed it on to me at the funeral reception. Such a kind gesture."

Robert flipped through the pages. "Here's one entitled 'Hallowe'en.'" He placed his finger on the page. "Burns writes in his footnote that this is thought to be the night when witches, devils, and other mischief-making beings are abroad on their baneful midnight errands."

Tess gave a hearty chuckle. "What a lot of nonsense. We've come a long way since those days. People believed evil spirits and witches emerged on All Hallow's Eve. They thought that masks, disguises, and offerings of treats would ward them off."

"Maybe, but tonight is special," Katherine said with a sparkle in her eye. "Hallowe'en coincides with a full moon this year. Shall we play some fortune-telling games?"

"Not as long as I am your vicar," Philip said in a stern voice.

Silence ensued briefly, which allowed Geneva to catch a soft scraping sound at the window. She jerked up straight. "What was that?"

"It's the fairies," Robert said in a sinister voice. "They're coming to get you!"

"Robert, stop teasing her," Tess scolded. "Don't worry, Geneva, it's only the holly rustling against the pane."

Jack stood to his feet. "Well, Philip, it was good having you and Claire join us, but it's nearly eleven so I think we ought to head up to bed."

Mary heaved her bulk out of the chair. "A very good idea. Come on, Grandmama Louise, I'll help you up the stairs."

Geneva followed Robert and Tess up the oak stairwell. Bidding them a good night, she entered her bedroom, warm and candlelit. After completing her ablutions and putting on her nightgown, she was stepping up into the canopy bed when she heard Pookie's pitiful meowing outside the window. He liked prowling the grounds and often climbed the magnolia to her window at bedtime, knowing she'd let him in.

Tonight as she opened the window, a gust of wind whooshed against her face. With a little chirrup, Pookie jumped from the tree to the windowsill and into her arms. His coat smelled wonderful—earth, moss, and dry leaves. While Pookie licked his paws near the hearth, Geneva snuggled down in her bed. Just as slumber overtook her, she felt the cat jump to the bed and nestle in the crook of her legs.

A few hours later, Geneva was awakened by the clanging of alarm bells, a thud of footsteps in the hallway, and several loud raps on her door. Getting up, she peered out the window as she pulled on her dressing gown. From the violently lashing trees, the wind had strengthened to gale force.

She dashed to the door and found an agitated Katherine on the other side, dressing gown untied and hair in a tousled mess.

"What is it?" she demanded. "What's going on?"

"The barn's on fire." Katherine wrung her hands. "Jack and Robert have already gone out with the servants to see what they can do. Stanway is rousing the tenant cottagers to fight the fire. Jack sent orders for the rest of us to stay here unless it appears there is any danger of the fire reaching the manor."

Geneva had already flung off her dressing gown and was reaching for her old work dress. "You can stay here. But if the servants can fight the fire, so can I. Ravensmere is my responsibility now. I need to help as well."

Katherine sniffed. "Very well. I know better than trying to change your mind. Perhaps I will go to the kitchen and see about arranging some refreshments. They will be needed when this is over."

Geneva pulled her jacket over her work dress, and stuffed her long tresses under her bonnet. With a hint of smoke already in the air, she had the bright idea of wetting a large handkerchief and stuffing it into a pocket before racing down the stairs. Once out in the courtyard, she gasped at the orange sky visible through the copse of trees.

Lifting her skirt, she ran full force across the lane and down the pathway into the chaotic horrors of the farmyard. Great tongues of fire rose up from a burning hayrick, which appeared to be the origin of the fire. Smoke swirled in a haze. A second fire raged across the thatched roof of the barn, and the wind carried thousands of sparks along its path.

The barn doors stood open wide, and horses and oxen milled frantically around the stable yard. Geneva could make out Burrows and a stable boy trying to herd the livestock away from the barn. Jack and Robert were nowhere in sight, but as Geneva looked frantically around, they emerged from the barn doors, dragging out a farm cart loaded with ploughs and harrows. Mr. Blackerby and his sons followed with carts filled with scythes, rakes, and shovels.

Jack called out, "It's impossible to save the barn, but we have time to salvage the contents. Just keep the water coming. And quickly. Every moment counts."

Glancing around, Geneva realized what Jack meant. A heavy-set, muscular man was pumping water at the well, while a line of laborers and house servants were passing buckets toward the fire and back to the pump for refilling. The smoke was now so strong Geneva could hardly breathe. She paused only long enough to tie the wet handkerchief over her nostrils and mouth before hurrying over to join the bucket line.

Geneva's arms were soon aching as she handed bucket after bucket to her neighbor, one of the housemaids. At the end of the line, each bucket was passed up a ladder raised against the barn to be thrown on blazing clumps of the thatched roof. But no matter how many buckets Geneva passed on, the fire only seemed to spread, fueled by the howling wind and scattering sparks that started new fires everywhere they landed across the thatched roof.

From the barn doorway, Jack raised his hands and shouted at the top of his voice, "Everyone get out of the barn! It's too dangerous. Containment is all we can do! Keep that water coming!"

Mr. Blackerby and his eldest son emerged through the barn doors with one last cartload. Just then, Samuel and Daniel Cavendish hurried into the farmyard, Peter Farthing and Edgar Baines on their heels.

Robert hurried over to the newcomers. "Thank you for coming. But there's nothing further anyone can do. We'll just have to let it burn. Thankfully, we got all the livestock and much else."

"I can't believe this!" Samuel shook his head in dismay. "That old barn has stood for a hundred years. What would cause it to catch fire now? There's been wind but no lightning I've seen."

By now, the hayrick with its cone-shaped dome had been reduced to smoldering embers, ashes, and scorched earth. The bucket line abruptly broke up as men leaped down from the ladder. Gratefully dropping her arms, Geneva saw the entire thatched roof was engulfed in flames. Moments later, a horrendous crack sounded throughout the farmyard. As every head turned to watch in horrified silence, the massive roof beams and timbers collapsed into a blazing pyre. Fresh billows of smoke belched forth, and ashes filled the air like a swarm of locusts.

The collapse actually proved useful as the remaining stone walls contained the inferno. Under Jack's direction, Mr. Blackerby called for a renewed bucket line to wet down the perimeter of the blaze. Meanwhile, Jack walked over to the recent arrivals. Geneva joined them, her wet handkerchief pressed against her nose and mouth to alleviate her coughing.

"Mr. Blackerby can take over here," Jack was saying when she reached the group. "It's vital for guards to watch for further fires as long as that wind is blowing. Until the last ember is cold, we'll need every pair of eyes we can get."

Samuel laid a hand on his shoulder. "At least no one was hurt. For that we can thank God. And it looks like you were able to get most of the barn's contents out."

"The most important things." Jack coughed repeatedly and cleared his throat before calling out, "A bucket over here? I'm parched."

A housemaid rushed over with one of the buckets Geneva had been hefting. She set it down, then scurried away. Lifting the bucket, Jack let it pour down his throat and spill over soot-blackened clothing before passing it to Robert. Only then did he seem to notice Geneva's presence.

"What are you doing here? I gave strict instructions for the women to stay safely inside until this was over."

Tugging the handkerchief down from her face, Geneva lifted her chin. "There were women servants helping here. Surely as the mistress of Ravensmere, I should be doing as much!"

"Hmmph!" Jack said nothing more, but Geneva caught an approving glance from Daniel. When Robert set down the bucket, Geneva scooped some water into her own parched mouth and over her sooty face. When she straightened up, she found Daniel watching with a wide grin. He winked at her as his father turned the conversation to the fire.

"This is such a loss for the estate. Does anyone know how it started?"

Robert wiped the water dripping from his chin. "Well, it may be All Hallow's Eve, but it certainly wasn't mischief-makers hanging about at midnight."

"What do you mean?" Samuel asked.

"What he means is that this was no act of God," Jack said. "It was arson."

"Arson?" Peter Farthing shoved his hat back. "Good grief, how do you know that?"

"Mr. Blackerby and his sons," Jack answered grimly. "Blackerby's dog is well trained. When he heard sounds in the farmyard that weren't the wind, he woke up the family with his scratching on the door. Blackerby and his sons got to the windows in time to see five men with torches igniting the hayrick. They loaded their shotguns and took the arsonists by surprise. Unfortunately, two managed to escape. But three are tied up in the cart shed right now waiting for the constable to arrive."

Geneva edged closer. "So who are these men? Not any of our workers, I pray!"

"Actually they are," Jack said even more grimly. "The three we caught were Harfield and his two usual lackeys, Norton and McGavin. It's pretty clear that Simon Harfield was the instigator. And it wasn't just the fire. We also discovered that the new threshing machine had been smashed beyond repair, evidently before the culprits set the fire."

He looked over at Geneva. "Despite my harsh words to Harfield last Wednesday, those three men have been valuable workers for many years. I doubt they would have done this if I'd been able to hire them for wattle fence business. It was indeed their right to work when wattle fence jobs became available."

His words felt like a kick in Geneva's gut. Was all this really her fault for having made Simon Harfield so angry? She felt completely justified for hiring Harry, Cyrus, and Charlie for her new business. They had treated her with respectful servility instead of rudeness and hate. Jack had persuaded Samuel Cavendish to hire them for that reason. And it was Jack who had stated publicly that Simon would never again be hired at Ravensmere.

Daniel stood close to Geneva and looked Jack in the eye. "If we're going to point fingers here, then your inflammatory words yesterday have done far more to rouse anger than Geneva. She has sought only to provide for the poor and needy. This is the outcome of Harfield's anger against *you*, not Geneva."

"That's enough, Daniel," Samuel interrupted. "Laying blame on anyone won't help the situation. These men chose to do what they did. No amount of anger over wages justifies such violence or mitigates their guilt. Speaking of which, is that not Constable Allenby arriving?"

At his words, Geneva turned to see a horse-drawn jail wagon rolling into the farmyard. Geneva recognized the driver as the constable who, with his deputies, had put an end to the market riot. The man stepped down from the wagon and approached. "Captain Everson, I've been informed you have some arsonists for me."

His arrival had been noted because a moment later Mr. Blackerby and his sons came forward, shoving three men across the farmyard. The men's arms were tied behind their backs, their feet hobbled so they could only walk at a shuffle.

"So these are your culprits," Constable Allenby commented. "Seems I've seen at least one of these men before."

"They were all participants in the riot four days ago," Jack said. "And they were caught red-handed starting this fire. I will send the witnesses along to make their statements."

Jack nodded at Mr. Blackerby and his sons, who directed the prisoners forward. Watching their slow progress with satisfaction, Constable Allenby spoke up. "Well done all around. First thing in the morning they will be taken to Morlington House to be questioned by Chief Magistrate Angus Fairfax. Following that, they'll be taken to Hawkley Castle Prison to await their trial at the next assizes."

As the prisoners drew close, two of them kept their heads bowed in submission, but Harfield glared defiance. Constable Allenby slapped his truncheon against a hand. "So what do you have to say for yourselves?"

"Say for ourselves?" Simon Harfield swung around on Jack. "I'll tell ya what! While you strut around with your jewel-studded walking stick, we've worked ourselves to the bone in your fields half-starved. We came to you with reasonable requests, but you were too pig-headed to give a care. This storm has caused far more damage than we planned, and we're glad 'cause you bloody-well deserve it!"

Simon shifted his glare to Geneva. "You too, miss! You come in here thinkin' you're so much better than the rest of us when you're nothin' but a low-class wench with a loose woman for a mother! I only wish we'd burned everything you own to the ground, not a measly barn!"

"Well, just think about this, Mr. Harfield!" Constable Allenby said. "While these good folks start rebuilding, you three will be on a prison hulk destined for Australia."

He gestured for two constables to load the prisoners in the jail wagon. Geneva turned away and started walking toward the manor. Every bone in her body ached from the stress of the night. She felt light-headed and deeply perturbed by Simon Harfield's hate for her. Daniel had been kind enough to defend her, but she couldn't help feeling guilty. Had her handling of Simon Harfield and her selection of men for the wattle fence business contributed to tonight's catastrophe?

Without warning, the sudden blast of a shotgun split the air. Geneva froze mid-step. "What was that? What's going on?"

Daniel hurried up beside her. "I'm so sorry, Geneva. One of your oxen suffered cruel injuries from the fire. Putting it out of its misery was the kindest thing that could be done."

For Geneva, that image of death was the last straw. The blood drained from her face. A moment later her trembling knees gave way. Daniel caught her just in time.

Gus McGavin had never felt such shame. Tears were for women and children, not men. Still, he couldn't stop them from coursing down his cheeks. His thoughts went back to the events of that morning. Even now, Gus could still smell the magistrate's breath reeking of onions and blood pudding as Mr. Fairfax had questioned the prisoners in the magisterial office of his stately home. With more than enough evidence against them, the three men had been taken by jail wagon to Ingleford's Hawkley Castle Prison.

No sooner had they passed through the doors than a sour-faced guard had taken them down a flight of stairs to a miserable dungeon. There in the cold, damp air that stunk of excrement, their hair had been shorn and their clothes stripped from their bodies. Then dressed in prison uniforms, each of them, barefoot and humiliated, had been led down dark corridors to separate cells.

Sitting on the straw-stuffed pallet that was all the bedding provided, Gus wiped his wet cheeks with his sleeve and watched a cockroach scaling the stone wall. A thin, moth-eaten blanket and a chamber pot pushed into the corner were the cell's only other furnishings. A tiny window with iron bars high on one wall provided a narrow shaft of gloomy light. But once night fell, the utter blackness would be unbearable.

Gus despised himself for being a weak-kneed coward. He hadn't wanted to take part in arson and vandalism. But he was a timid sort of person, and Simon Harfield, the biggest bully in the parish, had talked him into it—the worst mistake of his life. He cringed to think of the disgrace this would bring to his wife and family. Everyone knowing he was rotting in prison until the day he'd be shipped to the far side of the earth.

Could he even survive such an arduous journey? He'd been a sickly person all his life, picked on and ridiculed for his small frame, big nose, and pock-marked skin. Chances were he'd die of dysentery and have his body thrown to a watery grave.

Gus stretched out on the pallet and gazed at cobwebs hanging from the ceiling. But as the minutes passed and the shadows inched across the wall, his despair and hopelessness grew. Then it lifted as the only solution became clear.

Not wishing to delay any longer, Gus got up from the bed. After removing his trousers, he fashioned a noose that would slip snuggly over his head. With the knots pulled tight, he maneuvered the chamber pot beneath the window and upturned it. Using the pot as a stepping stool, he balanced himself on tiptoe until he managed to secure his makeshift noose around an iron bar.

But as Gus settled the noose around his neck, a fearsome thought crossed his mind. The Bible said, "Thou shalt not kill." Then Vicar Everson's frequent quote suddenly came to mind: "Fear God and keep his commandments for this is the whole duty of man." He must be out of his mind! He couldn't follow through with this terrible sin lest he face the wrath of God on the other side.

Choosing life over death, Gus lifted his shaky hand to the noose. But as he tried to loosen it, the chamber pot rocked beneath his raised toes. As Gus overbalanced, the pot crashed onto its side and rolled away. Gus fell forward, his dangling feet jerking and twitching until at long last they grew still.

CHAPTER TWENTY-ONE

Geneva could smell coffee. Delicious coffee—hot and creamy, robust and nutty. Finally realizing she wasn't in a dream, she opened her eyes to find Aunt Mary's plump face looking down at her.

"My dear, you've had such a long sleep. It's time to wake up."

Geneva lifted her head and saw steam rising from a cup on her bedside table. "Good heavens, how long have I been asleep?"

"A good six hours. Do you remember Daniel carrying you from the farm to the library? Mrs. Fox gave you hot milk with a little laudanum stirred in."

"Laudanum? What for?"

"Daniel told us all you'd done and the shock you experienced. You needed a good sleep. And it's certainly done you good. In fact, you slept right through All Saints' Day service this morning. We all slept late except for Philip. He had no choice in making it to the service. In any case, it's time you had breakfast and got yourself dressed. Jack wants to address the family and servants in the Great Hall as soon as you are ready."

Sitting up, Geneva pushed her tangled hair back. "I have two images stuck in my head, Aunt Mary. The roof of the barn collapsing. And those farm laborers hobbled with ropes. I know justice must be done, but I wouldn't want my worst enemy going to Hawkley Castle Prison."

"Hush, my dear." Aunt Mary placed the breakfast tray on Geneva's lap. "Don't get yourself into another state. Look, here's Pookie to see you."

Jumping onto the bed, Pookie sniffed at the sausages and eggs. Geneva stroked him and looked out the window. "I'm glad the storm is over, but I dread seeing the remains of the barn by daylight. And that poor dead ox!"

"You don't need to worry your head about that, dear," Aunt Mary said comfortably. "Jack is very capable. He'll see to it that everything is put right—just you wait and see. Now, I must leave you. Eat your breakfast and we'll see you downstairs."

An hour later, Geneva entered the Great Hall. The voices of the family and servants hummed throughout, all in a state of concern. Jack was perfectly groomed, sporting a black cravat that complemented his white waistcoat. He stepped forward from the fireplace, waiting until chatter gave way to silent attention before he spoke, his voice still hoarse from smoke inhalation.

"Thank you for gathering here this morning. First of all, I want to thank each and every one of you for your hard work in helping with the fire last night. We lost the barn but thanks to all your brave efforts, no other buildings or livestock. The fire is now completely out with no further losses. To compensate for lost sleep, you may enjoy a time of relaxation from two to four this afternoon."

He cleared his throat. "Now, the destruction of private property at the hands of arsonists is a serious matter. I have formulated a strategy to safeguard our community from further protests, violence, crimes, or possible Swing riots. I will be pushing for an increase in the number of village constables and having them armed with muskets. Also for the forming of a community watch. If a Swing letter is received, armed constables and watch volunteers will be dispatched to guard the property in question. In addition, I will pressure magistrates to bring the full weight of the law upon the perpetrators of these crimes, including capital punishment where applicable."

"With regards to the barn, we will rebuild immediately. Mr. Blackerby is already directing any workers without other urgent tasks to clean up the barn site. As soon as possible, construction workers will begin. During this time, I expect all of you to maintain a flexible and cooperative attitude." With a dismissive gesture, he finished, "That should do for now. Thank you for your attention. You may return to your duties."

As the servants dispersed from the Great Hall, the family gathered around Jack. Robert clapped him on the back. "Bravo. This community needs strong leadership. I'm proud that it's coming from you."

Aunt Mary nudged Geneva with her elbow. "See, my dear, everything will be just fine."

Geneva glanced out the window. "Look, Mr. Cavendish and his son are here."

"They've come to discuss the damage and a plan to move forward," Jack said. "Cousin Geneva, you have a right to listen in. Let's go down to my office."

A few minutes later, Stanway showed Samuel and Daniel into Jack's office. Jack shook their hands. "Thank you for coming. I hope you've caught up on your sleep."

"I certainly have, thank you." Samuel turned his gaze to Geneva. "May I hope you've slept well, Miss Geneva. We were worried about you last night. How are you feeling today?"

"I'm fine now, thank you. The sleep did me good." Geneva looked shyly at Daniel. "Thank you too. I was told you carried me from the fire last night. I'm sorry to have caused such trouble."

"It was no trouble," Daniel replied. "You had every reason to be in shock with all that had happened. I think I speak for all of us that it was brave of you to place yourself in danger fighting the fire last night."

Geneva went pink at the compliment. "As my father's daughter, I felt it my duty to set an example."

"We can all agree Miss Geneva showed herself a true Everson and mistress to Ravensmere," Samuel added warmly. "Meantime, we have several things to discuss. First of all, I received a message from Angus Fairfax. It's clear now that Simon Harfield was the leader of last night's destruction. His intention was to set the hayrick on fire and destroy the threshing machine that had taken their jobs. But the barn was unintentional, the consequence of last night's windstorm. It seems these men might rail against those in lawful authority over them, but they draw the line at hurting innocent beasts. Nevertheless, they will be duly charged under the law for the results of their criminal acts."

"Good, they deserve it!" Jack said vehemently. "Did they give up the names of the men who escaped?"

"No, they refused—another stroke against them when they are sentenced. As to the barn and threshing machine, it will not be an issue to release the necessary funds to replace those. Just provide me with the receipts and plans when you have them."

Samuel moved awkwardly in his seat and seemed to struggle for his next words. "There is one other matter I am somewhat reluctant to address, but as Miss Geneva's guardian and the one responsible for the prosperity of the estate, I have no option."

Jack frowned. "Whatever do you mean?"

Samuel cleared his throat. "First, let me assure you that your administration of the estate as Miss Geneva's land agent has been beyond reproach. But there has been a strong reaction within the community over the events at last week's market. Many prominent citizens witnessed your harsh words to the protestors. You may have echoed what any landowner would have said, but there is some sentiment that your words angered the protestors to the point of last night's arson. Whether or not that is so, news coverage on the two events in today's newspaper strongly takes that position."

Samuel shifted in his seat once more. "Now, I am not suggesting they are right or placing blame anywhere but the actual arsonists. The point is, Miss Geneva cannot afford to have such negative publicity directed toward Ravensmere or her own person. For that reason, I trust you'll understand my decision. From now on, if any farm laborers have grievances, Mr. Blackerby will direct them to Daniel. He will hear the complaint and decide if it has merit and what should be done. In consultation with myself and Miss Geneva, of course. I realize this is a major change in your duties as estate manager, but I hope you can see it's for the best of all concerned. The rest of your work is admirable, and I know Miss Geneva values and appreciates all you do as much as I do."

Geneva observed Jack's expression as he shifted his eyes to Daniel. The seething resentment in his cold eyes was unmistakable. She agreed wholeheartedly with her guardian's decision, but this could only make things awkward. Being demoted in authority where Jack had once expected to inherit had to be galling and humiliating. For once, she could almost feel sorry for her cousin.

With no verbal response from Jack, Samuel continued. "The arrest of Harfield and company will have a sobering effect on our community, but it won't ease the tension between laborers and landowners. I'm pleased to say that Daniel has a proposal for this issue."

He looked over at his son. "Do share it with us, Daniel."

"Yes, of course." Daniel turned to Geneva. "I believe the only way to ease those tensions is to get to the root of the matter. The key to doing that lies with the wattle fence business. The workers have become proficient at their job, and sales are remarkably good. Since they're qualified tradesmen, they deserve a wage in keeping with similar trades. I recommend that we pay them eleven shillings per week."

Geneva grinned. "They'll be happy to hear that."

Jack made a guttural sound in his throat. "Have you lost your mind? That is four shillings above what the others are making! How will that ease the alleged tensions your father spoke of?"

"I haven't finished yet," Daniel cut in. "With just three workers, we haven't begun to fill the market for wattle fencing left by the former maker's departure. He had a sizeable concern that sold in many area markets. In light of this, we need to bump up our rate of production by hiring three more workers and possibly more later. I've done the math and can say with confidence that the profits will not only cover the higher wages but provide additional income to restore our remaining laborers to their prior wages."

He smiled at Geneva. "When it becomes known that we have listened to the pleas of our workers, by providing well-paid winter work for the unemployed, those speaking against our past actions will be singing Ravensmere's praise—and the generosity of its new mistress. Especially when it also becomes known that Geneva is responsible for bringing the cottage industry to those same needy families."

Daniel sat back in his chair. "So what do you think? An added bonus is that every laborer receiving a fair wage will be one less family requiring poor relief, which will lessen the strain on the church's scant resources. That should lighten Philip's heart."

"I think it's marvelous!" Geneva exclaimed. "You've found a clever way to improve the lives of everyone on the estate without ruffling feathers about wages."

She turned to Daniel's father. "I hope you're in favor, Mr. Cavendish."

"Yes, I'm proud of Daniel's plan for several reasons. It will restore public confidence in the Everson name, ease the tensions of these past days, and benefit both the poor and the church."

"I disagree!" Jack turned to Geneva. "Cousin, I strongly urge you to reject this plan in its entirety. Daniel hasn't thought it through. He knows nothing about managing an estate like Ravensmere. His so-called proposal is far more complicated than he indicates. Business owners and the other landowners will object strenuously if we pay higher wages than other employers. It isn't just about the poor getting above themselves. The other landowners will see it as a push to force all other employers to raise wages accordingly. It would also greatly reduce the profits needed to run this estate. Your father and our forefathers didn't create Ravensmere to be a charity organization but a contribution to the British economy."

Geneva could understand Jack's position, but everything she'd endured in her short life made her lean toward Daniel's plan. She shook her head. "It would not hurt our family to go without a new wardrobe every year or the occasional banquet if that will improve the lives of our workers. If kindness and compassion bring on the wrath of our peers, then so be it. Perhaps it will prod them to reconsider their own decisions. I give my consent wholeheartedly."

Jack tipped his head back and laughed, but there was no mirth in it. Then he leaned forward with his face only inches from Geneva's and his voice low and hard. "Can't you see what's happening here? You don't have a clue what's going on! All these years, your father trusted me with the wellbeing of Ravensmere. He would be horrified if he knew that these two were sidelining me, stripping away even my authority as estate manager. Believe me, cousin, this is just their first step in a gradual takeover before you come of age!"

Geneva was outraged at the insinuation. She pulled back. "How dare you say that. My father trusted them or he would not have chosen Mr. Cavendish as my guardian. They wouldn't try to take over."

She turned to Samuel with a questioning frown. "Would you?"

Samuel opened his mouth to speak, but three raps on the door cut him off. A second later, the door opened, and Stanway stepped in.

"I beg your pardon for interrupting. A messenger just came with a letter from Mr. Fairfax. I was told it should be delivered immediately."

Jack got up to take it.

"Sorry, sir, it's addressed to the mistress of the manor."

Geneva's eyes widened. "For me?"

"Yes, Miss Geneva."

She took the letter. "Thank you, Stanway, that will be all."

She broke the seal. As her eyes darted back and forth across the page, she clutched her hand to her chest. "Oh, dear God, this can't be! Our farm laborer Gus McGavin, one of those arrested last night, is dead. He hanged himself from the prison window earlier this morning."

The letter slipped from her hand to the table. Tears splashed down her face as she visualized the gaunt, pockmarked man who'd resisted sharing in Simon's mockery of her. Geneva rounded angrily on her cousin.

"This wouldn't have happened if you'd listened to our employees' valid complaints. This was your doing. You made the decisions on wages, rent, and repairs these last years. My father was a generous man. He wouldn't have allowed matters to come to this. He would have been as generous as Daniel. Then Gus would still be alive—a husband to his wife, and father to his children. This is unforgiveable—totally unforgiveable!"

Tears streaming down her face, Geneva dashed from the room. As she stumbled down the hallway, she heard Daniel call to her. "Geneva, wait, please! Let me help you!"

She looked back with a distraught face. "There's nothing you can do to fix this. It's too late."

He came to her side and put his arm around her shoulder. "For Gus, yes. But you have every opportunity ahead to fix many other ills. Could we find a private place to talk?"

Geneva wiped her cheeks and nodded. "The library."

Daniel guided her in and closed the door. Geneva sank down onto a sofa. "I don't know what to think. I'm so muddled up. I don't know who to trust."

Daniel settled himself beside her. "I would hope that you can trust me and certainly my father. Adam would be the first to assure you so. Jack has cast both our characters into question. If you're doubting my integrity or my father's, then our actions will speak for us. But it's up to you to decide who to trust."

Geneva's mind flashed back to the protest at the market, the venom in Jack's eyes as he berated the laborers for their audacity in asking for more. That brought a memory of Daniel's very different and compassionate words facing a similar crowd of protesting laborers. Geneva was caught in the middle, powerless and vulnerable with only her good sense to guide her. But everything she'd witnessed of Daniel Cavendish assured her that he didn't have an untrustworthy bone in his body.

When had Daniel ever given Geneva reason to doubt him? The motives behind his plan couldn't be more honorable. Certainly nothing in it would financially benefit himself. And his father had endorsed that generosity wholeheartedly.

She turned her head to give Daniel a small smile. "I'm sorry for Jack's unkind words. I think he was grasping at straws in an attempt to redeem himself. Your plan reminds me of the golden rule—love your neighbor as you love yourself. Why doesn't everyone do that? The world would be a better place if they did."

"That's true. It would be paradise. I wish to follow it, but I often fail."

"I do too. But too many others don't care who they hurt. Like those rich, selfish landowners and that bully Simon Harfield. Or Nicholas Drake and my uncle Alex."

Geneva pushed her hair back to reveal the scar on her forehead. "See this? It happened one night when my uncle got drunk and violent. My head hit the corner of the cast-iron stove. This scar would not exist if Nicholas Drake hadn't gone to my mother's bedroom. That too is unforgiveable!"

Daniel shook his head slowly. "You have certainly had more than your fair share of troubles, Geneva. I'm so sorry for all you've gone through. It would be easy to become bitter."

"I'm not bitter," Geneva said. "But I do have negative thoughts about the past. They won't go away, and it's not easy to pray when I don't feel like it. That's why I need Pookie's calming effect."

"A loving pet can indeed be a great comfort." Daniel leaned back against the sofa to look more directly into Geneva's face. "Would you mind if I shared something from a past experience?"

"Of course, I'd like to hear it."

"Well, it was during my first year working at the bank. I'll spare you details, but a particular sin had crept into my life. I was self-deceived and didn't realize that it was hindering my relationship with the Lord. God chastened me with painful circumstances. Believe me, it wasn't fun. Eventually, one of Philip's sermons brought conviction to my heart. I repented of my sin, and God forgave me. It was incredible. A huge burden had been lifted, and I knew my fellowship with Christ had been restored. Geneva, I hope you understand that God chastens only those whom He loves as the Bible tells us in Hebrews chapter twelve."

Geneva knew the passage. "Like a father with his wayward son, it says."

"Exactly. I'm not saying that your troubles have come due to a prior sin as mine did. Nothing you could have done as a young child would merit the abuse your uncle inflicted on you. Whatever troubles you face, God loves you and permits them only for your ultimate good."

"Thank you for sharing. I will try to believe that." Geneva released a sigh. "There's something I should do. I'm glad Gus has an older son to take over as head of the family. But I want to help his wife by paying off any outstanding debts they have, and for her husband's proper burial."

"That's good of you to help financially. No one deserves a pauper's grave."

Geneva glanced across the library where the pianoforte stood proudly near a window. "Is there any chance you could do something for me?"

"That depends. What is it?"

"I haven't heard you play yet. Could you play a piece on the pianoforte?"

Daniel smiled. "I'd be delighted. Let's see... hmm. I think Beethoven's Pathétique Sonata would fit today's mood. Shall I play all three movements?"

"Oh, definitely, the more the better."

As Daniel took his place at the piano bench, Geneva moved to an armchair that faced the piano and made herself comfortable.

For a long moment, Daniel gazed at the keys in thoughtful medi-
tation. Then his hands came down in a colossal opening chord
that shook the piano on its legs. As his fingers moved over the
keys, his incredible virtuosity kept Geneva's attention. Finishing
the first movement, he continued into the second, a quiet, bittersweet lullaby with a dreamy sense of comfort, then into the
power and majesty of the final movement. Geneva marveled at
his dynamic command over the instrument as his nimble fingers
raced down the keys to a thunderous closing chord.

When the last notes died away, she stood up and clapped her
hands. "Oh, Daniel, that was truly superb. If the lords and ladies
of London could hear you, you'd be a highly honored guest in
their music salons. I've never heard anything so beautiful."

Daniel placed his hands in his lap. "That is very kind of you,
but let's give Beethoven the credit he deserves. What a loss for the
world when he died three years ago."

"Yes, but he'd be happy if he knew you were keeping his music
alive in such a talented way. Thank you for playing for me. You've
really lifted my spirits."

"Well, that's what it's all about—bringing joy and pleasure
to others. I expect my father is cooling his heels waiting for me."
Rising from the piano bench, Daniel walked over and cupped his
warm hands around hers. "Take care, Geneva. Things will settle
back to normal before long and don't forget, if you ever need help,
I'm here for you."

Later, after the rest period the servants had been given, the two
housemaids, Emily and Samantha, prepared a hip bath in Geneva's

bedroom. By the light of candles and a glowing fire, Geneva lowered herself into the hot water. At last, peace and silence reigned in the privacy of her enclave, shut off from dark hallways, estate affairs, rules, and protocol. With steam rising in soft wisps, she sunk deeper and felt her tension melting away.

The past week had revealed much about Cousin Jack. His poor judgement in handling the protesters. His calloused disregard for the welfare of Ravensmere's own laborers. If his kindness to Geneva was genuine, why didn't he extend it to others as well? What troubled her even more was the pearl necklace he'd given her. Its value alone could cover the additional wages and needed cottage repairs.

So far, Jack had been patient in not pressing Geneva for an answer to his marriage proposal. That couldn't go on forever. After his initial harsh words and accusations, not to mention his tyrannical behavior toward her at the protest, Geneva had to wonder if Jack's ultimate goal was not to win her heart but to win back his inheritance through their marriage.

If so, she knew her answer. Never again would she be used as a piece of property, as her uncle had done. She couldn't be certain of Jack's motives, but her doubts gave her a good reason to bide her time.

Geneva reached for a bar of scented soap Emily had set out. As she worked up a creamy lather, the room was filled with the glorious fragrance of a rose garden. Her thoughts shifted from Jack to Daniel. Despite Jack's insinuations, she had no uncertainty as to Daniel's character. He was a godly man of integrity, wisdom, and kindness.

Her mental catalog of Daniel's qualities shifted to an image of his tall, broad-shouldered frame. Of chocolate-brown eyes smiling down at her with tender concern. Of strong fingers creating beauty across a piano keyboard and strong arms carrying her up the path to the manor.

Geneva suddenly realized that her uncertainty about Jack's proposal had evaporated. Her heart belonged to Daniel and no one else.

CHAPTER TWENTY-TWO

At dinner the following night, Stanway served Stargazy pie. Geneva wasn't fond of the fish heads poking through the crust, but she knew the creamy filling of pilchards, bacon, eggs, and spices would be delicious.

Robert groaned with delight. "Ahh, my favorite dish. Cut me a big slog, Stanway. I ought to mention the chat I had with Jack this afternoon. I was shocked to hear about Samuel Cavendish's new business plan for the estate. If he continues expanding the wattle fence business, he'll desecrate our beautiful groves of hazels and willows. The estate's natural resources should be for the benefit and enjoyment of its landowners, not paupers and poor folk."

Katherine pursed her lips. "Excuse me, brother, but you're mistaken. In my work with the cottage industry, I have frequent visits with the wives of the fence makers. They've told me about their husbands' skillful method of harvesting the branches. It's called coppicing. It encourages plenty of new growth every year. I think it's wonderful to use the trees for a good cause. Don't you agree, Jack?"

Jack shrugged his shoulders. "It doesn't matter what I think. I'm just the estate manager, as others have been quick to remind me. But that isn't our concern right now. An hour ago, Mr.

Blackerby informed me of a racoon he had to put down. One of the dairy maids saw it behind the cowshed. It was foaming at the mouth and acting in a peculiar way, a strong indication that it had rabies."

Aunt Mary pressed her hand to her chest. "Good gracious, what frightening news. I hope the disease wasn't spread to other animals."

"So do I. Mr. Blackerby has instructed the farm laborers to keep an eye out. I've sent a message to Philip as well. The church-wardens will post signs to alert the villagers."

"Well, we mustn't take any chances," Grandmama Louise said. "Mary, you and I will have to curtail our afternoon walks until the danger has passed."

"That's wise," Geneva said. "On a brighter note, I've been thinking about hosting a special dinner in the near future. We could invite friends and community members to celebrate Ravensmere returning to normal, and the completion of the new barn. For entertainment, I thought I could hire the bagpiper and Scottish dancers from Ingleford. We could invite our servants and farm laborers for refreshments in the servants' quarters, and entertainment in the Great Hall—our way of expressing thanks for their help in fighting the fire."

"Excellent idea," Tess said. "We must invite my parents. A Scotsman like my father would love it. And I'll need a new dress for the occasion." She smiled down at her now well-rounded mid-riff. "None of those I have will fit anymore."

"So should I," Katherine added. "And don't forget about the Fairfaxes' winter ball. We'll need new gowns for that as well."

"Well, my dears, time is marching along," Aunt Mary put in. "Shall we plan a visit to the draper's shop tomorrow? I'm longing to see the latest fabrics."

"I'd love to go," Grandmama Louise said. "How about you, Geneva? You have only one ball gown. You'll need another for spring and summer events."

Geneva lowered her eyes. After her inner realization in the bath, she'd regretted increasingly that she'd agreed to have Jack as her escort to the Fairfaxes' ball. Nor did she want to think about more expensive clothing considering the needs on and off the estate.

"It sounds like a nice outing. But I'd rather not spend the day in Ingleford. I need to see Cousin Philip regarding Gus McGavin's burial. I've offered to pay for it."

"We're not going to Ingleford," Aunt Mary responded. "The draper's shop is in Porthaven. If you must see Philip, do it in the morning. We won't leave until after luncheon."

Geneva perked up. "I didn't know the shop was in Porthaven."

"Now you do," Tess said. "It's the best in the district for imported fabrics. Won't you come? After shopping, we'll collect my mother and have tea at Aunt Lydia's home."

Geneva rubbed her chin pensively. Daniel had promised to make inquiries about Nicholas Drake's fishing boat in Porthaven. Since she'd received no word from him, this would be a chance to do her own investigation. With the women focused on fabrics, she could walk to the docks and ask if anyone knew of him.

"Well, yes, I think I will come," she said with a smile. "I do hope the weather is fine."

The following afternoon, the Eversons' barouche carriage descended a hill and entered the narrow, winding streets of

Porthaven. Timber-framed buildings towered on both sides of the street. Laundry hung in dimly lit alleyways, and black-clad businessmen made haste as they dodged between shoppers and kidney pie vendors.

The carriage turned onto Mortimer Avenue, an elegant quarter of the seaport with classic Georgian buildings and specialty shops—an apothecary, a tobacconist, chandlers, milliners, and a sweet shop. At the end of the avenue, a sign elaborately painted in black, white, and gold announced: Ashley & Whittington ~ Domestic & Imported Fabrics.

"Ah, here we are," Aunt Mary announced. "Come along, ladies. I wonder what new delights are awaiting us."

Geneva followed her companions into the shop. It was definitely a popular place by the long queue of women making their purchases. Shelves and compartments rose from the floor to the ceiling, all filled with bolts of fabric in every texture and color imaginable. Hanging from rods, swathes of sample fabrics invited customers to touch the luxury of Indian sari silk, dazzling velvet, and the pearly sheen of satin.

Geneva tagged along cheerfully, but when the opportunity arose, she took Tess aside. "I noticed the harbor is just around the corner. I think I'll go for a stroll and a breath of fresh air."

"No, Geneva, you shouldn't go on your own. Wait and we'll all go together."

"That's not necessary. I walked all around Shaftesbury by myself. I'll be back before you're finished here."

The dock proved a short walk from the shop. The U-shaped harbor was a sight to behold with numerous fishing boats anchored in the sparkling water. A stone jetty protected the harbor's entrance, and not far from where Geneva stood, two cargo ships were tied up with dockside workers hauling crates into warehouses. Further down the dock, more fishing boats were tied up in threes with their broadsides parallel to the quay.

Geneva headed toward the fishing boats, clutching her bonnet against a gust of wind laced with the fresh smell of fish, salt, and seaweed. She passed a fishmonger with mackerel, pilchards, and crabs displayed in the window, then an industrial compound where masons hammered and chiseled massive rectangular stones. A sign above an office door read N. R. Spooner. This must be the stone shipping enterprise Jack's friend Nigel Spooner had inherited from his father.

Once Geneva reached the fishing boats, she approached several fishermen who were mending their nets. At her query, they shook their heads. On the far side of a group of three boats, an older man was scrubbing the deck of his boat with a long-handled brush. Clearing her throat, Geneva shouted above the clink of rigging and the squeak of timbers rubbing together, "Excuse me, sir, I'm looking for a fishing boat owner, Nicholas Drake. Do you know of him?"

The man straightened from his scrubbing to shout back. "Nicholas Drake? I sure do, the dirty, thieving rat! Haven't seen him in years. But you'll find his uncle, Dwight Martin, further up the dock. Green boat called *Zephyr*. He might be able to tell you more."

"Thank you, sir. I'm much obliged." Her hopes raised, Geneva pulled her cloak tight against the wind and continued on until she reached a boat with peeling green paint moored directly to the dock. Its name was so faded Geneva could barely make out the letters Z-E-P---R. On its deck, an elderly man with a long, straggly beard was sitting on a sea chest, gutting fish.

"Good afternoon, sir," Geneva called out. "I'm sorry to interrupt you, but are you Dwight Martin?"

The man set his gutting knife down. "And if I am?"

"Well, I'm looking for a man named Nicholas Drake. I was told Mr. Martin was his uncle. Do you know where I could find him? I need to speak with him concerning a private matter."

The man picked up his knife and returned to work. "Can't answer that, miss. I disowned my nephew twenty-two years ago."

Geneva walked a few steps closer. "I'm sorry to hear that. You must have had a good reason."

Mr. Martin shot a cold glance at her. "You bet I did. I found out he was stealing from my cash box. If you're a friend of his, that doesn't make me think so highly of you!"

"Well, I don't think much of him either. He brought terrible grief to someone close to me. Do his parents live nearby?"

"Nope, they died when he was a boy. That's when my wife and I adopted him."

Geneva waited for him to say more, but the old fisherman just picked up another fish and sliced off its head. "I don't mean to pry, Mr. Martin. This is important to me. If you could share more, I'd be very grateful."

"Very well, miss, if it means that much, I'll tell you what I can." Mr. Martin tossed the fish into a basin. "I have no sons, only girls. So I was glad to have a nephew who could help on my boat. I sent him to school, and I taught him everything to do with fishing, sailing, and navigation. From the start, he was a lazy lout. But when I found out he was a thief as well, that was it. He was eighteen by then, so I had no qualms in throwing him out to fend for himself."

"I don't blame you for being angry," Geneva said. "You were like a father to him. I've heard that he now has a fishing boat. Do you know anything about that?"

"So I've heard. That was a good five, six years after he left. Word gets around when someone has a big windfall at the racecourse. I guess he used the money to buy the fishing boat." The old fisherman gazed across the harbor. "Where's the justice in this world when lazy thieves prosper?"

"Would you happen to know the boat's name?" Geneva asked. "That would help in my search for your nephew."

Mr. Martin pulled on his beard. "It's been a long time, you know. Sorry, but if I ever knew the name, I can't remember."

"Well, at least I have more information than I started with. Thank you so much for taking time to speak with me."

Rising to his feet, he tipped his battered hat. "You're a nice lady, miss. Good luck with your search."

Geneva headed back up the waterfront toward the fabric shop. But she hadn't gone far when she heard a shout behind her. "Stop, miss! I remember now."

Geneva turned and headed back to the *Zephyr*. Mr. Martin leaned out over the railing, his eyes bright as he called out, "It just came to me. His boat was named after a constellation in the sky, *Cassiopeia*."

A huge smile broke out on Geneva's face. "Thank you, Mr. Martin. This will really help. God bless you!"

As she set off once more, Geneva's mind swirled. With this information, it shouldn't be hard for Daniel to find Drake. Harbor offices kept accurate records of moored boats and their owners. The purchase of the boat must have been after her mother was expelled from the manor, as he'd been working then as a coachman.

Given Drake's dishonest nature as a thief, could the supposed racecourse windfall have been a lie? Had he stolen the fishing boat, if that sort of thing was even possible? If so, it would have given him a good livelihood. Hopefully, Daniel would find that boat.

Geneva returned to the fabric shop just as Burrows was carrying the rest of the party's purchases to the carriage. Aunt Mary waved a hand as Geneva approached. "There you are. Gracious, your cheeks are red. I hope you didn't go too far."

"No, Aunt Mary, just far enough to see what I wanted. Are we going to Mrs. Northcott's home now? A hot cup of tea will do me good."

Four days later, on Saturday afternoon, Geneva was expecting Daniel to visit her on the farm for a private conversation regarding Nicholas Drake. For the past hour, she and Mrs. Fox had decided on a menu for the upcoming banquet. With some time before Daniel's arrival, she had gone to the kitchen to collect fresh baked fruit buns for the construction workers at the barn site.

Mrs. Fox followed behind her, sniffing the sweet aroma still lingering in the air. As she watched Geneva filling her basket, she turned to the cook. "My goodness, Lily, this reminds me of the days when you baked fruit buns for Billy Jasper. He worked long hours in the stables, and like most growing boys, was often hungry."

"Yes, I remember the little tyke," Lily said, wiping her hands on her apron. "What a shame he departed without saying goodbye. If he'd stayed with us, he might have risen through the ranks to coachman."

Geneva noted the doleful expression on the housekeeper's face. "You have a kind heart, Mrs. Fox. I can see you still miss the lad."

Placing a clean cloth over the buns, Geneva made her way to the farmyard. Since the fire six days ago, every vestige of the barn's charred remains had been hauled away in wagons. Now the construction was moving forward. Masons were laying stone and mortar on the original foundation. Not far from them, Jack had spread the blueprints on a pile of lumber for Mr. Blackerby to peruse.

Geneva lifted the cloth from her basket. "Good afternoon, gentlemen, will you have a fruit bun fresh from the oven?"

"Thank you, miss," Mr. Blackerby said. "I don't mind if I do."

After Jack and Mr. Blackerby helped themselves, Geneva carried the basket to the masons, who grinned as they reached into the basket with dusty hands. Once she'd made the rounds, she walked back to study the blueprints. "It's different from the original barn."

"That's right," Jack said. "This one has a central porch with four bays and an upper floor. Unlike the old thatched roof, this one will have slate tiles."

"That's good, less likely to burn. It was nice to see you, gentlemen."

"Our pleasure," Mr. Blackerby said. "It's unlikely we'll have further unrest and damages with Captain Everson's preventative measures in place."

Geneva still had buns in her basket. Circling around the dairy, she found the wattle fence makers busy in their workshop. Harry Whipple tipped his hat to her. "Good afternoon, Miss Geneva. Let me introduce our new apprentices. This is Clive Sykes and his brothers Cory and Fred."

Geneva smiled at the three newcomers and set her basket onto the worktable. "Lovely to meet you, and welcome to Ravensmere. Do help yourselves to a fruit bun."

Just then, Geneva heard a familiar baritone voice behind her. "Is there enough for a visitor?"

Geneva turned as Daniel walked up to the table. "I got your message, Geneva. Mr. Blackerby said I'd find you here." He broke off to greet each of the wattle fence makers with a handshake. To Geneva, he looked even more handsome than usual in his black top hat, brown overcoat, and toffee-colored boots with a light splatter of mud.

"Mr. Cavendish is the deputy trustee for the estate," she commented. "It was his idea to expand the business and hire additional workers."

"Thank you for that, sir," Clive said. "It's a privilege to learn a trade."

"Well, it's a profitable one," Daniel responded. "And I've heard good reports on the quality. Sales are doing exceptionally well at the market. You've earned this job by your own hard work. All of you. Ravensmere is blessed to have you working here." Daniel turned to Geneva. "Miss Geneva, I'm sure these men want to get on with their work. You had something you wanted to discuss with me. Shall we take a stroll?"

Leaving the farmyard behind, Geneva walked with Daniel through a coppice of birches where only a smattering of yellow leaves still clung to the limbs. Heavy clouds had moved in, but the air was still except for the gurgling sounds of starlings. Daniel smiled down at Geneva. "So what happened in Porthaven? I'm waiting with bated breath. Your note sounded mysterious—and pleased."

"Well, both of those are true. I learned more about Nicholas Drake, though a mystery still remains as to where he is." Geneva related her encounter with Mr. Martin.

"Well done!" Daniel said when she finished. "I couldn't have done better. I'll be out of town on business much of this coming week. But as my work allows, I'll inquire at the harbor offices, starting with Porthaven. If nothing fruitful comes from that, I'll check St. Aubrey."

Geneva clasped her hands together. "Goodness, you're so helpful. I couldn't ask for a better friend."

Daniel's eyes twinkled with an affectionate smile. "Well, I confess that I think of you often. Especially at the bank, my mind wanders to thoughts of you."

"Really? I do the same. I think of you playing your grand piano in the bay window at Wyncombe Hall."

"Well, isn't that interesting. I spend hours there. You know, Geneva, I truly believe God brought us together in Shaftesbury. If he can do that, then let's trust him to help us with this quest to find Drake."

Geneva peeled off a papery-thin piece of bark from a birch. "I've had thoughts about what you said at the market—that God never abandons us. I was foolish to think he had. I want to have a close walk with Jesus, but something keeps holding me back. I don't know what it is. Maybe it's a lack of faith."

"I can't help you with that, but God's Holy Spirit can." Reaching into his breast pocket, Daniel pulled out a tiny book. "Philip gave me this New Testament many years ago. You may already have a Bible, but this is one you can keep with you at all times. Having God's Word at my fingertips has been helpful in all kinds of situations. I hope it will help you as well."

Dropping the piece of bark, Geneva opened the well-used book. The print was small but perfectly legible. "I love this! Thank you for passing it on to me. I'll take good care of it."

She slipped the New Testament into the pocket in which she'd tucked Daniel's handkerchief that morning. It had become such a cherished keepsake that she moved it to a new pocket every time she changed her outfit. What would he think if he knew she carried it everywhere she went?

Just then, thunder sounded from the west. A moment later, the first drops of rain trickled down Geneva's face. Raising his collar, Daniel took her hand. "Come, if we don't make haste, you'll get soaked."

As they dashed through the coppice and up the path to the manor, the rain intensified. A down gust of wind tore at Geneva's bonnet, and a flash of lightning forked through the leaded skies. Reaching the rear courtyard, they took shelter in the cart shed where Daniel had left his horse Victor.

"Forgive me if I leave you now," Daniel shouted above the storm. "I have another appointment this afternoon."

"And you came all the way here just to speak with me?" Geneva exclaimed. "Of course, go. I would be most distressed to make you late."

Mounting Victor, Daniel smiled at the raindrops glistening on Geneva's cheeks. "Goodbye, Geneva. Stay strong in God's Word. He'll help us find that coachman."

CHAPTER TWENTY-THREE

Near the end of November, the family had gathered in the drawing room for their coffee after dinner. Jack was gone to Ingleford for dinner and a meeting with his political cronies. Robert and Tess were occupied with a game of backgammon. Since Geneva wasn't interested in her grandmother's chatter with Aunt Mary about gowns for the Fairfaxes' winter ball, she opened her tiny New Testament. Yesterday, she'd read a passage from the epistle of James that seemed to contradict conventional wisdom. But God's ways were higher than man's ways, so she wanted to read it once more.

> My brethren, count it all joy when ye fall into divers
> temptations; knowing that the testing of your faith pro-
> duces patience. But let patience have its perfect work,
> that you may be perfect and complete, lacking nothing.

Since Daniel had given her this book three weeks ago, she'd certainly needed patience. So far, he'd been unsuccessful in finding either Nicholas Drake or his fishing boat. Rather than giving in to discouragement during the gloomy days of November, Geneva had kept herself and the household cheerful with her frequent flute playing.

As Geneva read her Bible passage once more, Stanway appeared at the door. He addressed himself to Robert. "Sorry to interrupt, but Mr. Blackerby is here, sir. He wishes to speak with you."

"By all means, bring him in."

The estate bailiff stepped in, taking care to avoid the carpet with his muddy boots. Robert frowned as he rose from the backgammon game to greet him. "What is it, Mr. Blackerby? You look as if you've seen a ghost."

"I wish it was that simple, sir. Do you remember the raccoon I put down three weeks ago?"

"I remember," Aunt Mary piped up. "It had rabies. Gracious, don't tell us the disease has spread!"

"I regret to say you're right, Mrs. Everson. It's my dog, Max. He must have received a small bite. We didn't notice at the time, but today he began showing symptoms, drooling and acting aggressively."

Aunt Mary threw up her hands in horror. "Heaven help us, this is the worst news possible! Our banquet is only five days away. No one will dare to step out of their homes with a rabid dog on the loose!"

"I'm aware of that, ma'am," Mr. Blackerby replied. "I knew I had to put him down. I told my son to go inside and fetch the shotgun. But in the meantime, Max was so agitated and aggressive we couldn't hold him. Not without getting bitten ourselves. We chased after him until we lost sight of him down a cart track."

"Good grief, our entire community is in danger." Robert was already heading for the door as he spoke. "Have you notified the authorities?"

"Not yet, sir. I wanted to inform Captain Everson first thing, but Stanway tells me he is not home, so I thought I should inform you. My thought was to form a search party with every available man on the estate. Those of us who have shotguns should take them. The rest should arm themselves with a pitchfork or some other instrument for defence. We also need to send someone to notify the village as well as the authorities."

"An excellent plan," Robert said. "I'll have Burrows alert the chief constable. If Max isn't found within a few hours, I'll send word to Captain Everson in Ingleford. Meanwhile, let's get those search parties organized. The good news is that if Max is indeed infected, he will not be drawn to where there are people, noise, and light. He will seek a quiet hiding place."

Robert turned to the other family members. "I'm sure I don't need to tell anyone here to remain indoors until the threat is over."

The three men left the room to a chorus of assent. But Geneva's frantic thoughts raced to her cat. Pookie had eaten his supper at five. Then he'd gone outside for his night prowl. Every night was pretty much the same. Well before midnight, he would climb up the magnolia and wriggle through her bedroom window. A rabid dog was a threat to every creature, including her cat. The thought of losing him to such a dreaded sickness was more than she could bear.

Standing up, she announced, "I'm very concerned for Pookie. I need to find him and bring him inside where he's safe."

"Are you out of your mind?" Aunt Mary screeched. "Cats can look after themselves. You heard what Robert said. You're to stay indoors."

"No, Aunt Mary, any good cat owner would take precautions. Grandmama Louise, you love Pookie. Don't you agree?"

The old lady fiddled with the rings on her fingers. "I understand your sentiments, dear. But Robert is right and Samuel would agree that your safety is more important than the cat. Why don't you play the flute for us? That will calm you down."

Geneva pursed her lips. "Really, that's the last thing I feel like doing."

"Why don't you come and play backgammon with me," Tess suggested.

Geneva shook her head. "I'm sorry to be a poor sport, but I'm not in the mood for games. If you'll excuse me, I'd rather go up and have an early night. I'll see you in the morning."

Geneva made haste up the staircase. Her family members didn't understand. During the last five years of her tumultuous life with Uncle Alex, Pookie had been her only genuine source of comfort and joy. So whatever it took, she was going to find her beloved pet and secure his safety.

In her bedroom, Geneva changed from her evening gown to her woolen work dress. As she donned her bonnet, she peered out the window to the forest beyond her father's garden. The night was breezy with a waxing moon casting silver light on the swaying treetops. That forest was Pookie's territory now. He'd likely sharpened his claws on almost every tree, not to mention springing on slithering snakes and chasing rabbits and mice into their dens beneath tree roots. Without a doubt, that's where she'd find him.

Geneva tiptoed down the staircase. In the dining room, she slipped out the French doors and made her way to the gate in the walled garden. Stepping through, she crossed the grass and pushed through low-hanging cedar limbs. The forest floor was carpeted with fallen leaves. Only a few coniferous trees and naked limbs of ash trees blocked the moonlight. Glad to have this light, Geneva made her way deeper into the forest, calling softly, "Here, Pookie! Here, Pookie!"

Pookie knew her voice. If he was there, he'd come right away. She strained her ears for an answering mew. But she heard nothing except the moaning wind, the creaking of branches rub-bing together, and the crackle of dry leaves beneath her steps. Fur-ther on, she heard the plaintive hoot of an owl, then a loud crack followed by a swishing sound as a limb fell to the ground just a few paces away from her.

Panicked, Geneva plunged through the trees in the opposite direction. The tree trunks and branches were now thick enough she no longer had the meager light of the moon as guide, and she suddenly realized she had no idea how far she'd come or in which direction the manor lay. At any moment, the tossing, creak-ing branches overhead could drop another limb, and maybe this time it wouldn't miss. Perhaps Grandmama Louise had been right about the foolishness of this venture.

A snorting sound increased Geneva's fear. What if that was a rabid Max out there? Holding her breath, she listened. The snort came again—unmistakably a horse's snort. Moments later, she heard men's voices deep within the forest, then caught a twinkle of light flickering among the trees.

She let out her breath in a whoosh of relief. This must be one of the search parties Robert and Mr. Blackerby had sent out. If she could make her way toward them, they would help her find her way out of this wilderness. She moved cautiously toward the light, which retreated ahead of her as though someone was carrying a lantern.

The forest opened up abruptly so that the moon shed silver light ahead. No more than a dozen paces ahead, Geneva instantly recognized the outcropping where she'd discovered the tunnel exit. Off to the right, she saw the yellow glow of the lantern she'd been following. In fact, there was more than one lantern, along with the horses and men she'd heard. Three packhorses and three men, to be exact.

But instead of hurrying over with relief to join them, Geneva hesitated under the cover of a fir sapling. This was definitely not one of the search parties Robert had sent out. Not with the pair of crates roped firmly to each packhorse's back. Good heavens, it was Jack and his friend Nigel Spooner. What were they doing in the woods at this hour of night? Obviously something more important than the political meeting Jack had claimed to be attending.

Both men were dressed in smart overcoats and leather boots. But a third man she'd never seen before looked to be of a lower class. He wore a scruffy oilskin coat and rubber boots, and his long, messy hair was tied back with a leather cord. The three men were all standing in front of the netting that hid the entrance into Sir Callum's underground tunnel, their lanterns set on the grass at their feet. Geneva had no doubt that whatever was in those crates had been brought here for transport into the tunnel. Why had it not occurred to her that Jack was the most likely person in the household to know about the underground cavern?

Geneva debated moving into the open. As mistress of Ravensmere, she had every right to be here. But she could only imagine Jack's reaction to her being out alone in the woods at this hour. He might even think she was spying on him. No, better to wait until the men left. At least she now knew where she was and had no concerns about finding her way back.

Jack pulled out a large black key from his pocket. "Let's get this shipment inside. We're running late thanks to your French captain's tardy arrival."

Nigel was already lifting a crate. "Considering the sea conditions, I wasn't sure the *Étoile Polaire* would arrive at all. We should count ourselves fortunate. And Mr. Boisseau's letter promises another shipment within the month. That is far more than I anticipated."

"The challenge will be finding buyers for such bounty." Jack swung around as the third man let a crate drop to the ground with an audible thump. "Not so careless, Drake! I warned you tonight's goods are exceptionally fragile. If anything is damaged, believe me it will come out of your pocket."

"I've never broken anything yet," the man muttered with sullen insolence. "Not like some I could name!"

"You're getting full of yourself, Drake," Jack responded furiously. "That Ming bowl was cracked when I opened the box, as the buyer witnessed. Maybe you dropped that too. I should have taken it out of your hide instead of covering the loss myself."

The man answered with equal fury. "And maybe you're full of yourself too! You don't own me just because of . . ."

"Of what?" Jack stepped closer. "You think that I don't own you? That you can turn on me now? Should I remind you about the *kid*?"

For a moment, the two men stood chest to chest, glaring into each other's faces. It wasn't Jack who conceded first. Taking a step back, Drake shrugged. "Ah yes, the kid. Well, it goes two ways, doesn't it? I know plenty of things about you, Captain Jack Everson."

Stepping in between the two men, Nigel Spooner said calmly, "Hey, let's settle down. We can't afford to turn on each other now. In twenty-two years, we've had one loss. And we wouldn't be here without Nicholas."

"You mean, without his boat!" Jack muttered, lifting the net of vegetation. "Just keep in mind, Drake, there are other boats. You aren't irreplaceable, twenty-two years or not!"

Jack disappeared behind the net. The other two men followed, each carrying a crate. In a state of shock, Geneva braced herself against a tree trunk. Could she possibly have heard wrong? No! The names Nicholas and Drake had been spoken loud and clear.

The conversation had made it clear that these men had been associated for longer than Geneva had drawn breath.

The terrible truth hit Geneva so hard that hot tears rolled down her cheeks. Jack had lied to her when she'd asked about Nicholas Drake's whereabouts and what had happened that terrible night. He'd been working with Drake before her parents were married! Even before Drake became Ravensmere's coachman. What a betrayal to his uncle Adam who had been his benefactor and father figure for many long years. No possible excuse could justify such treachery and disloyalty.

Geneva wiped her tears away with Daniel's hanky. At least her search for Nicholas Drake was over, and now she longed to pour out the news into Daniel's sympathetic ear. Hopefully she would see him at church tomorrow. Meanwhile, she needed to make her escape before the three men emerged for another load. The outcropping had given her the necessary direction back through the forest to the garden wall.

Once she was far enough from the outcropping, Geneva resumed her soft calls for Pookie. She received no response, but when she finally emerged from the forest, a movement in the tall grass near the garden gate caught her eye. She froze when the movement coalesced into two glowing eyes. Almost immediately, she realized the eyes were too close together to be a rabid dog. "Pookie? Is that you?"

To Geneva's relief, her cat sprang from his hiding place. A fat mouse held in his jaws, he trotted over and dropped the lifeless creature at her feet. "Oh, Pookie, you're the best hunter. But, my goodness, do I have a tale to tell you!"

The next morning after the Sunday service, parishioners strolled outside to greet one another. Conversations abounded concerning Mr. Blackerby's poor dog Max. Within an hour, the search party had been successful in putting him down near the quarry. Philip had offered a prayer of thanks for the swift resolution, and the villagers had gladly resumed their normal activities.

Approaching Geneva, Daniel tipped his hat with a warm smile. "A good day to you, Geneva. Will you walk with me to my grandmother's headstone? It's been a while since I paid my respects, and I have some news you'll want to hear."

Geneva's face brightened. "I'd be delighted. Were you close to your grandmother?"

"Yes, very much so. Her love of the piano rubbed off on me."

At the grave site, he removed his hat. Geneva waited patiently while he stood in silence for several long moments. Then he stepped back from the grave and turned to her. "I mentioned I had news. You'll be interested to hear what happened yesterday."

"I have news to share as well. I learned something shocking on Friday. But you go first. I'm all ears."

Daniel settled his hat on his head. "Well, I went to my music practice in St. Aubrey as I always do on Saturday mornings. I was walking along the harbor wall with my horse when I noticed a fishing boat with the name *Golden Hind*. I thought nothing of it until I realized it might be Mr. Drake's boat."

"Why would you think that?" Geneva asked, puzzled. "His uncle said the boat's name is *Cassiopeia*."

"I'm aware of that, but the boat's original name had been painted over. I know because I was daring enough to scrape off a patch of paint with my pocket knife. The under layer showed the first three letters of the original name—C-A-S."

Geneva shook her head, even more puzzled. "I don't under-stand. Why did you even think to scrape the paint? What are you saying?"

Daniel's eyes twinkled down at her. "Think of history, Geneva. What was the name of Sir Francis Drake's galleon that he used to circumnavigate the world?"

"The *Golden Hind!*" Geneva's mouth fell open. "Of course! Drake fancied himself as a descendent of Sir Francis Drake. It makes perfect sense he'd choose that name."

"Exactly. Which is why I checked at the harbor office for the second time. *Golden Hind* was registered in the books, but the owner's name was recorded as Nick Dawson."

"Dawson? Do you think the owner is really Nicholas Drake, and he used a false name?"

"We can't be sure, but that fits the facts. If I can return to the boat when the owner is present, I could confirm the identity."

"This is incredible!" Geneva's breathing quickened. "I am sure you are right because on Friday night I learned that Drake was here at Ravensmere, and he most definitely has a boat. Let me tell you the things I've discovered."

Daniel listened with transfixed attention as Geneva described her discovery of the underground cavern, priest hole, and tunnels her reading had uncovered. She went on to tell how she'd stumbled upon the three men unloading goods in the forest and what she'd overheard. He shook his head in disbelief when she finished.

"I have never heard a whisper or rumor of tunnels under Ravensmere. But it's not surprising considering the manor's his-tory of smuggling. That secret was probably passed only from master to heir. Or maybe Jack uncovered that knowledge in the records as you did. Really, Geneva, I am astounded at your daring to go underground by yourself. I wish you had told me so I could have been with you. As to this news of Nicholas Drake, I am sorry for the pain this has caused you. Jack has indeed betrayed you grievously. A business connection with Nigel Spooner is understandable. Jack and Nigel have been close friends since school days. But I'm troubled that Jack has had a working relationship with Nicholas Drake since before the incident with your mother. The fact that it continues despite the dishonor Drake brought to your household certainly raises questions."

"That is what came to my mind." Geneva's voice shook with emotion. "If Jack was friends with this man when he testified as to my mother's immorality, the implications are horrendous. I must speak with that horrid man and find out what really happened with my mother. I'll ask Burrows to drive me to the docks at St. Aubrey. If Drake is there with the *Golden Hind* I will demand that he tell me the truth of that night."

"That is not a good idea," Daniel said firmly. "I understand how you feel. But confronting him in person is not the answer. He wouldn't admit to any wrongdoing. He could even become violent. I know what my father would say about permitting you to take such a dangerous step."

Geneva released a quick breath. "Then what was the point of searching for him?"

"All is not ended. Let me do some further inquiry as to the *Golden Hind* and its owner. I will speak with my father about pursuing Mr. Drake. His connections with Jack put a whole new light on the events of your mother's departure. He'll agree that needs to be explored."

Daniel looked unsmilingly down at Geneva. "But for your own protection, this must be done discreetly. If the man is hiding some guilt, we don't want him forewarned. As your guardian, your safety is my father's responsibility—and mine. When the time comes, I will accompany you to interrogate this man. But please promise me you will not attempt it on your own until I've had time for inquiries."

Geneva's shoulders slumped. "Yes, I'll wait provided it isn't too long."

Her face brightened somewhat. "In the meantime, I could go underground again. Maybe I will find something that sheds light on their activities and Nicholas Drake's connection to them."

Daniel's expression grew alarmed. "That is dangerous too, should they discover your snooping around." He paused thought-fully. "But an examination of just what they are up to would be helpful. If you are determined to do it, may I request the honor of accompanying you? I have no work afield this week. If you can find a time when Jack is not likely to stumble over us, just send me a note and I will ride over immediately."

Geneva's smile was now full strength. "Believe me, I have no great desire to go alone. Yes, Daniel, I will do that gladly."

CHAPTER TWENTY-FOUR

The following morning, Geneva left Mrs. Fox's sitting room, the two having completed their selection of desserts for the banquet. As she passed the butler's pantry, Geneva noticed Stanway had just begun cleaning the silverware, a task that took an hour or more. At breakfast, Jack had mentioned that he was heading to the Bell and Crown Inn for an eleven o'clock meeting concerning a quarry contract for an addition to the church in St. Aubrey. On hearing that, Geneva had immediately sent a note to Daniel asking him to meet her at the outside door to the wine cellar.

Geneva donned her winter jacket. Crossing the Great Hall and ante room, she took two steps down to the wine cellar. After entering with the master key, she locked it behind her, crossed the cellar, and unlocked the door leading outside. With it left ajar for Daniel's arrival, she was lighting two lanterns with a candle when she heard him arrive.

Daniel's greeting was warm with a hint of excitement as he stepped in. "I got your message. Are you sure it's safe to go down?"

"Oh, yes," she said eagerly, locking the door. "Stanway is busy in the butler's pantry. Robert is studying birds at Mr. Fairfax's estate, and the ladies have driven into Ingleford to shop for winter bonnets."

Daniel looked around with interest as Geneva retrieved the screwdriver she'd used before. "So where is this mysterious fossil?"

Geneva crouched down near the inside wall and placed her finger next to it. Daniel stooped over. "Ah, you are right, the perfect V shape. I'm amazed you deciphered the clue and found it all on your own. But please, let me go first. I'm not taking any chances with your safety."

Lifting the screwdriver from her hand, Daniel levered the trapdoor open, his handsome face alive with interest. Taking one of the lanterns, he descended the ladder. At the bottom, he opened the door that led into the tunnel. "This is truly fascinating. I wish I'd known about it when I was a child. What an adventure to explore what lies down here."

Geneva climbed down and eased the trapdoor shut above her. "There really isn't that much to explore. Just two tunnels and the cavern."

Geneva followed at Daniel's heels as they headed down the cold, dank passageway. With the light of two lanterns, she could see giant spiders scurrying across the arched ceiling. Their dark, hairy bodies and long legs made Geneva shiver. Daniel heard her footsteps faltering and looked back. "Are you all right?"

"Yes, just barely. I don't know which is worse—rats or spiders."

Pressing on a short distance, they came to the T-junction. Geneva gestured. "We turn right here. The tunnel straight ahead is a long one that leads to the exit door in the forest. If they brought goods inside for storage, they'll have carried them this way."

When they came to the cavern door, about twenty-five feet ahead, Daniel grasped the iron ring and pulled. As before, it was unlocked. Lantern held high, Daniel stepped through and walked around, taking in the simple furnishings and statue of St. Mary.

Geneva stepped in after him. The cavern was more crowded than when she had first entered. Six crates had been placed along the far wall, to the left of the tilting beam. Half of them were unopened. The other three were filled with crumpled-up news-papers and rags. What appeared to have been their contents had been set out on the table and covered with a white cloth.

"So what are we looking for?" Daniel made a 360-degree turn to survey the entire cavern.

Geneva approached the table and peered under the corner of the cloth. "My goodness, this for one. These must be the goods from Mr. Boisseau that Jack mentioned." Eyes bright with awe she pulled back the cloth carefully. "I never dreamed of anything like this!"

The light of her lantern illuminated the most glorious collection of perfume bottles. Some were decorated with gold ornamentation and precious stones. Others were enameled in vibrant colors and delicately painted floral sprays. Placing his own lantern on the table, Daniel picked up a snuff box studded with emeralds and diamonds. "I believe these things are what the French call *objets d'art*, generally owned by the very wealthy."

There were more snuff boxes along with an array of exotic pocket watches. Geneva admired the craftsmanship of mantel clocks with gold cherubim, porcelain figurines of French nobles, and miniature landscape paintings of the French Riviera. But after a few moments, she straightened up.

"Daniel, I don't understand. These things must have cost a fortune. How would Jack or Mr. Spooner pay for such costly shipments? Perhaps Mr. Spooner has such funds, but as far as I know, Jack has only his allowance and wages as estate manager."

"Yes, I'm baffled as well." Daniel stepped back from the table. "But there is nothing untoward here that I can see. If Jack and Nigel Spooner are transhipping goods from a French vessel to Drake's fishing boat, that is ordinary enough. But why at night by horseback to this hidden location? Why not simply sail up to the dock in Porthaven and unload? Nigel's offices are there. It would be far simpler."

Picking up his lantern, Daniel walked around the room, running his hand over the tilting beam, checking under the altar, around the prayer desk, and inside the two trunks. "Well, I don't see any ledgers or written documents here. If there were, it would give us insight into this business or Drake's connection. If we've seen everything, Geneva, I think it best we leave before we risk being discovered. All this certainly raises further concerns. First, Jack's unethical behavior in working with your disgraced former coachman. But also why bring these goods here in secret if their business is above board? Smuggling may have been part of Ravensmere's past, but none of these items are illegal to import openly."

Daniel helped Geneva lift the cloth over the costly items on the table. "What do we do next?" she said worriedly.

Daniel's smile was kind. "For you, nothing. I will do further investigations regarding the identity of Nick Dawson and the origin of the *Golden Hind*. But I will also see what I can find out about this Mr. Boisseau and his ship that brought the goods. The *Étoile Polaire*, you said? Meantime, carry on as you normally would, and please be discreet in anything you do or say that could put your cousin on alert."

Geneva picked up her own lantern. "Oh, I'll be discreet, all right. And I'll be patient while you make your inquiries. But I do need to speak with Jack on a personal matter. And don't worry, it has nothing to do with Nicholas Drake."

Later that afternoon, Geneva perused the long table set up in the Great Hall. Twenty-three seats were required for the banquet to be held tomorrow. After luncheon, she'd gone outdoors to pick stems of yellow witch hazel and hellebores in pink and speckled white. The winter florals looked wonderful in eight crystal vases placed on the starched white tablecloth. For an added flair of greenery, Stanway had helped her adorn the windows and doorways with garlands and swags of English ivy.

Over the last week, the invitations had been sent, the menu finalized, and the seating carefully determined according to protocol. But even the enjoyment of flower arranging had not eased Geneva's distress over Jack's betrayal of her trust in him. It felt like an ongoing slap on the face to know he was in regular contact with the man who had torn her parents' marriage apart and left people's lives in shambles.

Geneva smoothed out a wrinkle in the tablecloth and checked the time. Just a few minutes prior, Jack had walked down to his office. Now would be as good a time as any to speak with him. Before she could lose her resolve, Geneva hurried down the main hallway. Jack's office door stood open. Stepping inside, she found him working at his desk. "Cousin Jack, may I have a word with you?"

"Yes, of course, I can take a break." Laying down his pen, Jack stood up. "Let's make ourselves comfortable near the hearth."

As they took their seats in the wing chairs that flanked his celestial globe, he asked, "What is it, Cousin Geneva? Do you have concerns about the banquet?"

"No, that's all under control. I'm here regarding a personal matter between us."

His brow wrinkled. "Dear me, I hope I haven't been amiss with something."

Geneva twisted her hands in her lap. "It's not that. I want to apologize to you. I should have done it sooner, but time slips by so fast."

"Humph, I can't think of anything that would require an apology from you."

"It's concerning the birthday gift you gave me."

His eyebrows shot up. "Oh? You mean the pearl necklace?"

"Yes, I realize now I shouldn't have accepted it. It is far too expensive. It might have been different if I'd said yes to your marriage proposal, but I didn't, so I must return it to you." From her pocket, she pulled out the alabaster box containing the pearl necklace and placed it in Jack's hand.

Jack's eyes narrowed as his hand closed around the box. "This is completely unnecessary, Geneva. I hope you don't think I had ulterior motives in giving it to you. Your first birthday at Ravensmere was special. The gift was simply my way of honoring you."

"That may be, but it is still too much for me to accept. In any case, I've given it much thought, and I'm sorry to say that I cannot marry you. You have many admirable qualities, but we're not a good match. We wouldn't be happy. Our differences are too great."

Jack gave no immediate reply. He got up calmly, poured himself a shot of whiskey, and gazed out the window to the courtyard. Geneva threw a surreptitious glance at his desk, currently piled high with ledgers. Surely Jack must have some accounting for the goods she'd seen in the cavern, as he did for the estate transactions. Could Jack's private business ledger be among those he kept in this office? If so, they might reveal more about his relationship with Drake and their secret activities beneath Ravensmere. Maybe tonight if Jack went out again with his friends, she could slip in for a look.

Jack's face looked sorrowful and slightly pale when he finally turned around. He wiped at the corner of his eye as though brushing away an unbidden tear. "Well, Geneva, I must say I'm hurt and disappointed. I thought we were an excellent match with our common heritage, our love for the land, even our prosperous wattle fence business initiated by your bright imagination."

Sitting down again, he leaned over to take her right hand in his. "I shan't give up. I love you too much for that. We haven't known each other for long. Perhaps by summer you'll see things differently. And don't worry. There won't be any pressure on my part."

Straightening up, he glanced at the alabaster box on his desk. "You were quite right, my dear. I understand now. I was too ardent with the gift. I shall put it away and never lose hope."

His tone was sincere, his words persuasive. But this time Geneva refused to fall for his admitted charm. After seeing him with Nicholas Drake in the forest, how could she believe he cared for her and was not just trying to recoup his lost inheritance? She wanted to blurt out a demand that he explain his relationship with Drake, but Daniel had advised her to be discreet. Instead, she stood up and forced a smile.

"Well, I'm glad we've cleared this up without any hard feelings. If you'll excuse me, I must check with Mrs. Fox to see if our guests' table napkins have been ironed. Thank you for your time, Cousin Jack."

Feeling empowered by her actions, Geneva made her way to the housekeeper's sitting room. But before she reached it, Stanway intercepted her. "Miss Geneva, a letter has come for you in the post."

"Thank you, Stanway." Geneva immediately recognized her uncle's handwriting. Returning to the Great Hall, she sat at the head of the table and read the letter.

Dear Geneva,

Please excuse my atrocious handwriting. I'm in bed, propped up with pillows. Peggy has just brought my tea. She's been my housemaid since you left and invaluable during the last few weeks of my dreadful illness with the putrid throat. I knew death was just around the corner. The doctor made that clear. Somehow, I managed to survive. Geneva, I'm not ashamed to admit I was fearful of God's judgement awaiting me. In my suffering, I kept thinking about the past and how I treated you and your mother so badly. I am asking for your forgiveness for every harsh word and blow, especially the time you received that unseemly bruise on your forehead. Should you ever travel up this way, do drop by the pawnshop. I long to see you again to make my apologies in person. Best regards to you and your family.

Uncle Alex

Geneva got up and paced back and forth across the Great Hall. She was certainly relieved Uncle Alex had survived his illness. But what did he mean by the *bruise* on her forehead? Had he forgotten the doctor's visit and her cries of agony as the doctor sewed up the gaping wound with a needle and thread? She might forgive her uncle one day. But for now, it would have to wait.

Striding over to the fireplace, Geneva tossed the letter into the fire. As the flames rose up, she felt a twinge of remorse. But the feeling didn't last, and her thoughts turned to other things. Tonight, Lord willing, she would find Jack's private ledger. And tomorrow, she would host her first grand event at Ravensmere.

CHAPTER TWENTY-FIVE

Shortly after one in the morning, Geneva opened her lounge door and peered down the hallway. All was quiet, and not one light was visible beneath the bedroom doors. A shawl around her shoulders and a candlestick in her hand, she made her way down the stairs to Jack's office. Unlocking the door with her master key, Geneva stepped inside and locked it securely behind her. The room was chilly with just a few embers smoldering in the fireplace.

As she stood before Jack's desk, Geneva felt a pang of guilt. Not once had she ever snooped in her uncle's desk. She reminded herself that her reasons were not prying but virtuous. She sought only to find the truth about her mother, and Jack's lies had erased any obligation she felt to respect his privacy. After all, this office and its contents belonged to her, if not his personal correspondence. In this case, her intended end would have to justify the means.

Setting the candlestick on the worktable, Geneva opened the top right-hand drawer of the desk. As she expected, it contained the three ledgers Daniel and his father had audited. The lower drawer held numerous folders filled with rental papers, farming receipts, and reports from the Corn Exchange. On the other side, the drawers held six ledgers labelled Miscellaneous.

Placing the six ledgers on the worktable, Geneva sat down and began scanning their pages for anything pertaining to Mr.

Boisseau, the *Étoile Polaire*, lists of *objets d'art*, as Daniel had called them, or any mention of Nicholas Drake. By the time she'd gone through the last ledger without any success, she was not only disappointed but cold. Tightening her shawl around her shoulders, she stood near the fireplace, still warm enough for comfort.

Moments later, she was startled by the sudden half-hour chime of the brass mantel clock just inches from her face. As the tones lingered, she noticed something poking out from the back of the clock's brass base. Curious, she pulled it out—a chisel for carving wood, like ones she'd seen in her uncle's pawnshop. It seemed odd for Jack to keep such a tool behind the clock until she remembered the screwdriver she'd used to lift the trapdoor in the wine cellar. Of course! This must be Jack's version of that tool kept in a handy place for the same purpose.

Pushing it back into place, she looked around the office with a smile on her lips. The celestial globe was just a few feet away. She walked over until the globe was positioned at the same angle as she'd glimpsed it when she'd raised the trapdoor from the priest hole to see where it opened. This placed her beyond the perimeter of the Persian carpet on the flagstones shadowed by Jack's desk. Leaning close with her candlestick, she saw a similar crack to the one that marked the trapdoor in the wine cellar. One just wide enough to permit entry of the flat end of the chisel.

It was now very late and time to go up to bed. Tomorrow would be a taxing day with the banquet in the evening. Geneva returned the six ledgers to the drawers. As she was arranging them so they looked undisturbed, she thought she heard something. Holding her breath, she listened. Yes, there it was again—footsteps approaching rapidly down the main hallway. *It's just Stanway checking on something*, she tried to assure herself as she closed the bottom drawer. Heart thumping in her chest, she grabbed the chisel from behind the clock and placed her candlestick next to the trapdoor. Hands shaking, she lifted the trapdoor with the chisel and dashed back to the mantelpiece to slip it behind the clock.

The approaching footsteps were getting louder. Back at the priest hole, she lowered her legs into the hole. A key was rattling in the lock! It had to be Jack. She grabbed the candlestick, and scrambled down the rungs, tugging the trapdoor shut just as she heard the office door open.

Inside the stuffy confines of the priest hole, Geneva clung to the ladder, chest heaving for air and heart pounding madly. Had she been seen? Footsteps advanced across the carpeted floor and stopped. She waited with held breath. If those footsteps were Jack, surely he would not linger long at this hour of the night.

But to her shock, the next sound she heard was footsteps advancing toward the trapdoor. In renewed panic, Geneva scrambled down the rungs to the tilting beam that allowed access from the priest hole into the cavern. From the bottom she heard the trapdoor opening above. Heavy feet were coming down the ladder as she squeezed under the tilting beam. But as it settled back into place, the movement of air blew out her candle, leaving her in the dark.

Fighting back panic, Geneva let her fingers guide her along the wall until she bumped into one of the old trunks. She froze as lantern light emerged from the tilting beam. Falling silently to her knees, she crawled into the narrow space between the trunk and wall. Thankfully, this corner of the cavern remained in semi-darkness as the lantern's light flickered from the priest hole toward the worktable. Losing her own candlelight had proved a blessing.

As she dared to peek over the rim of the trunk, spying the tall man with a glint of light on ginger hair confirmed that it was indeed her cousin. Jack had easy access at any time from his office.

Why had he come down at this hour? He lifted the cloth and paused to finger some of the treasures on the worktable. Geneva suddenly realized the yellow light revealed far fewer items than had been there this morning when she and Daniel had explored here.

Picking up the lantern again, Jack walked over to the altar and reached into the niche that held the statue of St. Mary. Geneva couldn't see what he was doing, but a moment later she barely caught back a gasp. She had heard a clunk. Now a section on the wall was swinging open like a door, perfectly camouflaged in the rows of bricks and mortar.

Jack stepped through with his back to her. The lantern in his hand revealed a small chamber beyond, so small Geneva could see the far wall only a couple of paces beyond Jack's tall frame. Along with the tunnels and cavern used for smuggling, Sir Callum McCormack had evidently built an even more secret chamber for his private use. Could this be the information in Albert's journal that had been cut out with a sharp knife?

As Geneva watched, Jack placed the lantern on a table inside the chamber. Then he began pulling bank notes from his billfold. She could hear him counting to himself as he placed them one by one into a metal cash box. The missing precious items and Jack's presence at this late hour made sense. He must have delivered them to his buyers and was only now returning with his profits.

Jack closed the cash box and picked up a pen and a ledger. Turning the pages, he began to write. Despite her fear, elation filled Geneva. Daniel was right. It was logical for Jack to have a ledger to record his shipping transactions. And that he kept it down here in a hidden chamber was another strong indication there was something not right about whatever business he was conducting with Nigel Spooner and Nicholas Drake. If she could just get her hands on that ledger!

To her relief, Jack lingered only moments longer before closing the secret door and retreating up the priest hole. His exit plunged the cavern into blackness. Geneva was too busy thanking God for his deliverance to have time for fear as she felt her way from the cavern and through the tunnels to the shaft below the wine cellar.

Tomorrow, the household would be in a flurry preparing for the evening banquet. At her first opportunity, she would inform Daniel of her latest discovery. Then together they could decide how to explore yet another intriguing aspect of Sir Callum's secret world.

CHAPTER TWENTY-SIX

At eight o'clock on the last day of November, a hush came over the Great Hall as Captain Jack Everson stood to his feet to deliver a speech of gratitude to those who had fought the fire and to celebrate Everson Farm's newly designed barn. Jack was in his element, hair combed perfectly and dark-blue tailcoat cinched at the waist. Not to mention the pleasant fragrance of a nosegay pinned to the lapel.

For the occasion, Geneva had chosen an emerald gown of silk and organza contrasted with a gold neckline and broad waistband. Daniel had complimented her on how it accentuated the two colors of her eyes. Her hair was swept up in soft curls, and the only jewels she wore were diamond earrings that dangled against her slender neck.

Tonight's guests included the estate bailiff, Mr. Blackerby, and the two tenant farmers, Peter Farthing and Edgar Baines, each with their respective wives. The Eversons' closest friends had been the first to arrive—the Cavendish family, the Spooners, the Carringtons, and Mrs. Lydia Northcott with her son Edwin, who had just returned from Tahiti in the South Seas.

Servants in black and white livery presented the first course. Steaming bowls of Soup à la Flamond. Thin slices of turkey with chestnuts. Oyster sauce drizzled over partridge. Loin of veal à la Béchamel. Colorful French beans, squash, and asparagus. All looked and smelled delicious.

Cutting into a tender slice of partridge, Mrs. Lydia Northcott addressed herself to Aunt Mary and Grandmama Louise. "You have no idea how happy I was when Edwin arrived on my doorstep two days ago. I've been so worried about his illness with dengue fever."

"I can imagine," Grandmama Louise said. "Such a relief that he was alive!"

Aunt Mary reached for the salt cellar. "Thank the Lord that he recovered and was able to return home. We're so pleased you could join us tonight, Edwin."

The young man smiled. "I'm delighted to be here, Mrs. Everson, though I'm still adjusting to winter weather."

"How was your work in Tahiti?" Philip asked.

"Very challenging but greatly rewarding with the souls who came to Christ. However, my lingering health issues were a problem, so the mission's director urged me to return to England."

"You were wise to do that," Katherine spoke up. "I hardly recognized you with how much weight you've lost. I do hope you'll allow yourself plenty of time to convalesce."

Of average height with sandy-blond hair and a complexion tanned by the tropical sun, Edwin Northcott was indeed far too thin for his natural stocky build. But Geneva found something quite engaging in the kindly candour of his square, smooth-shaven features, cheerful smile, and warm hazel gaze. From the gladness lighting up Katherine's pale face, her cousin found the young returning missionary quite attractive as well.

"Thank you, Miss Katherine. I will. I was fascinated to hear about your charity work in bringing the cottage industry to Waterton. Both you and Miss Geneva have made a difference in people's lives. During the voyage, I had plenty of time to think about my future—possibly working with the Anti-Slavery Society or a teaching position at the London Missionary Society. I'm in no hurry, just waiting for the Lord's leading."

Samuel helped himself to more turkey and squash. "Speaking of London, do tell the others about your investment in a ship-building company, Daniel."

Daniel looked up with a smile. "Well, during my fortnight in London last month, I spent considerable time researching the company's records and history. They're constructing a new clipper designed for much greater speed. The science behind its design and structure is remarkable. It will reach New York and Bombay in record time, faster than any other ship. I was so impressed with the company that I didn't hesitate to buy shares."

Mr. Carrington gave an approving nod. "That sounds like a far-sighted investment. With a ship like that, imagine how much quicker Edwin's return journey would have been."

"Not to mention a more efficient postal system," Mr. Spooner said.

"That's a good point, Nigel," Jack spoke up. "Cross-channel deliveries to Porthaven would put a letter on your desk the same day."

Before long, silence fell as all turned to enjoyment of the food. Geneva savored the oyster sauce on partridge before offering a polite comment. "I walked past your stone-cutting enterprise the other day, Mr. Spooner. It appears quite flourishing."

Nigel Spooner beamed at the compliment. "Very much so. A large tonnage is shipped to Bristol on a regular basis. And Jack informs me your new wattle fence business is progressing very well."

"That's right. We have six tradesmen now with enough demand to consider hiring additional workers."

"Praise God!" Philip spoke up. "Between the new wattle fence business and cottage industry, tensions between Ravensmere estate and the community have improved significantly. What pleases me the most has been a reduction of families needing poor relief, which in turn means being able to help those truly in need more effectively."

He dabbed his mouth with his napkin. "Well, Cousin Geneva, this first course has been marvelous. I can't imagine what treats we'll have for second course."

Geneva rose to her feet at the head of the table. "Ladies and gentlemen, the servants will clear the table for the second course now. Shall we stretch our legs and visit with one another? If you wish to refill your glasses, Stanway is happy to serve you at the beverage table."

As the guests got up and moved about, Philip, Katherine, Aunt Mary, and several others gathered around Edwin, eagerly asking about the details of his missionary work. As hostess, Geneva chatted with as many guests as possible, then worked her way through the group to where Daniel was standing back, listening to Edwin's description of a revival among the whalers visiting Tahiti.

"Might I have a private word?" she asked in a low voice.

Daniel's chocolate gaze lit up. "In fact, I was hoping for the same. I have some news for you regarding our last encounter. Let's take a stroll, shall we?"

Geneva waited until a potted plant provided a partial screen between them and the guests before blurting out eagerly, "You will not guess what I learned last night! The cavern has a secret chamber. And you were right about Jack having a ledger for his private business. I saw him writing in one and counting out money. I am sure it was from the sale of the goods they brought in the other night."

Daniel looked as astonished as she could have hoped. "A secret chamber? And how did you discover all this since I saw you just yesterday?"

"Well, you mentioned the possibility of a separate ledger, so I thought I'd just take a look. I have my own key to Jack's office." Geneva hesitated, quite sure Daniel was not going to be happy with what she related next. She was right. His expression was thunderous by the time she finished.

"Do you realize how risky that was?" Daniel exclaimed. "How are we to keep you safe if you continue to place yourself in dangerous situations?"

"Well, he didn't see me." Geneva hunched her shoulders in a gesture of defiance. "And I will do what I must to uncover the truth about my mother. If he'd discovered my presence, it would have been embarrassing but hardly dangerous."

"I'm no longer so sure of that," Daniel answered flatly. "Not after what I myself have learned in the past day. I spoke to a gentleman at the bank this morning, a shareholder who serves on the board with my father. He was in the merchant marine for many years, so I asked if he had heard of Mr. Boisseau or of a ship named the *Étoile Polaire*. I was bowled over when he said yes."

He took a deep breath before continuing. "Apparently, it is a Frenchman, Henri Boisseau, who owns the *Étoile Polaire*. He has been long suspected by the customs authorities of smuggling since the Napoleonic wars. They've never had the opportunity to catch him, in part because he never comes close enough to the English coast for accusations to stand. It is their belief he must be working in partnership with an English vessel, which permits the offloading of goods without the risk of being spotted by a Customs revenue vessel."

Geneva gasped. "That explains why Nicholas Drake is valued by Jack and Nigel Spooner. The goods are transferred from the

Étoile Polaire to the *Golden Hind*, Drake's fishing boat. And—you said the Napoleonic wars? Why, that would be clear back to my earliest childhood. Or even when Drake was a coachman here before my birth. Jack said he and Nigel Spooner had been working with Drake for more than twenty years. Could they have been smuggling with Boisseau so long ago?"

Geneva glanced across the Great Hall to where Jack stood chatting with Nigel and his wife as well as Tess's parents, to all appearances the perfect gentleman. "We must get into that secret chamber and retrieve the ledger. It may shed light on the truth."

"Well, I don't want to risk any further danger to you," Daniel answered soberly. "But in this case, I am afraid you are right. We cannot turn back from seeking the truth. For now, let's enjoy the evening. You're doing a marvelous job as hostess. When it is over, we will make plans as to Jack and his activities."

Daniel held out his arm, and together the two returned to the table. The second course was followed by desserts—crème du café, savoy cake, and mince pies. Then guests and family retired to the drawing room for coffee and port while servants replaced the tables with rows of chairs in preparation for the Scottish entertainers. When they returned to the Great Hall, servants and estate laborers who had fought the fire had now finished their own refreshments and were crowding in.

The guests took their seats while servants and laborers found places standing at the back. Jack repeated a few words of thanks to the newcomers. Then all turned to watch the grand entrance of a piper and six other men in full Scottish regalia. Hand clapping welcomed them. Once they reached the dance floor, reserved at the head of the hall, the troupe turned to face their audience.

The piper filled his bag with a deep breath, and immediately the Great Hall was filled with thrumming and droning in a strange mixture of happy and sad. With ceremony, the dancers placed their arms akimbo, bowed slowly at the waist, and launched into an energetic and nimble performance of the Highland Fling.

In the back, servants and laborers grinned and clapped to the rhythm. Tess's father beamed from ear to ear at the glorious music and dancing of his heritage.

Geneva wasn't particularly fond of bagpipe music. As the minutes passed, she was beginning to feel lightheaded from the strain of the evening. She'd managed well enough in her first major event as hostess, but she'd also eaten too much, and the air was incredibly stuffy from the heat of the fireplace, burning candles, and so many people. She needed to get some fresh air before she fainted and disrupted the entertainment.

Slipping out of her seat, Geneva eased her way through the crowd toward the main hallway. As she did so, she saw Stanway bowing down to whisper in Jack's ear. Jack in turn leaned over and spoke to Nigel Spooner, seated next to him. The two men immediately rose and left the Great Hall. Geneva hung back briefly, then made her way into the entrance hall just in time to see them enter the dining room.

Still anxious for fresh air, Geneva stepped out the front door and through the entrance porch. The cold night air felt wonderful on her overheated, perspiring skin. And the scent of vegetation was like medicine clearing the fogginess of her mind.

The night sky was cloudless, revealing countless stars, and an orange-tinted half-moon. Drawing in more deep breaths, Geneva walked across the grass to take a seat at a bench set against the garden's stone wall. Just then, she heard a murmur from the perennial enclosure on the other side of the wall. She immediately made out Jack's confident voice, then Nigel's smooth tone. Of course! Stanway's interruption in the hall must have been some message for Jack—and Nigel too. From the dining room, they had stepped out the French doors to the garden.

Unwilling to eavesdrop on a private conversation, Geneva got up from the bench. But when a third voice rose clearly above the murmur, she stood motionless. "I was afraid Stanway would recognize me even after all these years. It was a risk I had no choice but to take. In any case, he did not seem to know me."

Nicholas Drake! Geneva no longer concerned herself about the ethics of eavesdropping. She listened all the more closely to the three men's voices floating over the wall. Nigel's voice complained, "We weren't expecting another shipment *this* soon. It has been but two days. I am not sure we can move such quantity in such a short period. Why has Boisseau changed the date?"

"He says the authorities are closing in." This voice belonged again to Nicholas Drake. "He had to get the shipment out of France immediately. If you do not want it, he will take it elsewhere. If you want it, he will rendezvous at one in the morning at the same coordinates. I already have my crew sitting off the cove. Let's hope the wind will be in our favor this time. Those rocks almost ripped the bottom off the *Golden Hind* last time."

"Have you ever not been rewarded for any loss you sustained working for me?" Jack responded in a hard voice. "That's how you got your boat to begin with, is it not? Don't ever forget where and what you were before I granted you such opportunity. Now, have you sent a man to bring the packhorses from the quarry?"

"Yes, they will be waiting," Nicholas Drake said sullenly.

"Good. I must see our guests off. Then I will meet you at the cove. Nigel, you'll need a change of clothes if you are to join us. I can help you with that if you can give your wife an excuse to remain for the night."

Nigel Spooner gave a crack of laughter. "My wife is used to my late nights with you. I'll tell her you've offered a few rounds of poker for select friends after the entertainment. Mrs. Northcott and her son will give her a lift home."

A pause followed, then Nigel Spooner spoke again. "Why the glum look, Jack? This shipment should take care of both our debts and a good margin besides. If you're concerned about Boisseau, our French friend hasn't remained a free man for over twenty years without knowing how to handle the authorities. If there is any hint of trouble, Drake knows to break off the rendezvous. Don't worry unnecessarily."

"I am not worried about the delivery," Jack snapped. "It's . . . well, if you must know, it's a personal matter."

"Personal?" Nicholas Drake sniggered. "Oh dear, I hope that doesn't mean the little lady rejected your marriage offer. Adam Everson's women keep coming between you and that birthright you're always going on about. Not that I'd care except you still haven't paid me what you promised once you had received your inheritance. Don't think I won't hold you to it!"

"You'll get your money, Drake!" Jack said coldly. "I handled it before, as you well know! One way or another, it won't be long."

"Except this time you can't just get her out of the house and wash your hands of it. What are you going to do? You can't force the woman to marry you. Even Captain Jack Everson doesn't always get what he wants. The joke was on you when daddy's little missy turned up."

"I handled that too," Jack said grimly. "And I will again if need be. Because Captain Jack Everson always does get what he wants. Don't you ever forget that, Drake!"

"Enough!" Nigel snapped. "You two can quarrel when we are safely out of this. Jack, we'd better get back inside before we are missed."

Geneva had listened to the conversation with horror. It definitely confirmed that Jack's long-term business relationship with

Spooner and Drake was illegal. And more shocking, the hint that Jack had something to do with Drake's affair with her mother.

But what did Jack's final words mean? What had he handled? Now that Geneva had refused his marriage proposal, how far was he willing to go to get his way? Certainly, that couldn't happen while she was alive and breathing.

Sudden fear overtook Geneva's horror. She made a dash toward the entrance porch and slipped inside. When she reached the Great Hall, the droning of the bagpipes had ceased and guests were again milling around chatting. Spotting her entry, Tess and her parents came over. Mr. Carrington's broad face was alight with pleasure. "Och, Miss Geneva, what a wonderful evening we've had. The dinner was superb, and you did me a great favor in selecting the Scottish dancers. I had goosebumps throughout the performance."

"I'm glad you enjoyed it."

"Well, we're on our way home now." Mr. Carrington bowed deeply. "And lang may yer lum reek!"

Tess laughed at Geneva's perplexed expression. "He's just wishing you the best for the future."

Geneva managed a smile. "Then I wish you the same, Mr. Carrington. It was delightful having you and Mrs. Carrington with us tonight."

As the Carringtons departed, Tess took Geneva's arm. "Are you all right, Geneva? You look quite worried for someone who has just enjoyed great success as Ravensmere's mistress."

"No, I'm fine," Geneva insisted. "I'm just tired from all the excitement."

"Well, everyone had a lovely time. Look at Katherine and Edwin chatting at the oriel window. Edwin was so hurt when she rejected his marriage offer. In spite of that, they seem comfortable with one another. I think they have more to talk about than when Edwin was courting her."

"It's nice that they can be good friends. Excuse me, Tess. I need a glass of water."

Geneva had caught sight of Jack and Nigel reentering the Great Hall. Keeping well out of their peripheral vision, Geneva circled around until she could approach Daniel. She didn't need to say a word. One look at her face, and he had taken her by the arm and was urging her out of the Great Hall.

"What is it, Geneva? What has happened? You're not taking ill, are you?"

Geneva shook her head. She didn't speak until she had steered their walk into the library. Stepping away to shut the door, she spun around on Daniel, hands clasped at her breast. "I am not physically ill, but my spirit is in anguish. I can only wish that I have misunderstood!"

She quickly related what she'd heard over the garden wall. "Have I made too much of the words I've heard? Could I be wrong in thinking Jack was behind whatever happened between Drake and my mother? He succeeded once in removing an obstacle to his inheritance. Will he now do the same with my person?"

"You are not wrong, Geneva. What you have reported changes everything, including all we believed about your mother—and more, I fear!"

Daniel's expression was grimmer than Geneva had ever seen it. "To ensure your safety, we must remove you from this household immediately. I will make arrangements for my mother to offer hospitality. I would suggest Philip and Claire, but they would ask questions and cannot be trusted to say nothing that would alert Jack."

Daniel took two long paces across the library, then back, his hand running abstractedly though his hair. "I have a plan. Since we know Jack's plans for the night, once you are safe, I will personally engage myself to follow him. That mention of bringing the pack-horses from the quarry gives me a good idea which cove Drake was speaking of. If I can be there before the time given, there will be no chance of being seen. Also, now that we know Jack and his conspirators will be busy with this shipment, it is the perfect time to take another look below for this secret chamber. You said your cousin inserted his hand around the statue of St. Mary before it opened?"

"I did. But if you think I'm going off with your mother while you go off to find out the truth about mine, that's not going to happen."

Geneva had listened meekly enough as Daniel laid out his plans for her safety and Jack's undoing. Now her chin rose and her back stiffened with determination. "If you're going to follow Jack, I'm coming too. *And* to look for that secret chamber. I'm the one who discovered the cavern—and Jack's plans. And it's *my* mother he has besmirched. Don't try to talk me out of it. If I must, I will simply go alone as I did before."

Daniel studied her face and the determined tilt of her chin, then broke into a smile. "Yes, you would, wouldn't you? Fine. If I believed there was real danger in simply following at a distance, I'd tie you up myself to prevent you. But I don't think a late-night stroll in the same direction as your cousin will offer any real risk."

He added warningly, "So long as you follow my lead and turn back immediately if I signal. Which I will do if I sense the slightest risk to your welfare."

CHAPTER TWENTY-SEVEN

In her bedroom, Geneva fastened the last button of her wool work dress, slipped the master key into her pocket, and donned her winter jacket and bonnet. Daniel had gone home to change out of his evening clothes. Stanway would not have locked the manor yet with servants still cleaning up after the festivities, so Geneva felt safe slipping down the stairs and out the French doors to her father's garden.

As prearranged, she made her way to the gazebo in her father's shade garden. Seated inside, she had waited for anxious, dragging minutes when she heard a low call. "Geneva?"

"Daniel?"

A moment later, Daniel ducked inside. "I left Victor tethered in the woods not far from here. I didn't want the risk of anyone in your household stumbling upon his presence. As I was coming through the woods, I spotted Jack and Nigel Spooner riding well ahead in the direction of the quarry, so we won't have to worry about being seen. Are you ready?"

Geneva pulled her jacket close. "In truth, I was worried you might go without me."

"I thought of it." Even in the dark, Geneva could hear a smile in Daniel's voice. "But I think I know you by now, and I wasn't about to risk you setting off on your own. Follow me."

Daniel led the way from the garden out to Quarry Lane. The half-moon had risen higher, and with billowy clouds scudding across the sky, the light was constantly changing at the mercy of the prevailing wind. Daniel soon directed their hike off the lane up into rocky terrain, occasionally pausing to give Geneva a hand over rough ground.

After an uphill walk, the landscape opened to grassland with stunted trees, heather, and gorse. Moments later, the quarry came into view—an abrupt interruption of nature that gouged into the hillside. There were no pounding sledgehammers and shouting men at this hour, just moonlit walls and chiseled columns of limestone reminiscent of an ancient castle. Geneva soon realized where Daniel was leading her.

"This is where I walked the day after I arrived," she whispered. "The day I met you at the ladder stile and went on to the Stillberry Stones. I saw Cox Cove from the cliff top. It wasn't far from the quarry, and there was a path down to the beach. I always meant to explore it."

"That was my thought for where Jack might be landing goods," Daniel whispered back. "I used to picnic down there with Robert, Philip, and Jack when we were boys. Robert told me once that family stories had Cox Cove as the place Sir Callum McCormack used to land his smuggling cargos."

He put out a sudden hand. "Shh!"

Not a light shone from the quarry or the foreman's cottage, but Geneva heard a distant clip-clop of hooves. Then three packhorses emerged from the quarry into the moonlight, the train of animals led by one broad, bundled-up form. Geneva held her breath as they clip-clopped at a walking pace from the quarry toward the clifftop.

Beside her, Daniel didn't move until the packhorses disappeared from view, seemingly straight over the cliff. Then he pulled out a pocket watch and angled it to catch the moonlight. "We have ten minutes until the *Golden Hind* rendezvouses with Mr. Boisseau's ship, assuming it is on time. Then whatever time it takes to offload their shipment and return to shore. That gives us time to find a hiding place. Now follow exactly where I step and make no noise."

Geneva followed on Daniel's heels as her companion flitted from one stunted tree to another. She heard the sound of surf crashing against rocks. Soon, they emerged between a rock outcropping. Just a pace ahead, the cliff dropped down to the sandy beach. Daniel's hand urged her down beside him in a prone position between clumps of heather. His breath tickled against her ear as he said in the softest of whispers, "We won't be seen if we stay low. Look!"

Inching slightly forward, Geneva saw the three packhorses making their way down a narrow, zig-zagging path to a small stretch of beach below, its white sand gleaming in the moonlight. Daniel reached into his coat and pulled out a long, metallic device. A spyglass, Geneva realized as he raised it to one eye. A long moment later, he handed the device to Geneva. Putting it to her own eye, she angled it down toward the beach.

She stifled a gasp as Jack and Nigel Spooner came into view of the lens, both of them standing together looking out over the water. Jack had a spyglass to his own eye. A third man unknown to Geneva led the three packhorses out onto the sand. If these animals came from the quarry, perhaps the man was the quarry foreman or some other employee there.

A blast of sea air swept across the clifftop, chilling Geneva's face and making her eyes water. The wind smelled strongly of sand, seaweed, and the odor of a thousand bird nests lodged in chalk crevices below. Further out to sea, the water was choppy with a light mist on the horizon.

Taking the spyglass back from Geneva, Daniel used a slow, sweeping motion to scan the horizon. A few moments later, he lowered the device. "The *Étoile Polaire* has arrived on time, as has the *Golden Hind*. It looks like they are transferring the crates now."

Geneva licked her salty lips. "May I have a look?"

Daniel passed her the spyglass. After searching back and forth, she spotted two dark masses floating on the sea in a misty haze of moonlight, one much bigger than the other. In a whisper, she asked, "Aren't they taking a big risk? Don't revenue officers search these waters?"

"They patrol the coastline. That is why they are making the transfer out to sea. Customs vessels are looking for French shipping, not English fishermen taking advantage of a moonlit night for fishing. Nor by treaty can they stop French-flagged vessels at sea without absolute evidence of smuggling. They need to catch them in the act of landing cargo. Unless someone knew of the trail leading down to this cove, they wouldn't mark it as a likely landing spot."

Just then a light went on at the bottom of the cliff. Its yellow glow revealed that Jack was holding a lantern high to mark the narrow entrance to the cove. A few minutes later, a single-mast fishing cutter eased into the sheltered waters offered by a rock bluff that formed one curving side of the cove.

"How convenient," Daniel whispered. "Any vessel passing up the coast won't see it."

Geneva could make out Nicholas Drake standing tall on the deck, his oilskin coat flapping in the breeze as he tossed the anchor into the water. A moment later, a dinghy was lowered into the water. Drake climbed down into the dinghy, then raised his arms to receive a crate that a crew member lowered over the side.

"Shouldn't we leave?" Geneva whispered against the shoulder of Daniel's coat. "We need to hurry if we are to look for the secret chamber before they return to Ravensmere."

"On the contrary," Daniel whispered back. "If we wait until they've stowed this shipment, we can search without concern of interruption. It's safer to wait until they're gone than to risk movement now."

Even with her wool work dress and warm jacket, Geneva was shivering with cold, alleviated only by the warmth of Daniel's long body at her side. But she stayed motionless, watching through the spyglass as the dinghy, now laden with crates, was rowed ashore by two crewmen and the line secured to a rock. Nicholas Drake clambered out and began swinging crates from the dinghy to the beach. Without a word, the man who'd led the animals down began lifting the crates to the horses' backs and tying down the loads.

Nigel approached Nicholas, his words floating up to the top of the cliff. "Was the shipment verified?"

"Yes, I made Boisseau open every crate before it was transferred. He's never let us down yet. This time he says he acquired valuable trinkets from a monastery. I didn't ask how." Nicholas chuckled coarsely as he handed Nigel what looked like a small satchel. "It's all listed here."

"Our customers will be intrigued. I'll come to the manor tomorrow afternoon, and we'll go over the finances and allocations."

With the crates secured to the packhorses, their handler led them up the path to the cliff top. Meanwhile, the two crewmen began rowing the dinghy back out to the fishing cutter. But Nicholas Drake joined Jack and Nigel in following the packhorses up the path. Geneva was following their progress through the spyglass when a zigzag of the path left the moonlight shining directly on Drake's upturned face.

Emily had described the one-time coachman as handsome. Even twenty years later, Geneva could see what she meant. But there was something unsettling in Drake's unshaven and swarthy appearance—a wild and ruthless element. His long, dark hair was tied back in a tangled mass, and a knife sheath hanging from his belt to the middle of his thigh added to the impression of a bandit or pirate. Perhaps that was just as well, or Geneva might have been tempted to rise from her hiding place and demand to know what had happened between him and her mother.

Instead, Geneva handed the spyglass back to Daniel and followed his lead in keeping her head down. She heard Jack speak curtly, addressing the animal handler. "Thank God we're nearly done. When we get to the bottom of Quarry Lane, wait for us where you did before. After we've unloaded in the forest, Mr. Nigel will bring the animals back and pay you for tonight's run. Just make sure the packhorses get back to the quarry stables before anyone knows they've been gone. Meanwhile, Nicholas and I will get this shipment under cover. We'll save the unpacking until we've all had some sleep."

Daniel would not let Geneva move until the pack train had moved out of sight over the hill. Then they made their way back to the manor, carefully skirting well away from the smugglers' route down Quarry Lane and into the forest. Arriving back at the gazebo, Geneva turned to Daniel. "What do we do now?"

"We wait," Daniel said calmly. He gestured toward an upper-floor window. "That's Jack's bedroom. When we see a light there, we'll know they are safely out of the tunnels. Then we can look for your secret chamber."

He leaned forward to look closely at Geneva in the moonlight. "You look exhausted. Perhaps you should go to bed and leave this last task to me."

Geneva straightened her slouched position. "Oh, no, I've got my second wind. You're not having this adventure without me."

Daniel chuckled. "Geneva Everson, you never cease to amaze me."

Reaching into his coat, he pulled out a water flask and a bag that proved to be filled with dried fruit and nuts. "Very well, if you're coming with me, then let's have a bite to eat while we wait. I don't want you fainting in the tunnel."

CHAPTER TWENTY-EIGHT

It seemed an eternity before Daniel and Geneva finally saw a light appear in Jack's bedroom and a tall, broad figure outlined against the window. No doubt he and Nigel were eager to get some sleep.

Daniel tapped her shoulder and indicated for her to follow him from the shade garden to the front entrance porch. Pulling out her master key, Geneva unlocked the heavy door and waited while Daniel entered. After listening for at least a minute, he beckoned for her to come in.

The Great Hall was dark and silent as they made their way to the wine cellar and shut the door behind them. Daniel lit the two lanterns they'd left behind on their last exploration. Raising the trapdoor, he cautioned, "Wait here until I check that no one remains below."

He disappeared into the shaft. Geneva heard no sound until he returned and called up softly, "The place is empty. But let's not linger any more than necessary."

With two lanterns and their familiarity with the passageways, it took little time to reach the T-junction and make their way into the cavern. As they set their lanterns on the worktable, Geneva noticed immediately that all the items from the previous shipment were gone. Their crates still rested on the floor next to the table, overflowing with crumpled newspaper and rags. The six still-unopened crates from tonight's delivery had been stacked in twos beside the empty ones.

Geneva pointed to the brick masonry wall on the left side. "That looks like an ordinary wall, but it's the section I saw open like a door."

Daniel had already walked over to the niche that held the statue of St. Mary. He felt around the back of the statue. Suddenly there was a click, and the brick wall swung open several inches. Pulling it further open, Daniel examined the back. "Look at this. A single layer of brick over solid wood with a spring-loaded opening mechanism. Ingenious!"

Each taking a lantern, Daniel and Geneva stepped inside the hidden chamber. The size was no more than three or four paces across. Its furnishings were even sparser than the cavern—a table, some wall shelving that currently stood empty, and a single wrought-iron chest positioned against the wall. The table held numerous things, including packages wrapped up with brown paper and string, each with a number scrawled in black ink.

Daniel picked one up. "I imagine these are items from the last shipment awaiting delivery to customers."

Next to the packages, Daniel found a metal cash box, a well-used green financial ledger, a cigar box, and a pen with an ink bottle. "Here's the ledger you mentioned. This is what we came for."

Daniel opened the ledger and shone his lantern directly on the pages. As he slowly scanned a page and turned to the next, Geneva occupied herself studying the packages. She would have liked to open one but doubted her ability to wrap it up again so that Jack wouldn't notice. Instead, she tried to open the metal cash box. It was locked, but the cover of the cigar box opened readily.

"Geneva, you ought to have a look at this."

At Daniel's soft call, Geneva moved to his side. "What is it?"

"Well, I'm not sure yet, but it's troubling to say the least." He flipped through several pages. "This ledger holds transactions that mention Mr. Boisseau and the *Étoile Polaire*. They go back for over twenty years. But that's not all. There are new transactions, specifically since Jack became estate manager two years ago."

Daniel continued as Geneva leaned over to study the page where his forefinger rested. "When my father and I did the audit, I noticed something odd in the quarry ledger. All sales were being shipped through Nigel rather than directly to long-term customers. It was also strange that both the quantity sold and the price received was sharply reduced from prior years. You remember Jack had a reasonable explanation. But these accounts here show that the actual tonnage sold and money earned is significantly higher than what's recorded in the official ledger. It is clear that Jack has been funneling the excess tonnage and profits through Nigel's stone-shipping enterprise. And the two men have been splitting the difference."

The neat columns of numbers on the page meant nothing to Geneva. "Are you telling me Jack is stealing money from my estate?"

"Yes, I am. It's called embezzlement. Whatever the particulars of Jack's shipping partnership with Spooner and Boisseau, embezzlement is a serious crime. This ledger gives absolute proof of Jack's guilt."

A shiver ran down Geneva's back. "This was well before Jack knew of my existence. He was stealing from my father before his expected inheritance! I can't believe he would do that considering all that his uncle had done for him."

Daniel looked up. "Let me finish perusing the ledger. There does appear to be a long gap in the entries. That would coincide with Jack's years in the navy. He was the heir apparent, so

Adam would have told Jack of this cavern and secret chamber. I can think of no reason your father would have bothered with Ravensmere's past. He was more interested in improving Ravensmere's future. But both Jack and Nigel were notorious for gambling debts in their school years. They would think it a joke to turn Ravensmere's history of smuggling into a solution for their own debts."

Seeing that Daniel was absorbed in the ledger's pages once more, Geneva returned to the cigar box. It contained two folded papers and a black medieval key at least five inches long. Jack had displayed a similar key the night she'd seen the three men at the outcropping. So this was likely a duplicate. No other doors on the estate would use such a key.

Geneva's first instinct was to show the key to Daniel. But he looked so engrossed in his columns of numbers that she pulled out Daniel's handkerchief, wrapped it around the key, and dropped it into her pocket. Then she picked up the first of the two papers. Opening it, she read the heading: *Christie's Auction House ~ King Street, St. James's, London, 8th February, 1811*

Under this heading was an itemized list detailing the sale of a set of rare Japanese Netsuke carvings. The sales price for the set was three hundred and fifty pounds. Geneva caught her breath when she saw the signature of the seller at the bottom—Mr. Nigel Spooner. She placed the paper on the open ledger.

"Sorry to interrupt, but it looks like that wasn't their only joint crime. Tess told me how a thief had broken in and stolen a set of carvings from a cabinet in the billiard room."

Daniel scanned the paper. "I remember your father taking the carvings out to show us when we were kids. Nigel couldn't have done this on his own. Jack must have faked the burglary and covered his tracks by having Nigel sell them on his behalf."

Geneva showed Daniel the second paper—a bill of sale for a single-mast cutter customized for fishing in local waters. The price of three hundred and forty-eight pounds had been paid in full with Jack's signature on the deed of sale. The date on the paper was the 9th of March, 1811.

Geneva blinked her eyes. "That date was just two days after my mother left Ravensmere. Oh, Daniel, do you think Jack sold the carvings so he could buy the *Golden Hind* for Nicholas Drake? His uncle told me Drake had a windfall at the racecourse. I don't believe a word of it. I think the boat was Drake's payment for getting into my mother's bed. That would explain the conversation I overheard."

Daniel gave her hand a gentle squeeze. "A bitter pill to swallow that your cousin could stoop to such levels. But at least you can be certain now that you are right about your mother's innocence. From what I can see here, Jack and Nigel's stolen goods are highly profitable. My guess is that they started with the embezzlement scheme when Jack returned from the navy. That was a pittance compared to these recent shipments. Then they somehow rekindled their smuggling operation with Mr. Boisseau and the *Étoile Polaire*. Jack is making so much money through smuggling that he hardly needs Ravensmere's income. He probably thinks he's entitled to it as he feels entitled to being Adam's heir."

Geneva set down the cigar box. "That still doesn't answer the question of what happened between Nicholas Drake and my mother."

Daniel smiled at her tenderly. "I'm sure everything will come to light. After all, just see how much we've already learned, thanks to your persistence and faith in your mother."

As he flipped another page, Geneva turned her attention to the wrought-iron chest positioned against the brick wall. Its thick layer of black paint had become dull and scuffed up from decades of use. Big handles were attached to either end, and riveted iron straps gave it extra strength. Its presence within the secret chamber indicated it must hold something of value. Other treasures like those in the crates?

Tucking her fingers under the lid, Geneva heaved up until the lid tipped back against the brick wall. But as she dusted her hands off and peered inside, she let out a scream. Daniel rushed over, putting his arms around her as she swayed dizzily. She couldn't speak, only point to the bottom of the wrought-iron chest.

Daniel's mouth opened and shut without speech as he saw what had spooked Geneva—a human skeleton lying curled up in a fetal position. No hair or flesh remained on the skull, just hollow eye sockets and a wide-open jaw with protruding teeth. The clothing was reasonably intact and appeared to be the humble attire of a laborer, but the flesh where arms and legs protruded showed only brown leathery strips clinging to the bones like horror stories of some Egyptian mummy.

"Dear God, help us!" Geneva exclaimed, clinging to Daniel's strong embrace. "That isn't a man. It looks like no more than a child. I don't understand. Why would Jack keep such a terrible thing in here? Who could it be?"

Daniel guided Geneva out of the secret chamber and into the cavern. "It's all right, Geneva. You've had a terrible shock. Take a deep breath and let it out slowly."

"I can't! I'll never forget that image. That poor, poor child!" As tears rolled down her cheeks, Geneva pulled out Daniel's hanky and dabbed at her eyes.

"Shhh! We'll find out who it is. Just relax and breathe." Daniel's deep voice was tender and soothing, his arms warm about her. Geneva let her head fall against his broad chest, thankful for his presence. If she'd been alone when she uncovered that body, she'd have gone totally berserk.

As her tears subsided, Daniel lifted the corner of the handkerchief and ran his thumb over the embroidered initials. "I had no idea you'd kept this since we met at the ladder stile."

Wiping a hand across her eyes, Geneva straightened up from his embrace. "Of course I did. It's my special keepsake—a reminder of your kindness to me."

"Really?" Daniel gently wiped a lingering tear from Geneva's cheek. "That gives me hope your affection for me might be as strong as mine is for you."

A flame in her heart banished any further desire to cry as Geneva raised her tear-washed eyes to his tender gaze. "I'm sure it is. You're so special to me I can't imagine life without you."

Daniel drew her closer. "Geneva, I'm so happy to hear that. I fell in love with you on your birthday when you played your flute so beautifully. Or maybe even that first day we met when I witnessed your tender heart toward those less fortunate. I love you with all my heart."

"And I love you too, more than I ever dreamed I could love!"

Daniel bent his head slowly, but not to her lips in their first kiss as she'd expected. Instead, he placed a gentle kiss on the palm of her hand, then folded her fingers around the kiss. "Are you feeling better now, my dearest?"

A small smile crossed Geneva's lips as she recognized what a true gentleman Daniel had been not to take advantage of her emotional outburst. Standing up tall, she released herself from his gentle embrace. "Yes, much better, thank you."

His hands dropped to his sides and reached for a lantern. "Then can you handle going in there one more time?"

Geneva drew in a deep, shuddering breath. "I believe I can if you feel it necessary. Why do you ask?"

"I noticed something else in that wrought-iron chest. We need to find out what it is."

Geneva followed Daniel back into the secret chamber. She had no desire to see the dead body again, so she hung back as Daniel lifted out a cloth pouch that had been lying at the foot of the wrought-iron chest. As he opened the drawstring, Geneva wondered what other horrendous find would lie inside. But what he pulled out was just an inexpensive piece of jewelry—a pendant attached to a broken silver chain.

"A St. Christopher." Daniel showed Geneva the pewter image of a man carrying a child on his shoulder. "The patron saint of protection."

He turned the pendant over. "There's a name engraved on the back—Cecilia Jasper Fox."

Daniel handed it to Geneva, then reached back into the pouch and pulled out a crumpled paper. He smoothed it out on the table. There was a message on it scribbled in pencil and barely legible.

> Jack— Billy overheard our conversation. He was asking
> too many questions. I had no other choice. His body is
> behind the forest net. Bury him. I don't have time. ND

Geneva gasped as she read the words. "The kid! That's what Jack said to Mr. Drake that first time I saw him in the forest. I didn't know what he could mean. But this must be Billy Jasper's remains, the stable boy Mrs. Fox believed to have run away. If Nicholas Drake killed him, then Jack must have kept all this as some form of power over him. But why would Drake kill a child? What questions had he asked?"

"I think I can guess from what you overheard," Daniel said soberly. "Look at the name on this pendant. I happen to know Mrs. Fox's first name is Cecilia. Don't you think it's interesting that Billy's surname is Mrs. Fox's middle name?"

"Of course!" Geneva exclaimed. "She told me how she took him under her wing. She still has a picture of him on her mantelpiece."

"Well, if the child was a member of her family, she would admit it or adopt him openly."

"Yes, I think he must have been Mrs. Fox's own son," Geneva agreed sadly. "Since she wasn't married, she placed him in an orphanage with Jasper as his surname. Then she waited until he was old enough to be hired as Ravensmere's stable boy. It was clear in her speech how much she loved him and still misses him."

Daniel shook his head grimly. "Well, the broad picture is much clearer now. Jack doesn't trust his partners. He'll do anything to protect himself. Since the chain on the pendant is broken, perhaps he found it somewhere and decided to use it as leverage over Mrs. Fox. The auction receipt is his leverage over Nigel. And more importantly, Billy's remains and this note serves as his leverage over Drake. That would seem to be his pattern."

"If Jack did use this against Mrs. Fox, then it can only have been around the same time that my mother was thrown out," Geneva said thoughtfully. "Mrs. Fox said that was the general time when Billy disappeared. He must have overheard Jack and Drake plotting to disgrace my mother. But what role could Mrs. Fox have played in any of this?"

"That is something else to be investigated." Taking the two papers, Daniel tucked them into the green ledger and dropped the pendant into his pocket. "But not tonight. This is now far beyond embezzlement or even smuggling. This is evidence of murder and proof that your cousin is a very dangerous man. I'm taking this evidence with me and going straight to Constable Allenby. I want you to go to your bedroom immediately and lock yourself in. Jack may be sleeping, but I do not wish to take even the smallest risk with your safety. Once I've shown all this to Constable Allenby and sent word to my father and Mr. Fairfax, I'll return to the manor."

Daniel drew Geneva into another embrace before releasing her. "Meanwhile, promise me, my dear Geneva, that you will stay safe until my return."

CHAPTER TWENTY-NINE

Geneva's second wind had long since run its course by the time she and Daniel climbed up the ladder to the wine cellar. Her turmoil over Jack's betrayal added to her fatigue from the long night. "Daniel, I prayed that God would reveal the truth about my mother. But I never expected this much truth. In a way, I wish I was still in the dark, knowing nothing."

Daniel blew out his lantern. "That's understandable, dear heart, and the reason why I want you safe in your bedroom. But may I give you a word of advice?"

"Yes, you know I always welcome it."

"Then may I recommend that you turn this over to God and do his will."

His words weren't what she expected. Geneva wrinkled her brow. "What is his will?"

"His will is that you trust him and know he's in control of everything that happens. If you have any unconfessed sin, ask for his forgiveness, then keep your heart focused on Jesus. He will resolve this in his own perfect way. After I've gone, go upstairs and lock that door of yours. I'll retrieve Victor from the forest and ride into the village. If all goes well, I'll be back within the hour."

Geneva squeezed his hand. "I will be praying for your safety and success every moment until you return. Godspeed."

As Daniel departed and sprinted down the drive, Geneva closed the door and left it unlocked for his eventual return. Lantern in hand, she made her way to the staircase. But Daniel's words of advice had pricked her conscience so much that she turned back to the Great Hall and stood below the portrait of her father. Lantern held high, she looked at Adam's youthful face in the painting and was immediately struck with the ugly truth she'd suppressed for far too long.

Behind her cheerful and charitable exterior, Geneva had disobeyed God. Bitterness and malice resided in her heart. So often, it had reared up in anger, blaming, and judging. All the while, she'd fooled herself into thinking she didn't have to forgive Uncle Alex or her father. Both men had apologized sincerely, yet her stubborn heart had resisted. If Jesus could forgive the soldiers who'd pierced his hands and feet, could she not forgive those who had sinned against her?

Tears trickling down her face, Geneva confessed to God the grudge she'd held against her father when she should have forgiven him and done her utmost to build their relationship. She repented of her sin in not writing back to Uncle Alex. Finally, she gave Ravensmere to God in faith that he would carry out his perfect justice.

Comforted in the knowledge that she'd made things right with God, Geneva turned away from her father's portrait and made her way back across the Great Hall. But as she turned down the hallway and approached the staircase she heard the creak of a door opening, then footsteps and a murmuring of male voices.

In a split second, her tranquil state was torn away at the sight of Jack, Nigel Spooner, and Nicholas Drake advancing toward her. Jack was carrying a lantern. His gaze narrowed as he set his eyes upon her. "Cousin Geneva, what are you doing down here at this hour?"

Geneva was suddenly mindful of her work dress, its wool marked with dirt, twigs, and bits of heather from her time on the clifftop. She also realized that while Nicholas Drake looked as unkempt as before, both Jack and Nigel Spooner had changed out of the rough work clothing they'd worn at the cove. A strong odor of whiskey wafted from all three men.

So that was the explanation of the light in Jack's bedroom window. He and Nigel hadn't been retiring to bed but changing out of their surf-dampened, dirty clothing. Then they had gathered in Jack's office to laud their latest success with what was clearly more than one celebratory drink.

If she'd reacted sooner, she might have blown out the candle in her lantern to avoid them noting her disheveled state. But Jack had already raised his lantern high, the beam playing over her rumpled, soiled appearance. So she chose instead to brazen it out, walking forward to push past the three men toward the staircase. "I could ask you the same question, Cousin Jack. But right now I'm too tired. I'm going to bed. Good night."

But before she could get past, Jack grabbed her arm and pulled her to a halt. "Hold on a minute. What are you doing dressed like that and all filthy like you've had a roll in the bushes? You haven't been outside for just a stroll in the garden. Have you been out for a tryst with someone?"

Geneva dropped her lantern as she tried to tug her arm free. The candle blinked out as it rolled across the floor. "A tryst? I've done nothing of the sort. I couldn't sleep so I went out for a walk in the fresh air. I stayed out longer than intended. I didn't mean to disturb anyone. I had no idea you were still up or had friends here."

Geneva knew she was babbling. She tamped down terror as she glanced over at Nicholas Drake. His tangled mass of hair, filthy coat, and unshaven face no longer screamed outlaw to her but murderer. Could he read her knowledge of his guilt in her expression?

Jack's eyes narrowed further, and he tightened his grip. "The manor is locked. How did you get out or back in?"

"I have my own master key. Stanway gave it to me." She yawned and patted her mouth. "This is my home, after all. If I choose to go out at any time of the day or night, why should I not? And now, if you don't mind, I'm going back to bed."

"She's lying!" Geneva hadn't realized Nicholas Drake had moved so close to her until his leg bumped her pocket that held the five-inch key she had found in the secret chamber. The former coachman moved to block her in between his large body and Jack. "She recognizes me! I saw it in her eyes. Now why would Miss Elizabeth's daughter I've never met know who I am? And that isn't just grass or twigs on her dress. It's heather! Like what grows up by the cove, not down here!"

Drake snatched at her pocket. "And what does she have here?"

"Nothing, just my personal things." Geneva's step back only brought her hard against Jack.

"I don't believe you. You're afraid. I can see it in your eyes." Before she could make another move, Drake's hand had gone into her pocket and come out again. He tossed the New Testament she kept there to the floor, then shook loose Daniel's handkerchief from the five-inch key. Lamplight shone brightly on the exquisitely embroidered initials.

"Well, well!" Jack sneered. "So that's who you've been catting around with—Mr. Daniel Cavendish. So he's not such a Puritan after all!"

"Not just catting around, boss." Drake held up the key. "Seems they've been where they shouldn't."

Jack wrapped his large hand around Geneva's throat. "So the truth comes out! You two have been spying on us! Drake, go after him. If Miss Prissy here is just heading to bed, he can't be far."

"No, Daniel knows nothing about this!" Geneva's fear for her own safety was now swept away by terror for Daniel's. She must secure him time to get away. "I did follow you, but I did that on my own. I learned about the tunnels from Albert Everson's journal. And I saw you and Mr. Spooner with this man in the woods when I was searching for Pookie. I heard his name mentioned. That's how I knew who he was. I only had Daniel's handkerchief because he bandaged my cut finger. I kept it because I *love* him, and he loves me too!"

Jack's handsome face twisted with fury and hate at Geneva's words. "So Cavendish is why you turned me down! And the key? You think I don't know where you got it? Don't tell me you found that little secret in Albert Everson's journal. I made sure that was impossible! Well, bad news for Cavendish. If you won't marry me, there isn't a chance in hell I'll let you marry him any more than I should have let your mother marry Uncle Adam. I corrected that mistake, and I'll correct this one."

Geneva had guessed right. Jack was the one who had cut out the journal page. And was clearly responsible for her mother's misfortunes. He shifted his grip to cover her mouth and snapped at the men. "Come on, help me get her below."

As they took her down the hallway, Jack's hand across Geneva's mouth was too strong for her to cry for help. Nigel Spooner had taken Jack's lantern. He opened the office door while Jack and Nicholas Drake manhandled her inside. Still gripping Geneva tight, Jack gestured for Nigel Spooner to lock the door while

Nicholas grabbed the chisel and pried open the trapdoor to the priest hole.

Geneva no longer struggled. Resistance against three strong men was pointless. Her only thread of hope was her trust in God's mercy—and Daniel galloping on Victor to alert the authorities. If she could just keep her captors distracted until he returned!

Geneva tried to keep her balance as Jack prodded her down the ladder and through the tilting beam from the priest hole into the cavern. Nicholas Drake had gone in front, Nigel following at the rear with the lantern. Jack pushed Geneva ahead of him until they'd reached the worktable, where he shoved her down into a chair.

"Dear Cousin Geneva, I suggest that you make things easy for yourself by not doing anything foolish. Sit on that chair and be quiet. Nigel, one lantern isn't enough in here. Light those three whale oil lanterns on the table. Drake, don't take your eyes off her."

Jack dropped the key and handkerchief onto the worktable. Walking over to the shelf that held the water crock, he picked up a pewter mug and turned the spigot to release a small amount of water into the mug. Then he pulled a small medicine bottle from an inner breast pocket and opened it. As he added its contents to the mug, Geneva caught sight of the label: Tincture of Digitalis.

Terror rushed through Geneva's body. That was the medicine her father had used for his heart condition. A medicine that was deadly poison if not taken in the precise dosage prescribed by a physician. So that was Jack's solution—to poison her to death!

Catching her expression, Jack spoke mockingly as he slid the bottle back into his inner breast pocket. "I didn't think I'd need this again after I said a fond goodbye to your father. Until you made clear yesterday I wouldn't be getting Ravensmere back through marriage."

At Geneva's shocked gasp, he added with a sneer, "Oh, yes, a few extra drops in your father's lemonade did the trick. Funny thing is, I went to all the trouble of using dear Uncle Adam's own medication so that any investigation would point to an accidental overdose. I might have spared myself the trouble since the police didn't even suggest foul play. Of course I'd no idea Uncle Adam had already made a new will."

Nigel Spooner spoke up for the first time. "Are you sure you want to do this, Jack? You've never gone this far! I mean, a woman, for heaven's sake!"

"Elizabeth was a woman, and you had no objection!" Jack snapped. "What else do you propose? She knows too much to set her free. Would you suggest white slavery? I'm sure Boisseau would oblige, but I think little Miss Prissy would prefer this."

Picking up the cup, he strode over to loom above Geneva. "You're a pretty lady and I really would have been willing to marry you. Everything would have been all right if you'd just said yes!"

Geneva tried to jump up from her chair, but Nicholas Drake's powerful hands on both shoulders held her down. She fought to muster courage or at least defiance, but her voice trembled as she spoke. "It won't do you any good to kill me. I lied to you. Daniel and I both saw your shipment tonight. He knows all about Mr. Boisseau and how you've been smuggling on his ship all these years. We also both know about your secret chamber. If you kill me, he'll know it was you. You'll hang for it! And so will Mr. Drake when they find the boy's body."

Jack threw his head back in a derisive laugh. "Good try, Geneva. But that's where you're wrong. The moment I saw the key, I knew you'd found the chamber. When the time comes, your lover Cavendish can search down here all he wants. He won't find one shred of evidence, including you."

He moved forward with the cup. "Drake, hold her tight and open that big mouth of hers."

But instead, Drake released Geneva's shoulders and took a step back. "What secret chamber is she talking about? Where did she get that key?"

"Yes, what secret chamber?" Nigel Spooner echoed. "Have you been holding back?"

"Can't you see she's bluffing?" Jack said impatiently. "I had the second key hidden behind that statue. She must have found it snooping around."

"No, I didn't." Geneva's eyes flashed from Nicholas Drake to Nigel Spooner. "If you reach behind the statue of St. Mary, there's a lever that opens a secret door in the wall over there. Jack keeps things in there he doesn't want anyone to see. Like his ledger for his smuggling business. And proof of your own crimes. *And* the remains of Billy Jasper's body in a wrought-iron chest."

Drake swung around furiously on Jack. "You slippery snake! You were supposed to bury him in the forest. You told me you had."

Jack set the cup down on the table. "Settle down, Drake. I took care of it, didn't I? How I did it is my business. *I'm* the one in charge here, and don't you forget it. Have you not prospered since the day your uncle kicked you off his boat?"

"Oh sure, with Billy Jasper held over my head for going on twenty years! Did you know about this, Spooner? I want that body gone today. And any other evidence."

"You don't give me orders!" Lunging forward, Jack shoved at Nicholas Drake.

"And I'm sick and tired of you giving them!" Drake's swarthy features were suffused with rage as he pushed back. Their shoving match moved both men away from the table where Geneva sat.

Nigel stumbled backward to get out of their way, leaving Geneva suddenly free and unnoticed in her seat. A swift glance revealed her opportunity. Springing toward the table, Geneva snatched up the whale oil lantern and threw it at the heap of emptied crates. At the same moment, her other arm swept the two unlit lanterns and extra bottle of oil to crash onto the heap.

The result was far more than she hoped. As the glass of lanterns and bottle shattered, burning oil ignited the wrapping material in a great whoosh of orange flames and heat. The explosion scattered flaming debris, glass, and oil toward the new crates as well. In the next instant, Geneva grabbed Daniel's handkerchief and the black key. Her first instinct was to escape through the priest hole but the men's aggressive confrontation blocked her way. Instead, Geneva raced to the cavern door.

Behind her, she could hear her captors' furious shouting, no doubt struggling to prevent their new shipment from going up in flames. Hopefully that would stop them from coming after her immediately. Reaching the door, she pulled it open, dashed over the threshold, and slammed it shut. Her fumbling fingers found the keyhole. As the key slipped in, she turned the lock and swung around to face nothing but pitch-black darkness.

CHAPTER THIRTY

Geneva thanked God for her narrow escape as she dashed down the tunnel, tapping the key repeatedly on the wall to help herself stay on track. Her head start wouldn't last for long. Jack had a key and would surely come after her. As she neared the T-junction, her mind screamed at her to make a choice. Left or right?

Jack had already caught her once indoors, and he'd do it again if she tried to escape out the wine cellar. If she could escape out the forest door without being caught, Geneva could hide in the forest until Daniel returned. At the junction, Geneva turned right and sped down the long tunnel. There was still no sound of pursuit. In her mind, she envisioned the three men trying to douse the fire with water from the crock and dragging the new shipment to safety. *Dear Lord, just a little more time!*

Geneva forged on, her heart pounding as her ankle twisted over bits of rubble. On reaching her estimated halfway point, she slowed just enough to look back. Lantern light flickered in the distant darkness and with it the muffled din of her approaching enemies. *Oh, dear Lord, help me!*

Picking up her pace, Geneva streaked ahead until she finally felt the tunnel's upward incline. She knew the stairs were near but didn't slow down soon enough. Stumbling into them, her hands and knees bashed against the stone steps. She was too panicked to feel pain as she scrambled up to Sir Callum's arched door to the forest.

By now, her pursuers were closing in with angry cursing and pounding feet echoing up and down the tunnel. Geneva fumbled to find the lock in the dark, almost dropping the key in her haste. When the door finally swung open, she dashed to the other side, slammed it shut, and turned the key in the lock.

Geneva had no time to rejoice in her brave escape into the fresh night air. Without wasting a second, she was ducking out from the forest net and pushing her way through brush into the trees. As in the tunnel, she used the key to feel out tree trunks before she could run into them. So long as she headed directly away from the outcropping, she should come out somewhere on the grassy verge dividing the forest from the garden wall.

But she hadn't progressed far when she heard angry voices behind her. The three men had clearly emerged from the forest net. Which way would they go? If they were headed her way, she'd see lantern light by now. More likely they'd take the path used by the packhorses. Once on Manor Lane they'd try to cut her off at the edge of the forest.

One thing was certain. Jack wouldn't give up. His bungled attempt on her life would drive him even harder to finish the job. Taking shelter at the manor was out of the question, at least until Daniel arrived, hopefully soon and with reinforcements. Daniel needed to know Jack was forewarned before he walked into a possible trap. What if Jack turned his violence on Daniel? What if the others had a gun? The last thing Geneva wanted was for anyone else to be hurt on her account.

Hunching to avoid low-hanging branches, Geneva continued feeling out one step at a time. Sticky cobwebs clung to her cheeks, prickles snagged at her jacket, and she could feel a bird's nest of twigs and dead leaves in her hair. It seemed an eternity before she reached the grassy strip separating the forest from the garden wall. The moonlight allowed her to straighten up and move more quickly, weaving around fir saplings and cedars until she reached a spot near Manor Lane and the pebbled drive. This was a good place—well out of sight, where she could wait for Daniel's return to the manor.

Now that she was no longer moving in a panic, Geneva realized she was still clutching both Daniel's hanky and the key. She was stowing both back into a pocket when she heard the distant sound of horses on Waterton Road. Fear banished by relief, she shoved back cedar limbs to step out onto the road. Daniel must be warned as soon as possible.

But her relief turned back into terror as she heard a loud rustle in the underbrush, then felt powerful arms grabbing her close. As she fought back, she heard Jack's sneering voice. "Stop, Geneva! You know it's hopeless."

Geneva kicked back at his shins, but his vice-like grip tightened until she thought her ribs would break. Raising his voice, Jack called, "Drake, Nigel, over here!"

She heard a fresh crashing in the brush. As Drake broke into the open, Jack said derisively, "I gambled you'd come this way if you were really hoping Cavendish would ride to the rescue. You just can't win, can you? Drake, you take her!"

Drake's big hand smothered Geneva's mouth, his stinking, sweat-drenched body pressing against hers. Jack reached into his coat. "Well, Geneva, I guess you're wishing you'd accepted my marriage proposal." He pulled out the brown medicine bottle. "Glad I didn't use all of this. No matter. It will work even better undiluted."

Geneva moaned desperately in the back of her throat, causing Drake to press his filthy hand even harder upon her mouth. Jack removed the cap from the small bottle. "Moan all you want. No one will hear you. Your demise will give me exactly what I want. Ah yes, you will have gone wandering in the night and slipped from the cliffs to your death."

Geneva had passed from terror to resignation. If the next moment was to take her into God's presence, had she not an hour ago submitted her life to God's will? *Just protect Daniel, dear Lord! And please don't let Jack get away with this!*

As Drake moved his hand from her mouth to pinch her nostrils, Jack held the medicine bottle close to her mouth. For just one instant, opportunity opened before her. With a quick jerk of her head, Geneva sunk her teeth into the fleshy base of Jack's thumb and bit down as hard as she could.

Jack stumbled back with an angry shout of pain. The medicine bottle fell from his hand to the ground. Geneva kicked backward with all her strength. A yelp of pain told her the blow had landed on Drake's shins. Twisting herself free, she ran full force toward the manor—under the stone archway and down the pebbled drive, screaming at the top of her lungs to awaken the household.

She could hear pounding feet and angry cursing behind her. But now she also heard the thud of hoofbeats galloping down the drive. Jack's hand came down on her shoulder like a claw. But only for an instant. As a horse knocked him aside, the most welcome voice in the world called out, "Give it up, Everson. The authorities are here. They know of your crimes."

Leaping from his horse, Daniel landed on Jack, wrestling him to the ground. Now other hoofbeats were approaching. At least eight men with lanterns rode down the drive, led by Constable Allenby. Surrounded by mounted constables, Nigel Spooner raised his arms in defeat, but Nicholas Drake took advantage of the commotion to break away.

"Daniel, Drake's getting away!" Geneva called out urgently.

Releasing Jack, Daniel vaulted back onto Victor. Drake had sprinted out to Manor Lane, heading toward the village. Victor caught up easily, pressing the fugitive against the stone fence that bordered the lane. Reaching down, Daniel grabbed his collar and literally dragged him back to the manor.

By the time he arrived back, the front drive was filling with people, not just the party that had arrived with Daniel but the servants and Geneva's family, all in their dressing gowns and slippers. As Daniel dragged Nicholas Drake in and released him next to Jack and Nigel, Constable Allenby swung down from his horse and raised his booming voice. "Captain Jack Everson, Mr. Nigel Spooner, and Mr. Nicholas Drake, I hereby declare that you are under arrest for serious crimes."

He gestured to his constables. "You, you, and you, seize the prisoners and take them into the Great Hall." He nodded at two others. "Take the horses. The rest of you come with me."

As the constables clapped handcuffs on the three men, Daniel hurried to Geneva's side. "Are you all right? Things didn't go as I thought."

Geneva clung to him for just a moment. "Yes, but thank God you came just in time."

She handed him the medicine bottle she'd retrieved from where Jack had let it fall. In a voice that still shook, she filled Daniel in on what had happened since his departure. By then, the prisoners were being herded toward the entrance porch, the family and servants standing back in astonishment to make a pathway for them. After their hunt for Geneva in the forest, Jack and Nigel looked as much a mess as Drake in scuffed-up boots, dirtied tailcoats, and tangled hair.

Taking her arm, Daniel led Geneva indoors on the heels of Constable Allenby. Inside the Great Hall, servants were lighting candles. Constable Allenby was calling for chairs and directing the prisoners into them. By the time they were settled, several more horsemen had arrived at a gallop, including Samuel Cavendish, Angus Fairfax, and Philip.

As they entered the Great Hall, Aunt Mary surged forward. "Mr. Fairfax, Mr. Cavendish, a terrible mistake has been made. You tell them, Philip! This is outrageous. My son is a decorated war hero, not a criminal. How dare you treat him like this!"

Robert put his arm around her. "Please, Mother, don't shout. I'm sure you're right. Constable Allenby is simply doing his job. Mr. Fairfax will make sure everything is cleared up quickly."

The chief constable stepped forward. "I'm sure this is a great shock to your entire family. Yes, Daniel Cavendish has made serious allegations against the captain and these others. But I can assure you we wouldn't arrest them without evidence."

He turned to Daniel. "I believe you have more to show us beyond this ledger you presented earlier. Now that the chief magistrate has arrived, perhaps you can explain fully why we are all here."

"Yes, Daniel!" Robert interrupted in a hard tone. "You've pulled us out of our beds at an ungodly hour this morning. Whatever you have to say better be of some consequence. If not, your credibility will be forever lost."

CHAPTER THIRTY-ONE

Daniel and Geneva drank the last few swallows of hot tea Emily had prepared, thankful for the quick surge of energy that would keep them going a little longer.

After the prisoners had been handcuffed to chairs at the head of the Great Hall and surrounded with six guards, the family and servants had gone upstairs to dress quickly.

On their return, Daniel nodded to the family and stepped forward to address Chief Magistrate Angus Fairfax who had been waiting patiently. "Sir, believe me I would not rouse you or anyone else from their beds without great cause. What I have to say gives me no pleasure whatsoever. I only wish none of this was necessary."

Daniel pulled Jack's secret ledger from his coat and held it up. "This is the ledger in question. Its contents make clear that when they were barely more than schoolboys, Mr. Nigel Spooner and Captain Jack Everson formed a private smuggling operation with one Henri Boisseau, bringing over French brandy and other goods during the Napoleonic wars. The goods were brought to Cox Cove near Everson Quarry. At the manor they were carried through a tunnel to an underground cavern, built centuries ago for the purpose of smuggling. Jack, as heir apparent to Ravensmere, had been given this knowledge."

Geneva glanced at Jack as Daniel spoke. Her cousin's expression held nothing but arrogance and contempt. Daniel went on, "After Jack became the estate's manager two years ago, he also conspired with Spooner to defraud the estate of quarry sales. More recently, they have turned to shipments of high-value objects of art looted from French aristocrats during the war. These goods are being transported by Mr. Boisseau in his ship *Étoile Polaire*."

Daniel opened the green ledger and took out the auction paper. "It has also come out that Jack and Nigel Spooner are responsible for the theft of Adam's Netsuke carvings almost twenty years ago. This is proof of their sale at Christie's Auction House for a grand total of three hundred and fifty pounds."

Amidst the family's astonished murmurs, Robert stepped forward and raised his voice again. "What a horrendous accusation to make! My brother wouldn't steal from his own family. Why would he do any of the things you claim? He was no pauper but a young man from a family of wealth and privilege."

Fists balled, he glared at Daniel. "How do we know you aren't simply inventing accusations for your own purposes?" His angry glance went to Geneva. "First you bring this woman here to snatch Jack's inheritance. Then you conveniently accuse him of crimes no one else knows of. Maybe this was planned all along between you and our so-called cousin to seize control of Ravensmere."

Samuel stepped forward and raised a warning hand. "Show some respect, Robert. Miss Geneva has been proven Adam's daughter by every possible measure. And my son wouldn't jeopardize his reputation with unfounded assumptions. You can look at the evidence yourself if you don't believe it."

Daniel continued in a cool manner. "As to why Jack, an eighteen-year-old with rich prospects, would steal, that answer lies in Miss Geneva Everson's absolute faith and insistence since her arrival that her mother was innocent of any wrongdoing, as she was accused of so many years ago. Not many of you will recognize the man seated next to Captain Everson. Twenty years ago he was the family's coachman, one Nicholas Drake. Captain Everson used the money from the stolen carvings to purchase a fishing cutter for Drake's use. I have the bill of sale here."

Some of the arrogance had left Jack's expression, but he made no attempt to defend himself, perhaps because there was nothing to say. He just stared ahead stony-faced as Daniel went on. In contrast, Drake's face went from dark fury to paled fear as Daniel held up the second paper.

Stanway stepped forward to peer into Drake's face. "This man brought a message for Captain Everson last evening. I wouldn't have recognized him after all these years. But on closer look, you may be right."

"What's your point in all of this?" Robert snapped.

"I'm about to prove that a serious injustice has been perpetrated on your family—and especially on Miss Geneva. Since 1808, Nicholas Drake has served as Jack and Nigel's henchman in their smuggling operation. Twenty years ago he was hired as the family's coachman. Is that not true, Stanway?"

The butler was taken aback. "Yes, sir, that's true. But I knew nothing of any smuggling. The captain was just a lad at the time. He informed me that Nicholas Drake was a trustworthy coachman who had served in Mr. Spooner's household. The former coachman had left unexpectedly, so I took Mr. Jack at his word and hired him."

"And how long did Drake serve as coachman?"

"Just a few weeks, sir."

"Is it true that Mr. Adam dismissed him for unseemly conduct with his wife?"

"Yes, sir. We were all shocked by it."

"Indeed," Daniel said. "Let's put the facts together. Jack saw to it that Drake would be hired as coachman. Jack bought him a fishing boat for one reason—to pay Drake for setting up Adam's wife as an adulteress."

Grandmama Louise let out a pitiful cry. "Stop what you're saying! You're twisting the truth. My grandson is a highly respected member of society. He would never do such a thing."

"With all due respect, Mrs. Everson, Jack did those things for the same reason that he tried to take Miss Geneva's life not a half hour ago. He had one goal and one motive, to win back what he considered his birthright—master of Ravensmere estate."

Babbling voices, groans, and cries made a terrible din in the Great Hall. In the midst of it, Geneva knew her moment had come, the chance to fulfill her reason for getting in the carriage with Mr. Bradshaw and coming all the way to Waterton.

As she approached the scoundrel seated next to Jack, the clamor and uproar gradually faded, all eyes turning her way. Even handcuffed and stripped of his knife belt, Drake looked so furious and dangerous Geneva paused several feet away. "Mr. Drake, I wish to speak with you. Will you please look at me?"

Drake lifted his eyes. In the struggle of his capture, his tangled mane had come loose from its binding, making him peer at Geneva through wild strands of hair.

Firmly, Geneva addressed him. "I never thought such wickedness could happen at Ravensmere. I want to know what happened between you and my mother. Tell me—right now!"

Silence ruled over the Great Hall except for a rooster's crow heard through an open window.

"Don't speak!" Jack hissed at Drake. "There is nothing they can prove."

Drake gave him a long, cool look before turning his gaze back to Geneva with a shrug. "There's not much to tell. Yes, if you must know, I got into her bed, but *nothing* happened."

He raised his voice. "I'm innocent!"

Geneva gritted her teeth. "You are *not* innocent. Explain yourself."

"Nothing happened because she was drugged with laudanum that put her in a deep sleep. Mrs. Fox did that. She's the one to blame. Question her, not me!"

Geneva walked past the dumbfounded servants to Mrs. Fox. The woman seemed to be in a daze, edging backward until Stanway stopped her from going any further.

"Mrs. Fox," Geneva said. "You heard what Mr. Drake said. Is he correct?"

The housekeeper glanced fearfully at the other servants. "I am not to blame. I was following Mr. Jack's orders. He told me to put the drug in her bedtime hot chocolate. He said she was having difficulty sleeping."

Geneva's tone hardened. "That's highly irregular. If my mother needed medicine, that was none of Jack's business. Why would you obey him for something like that?"

The housekeeper's hands trembled as she picked at her nails. When she didn't respond, Daniel pulled out the St. Christopher pendant and held it up by the chain.

"Mrs. Fox, this pendant has your name engraved on the back— Cecilia Jasper Fox. The captain had this hidden with the other evidence we uncovered. We believe he kept it to blackmail you in case you were tempted to reveal his plan concerning Elizabeth Everson. Do you have anything to say about that?"

The housekeeper fixed her gaze on the pendant and broken chain. "Yes, that's my pendant. I lost it many years ago. You can ask

Stanway and any other staff here at the time if I didn't search high and low for it."

"Mrs. Fox, I know you don't want to get Captain Everson into trouble—or yourself," Daniel said gently. "But there's something else you should know. We found this note with that pendant. It was written by Nicholas Drake to Mr. Jack following his dismissal as coachman. Constable Allenby, would you read this aloud?"

As the chief constable read the scribbled words, Mrs. Fox covered her mouth with shock. When he finished, the housekeeper let out an agonized scream. "Oh dear God in heaven! He killed my Billy! He didn't run away as I thought. He was murdered! Please God, don't let this be true!"

Geneva put her arm around the housekeeper. "I'm sorry, Mrs. Fox. It's true, and we have proof. Jack was an accomplice to his murder. He hid the child's body in an underground cavern beneath this very hall. He did it so he could blackmail Nicholas Drake, just as he kept your pendant in case you ever tried to speak up."

Mr. Fairfax strode over to Jack. "Is this all true, Captain Everson?"

Jack attempted to get to his feet, only the handcuffs forcing him back into the chair. No longer stony-faced, he shouted at his family, "Are you all this gullible? Yes, I may have done some smuggling. Since when is that considered a crime at Ravensmere? Our family fortune was built on smuggling. But I'm not guilty of anyone's blood!"

Rushing to the head of the hall, Mrs. Fox slapped Jack across the face. "You're a double-crossing liar! It was almost twenty years ago when I lost my St. Christopher that my father had given to me. You're the one who found it! Mr. Daniel is right. You used it to blackmail me into putting laudanum into dear Miss Elizabeth's hot chocolate and to stop me from speaking about your wicked plan. Yes, Billy was my son, and I was a stupid fool to obey you just to keep my job and reputation in the community. I don't care anymore."

She turned to the sea of faces watching in stunned disbelief. "I loved my Billy dearly. But Billy's death isn't the only murder that's taken place at Ravensmere. Captain Everson murdered his uncle! Is there no end to the wickedness in this place?"

"What are you saying?" Angus Fairfax demanded. "The physician said Mr. Adam died of a heart attack."

"A heart attack, yes. But not a natural one. I prepared the fresh lemonade that day when the master asked for drinks to be brought to the garden. The captain was in the kitchen. I saw him fiddling with his uncle's glass when I was getting Miss Geneva's grape cordial. He had a little brown bottle in his hand. He doesn't usually come to the kitchen. I asked him what he wanted. He told me to stop dawdling and take the beverages out."

She burst into tears. "I didn't know for sure, but I wondered because the bottle looked just like your father's medicine, and his bottle was missing when we cleaned out your father's lounge after his death. I didn't dare ask the captain, but after what happened with Miss Elizabeth all those years ago, I couldn't help wondering."

Geneva was probably the calmest person there, only because she'd already processed the shock of Jack having murdered her father. The color drained from Samuel's face. The women of the family were in hysterics. Grandmama Louise slumped into a faint, Aunt Mary and Katherine trying to hold her up until Robert and Philip hurried over to help. The constables looked as shocked as the servants. After all, Captain Everson had been one of the most prominent men in the area.

Geneva saw tears rolling down the housekeeper's face. "Mrs. Fox, you've had a terrible shock. You must lie down. Emily will take you to your room and bring you tea."

Mrs. Fox shook her head stubbornly. "Thank you, Miss Everson. I don't deserve your kindness. But if my Billy is under these floors, I want to see him."

Constable Allenby approached Samuel Cavendish. "Sir, since you're the trustee of the estate, may I and a few others have your authorization to enter this cavern your son and Miss Geneva spoke of? The court will want two witnesses to testify to the child's remains."

"Of course," Samuel responded, still looking shaken at the revelations. "Daniel will guide the way."

"Philip and I want to look in that cavern too," Robert announced. "If our brother truly has committed a crime, we want to see the evidence for ourselves."

CHAPTER THIRTY-TWO

A half hour later, Constable Allenby, Mr. Fairfax, Robert, Philip, Samuel, Mrs. Fox, and Daniel emerged from the wine cellar into the Great Hall. Guards were maintaining their vigilant watch over the prisoners. At the other end of the hall, Stanway was serving coffee and tea from the sideboard to the family and remaining constables. A roaring fire had eased the chill in the air.

Geneva was finishing a third cup of tea when Mrs. Fox rushed past her, sobbing on her way to her sitting room. The rest of the group joined the family.

Mr. Fairfax spoke up. "What amazing history lies beneath this manor. But I deeply regret Miss Geneva and the mother being exposed to the horrendous sight of the child's remains. Mrs. Fox identified her son by his clothing, which she had purchased for him. Billy's neck had been broken, so at least she has the consolation his death was quick."

Robert brushed dust from his hands and shoulders. "I'm astonished at the length of that tunnel. It's monstrous to think that Jack was hauling in stolen goods while we were sleeping in our beds."

"I am not truly surprised that Jack could be so deceitful." Philip cast a scathing glance at his brother. "I remember well his lies and gambling debts in our youth. But to murder our uncle who took us all in when our father died, to conspire to destroy his happiness with his bride—it is unconscionable. God help our parish. It'll be turned upside down when the news comes out."

Samuel was turning the pages of Jack's secret ledger as Mr. Fairfax stepped closer. "Samuel, can you confirm your son's assessment of that ledger?"

"Definitely. It helps that Jack's work is clear and well-organized. There's more than enough evidence for embezzlement against both Captain Everson and Nigel Spooner. The issue of smuggling and the importation and sale of looted goods will, of course, need to be taken up by revenue agents as that is not my field of expertise."

"Good enough," Mr. Fairfax nodded. "In any case, we found ample evidence below, including a clear identification of the deceased child. Mrs. Fox has expressed willingness to testify in court as to Captain Everson's role in the case of Elizabeth Everson as well as Adam Everson's death. Combined with Miss Geneva's testimony of the captain's direct attack on her, this will give ample case for a trial at the next quarter session. In the meantime, Captain Everson, Mr. Nigel Spooner, and Mr. Nicholas Drake will be held at Hawkley Castle Prison."

The chief magistrate turned to Geneva. "Miss Geneva, I promise to do all I can to quell the gossip and news reporters who will be swarming to a story like this. But it may not be possible."

"Thank you, sir. In truth, I want all to know that my mother was innocent of the scandal whispered against her all these years. If that means news stories, so be it. I hope you'll understand if I don't attend your winter ball next week. I don't think I could handle all the stares and questions."

"Not at all, Miss Geneva. You are a grieving family in need of privacy. My heart won't be in it, but what can I do? Everything is prepared."

As Stanway stepped forward to offer coffee, Robert took Daniel and Geneva aside. His face was so pale and drawn that he seemed to have aged ten years overnight.

"I owe both of you an apology. Daniel, I'm sorry I called your integrity into question. We owe you a debt of gratitude for helping Geneva uncover Jack's crimes. I'm embarrassed and full of regret. If I'd been more involved in my brother's life, I might have noticed something was amiss. And Geneva, I'm sorry I resented your presence when you first came to us. If you hadn't become part of this family, we'd still be in the dark."

Aunt Mary came to Geneva with puffy, red eyes and her hanky pressed to her bosom. "My dear girl, I have to speak with you. I'm terribly sorry for all the times I criticized your mother."

Katherine pushed in as well. "We should have believed you, Geneva. You knew her far better than we did. Will you forgive us?"

Geneva gave them each a hug. "I certainly will."

Lastly, Grandmama Louise beckoned to Geneva from her armchair.

"I don't know what to say, Geneva. I thought I had overcome my grief in losing Adam. With this latest—oh dear, I don't know if I'll ever get over the shame and heartache Jack has brought us."

Geneva lifted Pookie onto her grandmother's lap and leaned down to kiss a withered cheek. "Don't worry, Grandmama Louise. Love and time will conquer our sorrows and heal the past. You'll see."

Geneva turned around and made her way to the prisoners. Only Jack dared to look her unrepentantly in the eye. Drake remained in a slumped position, head down and knees wide apart.

Geneva cleared her throat. "I have a few things to say to you three. First, it's right and fitting that you've been brought to justice. I just wish things could have been different. Mr. Drake, you should have been grateful for what your uncle did for you. If you'd loved and respected him, you might have a fleet of fishing boats and children bouncing on your knees by now.

"Mr. Nigel, your crimes were not against me personally, so I absolve you of that. But you, Cousin Jack, you had so much going for you. You are intelligent and gifted and could have made something great of yourself if you chose. Instead, you became consumed with acquiring Ravensmere. You broke up my parents' marriage to prevent my mother from producing an heir. You thought to get rid of my father before he changed his will. Little did you know on both accounts that it was already too late. Now you must face the consequence of your sins."

Geneva looked at each of her tormentors in turn. "At least I am now free of you all. I forgive you, and I pray that God will have mercy on your souls."

Walking away, Geneva intercepted Emily and Stanway, who had just finished handing around cups of coffee to the new arrivals. "Stanway, I must tell you that as of now, Mrs. Fox is no longer my employee. I understand her reasons for what she did, but I cannot have her continue serving in this household. She may stay for Billy's proper burial. After that, I'll give her sufficient funds to manage until she can find a new situation."

Geneva turned to the head housemaid. "Emily, you've worked here for a good twenty years. Will you accept the position as Ravensmere's new housekeeper?"

Emily's face broke into an astonished smile. She gave a deep curtsey. "Yes, miss, thank you for the privilege. I would be honored."

"Forgive me, Emily, but I never learned your surname. What is it?"

"Bathgate, miss. Emily Bathgate."

"Well, Mrs. Bathgate, it's good to know I can count on you and Stanway during this trying time."

Just then, Geneva heard a commotion outside. As she glanced out a window, the first paling of dawn revealed a jail wagon and team of horses pulling up at the entrance porch. At a shouted order from Constable Allenby, the prisoners were uncuffed from their seats, re-cuffed, and led across the Great Hall. Jack kept his eyes averted from his mother and grandmother, who rushed to the front entrance, weeping, as he was led outside.

The entire family gathered on the pebbled drive, watching somberly as the three prisoners were assisted into the wagon. The door was secured with a padlock, then with the driver's flick of the reins, the horses clip-clopped into movement. As the wagon clattered down the drive, Geneva saw Jack's face pressed against the bars of the rear window. The arrogance was gone from his handsome face, and his eyes were filled with tears as he viewed his ancestral home and family for the last time.

CHAPTER THIRTY-THREE

Geneva gripped the edge of her seat as the carriage took a sharp turn in the road. There to her left, she beheld the hilltop town of Shaftesbury—a lovely sight on this sixteenth day of April. St. Peter's church tower stood out against a pale-blue sky. The white-washed cottages of Gold Hill caught the afternoon sun. Further down the hill, crab apple trees were dressed in a profuse display of pink blossoms.

The carriage journey from Waterton had been enjoyable, Daniel seated next to Geneva, Robert and Tess across from them. Their baby girl had been left in the care of her nanny. Amiable conversations had made the time pass quickly. Now Geneva was only minutes away from a visit with Uncle Alex.

Robert craned his neck to see the view up ahead. "I can't understand why you'd want to see that grumpy old codger again."

"She has personal reasons," Tess said. "It's been eight months since Geneva left him and came to Ravensmere."

Daniel raised his brows. "And exactly four months since Jack and Nicholas Drake departed from this world."

Robert surveyed the passing scenery. "Spooner got his just deserts with a prison sentence. As for Jack, his trial wasn't for me. I'm better off without memories like that, especially the announcement of the jury's verdict."

Daniel tipped his head to view the town. "On a brighter note, shall we have tea at Shaftesbury's inn? That will fill in the time while Geneva has her visit."

Robert nodded. "Jolly good idea. I hope they have sponge cake as good as Lily's."

As their carriage ascended the hill and entered the cobbled streets, Geneva took in the familiar sights of her birth town. At the town square, Burrows brought the carriage to a stop. Daniel took her hand to help her down.

"Well, here we are," he said with a grin, "back where we first met."

Geneva lifted shining eyes to him. "Who would have known that we'd be here today with our wedding just two months away!"

"Indeed, aren't God's ways mysterious?"

Playing with the diamond ring on her finger, Geneva turned her gaze to the very spot where Daniel had approached the farm laborers. She'd never forget that sweet memory—his handsome face, his tailcoat in a smart shade of maroon, and the troubled laborers who'd stood back in fear until he spoke to them with kindness and compassion. Just three weeks ago, he had proposed to her at the Stillberry Stones—the most joyful moment of her lifetime.

With tear-brightened eyes and a smile on her face, Geneva turned to her companions. "You'll find the inn just around the corner. I'll meet you there a little later."

Geneva walked up High Street and came to the pawnshop with the three brass spheres above the door. The shop was busy as always on a Saturday afternoon. Looking up from his paperwork at the counter, Uncle Alex squinted his eyes and scratched his whiskers.

"Geneva? By gum, I didn't think I'd ever see you again."

Geneva approached the counter. "It's lovely to see you, Uncle Alex. I'm sorry I didn't answer your letter. I've come for a short visit. Could we have tea at the back?"

"Yes, I could use a cup. Peggy will make it for us. She's my housemaid, but not live-in, thank the Lord. I can only take her in small doses."

Leading the way through to the parlor, he called out, "Peggy! Bring tea for two." He gestured to the chairs. "Shall we sit down?"

As Geneva took her seat near the hearth, her uncle looked her over. "Aren't you a well-dressed young lady! What's been happening in your life?"

"Well, things changed a lot after my father died."

"Humph, I was told that he died before your mother came to live with me. What was that all about?"

"It was a big misunderstanding, Uncle. I can assure you that Mother's name is held in high regard by my family. After I leave here, I'm going to the church to pay my respects at her grave."

"I see. Well, do tell me what rich folk do all day."

"I'm always busy. My idea for a wattle fence business was well received. The employment has helped numerous families leave poverty behind. I'm playing the flute in church like I did here. Best of all, I'm engaged to be married."

"Married? That was quick. To whom?"

"A family friend, Mr. Daniel Cavendish. He's a wonderful man. The wedding is set for June fifteenth. I hope you'll come."

"Hmm, I have a horse and carriage now. I suppose I could."

The housemaid brought a tea tray and disappeared quickly. Geneva poured and handed the teacup to him. "Well, Uncle Alex, I need to talk to you about the main point of my visit. I admit I resented your harsh treatment while I was growing up. When your letter came, I could hardly believe that you would apologize. I was glad you had recovered from your illness, but I was too bitter to forgive you. It took God's chastening for me to finally see that I'd been disobeying him."

She set her cup down. "Uncle Alex, I truly forgive you, and I hold no grudge whatsoever."

"Ah well, nice of you to say so. Now we can forget about it." He glanced down at her bag. "What have you got in there?"

"Oh, I brought you some gifts." She placed an assortment of wrapped cheeses on the table. "They're from Everson Farm. I hope you enjoy them."

Alex gave one a sniff. "Not bad at all. A few slices will go well with my whiskey each night."

For the next forty minutes, Geneva sipped her tea and listened to her uncle chatter about his customers, the annoying staff, and the rare coin collection that had come in the previous day. When the time came for her to leave, he walked with her to the side door.

"Thank you for visiting. I can't guarantee I'll come to your wedding, but I would enjoy a letter from time to time."

"I will, Uncle Alex. Take care of yourself, and God bless you." Geneva gave him a kiss on his prickly cheek. Waving goodbye, she departed down High Street with a joyful spring in her step.

The following afternoon, the party of four returned to Ravensmere. They were greeted by Stanway, who hung up their coats and hats and helped Burrows bring in their luggage.

Mrs. Bathgate scurried up the hallway. "Welcome back, Miss Geneva. How was the trip? Were the roads good?"

"Yes, as far as I know. I fell asleep part of the way home. Mr. Cavendish's shoulder was a comfortable pillow for my head."

"Well, you'll be excited to hear what happened earlier this afternoon. Come through to the Great Hall. Mr. Northcott is here for dinner, and the family is waiting for you."

"Edwin's here again? That's wonderful. I have a feeling he'll pop the question to Katherine any day now."

As they entered, Aunt Mary came forward quickly, her shoes clicking on the stone flags. "My dears, welcome home. Philip, come and tell Geneva what happened. And Katherine, don't blurt it out."

"Really, Mother, why would I do that?"

"Hush, let Philip speak."

Philip massaged his hands together in a calm manner. "Claire and I brought the children for a visit earlier. They've gone home now, but while they were here, an unexpected visitor came to the manor. A total stranger by the name of Mr. Sparks. He brought something for you, Geneva. It's over there on the chair."

Geneva looked over her shoulder. "What is it?"

"That's for you to find out," Grandmama Louise said. "Go and take a look."

Geneva crossed the room, her family following behind. Propped up on a chair was a large, flat rectangular shape draped in a blanket. She had an inkling what it might be even before she pulled the blanket loose. Dropping the blanket to the floor, she clapped her hands to her cheeks and cried out, "Mother! Oh, it's too beautiful for words!"

Leaning forward, she touched the canvas of an exquisite oil painting—a masterpiece portrait. "It looks exactly like her as if she were right here with me. Look at the light on her cheek and the shimmer in her satin gown."

"I remember it now," Aunt Mary said.

Grandmama Louise moved in for a closer look. "So do I. I remember her posing in the oriel window. The artist kept telling her to sit still."

"She was a beautiful woman," Daniel said. "Who is this Mr. Sparks?"

"He lives in Blandford Forum," Philip said. "Twenty years ago, he viewed the portrait at an auction and liked it so much that he won the bid. Last December, he read the newspaper article about Jack's criminal charges and how he broke up Uncle Adam's marriage to Elizabeth. He was shocked because her name was written on the back of the portrait. He didn't want to give it up, but in the end, his conscience won and he made the trip to Waterton."

Daniel tilted the portrait forward and looked behind. "Yes, there it is—her name."

Geneva peered around for a look and placed her hand on the gilt frame. "I want it hung up right away."

"Lovely idea," Mary said. "How about the library?"

Geneva looked around the Great Hall. "No, it belongs in here next to Father's portrait—that one where his elbow is resting on the saddle of his horse. That must have been painted around the time when he married Mother."

"Shall I hang it for you, miss?" Stanway asked.

"Yes, please do." Geneva stood back to watch. When the portrait was in place, tears welled in her eyes. "That's how it should have been a long time ago—the master and mistress of Ravensmere, side by side, loving each other, with no man putting them asunder. But God is so good. He's answered my prayer. If Mr. Sparks read about my mother, then think how many more now know that Elizabeth Everson was a fine and honorable lady."

CHAPTER THIRTY-FOUR

Four months later on a Saturday afternoon in mid-August, Daniel brought Victor to the mounting block and helped Geneva into the saddle, her legs dangling to one side. He seated himself behind her, then they set off for a slow, easy ramble around the estate.

The day was perfect. Fluffy white clouds moved across an azure sky, and the song of a woodlark proclaimed the glory of the day. As they crossed Raven's Lane and rode through the coppice of trees, Daniel kissed Geneva's cheek, warm from the sun's rays.

"I received a letter this morning. Mr. Fairfax had another meeting with the tenant farmers and landowners. They've agreed to my proposal for the farm laborers' wages."

"Really? I can hardly believe that those stubborn men would concede. What's the new wage?"

"Eleven shillings."

"Eleven? That's marvelous. I hope other landowners do the same. How did you convince them?"

"Well, this is where my banking background helped. I spread the papers out and explained my deep financial analysis. They balked at first until one of them acknowledged the logic and benefits of the plan. After that, more caught on one by one."

Geneva slipped her arm around him. "I'm so proud of you, darling. Now the laborers will have enough food for their families and money to save for decent clothing and shoes."

They trotted on to the farm, circling around the buildings until they came to the new workshop with its colorful sign hanging above the double doors: Ravensmere Wattle Fence Company. Harry Whipple was loading hurdles into a wagon with the company's name painted in bold letters. He had put on weight, and his flaxen hair now had a glossy sheen. He glanced up with big smile on his freckled face.

"Good afternoon, Mr. and Mrs. Cavendish. You'll be pleased to hear this is the biggest order we've ever had. A sheep farmer east of St. Aubrey sent the order."

"Excellent news," Daniel said. "How are your reading lessons coming along?"

"Very well, sir. I can read faster now. My kids love hearing Bible stories at bedtime."

Daniel chuckled. "Well, I've thought it over. By Michaelmas, you'll be ready for a promotion from tradesman to assistant manager."

"Lawks, my Anna will dance a jig when she hears that." Harry reached for another hurdle. "I better get on with this delivery, sir."

Leaving the farmyard behind, Daniel and Geneva set off on a cart track through green pastures thick with the scent of wild flowers and the pleasant sound of jangling cow bells. As they turned west, Victor plodded along a footpath to the shimmering waters of the lake.

"Do you remember my trip to London for an investment opportunity?" Daniel asked.

"I do—the shipbuilding company with a clipper faster than any other."

"That's right. My shares have done exceptionally well. Now I have a proposal."

"Goodness, you're full of surprises today," Geneva said with a smile. "What is it?"

"Well, I've always thought that an education would raise the living standards of the poor. I want to use my savings to build a charity school for the village—not just for education but for winning souls to Christ. With the increased business from the wattle fence company, I thought perhaps we could direct some or even all of the profits to the school's operational costs. What do you think, my love?"

Geneva lifted her gaze to his tanned face. "I don't need to think. It's a wonderful idea. Everyone will applaud you for it, especially your father. He might want to contribute as well."

As they talked about the possibilities, Daniel guided Victor off the path and up a gentle slope through tall, swaying grasses. At the top, they stopped their conversation to view the lake. Ducks swam between lily pads. The splash of a trout sent ripples across the smooth surface.

As Daniel wrapped his arms tighter around his wife, Geneva revelled in his loving embrace. The beat of his heart against her chest. His wonderful scent like pine needles in a rain-drenched forest. The way he kissed her mouth—warm, sweet, and passionate. Several blissful minutes passed before the two turned their gaze to the lake once more.

"I've spoken to Edwin about the school," Daniel said. "Now that he and Katherine are engaged to be married, he believes God has given him a mission field right here in Waterton. He asked if he could have the position as the school's teacher and manager."

"Really?" Geneva exclaimed delightedly. "This is coming together so well. I'm sure Katherine would want to work with him. They'd make a great team. Have you thought about where we would build it?"

"Yes, I want it close to the village and the manor. A place where the children could have room to run and play and have sports."

Geneva craned her neck and looked all around. "I know why you brought me here!"

The corner of his mouth lifted in a smile. "You do?"

"Yes, you want to build the school right here next to the lake."

Daniel chuckled deep in his throat. "Why not? If it's well-designed and landscaped with beauty in mind, I can't think of a better place."

"Oh, Daniel, we have so much to look forward to. I wish everyone could have the joy I feel today."

"Well, my dearest, this estate belongs to our heavenly Father, and we are his stewards. With his help and guidance, we'll use Ravensmere to raise our family and to bless our community—all for his glory."

Geneva's eyes shone as bright as the noonday sun. Leaning into his embrace once more, she nestled her head in the crook of his neck. "Speaking of raising our family, Daniel, my dearest, I have something to tell you."

The End

Printed in the United States
by Baker & Taylor Publisher Services